Traveler

BREEANA PUTTROFF

FIRST EDITION
ISBN 13: 978-1-940481-22-7

~~~~~~~~~~~

Cover Design: Mallory Rock

Formatting & Layout: Mallory Rock

Editor: Jennifer Severino

~~~~~~~~~~~

Thirteen Pages Press
P.O. BOX 350944
DENVER, CO 80035

For Mallory,
My dear friend and amazing artist who helps me bring
other worlds to life.

ONE
THE WOODS

Ellarowan lockwood hated waiting.

It wasn't because waiting was boring—though, of course, it could be. And it wasn't because she was impatient—even if she sometimes was.

What she hated about waiting was that feeling she got, deep in the pit of her stomach, that *something* was about to happen, and it was too late to do anything about it.

Waiting was like knowing a secret existed, and knowing that learning the secret could change everything. It was wanting to know something and not wanting to know it all wrapped together in a too-fast heartbeat. Waiting was the dangerous time. The moment between the life she had now and a future that could either go on as planned or be changed forever with a single whisper.

She'd had plenty of practice hating to wait. She'd had no choice; her father was guildmaster and was constantly traveling. Waiting was the worst when his return was imminent, and that feeling would take hold of her stomach like a fist, kneading and churning everything inside her. Anything could happen when he was away. An airship could crash, a carriage could overturn, the river could be too fast and too deep....

The feeling would never go away until she knew he was safely back at their estate.

She had already lived through the feeling of waiting once today. Her father had just returned from an extended visit to the other guildhavens. She hadn't seen him yet—wouldn't see him until dinner—but she knew he'd arrived safely, and her time of waiting was over. Or it could have been.

But here she was, in a clearing in the woods, waiting for someone yet again. This time, it was her choice.

Loric was late, which did nothing to calm the rumbling and roiling in her midsection. It meant nothing, she knew that, told herself that over and over as she paced. People were late sometimes. There were hundreds of reasons he might be late. She did it to him just as often. It wasn't always easy to slip away from their duties and their families to meet out here in the woods in secret. Chances were, he hadn't fallen and broken his leg, or been eaten by a dragon, or, worst of all, simply decided he no longer wanted to come.

It was irrational to be so worried. *Don't be irrational,* Ellarowan told herself, sitting down on a large rock and opening her bag.

Drawing never failed to calm her. She pulled her sketchbook and charcoals from her bag, flipped through the pages until she found a blank one, then took a deep breath and began to draw.

She'd managed to get two whole parallel lines drawn when the telltale crackling of shoes on dried leaves made the charcoal fly out of her hands, and she let the sketchbook fall with it as she stood and turned.

"Hello," Loric said, with the smile that made her insides melt in an entirely different kind of way. "Sorry I'm late."

"You ought to be," she smiled back and crinkled her eyes in the way that let him know she was teasing. "I was about to give up on you. I have to leave in half an hour if I'm going to change and make it to dinner on time."

"Well, we'll just have to make the most of the next half hour, won't we?"

In three quick steps, she was in his arms, and the next several minutes made her forget she'd ever been worried at all.

Waiting was terrible, but sometimes, it was worth it.

"I brought you something," he said when they finally managed to break away from each other, at least for a moment. "A birthday gift. I'm only three weeks late, sorry." He reached into his pocket and pulled out a little piece of orange silk.

She raised an eyebrow and held out her hand so he could gently set the little bundle in it. "You didn't need to get me anything. It's bad enough that I wasn't even able to invite you for dinner that night."

"I knew what I was getting into when I began courting you," he said. "Your father wants only the best for you. Someday, he'll learn that's me."

She smiled and stretched up to kiss his cheek. "Still, you're enough. You didn't have to get me a gift."

"A girl only turns eighteen one time," Loric said. "I thought you needed something to commemorate the occasion." He pulled apart the edges of the cloth, revealing something small and shiny inside.

Ella gasped as she picked up the little silver charm. "It's an airship." It was a perfect replica of the enormous ships docked at the bay. The kind Loric helped build, and her father often rode in, though Ella had never seen the inside of one herself. She ran her finger over the sleek shape of the cabin on the charm. Unlike regular ships, these could rise into the air, easing travel in the stormy seas and over the peninsulas that made it so difficult for regular ships to navigate between the guildhavens.

"Do you like it?" he asked, his voice unusually shy.

"It's beautiful."

"I crafted it myself."

She sucked in a breath as she looked up at him. He was talented, she'd known that, but she hadn't imagined he could make something so perfect. "Loric, it's amazing. I'm going to put it right on the table by my bed so that you're the last thing I think about before I go to sleep and the first thing I see in the morning."

There was no talking for a while after that. Perhaps too long a while, because by the time Ella was thinking straight again, the angle of the sun had shifted, and she knew it was time.

She didn't need to tell him. Loric's face fell as he read the look in her eyes.

"Must you really leave so soon?" He took a lock of her hair between his fingers, gently twisting the red and black strands together. "It never feels like I have enough time with you."

His eyes were almost the same color violet as hers were; it was one of the first things she'd noticed about him. As she looked into them, she wondered if her irises were just a single shade lighter, right between the spokes of the star-shaped pupils, the way his were. She could have stared at them forever. "Would any amount of time be enough?"

"No," he said, laughing and leaning in to kiss her cheek. "But if I could just have another hour…"

"My father is home tonight. You wouldn't want me to miss dinner with him because I was with you, would you?"

"No." He cleared his throat and let go of her hand. "No, I definitely would like to be on your father's good side. I just wish I had more time with you right now, that's all. I'm not ready for you to leave."

Ella wasn't ready to leave, either. But then, she wouldn't have been ready to end a visit with Loric even if it was midnight. Still, the sun wasn't setting yet. There were a few more minutes to stall here in the woods. "You're the one who was late, remember?"

"You haven't asked me why."

"Was there a special reason?"

The grin that played at the corners of his mouth reminded her of a child on the morning of Festival, and she wondered how she could have missed it before. It was so infectious, she found herself smiling along with him, even before he answered.

"After I finished my work today, Gaius took me aside." Loric's expression was growing brighter by the moment.

"And?"

"He wants me to take over all the orders for the Third Fleet."

Her grin was in competition with his now. "Take them *over?* You mean…"

"My apprenticeship is finished."

"But you're—"

"The youngest to complete the apprenticeship ever, yes."

"By a lot, aren't you?"

He shrugged one shoulder. "Only by one cycle. The youngest before me was twenty-one."

"You're being modest. A cycle is a long time in an apprenticeship. You only turned twenty last moon."

The dimple in his chin always grew deeper when he was trying not to be prideful. "Of course, we've been needing a new shipwright badly. With the pressure lately from Silver Island, we couldn't keep up with production."

"Loric…"

"But there *were* fifteen apprentices to choose from, and Gaius chose me."

She squealed and threw her arms around him. Unable to contain his excitement any longer, he wrapped his hands around her waist and twirled her, lifting her into the air as he did so. They laughed and spun until they were both dizzy and then he set her back down again and pressed his lips against hers.

He'd never kissed her quite so long or so deeply before, and it took a long time before she remembered she was supposed to be leaving and was able to pull away.

"I still have to go," she said, though her voice betrayed just how much she didn't want to.

He was still grinning. "I know, but it's okay. Soon, everything will be different. Your father won't be able to say no to his daughter courting the youngest shipwright in the history of Ravensguild."

It had never been easy to walk away from Loric, but this time was the hardest yet. She wanted to stay, to hear more details about his new job—or at least to memorize more details about that long kiss—but she knew that "five more minutes" could have melted into five hours, and there just wasn't time. Still, she couldn't stop grinning as she ran up the path, darting between the familiar trees of the forest at the edge of the Guildmaster's Estate. She even giggled to herself as she thought about his words, just before their last kiss. "Soon, we won't have to hide."

Just as the corner of the old, unused guest cottage came into sight, she realized that her giddiness had distracted her a little too much.

She'd forgotten what he said *after* the kiss. "Be careful walking back. I've kept you a little too long. You know one of the apprentices disappeared last moon."

As always, she'd promised him she would be careful. But this day she'd been distracted.

The river marked not only the edge of the Guildmaster's Estate but the boundary-line of Ravensguild. There was nothing on the other side of it, save wilderness and danger, all the way to the Crimson Mountains. The realm of the magic ones.

At least, those were the rumors about why it was unsafe.

She'd never been afraid of the river for those reasons. She knew the real dangers were the currents that could sometimes be swift. Still, she always remained wary and watchful.

But tonight, she hadn't. Tonight, she'd been thinking about the way Loric's tousled brown hair framed his face when he looked at her, and she'd wandered just a little too close to the river, past the line of trees that marked places long forbidden.

During the day, this wouldn't have been a grave mistake. The boundaries were more caution than anything. In the middle of the day, so long as one watched where they were going, made noise, perhaps carried a weapon, coming out this far was mostly an adventure. Out here she was free from the watchful eyes of her father and the servants, free from responsibility and obligation.

But the protective rays of the sun had faded into evening shadows, and she hadn't been paying attention—hadn't been *listening*—and she'd missed the early warnings that something wasn't right. Everything was quiet. The symphony that normally kept her company on her way back to the house was absent. No birds chirped and cooed in the trees. Nothing rustled in the bushes near her feet. The only sound was the flowing water of the river, much too close.

She stopped walking to check her surroundings now, her hand moving instinctively to her leather pouch and the small knife hidden within. Before she could pull the weapon out, a horrible shriek broke the silence of the dusk. Even over the rushing of the water, the panicked scream of the animal was heartrending.

Her whole body reacted, tensing, as she spotted the threat. A panther, twice her size at least, crouched just on the edge of the river, its eyes locked on an iber. She froze, torn between the terrible urge to rush forward and rescue the iber and the instinct to run as fast as she could away from the danger. So torn, that all she could do was stand there and watch as the giant cat moved closer, cornering the small, quivering creature against a rock.

Don't run. The voice in her head finally kicked in, thundering the advice she'd heard so many times. Her body's decision to freeze seemed a strange thing to appreciate, but at the moment, she was grateful for small favors. *If you run, the panther will notice, and it will go for the larger prey instead. Don't make any sudden moves.*

She knew what *not* to do, but she didn't remember what she *was* supposed to do. She stayed frozen as the nightmare scene unfolded in front of her. The panther's jaws snapped shut, and the iber stopped screaming.

In the next instant, everything changed. Ellarowan hadn't moved—*she knew she hadn't*—but something made the cat stop in its tracks and look upward, right to where she was standing. The hair on the back of her neck stood straight up, tingling in the slight breeze. Now it was far too late to flee. The panther's eyes were a terrifying shade of yellow as they locked on to hers. The iber, still wriggling, dropped from its mouth, terrifying her even more. The snapping of the massive jaw should have killed the iber instantly—if the panther was only hungry. This cat wanted to play.

Everything went silent. Even her heartbeat, which had been thundering in her ears only a second before, seemed to have stopped.

Get small. No, that's not right. Get big. That was what she was supposed to do. Look big and threatening, but not run. *And don't make any sudden moves. Right.*

Her hands had clenched into fists without her even noticing. Now, she slowly unfurled each finger. The temptation to wipe her sweaty hands on her pants was great, but she avoided making that movement. Instead, she raised her hands slowly up. *Slowly, slowly.*

A hint of pink appeared at the bottom of the cat's mouth and flicked across its jaw. It blinked lazily as it continued to stare. The message was clear. *You're welcome to try.*

It took everything she had not to run and to keep raising her arms. *Please run away, please run away.* The refrain beat inside her mind.

When her hands were almost halfway up, stretched out to the sides as wide as possible, she turned her palms forward. "Please run away." This time, the words came out in a whisper as she concentrated her fear into actions. The cat's mouth closed and it dropped its gaze from her eyes.

Finally finding her voice, she took the only chance she was going to get. "Go!" she screamed.

And it did. With a last glance at her hands, now as high as she could lift them, the panther lowered its head, turned, and retreated into the trees.

She blinked several times, trying to decide if what she'd just seen was real. Sound slowly returned over the roar of blood past her ears. First the swishing movement of the water, then the calls and chirps of evening insects. She lowered her now-aching arms and stood there for a long time, long after she'd watched the tail swish in the distance until it vanished. The pounding rush of blood in her veins slowed and quieted well before her feet would cooperate and move.

The smart thing to do now would be to run up to the main house as quickly as possible. There was no way of knowing if the panther would come back, or if the bloody iber would manage to attract something much worse.

The sun had almost entirely disappeared behind the trees, and the orange glow of sunset was fading into blues and purples. This was the most dangerous time of day. There were more than just panthers in those woods. And already, her father would be expecting her at the table. Returning home immediately was the only logical choice.

And that was the choice she meant to make. She meant to turn and leave and do the right thing—the proper thing.

But once again, her feet didn't behave; her body didn't listen. Instead of moving toward the house, she found herself hurrying toward the river instead, to the spot where the wounded iber still lay.

Ibers had always been her favorite animals to spot out here in the forest. Tiny creatures hidden in enormous balls of fluff. Though she'd always wanted to hold one, she'd never been close enough to even see an iber's eyes. She knew they had them—and also little claws buried beneath the mountainous strands of silky hair—but she'd never seen either. Until now.

One of this iber's shiny black eyes was exposed; the brown-gray hair that normally hid them so well was matted back with the blood that oozed from two puncture wounds along the nape of its neck. At least, Ella supposed that was its neck.

She barely breathed as she stretched her hands toward the iber, terrified of startling it and incurring its wrath—or damaging it further. The claws, however, remained hidden, even as her fingers made contact with the trembling fur. Its one visible eye watched as she carefully slid both hands into the damp fur and under its tiny body. She braced herself for its reaction as she lifted it—holding it carefully away from her in case it panicked. The iber was so much lighter than she'd been expecting that she almost accidentally tossed it into the air instead of lifting it gently into her arms.

The iber didn't move; it just kept staring.

A horrible shiver tore through her as she realized its lack of reaction probably meant she was too late, but since the animal was still warm and quivering, she pulled off her shawl with one hand and wrapped it inside, still mindful of the hidden claws as she pulled the animal in close to her.

As soon as she brought the creature to her chest, its eye closed. The trembling stopped, but she could still feel the small sensation of fur moving as it breathed.

Now she was able to run. Her feet cooperated in getting away from the river as quickly as possible without damaging the little animal more.

There was only one place to take it. Ella was out of breath when she reached the creaky porch of the old guest cottage and tried the knob.

A lock wouldn't have stopped her, but the door swung open easily revealing a neat little furnished room complete with a fireplace and a small washroom off to one side. There wasn't nearly as much dust as she'd expected, considering nobody came out here anymore. This building had fallen out of use when she was eight or so, after the construction of several new guest houses on the other side of the property, closer to town than to the forest. Her father didn't want guests so near the river.

It was to the washroom that she took her little bundle, wiping clean space on a small washstand before she set it down. She figured the old lamp in there would be out of oil, but when she tried lighting it, it flickered into feeble life. The darkness of the room reminded her how late she was. If she didn't hurry, someone might come looking for her, and her secret meeting spot with Loric would be ruined.

She couldn't think about that now.

Her older brother, Tallen, had once caught an iber. He still had the faint scars on his forearm to show for it. Ella kept this in mind as she gently peeled back the shawl to peek at the animal.

She knew nothing about healing, but telling her father about her near run-in with the panther was a risk she couldn't take; she'd never be allowed out into the woods like this again if he knew, so she'd have to do what she could. The ancient pump in the washroom still worked, even though it made a terrible noise as she primed it, and there were worn towels in the basket under the washstand. She knew where these came from. Many cycles ago, she and Tallen had turned this old building into a playhouse, and she'd rescued many items from the main house for their pretend play. So many hours she'd spent folding towels and arranging blankets on the small bed for her dolls.

The iber was still breathing, which she supposed was a good thing, and it looked like the bleeding had stopped. Also good.

The iber's claws never made an appearance as she took a towel and did what she could to clean up its fur and to wrap a towel around the cut. She knew she needed to hurry, but she couldn't make her hands move any faster as she tended the animal. For several minutes, for no reason she could think of, she just stood there, holding both hands over the center of the iber, on the spot where she thought its heart must be. The quivering stopped, and its breathing evened out. It was probably going to die tonight anyway, and it wasn't her fault, she told herself, but still, her hands lingered over the bandage for several minutes; she couldn't tear herself away.

Now, she wet one of the towels and used it to gently clean the blood from the iber's matted fur. Then she retrieved a doll-sized plate from the cupboard near the fireplace and covered it with a layer of water.

Once she'd finally managed to set the creature on several towels on the floor and left the plate of water near its head, she ran toward the house faster than she'd ever run in her life.

Unlike the nights when her father wasn't home, the big house was lit like a beacon against the fast-darkening sky, light poured from most of the windows on both floors, and the front porch blazed with a brightness better reserved for midday. Therefore, the figure leaning against the porch rails was visible before she even reached the gravel path leading to the steps.

Ella stopped running. There was no point; she was only going to muss herself further before dinner.

Tallen crossed his arms across his chest as he watched her approach.

"How much trouble am I in?" she called up to him once she'd finally reached the massive wooden steps.

"Father hasn't called us for dinner yet."

Her head snapped up, and she jogged the last few steps. "He hasn't?"

"You have the luck of a dragon, El. Where have you been?"

"Just out for a—"

"What happened to you?" Her brother's voice interrupted her in a panic. "There's blood all over your blouse!"

She looked down. Sure enough, there were streaks of iber blood everywhere. She should have thought to clean herself up a bit, too. Though there was enough of it, there was probably no help for it. "I found an injured iber."

"And you *touched it?*"

Any other time, she would have hated giving Tallen something to scold her for, but tonight she was only relieved. She'd much rather fight about touching an iber than tell her older brother what she'd really been doing.

"I'm fine. None of the blood is mine."

Tallen was lucky their father wasn't out here to hear the word he mumbled under his breath. "You are…something, El. I would hurry and change out of those clothes and get cleaned up for dinner if I were you. Father's going to call at any moment."

"Thanks, Tal." She ran past him and into the house. Although her brother fancied the five cycles between them as an excuse to direct and scold her, he almost never could bring himself to tell on her to their father.

In her haste to get upstairs, she nearly tripped and sent herself sprawling back down the stairs, so she took a breath and slowed down a bit. Winding up covered in her own blood was the last thing she wanted to do before dinner.

Just before she reached her bedroom, she came to a dead stop. The door was open when she knew she'd closed it, and, moreover, all the lamps inside were lit.

She felt as if she were facing the panther all over again. Her legs turned to lead as she tried to drag herself the last few steps down the hall. *Her father knew.* It was all she could think. He knew she'd been lying, that she'd been sneaking out to the woods to meet with Loric. She'd been caught doing something not only against his wishes, but also dangerous. She was going to walk into her bedroom and find him sitting on the bed, waiting for her.

It took every ounce of courage she had to cross the threshold into the room.

But her father wasn't in there. Nobody was.

Someone had been. Most likely one of the servants had been sent up to turn on the lights and to deliver the box that was sitting on her bed.

The stress of the last—she didn't quite know how long— seemed to hit her all at once, and her legs and arms felt shaky enough that she sat down on the bed to open the gift.

She didn't need the note to know who it was from, but she read it anyway.

> *Ellarowan,*
>
> *I saw this in a shop while I was in Silver Island. As soon as I saw it, I thought of you and had to get it for you. I hope you like it as much as I think you will.*
>
> *Love, Father*

Inside the box was a dress made of a soft, satiny material in a rich black color, with red threads that shone through in the lamplight. She'd never seen anything like it, and she loved it immediately.

"Ellarowan, where have you been? Dinner is in ten minutes."

Ella turned around to see her caretaker, Sabelina, standing in the doorway of her bedroom. "I know. I'm sorry. I lost track of time."

"I know you didn't forget he was going to be home tonight." Sabelina's voice carried across the room as she hurried into Ella's private bathing room. There was the sound of water running and then she returned with a damp washcloth. "Blood, Ella? What have you been doing?"

Ella shrugged out of her stained shirt and reached for the washcloth. "Would you believe me if I told you I found a wounded iber and tried to rescue it?"

Sabelina scoffed. "Perhaps next time you'll wrestle with a panther instead and save me the trouble of having to clean you up." She lifted the dress from the bed and shook it out.

"You'd still have to clean me one last time for the funeral," Ella pointed out, holding out her arms so Sabelina could help her into the dress. "Besides, what do you think got the iber?"

"*Vosh*, Ella, you will be the death of me someday. Running around and sneaking off late on an evening you're supposed to have dinner with your father…" The hairbrush was now in her skilled hands, and Ella sat down on the dressing table bench.

"It's hardly sneaking off. I'm eighteen. Of age. I'm free to leave and do as I please."

"That may be, but it is disrespectful to your father. Do you really think he deserves that? Sabelina set the brush down and ran her hand along the silky half-sleeve of the dress.

"No." Ella sighed, staring down at the shimmery material of her skirt.

"He's not perfect, I know. He's strict, Ella, but…"

"…he does try." Ella finished. She knew the rest of it, not because it was a lecture, but because the thoughts played in her mind often enough. He was the only parent she had left, after all, and he'd been raising her and Tallen on his own, no easy task.

A moment ago, she'd been terrified and starving, now she wasn't so sure she'd be able to stomach dinner. Was sneaking around and lying and nearly getting eaten by panthers really how she wanted to repay her father's thoughtfulness?

He tried, Ella knew, and this certainly wasn't the first time she'd come home to discover an unexpected gift from him. It would be useless to even thank him for it. She knew if she tried, her father would brush it off, pretending he didn't know what she was talking about, though the patches of skin just behind his ears would turn scarlet.

He loved her, the best he knew how. He didn't deserve to be deceived.

It was time to stop lying to him and tell him the truth about Loric. Surely now that Loric was no longer to be an apprentice, her father wouldn't have objections. *Yes,* she decided, *she would tell her father tonight, and tomorrow she would invite Loric over for dinner.*

"Let's get you downstairs," Sabelina said.

TWO - AN ANNOUNCEMENT

ALTHOUGH SHE MADE IT to the dining room only five minutes late, Ella was surprised to see that her father and brother weren't yet seated. Mealtimes were important to Marius Lockwood. Either you were on time, or everyone began eating without you.

Tonight, however, there was no mention of her tardiness, even as she replaced the shoe that had come off in her haste and tucked a still-wet strand of hair behind her ear.

Instead, her father smiled warmly as she entered. "Hello, darling, you look lovely. That color is stunning on you."

"It does match your hair—with those little red streaks," Tallen agreed.

Ignoring her brother, she went into her father's outstretched arms for a long hug. "Thank you, Father. It's so good to see you."

Her father leaned down and kissed the top of her head before taking a step back. "I trust you've been well? Not gotten into too much trouble?"

"Why? What did Sabelina tell you?" she asked, giving him her best impish grin.

"Fortunately for you, I received no messages from home while I was away." He smiled back in the way that told her he was joking. "Shall we eat?"

She'd been almost certain she was safe when she saw the gift on her bed, but it was still a relief to know for sure she hadn't been found out. Tallen raised a knowing eyebrow at her as they walked to the table, but she was feeling generous enough to not bother jabbing at him with her elbow.

The food was already laid out when they sat down, and as soon as the first lid was lifted from a serving dish, Ella found her appetite again. While dinners with all three of them together were always special, and they all had similar tastes, it was as the menu had been deliberately prepared to include *all* her favorite foods.

"How was your trip, Father?" she asked.

There was even a glass of her favorite tea, the kind Sabelina brought up for her every night before bed. This was the oddest addition to her meal, but she was grateful. Taking a sip calmed her; it had been a while since she'd enjoyed it cold.

"Busy. I only had one afternoon to look in the shops." He smiled again, letting his gaze fall on her dress for only a second. "I'm glad to be home. I shouldn't have to leave now for at least the next moon."

"That's good news," she said, smiling. She didn't believe him, not entirely. He was never home for anywhere close to a moon, but perhaps he'd stay for a few days this time, at least. She worried about him less when he was at home.

And if he was going to be home for a little while, perhaps she didn't have to tell him about Loric tonight. She would have time, now, to figure out the best way to do it, rather than spring it on him while he was unprepared.

Perhaps she would start with inviting him to dinner tomorrow. Inviting guests was common—there was no reason she couldn't invite a young man. Her father would be impressed with his skills and knowledge of the airships. Loric knew how to be impressive and charming in all the right ways. Her father would have trouble resisting him once they'd spent time together.

By the time the meal was drawing to a close, Ella was more relaxed and optimistic than she'd been in a long time. Soon she wouldn't have to hide things or lie to her father.

"Sunfruit cakes?" she exclaimed when she lifted the silver lid of the dessert platter. "I don't remember the last time we had these!"

"They were always your favorites when you were little," her father said. "I asked Flora to make them for you especially for this evening."

He grinned at her expectantly, obviously pleased with himself for arranging the surprise for her, but suddenly she wasn't in the mood for sunfruit cakes. Something wasn't right. Her father never had a hand in meal planning. So long as dinner appeared on the table at his appointed time, he was unconcerned with the specifics. Now, all of it—the dress, the foods, the sunfruit cakes, felt too intentional. Something wasn't right. Suppressing a shiver that wanted to travel all the way through her insides, she looked at her father. "I thought we couldn't get sunfruit ever since Silver Island…"

Her father cleared his throat. "Our difficulties with Silver Island are resolved now."

She raised an eyebrow and looked at Tallen, but her brother didn't look surprised. His face was a strange, dusky color, and his eyes wouldn't meet hers.

"That simply?" she asked. Every conversation she'd ever overheard about Silver Island in the last ten cycles had been about the uneasy truce between the almost-mythical overseas guildhaven and her own. She'd slept poorly every time her father ever had to travel there on diplomatic missions. More than once, the winds had whispered words like *treason* and *war* when the topic of Silver Island arose.

It had never seemed like the kind of problem that could be solved in a day.

Not peacefully, anyway.

"We're to be allies." There was no mistaking it, something was *off*. Everyone in this room knew something she didn't. Although her father would at least look at her, the expression on his face filled her veins with ice. A desperate desire to be in on the intrigue warred with a terrible suspicion that she didn't actually want to know.

Curiosity won. "How so?" She only just managed to keep her voice from shaking.

"You shouldn't look so frightened, Ellarowan," her father said with an unconvincing chuckle. "It's quite good news. It means peace and the strength of combining our troops. It means having sunfruit at the table again. Anytime you like."

But she wasn't fooled. "What else does it mean?"

"Well, that's another bit of good news. It means you're to be married."

All the glasses on the table remained intact, so she had no idea what could have made an enormous shattering sound, but she heard it. Immediately after the shattering, the room grew frosty despite the evening's heat. She couldn't force her mouth to form words, but her father began answering the questions she would have had if she could speak.

"Padraic Stone is the guildmaster of Silver Island."

The name wasn't familiar to her, but she didn't know if it was because she'd never heard it, or because she didn't understand anything right now. All she could do was sit there and try to listen over the fear and rage building up inside her.

"Padraic's son, Cayloken, is of age and is said to be a fine and capable young man. He should be a very good match for you. I think you'll be pleased."

This wasn't real; it couldn't be happening. Maybe she was dreaming, or maybe she hadn't escaped the panther. Perhaps she'd been attacked instead and was dead now. If so, this punishment the afterlife had devised for lying to her father seemed extreme.

There were other possibilities for what was happening, but this situation being real wasn't one of them. Ella's father had always been strict about the very idea of her courting—she'd never been allowed to accept an invitation from *anyone*. "There are too many with ulterior motives for getting close to the daughter of the guildmaster," he always said. That was why she'd hidden her relationship with Loric from him for so many moons.

And now he was suggesting she marry someone who definitely had ulterior motives, who they *knew* they couldn't trust?

Impossible. Ludicrous. This wasn't happening.

"…the Stones and their retinue will arrive here in a little over a fortnight. There's to be a grand engagement party. You can have whatever you like."

Obviously, she'd missed most of her father's speech, but these last few words somehow broke through her surreal haze. "A party? You're talking about destroying my life, and I'm supposed to think about a *party*?"

For the smallest fraction of a second, there was a break in her father's perfect, stoic expression, but he immediately hid it with another smile. For the first time in her life, she considered smacking the smile off her father's face.

"You're the guildmaster's daughter, Ellarowan. There were always going to have to be some sacrifices. This is a small one, all things considered. It's not necessary to be so dramatic about it."

"Getting married is a *small thing*?" She felt like she was yelling, but the sound that came out of her mouth was more like a strangled squeak. A painful pounding started in her head, and the lights in the dining room were suddenly overwhelming. She closed her eyes.

"I'm not asking you to care for him if you don't choose to. I've heard he's a strong leader and an excellent hunter, and you might actually enjoy his company. But if you'd prefer to continue to spend your free time with that shipwright's apprentice of yours, that's fine, you'll just have to be a bit less public about it. You'll still have a comfortable home and all your things. I'm hardly asking you to 'ruin your life' as you put it."

"I…" She tried to respond, but no words would come. The table in front of her seemed like it was moving; she set her hand down on the tablecloth to steady it, but somehow ended up face down on the scarlet silk.

"We can resume discussion of the details later when you're finished with your tantrum. This could be a very good thing for all of us if you can manage to embrace it."

Tantrum. The word rankled enough to make her coherent again. *Tantrum?* As if her feelings about being forced to marry a stranger were equivalent to those of a toddler refused a cookie. She looked up now, her head still pounding furiously. She couldn't see straight, but she thought that if she could, rage would be pouring from her eyes like dragon fire, but her father was already gone.

His plate still sat on his placemat, a half-finished fillet next to an untouched sunfruit cake, but no servant rushed to clear it, even though Marius was no longer in the room.

She shifted her gaze to Tallen.

Her brother's face was a shade of gray she'd never seen before, and she knew he wished he'd executed such an efficient escape.

"You knew." She'd found her voice again; it rang darkly to the corners of the room. The servants might decide the dishes would keep until morning.

"Only five minutes before you did. Father told me while you were upstairs changing."

"And you didn't put a stop to it?"

Tallen raised an eyebrow.

"Or at least *warned* me?"

"What good would that have done, Ella? Do you think running away before dinner would have stopped this? It's already done, already arranged. You're lucky he's even given you a fortnight to prepare yourself."

"He can't just *do* that, can he? Tell me who to marry? Make me do it?"

"Of course he can. He's the guildmaster. Your match has already been approved by the council."

"He hasn't made you marry anyone." She didn't entirely understand the words coming out of her mouth. At this point, she was mostly speaking to try to wake herself from the nightmare she was having. Because, surely, that must be what was happening.

"I'm sure it's not for lack of trying, El. He just hasn't found a suitable match for me that will also put our family inside another Guildmaster's Estate."

She blinked, trying to make his words make sense.

"Surely you understood that, Ella. Your husband-to-be is the future guildmaster of Silver Island. Our family will have power over two guildhavens."

"And I get no say in this, whatsoever?"

"If you handle it right, eventually you'll get a lot of say, as the guildmaster's wife."

The look she cast on her brother then was so wilting that she didn't even need to say the words, but she did, anyway, just to do as much damage as she could. "Yes, that position works out so well for everyone."

Her dagger hit its mark. The light in Tallen's eyes disappeared completely for several seconds. She might as well have punched him, and for that moment, it was worth it— even if the thoughts she'd roused weren't any easier for her.

They wouldn't talk about it, she knew. Tallen wouldn't make her answer for her remark; that wasn't even a possibility. A moment later, his voice was as steady as if she hadn't said anything. "Anyway, it's done. You might as well get used to the idea before they get here, and enjoy your time until then. Father left money for you." He nodded toward the sideboard.

Something else had occurred to her as he talked that kept her from looking for the money—which she didn't want anyway. "Did *you* tell Father about Loric?"

Tallen's eyes went as wide as River Rinn. "*Loric?* You've been seeing Loric Allsdale?"

She froze. Tallen was better than she was at covering his tracks and feigning ignorance, but he seemed truly surprised at this information.

"You thought you were going to accomplish *that* without Father finding out?"

"Apparently I managed to hide it from you all right."

"Yes, but…" He let out a low whistle. "What did you think, El? That you were just going to invite him here for dinner one night and announce your courtship and the whole thing would just m— just work out?"

A terrible warmth flooded from her head to her toes, and she felt sick to her stomach, but that wasn't the worst part. Some of the heat was beginning to congregate behind her eyelids, and that was something she could never allow to happen. She didn't care that she nearly knocked Tallen over in her haste to escape the dining room. If he said anything as she departed, she didn't hear it.

Furious as she was, though, she stopped when she reached the bottom of the stairs. Tallen hadn't followed her, and nobody else was in the foyer, so she stood there, staring at the black and gray streaks in the stone floor, trying to make patterns from the senseless squiggles. After a few minutes, everything was quiet again. Her breathing was steady; her heart settled back into its familiar rhythm, and her face was as cool as it should be. By the time she returned to her room, her mind was clear.

Closing the door behind her with her foot, she used her hands to lift the dress over her head, ripping it in half as she did so. Halfway to her bed, she stopped, realizing that if she stuffed the garment under the edge, Sabelina would find it there, and probably mend it. But the fabric was still good; it would make a nice gift for someone if they wanted to take the seams out and make something new.

Now that she thought about it, her friend Shea would adore the dress, and have the discretion never to wear it in front of her. Sighing, she shoved the thing under the edge of the end of her bed, where she wouldn't risk seeing it tonight when she returned—if she returned—but Sabelina would easily spot it tomorrow morning.

Five minutes later, she was dressed again and headed back down the stairs.

"Do you want to talk about it?" Tallen's voice cut through the night as she passed by him on the porch.

She didn't even flinch as she ignored him and kept walking.

"Would you like me to go and get Bastian for you?"

It was a challenge, but she didn't turn and say, "Why? So later you can press him for details about where I went, and who I was with?" Really, the only thing that kept her from blurting that out was her knowledge that Bastian would *never*. Her feet did come to a stop, though, and she held her hand out toward the drive yard.

When Tallen returned a moment later, he leaned up against the railing near her, but he didn't say anything. Maybe he'd wised up. He did, however, hold out a stack of notes so thick they almost couldn't be folded in half and shrugged one shoulder.

Ella bit the inside of her cheek until she tasted metal. She didn't want her father's gifts; she didn't want to be paid off—but she also didn't want to spite herself for no reason. Her father was the one who had taught her long ago that, "A gift freely given doesn't constitute an obligation." She wasn't sure he thought that rule applied to gifts given by *him*, but, it worked for her now. So she reached for the money and shoved it into her leather pouch without saying a word.

Bastian readied the carriage with merciful speed, so she only had to stand there in stony silence with Tallen for a couple of minutes before he pulled to a stop just in front of the porch stairs.

Although their carriage driver was usually chatty and amiable, he was also perceptive, so he, too, was quiet as he opened the door and helped Ella onto the plush cushioned seat inside. He only spoke once he'd climbed up into the driver's seat, and only to ask the single necessary question. "The Dozy?"

"Yes, please."

THREE
THE DOZY

THE DOZY'S TRUE NAME was *The Dozing Port*, but nobody ever called it that. Ella supposed the wooden sign hanging outside the low stone building on the edge of town had once contained the full name of the taberna, but wind and rain had long ago washed away everything except a *d* and a *z*. The Dozy wasn't a typical taberna, either.Most of the drinks they served were mild, and the patrons were far more likely to be found playing rex lusus at the comfortable tables or listening to the storytellers around the campfire than brawling on the back lawn, but there wasn't a word that described it better.

If she had been forced to give The Dozy a label, the word Ella might have chosen was *home*.

Bastian drove the carriage through the narrow ruts of the lane that led to The Dozy's drive yard. The little road desperately needed to be graded again, but that was unlikely to happen anytime soon. The outside of the establishment was uninviting by design, Ella thought—nobody here much cared for anything likely to draw in scores of unknown visitors. The property was secluded, hidden from the rest of Echo Bay by its ring of ancient, towering cypresses.

Ella suspected that she wouldn't even know about the existence of The Dozy if it hadn't been for Bastian taking pity on a tiny girl who was missing her mother. She still remembered the evening he'd discovered her hiding in the stables so nobody would catch her crying and set her to lessons for distraction.

"I was just about to ready the carriage to take a ride, child," Bastian had said, crouching down beside her in Tasia's stall. Her mother's horse seemed to be the only creature in the house who was just as confused as Ella. "Would you like to come with me?"

She'd nodded.

"Let me just go and tell Sabelina you're with me. You've had her worried for a bit, but she'll be glad I found you."

The driver had never been much for talking, not even back then, but he'd helped her into the carriage and driven her to the strange, dilapidated building. Once inside, he deposited her at the back counter where she'd immediately been fed and attended to by Old Cecil and his wife.

That was her memory, anyway. These days, Bastian would say he didn't recall any of it, that memories were tricky.

The past wasn't something anyone talked about much, anyway.

Tonight, climbing the steps to the wide porch was more comforting than usual, though it was only once she'd passed through the unassuming wooden door that some of the evening's tension began to melt from her.

The first time Ella had entered The Dozy, on that long ago night when she was so young, she'd actually squealed aloud at the difference. Whatever the outside lacked in comfort, the inside made up tenfold. Though the outside door was weathered and worn, the side that closed behind her gleamed with such a shine she could see her reflection in the fresh oil.

The large main room glowed with the warm light of glass lanterns affixed to the walls over each of the cozy tables that ringed the outer perimeter. Illuminated glass globes hung suspended over each of the gaming tables that dotted the center of the room, casting soothing, flickering candlelight over everything. Old Cecil, the proprietor, would choose to spend the last day of his life scraping the wax from the dozens of glass balls before he'd surrender The Dozy to the "blight of the deathly current," as he called the power that now flowed to nearly all of Ravensguild.

"Ella!" The sound of Shea's voice was a welcome respite from the turmoil of thoughts in her head, and Ella smiled as she hurried over to the counter where Shea was setting down a tray.

"It's late," Shea said, brushing her thick brown hair out of her face after they'd hugged. "I was afraid you weren't coming tonight since your father got back today."

The mere mention of her father sent a white-hot thrill of anger coursing through her chest, but she tried to ignore it, forcing herself to smile instead. "Well, I'm here now."

"What's wrong?" Shea's chartreuse eyes narrowed in a mixture of suspicion and concern.

"Nothing." She didn't want to talk about it—wasn't even sure she could. Not yet. If she said the words, then it would become real, like something that was actually going to happen, and she had no intention of accepting it.

"Is Loric coming tonight?"

"I hope not." The words were out of her mouth before she realized what that would sound like. A word that would have shocked Shea nearly followed that slip, but she tried to cover it. "I mean, I didn't think I'd be able to come since my father just got back, so we didn't make plans."

Shea stood staring at her in silence for several seconds before she grabbed hold of Ella's wrist and dragged her to the far corner of the room, where she peeked around a giant bookcase before pulling both of them into the alcove behind it.

There was a small couch in the middle of the alcove, hidden from view of the rest of the patrons, but they didn't sit. Shea wasted no time getting to the point. "What happened with Loric?"

"Nothing happened. Actually, that's not true. He got promoted to shipwright."

The immediate joyful surprise on her friend's face was a crushing reminder of what tonight *should* have been like. Ella should have been dancing as she came into The Dozy tonight, sporting a smile that would last a week. Instead, hot moisture pricked at the insides of her eyelids.

"Oh, Ella…"

It had been a while since anyone had said her name in that pitiful tone, and the memories *that* brought up did nothing to help with the dampness in her eyes. She bit the inside corners of her lips to keep them from trembling.

"Did he… Did he break things off with you then?"

Her head snapped up. "What? No! Why would you think that?"

"Well, when you said you hoped he wasn't coming…"

She had said that. It didn't matter that she'd corrected herself, Shea would have caught that she'd truly meant it. Not for any reason, her friend suspected, though. Seeing Loric was the one thing that might have calmed her and restored her good mood tonight. She still wanted to hear more about the end of his apprenticeship, and she definitely wouldn't have minded revisiting that kiss they'd shared earlier… But there was no way she could face him now, no way she could tell him what had happened at dinner tonight. The very idea made her stomach churn. Her legs felt so wobbly just thinking about it, she had to lean against the back of the couch.

"Then *what happened?*"

Some part of her must have wanted to tell Shea everything, or she never would have come here tonight. It was ridiculous to pretend otherwise.

At first, she maintained her composure as she told Shea all about the terrible dinner, the dress, the food, her father's absolute dismissal of any argument. But somewhere in the middle of sharing the burden with someone else, her anger mingled with fear and powerlessness, and a single dreadful tear went racing down her cheek. She almost stopped everything right then and headed back to the carriage—only the fact that Shea pretended not to see it kept her there.

She would *not* cry.

She wasn't sure how they ended up sitting on the couch, but by the end, Shea had her wrapped in a blanket and had somehow managed to produce a mug of baymallow tea, which Ella sipped at as she tried to calm herself.

"Can he make you do that? Marry someone you don't want to?"

She wanted to say no, wanted to keep arguing against it, to not believe it was the truth, but the ride had given her time to think and face the reality of the situation.

"Of course he can. Tallen said the match has already been approved by the council."

"You don't have to agree?"

She shook her head, knowing even as she did that Shea wouldn't understand in the same way she did. Shea's father worked maintaining the small boats that ferried travelers between the nearby islands. He wasn't the guildmaster or even a landowner. Although the two families resided in the same guildhaven, they occupied vastly different worlds. Shea might not wear rubies on the day she wed, but she would have full freedom to choose her partner.

Ella had always known that she would need her father's approval for any match. If she'd been honest with herself about it before now, she probably would even have realized that the council, too, would have to give their consent before she went any further than an official courtship with a suitor. She was the guildmaster's daughter, second in line to the position herself. It wasn't a secret that her marriage must someday reflect that. But it had never occurred to her that she would have no say in the matter at all—that someone would be chosen for her and she would have no choice but to accept marrying a complete stranger.

"And there's nothing you can do about it? At all?"

She held up a hand in defeat.

"What if you refused? He can't make you say the vows or sign the contract."

Ella bit her bottom lip, contemplating this. "He'd disown me. I'd have nothing, probably not even a home."

"So? Come live with me."

She narrowed her eyes. "Don't be ridiculous, Shea."

"I'm sorry. That was stupid. I just…I don't know what to say."

"At least I know you'd let me if I could." She understood where the sentiment came from. Shea's life was so different from hers, it must be difficult for her to comprehend the situation Ella was in. It was tempting to imagine it was really that easy, that she could walk away from everything. But she was the guildmaster's daughter. Nothing would ever be quite that simple—and worse, even if she could have given it all up, she wasn't sure she would have *wanted* to. "If I refuse, there's a chance I'd start a war with Silver Island."

Shea's eyes widened. "Do you really think so? That seems extreme."

"I don't know. More likely, I'd be arrested for defying the council's orders—and then my father could probably make me do it anyway."

The sudden sound of someone clearing her throat made both Shea and Ella jump. Ella looked over and saw Andela, one of the other servers, standing there. "Loric is looking for you, Ella," she said. "I told him you were outside; it looked like you wanted a bit of privacy, but he'll realize in a minute."

Less than a minute later, it was as if they'd never had the conversation in the alcove. Shea produced a handkerchief and carefully eliminated every trace of salt from Ella's face before applying a light coating of powder.

Ella allowed her friend to tidy her hair, too, but when Shea reached into her small bag and pulled out a vial of berry-wax to tint her lips, she shook her head. "This is hard enough. Thank you, but I should just go."

"You're going to tell him *tonight?*"

Yes, she was going to tell Loric tonight. There was no sense in waiting; it wouldn't get any easier. Or at least that was what she told herself as she walked, trembling, across the main dining room of The Dozy and through the door that led to the back porch and lawn.

The evening's storytelling had already begun, down below in the yard. Up on the porch, the shadows danced in the flickering light of the great fire, and Henric's powerful deep bass echoed through the clearing. Normally, this whole scene was Ella's favorite thing to witness, but tonight, she didn't notice any of it. Tonight, all she could focus on was Loric's lanky form draped over the wide railing and the way his mane of brown hair swung to and fro as he scanned the gathering crowd.

Beside him on the railing perched two heavy pewter mugs filled to the brim, she knew, with sweet cinnamon farrago. He wouldn't even sip at his until he found her. For a moment, she couldn't breathe as she remembered the first time she'd seen him standing there, in almost that same spot.

"Who is that?" Shea asked, looking sideways up at the porch.

Ella's head spunin that direction before she stopped to consider that she might regret it.

Shea's elbow jabbed into her arm. "Ella! Don't let him see you looking!"

But it was too late to avoid that. The stranger's eyes had already locked on hers, and he flashed a crooked grin at her before she could look back away.

He wasn't truly a stranger, of course. Unfamiliar to most of the patrons of The Dozy, perhaps—and such things didn't go unnoticed here—but Ella had seen him before. She couldn't remember his name just then but knew they'd been introduced at least once before, at a pre-Festival party, if her memory was accurate. The young man's father was… Yes! That was it. His father was Frederic Allsdale, a landowner, though Ella didn't know much more. She'd probably seen the son more than once over the last cycle, but never at a time they'd been able to talk.

Apparently, that was about to change, though. Ella could feel Loric moving closer to her, even though her gaze was now fixed on Shea.

"What am I doing?" she whispered to her friend.

Shea only laughed. "Flirting, apparently."

If Loric was as nervous as she was, he didn't show it. He sauntered right up to the two girls as if they'd been expecting him. "Ellarowan, right?"

Her cheeks and chest flamed hotter than the embers of the fire, but she managed to smile and hold out her hand. "It's Ella, please."

He pulled her hand to his mouth, brushing his lips over her knuckles, lighter than a feather. "Loric Allsdale."

Sighing in relief, she let her smile grow wider. "Yes, it's good to see you again, Loric."

"The pleasure is mine…Ella." His eyes twinkled in the firelight. "And who is your lovely friend?"

She'd stayed late that night at The Dozy. Later than she'd ever have dared to had her father been home, but he'd been away then.

Loric was a fine companion to both her and Shea; he'd never sat around the fire before to listen to the histories and the poetry, and he was fascinated with all of it. They'd talked—and laughed—until the flames burned to ashes and Shea had quietly disappeared, letting them get to know one another.

Ella closed her eyes, remembering that night—and the ones that had followed—willing herself to believe that nothing had changed, that this was just a normal night at The Dozy and she and Loric could listen to the stories and then sneak off to hide behind one of the trees for a while. But when she opened them again, it wasn't a normal night. It wasn't a moon ago. It was tonight, the night she'd learned she was betrothed to someone else, and he was still there, looking for her, and she had to face him. She took a deep breath and then put one foot in front of the other.

He must have heard her footsteps on the polished wood because he turned around to face her when she was still several feet away.

"Ella." His whole face—his whole body, really—lit up with a smile of pure, unadulterated joy, and he closed the distance between them before she had time to remember what she'd come out here to say.

He scooped her into his arms, radiating happiness that enveloped her as he pressed his soft, warm lips against hers, smiling even in his kiss. And then, there was nothing in Ella's mind except him. Nothing except the way his hands—rough and calloused from the work of the shipyard—felt like feathers on her cheeks as they cradled her face. He tasted of cinnamon and soap, and she couldn't get enough.

She couldn't tell him, not tonight. Today was his day to celebrate his incredible accomplishment; it wouldn't have been right to mar it now. And, after a few more kisses like that one, she couldn't quite remember what she'd been going to say, anyway.

Forgetting what she was supposed to say to Loric had been easy. Remembering later, halfway home in the carriage, tied her stomach in such knots she had to lean out the window, gulping in the cool night air so she wouldn't be sick all over the velvet seats.

For a brief moment, she considered that her father would deserve it if she ruined the interior of the expensive vehicle. But before she ever pulled her head in, she realized Bastian would be the one to clean it up. Marius would likely never even know.

In any case, the nausea passed without incident. By the time Ella arrived back at the estate, she was calm again, at least outwardly. Her dinner stayed locked soundly where it belonged as she climbed the steps to her room.

The hallways were dim now, illuminated only by a series of small lights near the floor. Her father was especially proud of this invention; it took a great deal of Ella's strength not to kick each light as she passed.

She was concentrating so hard on this task, though, that she nearly tripped over something large just outside her own door.

"Ooof!" Tallen grunted.

"See what happens when you lurk in people's doorways?" She stepped over her brother's legs and pushed her bedroom door open. Not in the mood to discuss the evening's events with him, she hurried to shut the door behind her quickly, but it wasn't fast enough. The hard wood slammed into Tallen's chest, earning her another quiet exclamation—though not the shouting she would have expected.

"Ella, I'm sorry."

This declaration was so far from anything she'd anticipated that her arm paused midway to slamming the door on him again, and her eyebrows knitted together. "You're sorry, or you're here to tell me I should calm down and not *throw a tantrum* and make things easier on Father?"

For a moment, he looked as if she'd punched him instead of spoken, and she started to wonder if he was sincere. She also kind of wondered if she *was* being awful to him.

"I deserve that, I guess."

She took several steps backward into her room, feeling like everything was turning upside down all over again.

When Tallen followed her, she didn't try to stop him.

The small bedside lamp was on its low, night-light setting, casting just enough light to give the area near the bed a reddish-pink glow while the rest of the room remained cloaked in black shadow.

When they were little, in the cycles after their mother died, Tallen would slip into her room every night. He would turn on that lamp for her and then sit at the foot of the bed, his hand on her feet until she fell asleep, keeping those shadows at bay. It had been a very long time since he'd last done that, though; she wasn't sure why she remembered if now.

"I thought you knew," he said quietly.

Ella sighed and leaned back against the edge of her bed. "I should have. It should have been obvious to me a long time ago that Father was just waiting for the right match and he would never allow me to choose for myself."

"You knew he could."

"Yes." She stared down at her hands, picking at a loose thread on her star-patterned quilt. "Of course I knew that he *could* choose my husband. I guess I just didn't let myself believe that he *would*. Nobody chose for him."

Tallen sucked in a breath and shook his head. "I wouldn't have drawn the same conclusion from that fact you seem to have. If anything, I should think Father would be less likely to let you make the same mistake he did."

Ella's stomach churned, and her whole body felt suddenly hot. If she could have shot fire at her brother, she would have. "Really? That's how you see it?"

He looked slightly remorseful, but not enough to appease her. "That's not what I meant, El, but I think it's how father sees it. If he hadn't married mother, if he'd married someone of his own station, he would be greatmaster by now. He'd never have lost it to Amalric Sandrez. And then she died, leaving him to raise two small children on his own. And no family or money of our mother's to help…"

"That's hardly mother's fault. Father doesn't have family, either."

Tallen gestured around the room with his hand. "You think the guildmastership and this estate came out of nowhere? Father's mother died in childbirth, but still, her family and connections preserved and added to all this. Their money is the reason Ravensguild was the first guild to add airships to the fleet. Surely you realize all this."

"I'm not too stupid to understand it, Tallen. I just think there are more important things than money sometimes."

"Says the girl who's never lived without it. I notice you're not fancying yourself in love with some poor vegetable seller. Loric Allsdale is almost as much a catch as you are—but not quite. Forget it, Ellarowan. You're never going to win that argument."

She chose to ignore the jab, only because it was late at night and pulling his hair out would cause servants—and possibly her father—to come running. "So you're saying I have no choice then. There's nothing I can do?"

"Begin preparing for your wedding."

"What if I went to the council myself and told them I didn't want to be married at all?"

Tallen rolled his eyes—which made Ella want to claw them out of his face. "How would you be planning to do that? The council doesn't meet again for another two moons, and the next meeting is not in Ravensguild. Besides, even if you could get there, father will be there. He has a vote, too."

She knew all this of course. Her father was one of the more powerful members of the council. She was grasping for any solution, no matter how absurd and failing spectacularly.

"Also, not getting married at all is not a solution to continuing your relationship with Loric."

At this point, he was just rubbing it in. She turned away from him and walked over to her dresser, pulling pins from her hair as she went.

"Even if it would work, Ella, I wouldn't try it. Peace with Silver Island is no small matter—and neither is peace with Father."

"You can shut up now, Tallen. Go bother someone else or go to bed. I'm not interested in peace with Father."

He was quiet for a moment before he responded. "Yes, you are. You can be as angry as you want, for as long as you'd like. Launch your battles if you must, but don't mistake that for being able to win a war."

"Not to mention that it's easier for you if I concede without a fuss," she said, twirling around to look at him again. "My being safely married off and our guildhaven at peace with Silver Island will only benefit you when you become guildmaster."

His lips pressed together in a tight smile. "All of that can be true without my being wrong, you know."

"I'll never forgive him."

"You don't have to."

"And maybe not you, either."

"That won't change anything. You should get some sleep. Drink your tea." He nodded toward the mug on her night table. Sabelina had clearly left it for her.

She was strongly considering throwing the cup at him, but he wisely ducked out of the room as she reached for it. The tea was still hot; it would have been a shame to waste it, anyway.

FOUR
AFTERMATH

ELLA WASN'T INCLINED TO take any of her brother's advice that night—including sleeping. Not that she had much choice in that matter. The bliss of unconsciousness eluded her for most of the night as she fretted over what she was going to say to her father in the morning.

A bare hint of yellowish light shone through the edges of the shutters on her windows by the time she finally dozed off, but still, the first sounds of the breakfast dishes being moved around in the kitchen below roused her again. Sabelina wasn't even upstairs to help her yet, but she didn't care. She dressed quickly and hurried to the dining room, ready to ambush her father before the careful words slipped from her mind or he found something more pressing to do. But when she reached the dining room, there were only two places set at the table.

The space in front of her father's seat was empty.

The pounding and rushing in her chest grew stronger—a feat she hadn't believed possible.

"He left just an hour or so ago." Sabelina's voice from the doorway didn't even startle her; it was as if she'd been expecting it somehow. "He said he'd send word before we're to expect him to return but not to hold dinner for him tonight."

Last night, he'd told her that he wouldn't need to leave again for at least the next moon, but it didn't matter. She wasn't surprised; she merely nodded and slumped down into her own chair.

Sabelina moved behind her, gathering up the back of Ella's hair in her sure, cool hands, and pulling a comb from the bottomless depths of the pockets of her apron. "You were in quite a hurry to talk to him, weren't you?"

"And all for nothing." Ella pulled her legs up and hugged them to her chest as Sabelina worked through her curls with the comb.

"Your father left directions to prepare the house and the guest cottages for a large contingent from Silver Island—and to begin preparing for a betrothal party and a wedding." The comb stopped moving, and Sabelina's hand landed on Ella's shoulder.

"I'm sure he did." She reached up and took Sabelina's hand in her own as the tears began to roll down her cheeks—only now would she let them.

Sabelina let go of her for just long enough to cross the dining room and close the door, pulling the latch snugly. When she returned, she pulled out the next chair and sat, pulling Ella's head into her lap, rubbing her back and rocking her as she cried.

It had been a very long time since Ella had wept at all, and the last time had also been in her caretaker's arms—the only place she'd allow herself to do it at all. This storm, fueled as much by anger as it was by devastation, calmed quickly and used the corners of her apron to dab at Ella's eyes once the last tear had fallen. "I'm sorry he's done this."

"Is there nothing I can do?" she asked, once her voice was steady again.

"I don't know, dear one. I imagine any question of that will have to be answered whenever your father decides to return."

Ella scoffed. "I know it's not possible with my father, but surely *you* know of some other way? Someone I can talk to? Something?"

She hadn't expected to get the answer she really wanted, but her jaw nearly fell on the floor when Sabelina seemed almost to ignore the question completely. "I wish I had better news," was all she said as she resumed her task of untangling Ella's unruly locks.

It wasn't like Sabelina to support her father's more outrageous stances without question—not when he wasn't home, anyway. Anger and fear bubbled inside Ella as she stared at the red-and-black pattern that ringed the plate in front of her, trying to contain herself. Unsuccessfully. "What do you suppose my mother would have had to say about this?"

The comb slipped from Sabelina's fingers, landing on the stone floor with a metallic clang, but this was the only pause in the caretaker's response. "I don't know if it would have mattered. Your mother did, after all, decide that there was only one way to escape your father's commands."

The answer was like a physical blow, slamming her into the back of the chair. Conversations about her mother's death were avoided at all costs in their house. Her father wouldn't permit such discussions around him, and Ella didn't much like hearing—or talking—about the circumstances surrounding her death, either. *Nobody* had ever come out and said that her mother had taken her own life, although it had been implied once or twice the way her caretaker seemed to be doing now.

So Sabelina *didn't* support her father's decision completely, but wouldn't speak out against it at all. This was more serious than Ella had thought.

She regretted starting the conversation.

Sabelina only bent to pick up the comb and then resumed her work braiding Ella's hair."Perhaps something can be worked out when the guildmaster of Silver Island arrives. We don't know what his son has to say about any of it after all, do we?"

For the first time since dinner last night, she felt a small bubble of hope, though she knew the idea was likely futile, it was at least something to hold onto.

"In the meantime," Sabelina continued, "I suppose we might as well spend as much of your father's money as we can manage, eh?"

The first part of the day passed far more quickly than Ella would have expected it to. She suspected much of this was because her lack of sleep made it hard to concentrate and gave everything a kind of dreamlike quality. Her father's absence also helped; angry as she was at him for leaving and ignoring her wrath, it was easier to pretend all the measuring for clothing and searching through dinner menus was for a normal party with him gone.

Perhaps the thing that sped the day most of all, though, was her apprehension at what the late afternoon held in store. She'd often complained that enjoyable days seemed to pass far too quickly, but it turned out that a day with something to dread at the end disappeared like salt in hot water.

Regardless of her feelings on the topic, the sun refused to stay directly overhead, and instead sped to the west until her bedroom glowed with hot, golden light, and she knew she couldn't put it off any longer. After asking Sabelina to hold her dinner in the kitchen until she asked for it, Ella slipped outside and headed toward the clearing.

Every danger the forest held at dusk and beyond was matched by a wonder in the late afternoon.

The sun that poured through Ella's windows with a blinding, blistering light was filtered through the leaves of towering, ancient trees here, casting dapples of green and gold between wavering shadows that chased each other playfully over the ground.

High up in the branches of the trees, birds chittered and squawked, calling out greetings, searching for mates. There were the noises of other small creatures, too, as they hurried to conduct the last of their business in the safety of the sunlight before the predators came lurking.

The heat of the day had long since baked off the overnight buildup of moisture, and now everything smelled of the rich musk of soil and the honeyed scent of the nectar in the great blue and yellow hiranthia flowers that climbed in vines over so many of the tree trunks.

Usually, Ella took her time walking through this part of the woods, perhaps stopping to watch an animal at its work or to pluck off a hiranthia bloom that was just beginning to wilt, to feel the velvet-soft petals against her skin. But today she couldn't bring herself to enjoy any of the forest's offerings.

Rushing to arrive at their meeting place too early was often an exercise in disappointment, but today her feet didn't care; they darted over the rocks and roots with little thought of anything but reaching her destination. A large part of her didn't even want to go to the meeting place; she wasn't ready to tell Loric. She knew everything was going to change once she did, and the bliss of their secret meetings would be destroyed. But the only thing worse than living through a terrible event is waiting for one to happen. In the end, her desire to end the torture of waiting was greater than her fear of what would happen, and when she reached a spot where the rough terrain leveled out, she broke into a run.

Loric wasn't there when she reached the clearing, of course. There were still a few minutes before their usual meeting time, and while some days he'd show up a bit early to surprise her, surely the first day of his new job wouldn't be one of them. It didn't matter. She felt better just being there. While she wasn't at all looking forward to what she needed to do, at least it would be done, and she could begin the concrete work of dealing with the fallout instead of the terrifying anxiety of waiting and wondering.

Trying to keep herself calm, she made her way over to a large tree stump, sat down, and pulled her sketchbook from her leather bag.

At first, she sat there on the stump, staring at the blank

paper, rolling the stick of charcoal between her thumb and forefinger until both were black as midnight, but after several minutes the idea came, and her hand moved over the page almost on its own.

She kept her eyes on the paper and her ears on the surrounding forest, waiting—hoping—for the interruption of Loric's boots crunching through twigs and rocks. The page filled, first with soft lines, then more definite strokes. Eventually, swirls and shadows appeared, nudged gently into place by her coated fingertips. But the forest floor remained silent.

Finished, restless, she stood and paced the clearing, from edge to edge and back again, working her way around the lopsided circle, but her motions didn't change anything. He wasn't here. And now that the rays of sunlight were growing feebler and coming fully sideways through the lower branches of the trees, she knew he wasn't coming.

There had been other times he hadn't shown. They were few and far between, but since they didn't dare use the wires to send messages to each other that could be intercepted, there was no easy way to communicate between their meetings. This meant it was inevitable that occasionally one or the other of them would be waylaid past dusk. But this time, she knew it wasn't chance. This time, she knew it was her fault, knew she'd done the wrong thing in not telling him last night. And she wasn't sure it could be fixed.

Seeing no other options, she pulled the paper from her sketchbook, scrawled some words on the back, folded it once, and tucked it under a rock in the middle of the clearing, leaving the white edges sticking out where they'd catch the light, making sure the drawing wouldn't be missed.

The sharp emotions of last night and this morning had

faded into a kind of dull, aching numbness. Part of her thought she should feel devastated at Loric's absence, but it was overruled by the larger part of her that had known, deep down, that this consequence was likely. And what did it matter, anyway? Unless she could find a way to escape her father's mandate, prolonging the inevitable with Loric was only going to hurt him more.

The panther incident was still fresh in her mind as she started back through the woods, so she should have steered well clear of the river, but she didn't. Instead, she found herself wandering down almost to the edge of the water, her eyes traveling the bank for signs of the attack she'd witnessed.

She expected to find the place easily; the struggle between the panther and iber loomed in her memory like a massive battle that should have left trails of broken branches and blood in its wake. But the evidence along the riverbank—or rather, the lack thereof—told a different story, reminding her how quickly it had all happened in reality. Surely, she thought, there would be a patch of broken twigs and mangled leaves, dotted with small drops of blood, but if there was, she couldn't find it.

The whole area was calm and peaceful, reminding her that she hadn't always been frightened of dangers lurking beyond the river.

When she was a small child, nobody had such worries. Back then, the river wasn't a boundary, dividing the land in two. If the great Rinn Forest had held threats back then, they'd never come this close. The lawns and woods behind the Guildmaster's Estate had been a lush retreat in those days, dotted with hammocks and picnic tables, scattered with toys. Ella and Tallen had played out here every day from the moment their lessons were finished until Sabelina's bell dragged them back inside for dinner.

And their mother. She knew her mother couldn't have possibly spent every moment out here with them when she had other duties. Of course she couldn't. But in Ella's memory, her mother was always there, reading stories and poetry while they stretched out on blankets, the willing victim in their rescue adventures, helping search for flowers to make crowns for Ella's hair.

The only true danger then, it seemed, had been the river itself. Ella and Tallen had been forbidden to play there alone—not because of panthers or the other dangers that lurked somewhere far on the other side, but for the same reason they were watched at the seashore. Careless children and water didn't mix. Although most of the time the river was narrow and shallow where it touched their property, on occasion it would remind them that it was a tributary of the great River Rinn, especially when the heavy rains fell, swelling the banks, making the depths of the river swirl and churn.

Lyonet Lockwood had mitigated even this peril, taking her children to play there when the water was shallow and calm, keeping a watchful eye as they splashed and swam. Besides taking them often enough they wouldn't be tempted to go without her, she'd taught Ella and Tallen how to recognize when the water's movements warned of trouble, taught them how to swim and how to rescue someone who was struggling. This had been their favorite game, one pretending to drown while the other dove in and pulled them to shore, inevitably dissolving into a pile of tickles and giggles back on dry land.

Despite the difference in age and size between the two of them, Ella had always been just as good as Tallen on the rescue missions.

Ella hadn't been afraid of the river then. Cautious, yes, but never scared. She knew that so long as she followed her mother's directions, she would be safe near the banks.

Or, at least, that was what she'd believed, right up until the river had stolen her mother.

There was no evidence of *that* struggle along the banks of the river now, either. She wondered if there ever had been. She'd been only three cycles old when it happened, not old enough, Tallen always said, to remember what things had really been like. And perhaps he was right. Maybe she was simply too young to have known about the predators in the woods, or about the strange lights that sometimes moved in the trees late at night, or the rumors the demons, the magic people who stole others away. It was possible the peace and playfulness of her memories were only the daydreams of a young child.

But she didn't think so. Some of her memories were just too clear—and at least some of them were indisputable.

The old guest cottage still stood there, just a couple dozen yards from the river, a wooden monument to the days this part of the estate was a warm and playful retreat and not a shadowy zone of mysterious threats.

Ella had been avoiding thinking about the cottage today, for much the same reason she'd spent the day trying to chase thoughts of Loric from her mind. She wasn't sure she was ready to come face-to-face with the consequences of yesterday. While she'd done everything she knew to do for the little iber, she wasn't stupid. The creature had been attacked by a panther. When she opened the door of the cottage again, it would be to clean up the iber's remains.

She'd given it a cozy, safe place to die, and she'd denied the panther a meal on the edge of the estate, hopefully deterring it from hanging around, but an iber that had spent time between the jaws of a giant cat was a *dead* iber.

Unpleasant as that task was going to be, though, she knew that delaying it wasn't going to make it any easier. Unless she planned on avoiding the cottage forever—and though she knew that perhaps she *should*, she also knew she *wouldn't*—the best time to deal with it was right now.

So she sighed and headed for the little wooden building, wishing she'd at least brought along a spare set of grubby clothes.

She'd just reached the top step of the porch at the little cottage when she heard a loud thumping noise that nearly made her jump out of her skin. She whirled around, looking for the source; it took her a minute to realize that the noise had to have come from *inside* the cottage, which shouldn't have made sense. The only thing inside the cabin was an iber, and it was dead.

Or was it? She held her hand over the doorknob, trying to work up the courage to turn it. Was it possible? Could the iber still be alive in there? Or... she paused at a new thought. Could something else have gotten in?

Grateful this had occurred to her before she opened the door, she walked the length of the porch and then down around the outside of the cottage, checking all the windows. Everything was closed up tight. Unless something had made it in the front door—something with thumbs, capable of turning that knob and then closing it back up again—only the iber could be inside. Taking a deep breath, she turned the knob for herself.

Half expecting something—some*one*?—to jump out at her, she was nearly startled again by the silence that greeted her inside.

Quiet and still as it might be at the moment, the room didn't look much like the place she'd entered last night. Immediately, she saw what must have made the thumping noise. One of the bedside tables was now on its side. The covers on the bed were rumpled and strained, pulled down nearly to the floor at one of the corners, revealing linens underneath that were crisper and cleaner than she would have expected, despite the fur on them.

The rugs, too, looked like something had stomped and skittered through them—because, of course, something had. And the seam on one of the curtains was ripped to shreds, making it a terrible hiding spot for the small creature huddled underneath, its little body quivering as badly as Ella's hands were.

The iber was very much alive.

She didn't know how, but the creature wasn't *just* alive—it was up and moving, wreaking havoc in the cottage, clearly not even on death's door.

Now the question was, how was she going to check its injuries and get it out of here? Dealing with a stunned, dying iber was one thing. An alert, terrified one was another story altogether.

Cautiously, she took a couple of steps toward the animal, holding up her hands where it could see, talking in what she hoped was a soothing voice. "Hello. I'm glad to see you're okay. I'm not going to hurt you." It felt ridiculous to talk to the creature as if it understood her, but apparently, the iber didn't think the idea was as terrible as she did. By some strange miracle, it didn't run or jump away as she approached. In fact, as she got closer, the iber's trembling seemed to slow a little bit, and it raised its head, those black, liquid eyes blinking up at her.

The fur under its eye was still a dull brownish-red where last night's blood had dried into the soft strands, but there seemed to be less than yesterday. The eyes themselves were wholly undamaged. In fact, aside from the dark patches in the fur, she wouldn't have had any idea the iber had tangled with a creature ten times its size just the day before.

Incredibly, the closer she got, the calmer the animal appeared to become. By the time she reached the window and lowered herself gingerly to her knees, the iber's fur was utterly still except for the slow, regular motion of its breathing.

Even more impossibly, when she ever-so-slowly reached her hand out near it, the thing took a step of its own, right toward her hand.

That the iber wasn't frightened was absurd enough, but even more shocking was the fact that *she* wasn't at all scared either. She should have been—small as it was, the iber could inflict plenty of damage if it wanted to. But, somehow, she knew it didn't want to.

Her breath stalled and silenced; her whole body went still and quiet as the little iber took one tiny step in her direction and then another.

Before she understood what was happening, soft fur brushed up against the underside of her hand; the warmth of the little animal seemed to flow from her fingers up through her arms and then down again into the center of her being. They stayed that way for several minutes, creature and girl, until her knees complained and she began to fear she'd tip forward onto it. She edged down from her knees and into a sitting position, afraid to breathe as she did so, lest she frighten the iber and send it on another destructive spree through the cabin—or worse, through her skin.

But the creature wasn't bothered by her movements at all. It remained in the same place, just watching her until she was sitting down, and then, it moved even closer to her. Before she really understood what was happening, the iber—this small, wild creature of the forest, the clawed ball of fur that could do serious damage to her face if it decided it wanted to—was nestled in her lap.

After a moment, the iber rested its face against her leg, and the whole cabin filled with a deep rumbling noise that shook her body, reverberating against the floor.

She didn't know what the noise was—hadn't even known that ibers were capable of making such a sound. But she did have an idea of what it meant. If the creature she was holding had been a cat, she would have said it was purring.

The whole thing was, arguably, the most surprising event she had ever experienced, and yet she didn't *feel* surprised at all. Instead, it all felt right, as if the iber had perched in her lap a thousand times before and would do it an infinite number of times in the future.

Of its own accord, her hand went to the creature's head, touching the warm, wispy fur there before stroking down the length of its little body. It was so, so soft. When she closed her eyes, she almost couldn't feel the fur; it was like touching a cloud—mist that would disappear if you tried to hold it. But she *was* holding it. The warm weight of the animal was quite real against her legs.

All her caution gone now, she kept petting it with one hand while she used the other to lift the fur near its eyes and neck, searching for the wounds it had sustained the night before.

It took several minutes of carefully feeling her way through the long fur to find them, but the wounds were there—two hard little lumps buried deep in the piles of thick fur, spots where the panther's teeth had cut into the iber's skin.

The animal didn't flinch even when she touched these spots. Oddly, though she knew exactly when they'd happened, the injuries felt much older than a single day. These were scabbed over, nearly healed. And the little iber was healthy and whole. She didn't understand how, but she was grateful.

After what felt like a terribly long time of petting the creature, she decided to try to stand.

The iber didn't object even to this. It sat calmly in Ella's arms as she rose to her feet, and it allowed her to carry it outside onto the porch.

For the briefest of moments, she considered keeping the thing—perhaps taming it as a pet—but she knew that would be impossible. Though they might be fluffy and cute, Ibers were wild creatures, none had ever been successfully tamed. And they were social animals—somewhere out there in the woods, the iber's pack would be searching for it, calling with the high-pitched squeal she'd thought was the only noise it could make.

Still unwary, she walked down the steps and then lowered the iber gently to the ground, giving its fur one long last pet before letting go.

For several minutes, the critter didn't move. It stood still, the way it had underneath the curtain, blinking up at her with the hint of shiny black eyes, mostly hidden now by the long fur and the encroaching dusk.

From where she stood, Ella could see a good section of the river. Her eyes swept up and down the bank, but she detected no dangers. Birds still chattered loudly in the trees, their calls turning toward the final search for food and shelter for the evening, not warning of predators. Bright oranges and golds reflected in the gentle flow of the river, the last of the day's sunlight shimmering and dancing.

"Go on," she coaxed the iber in her softest voice.

She'd never before had the opportunity to see an iber walking up close. The movement was so strange that for a moment she wanted to giggle. It had legs, she knew this for sure, so it had to be stepping like any other animal, but its feet were hidden in the massive fluffs of fur, so when it moved, it appeared to be floating along the ground, like a feather duster. But Ella only got to see the movement for the briefest of seconds. The iber only made it about a foot away before it stopped again, staring back up at her.

"Well, I'm not putting you back in that cottage if that's what you're thinking. Another night in there and you'll have it falling down around you."

It blinked.

"Look, it's safe. There's nothing out here." She held her hand out toward the river, feeling ridiculous even as she did. The creature wasn't *acting* scared, anyway. It wasn't trembling or watchful. Its fur moved up and down in a slow, steady rhythm as it breathed. She didn't think it was scared, at all. It was just...sitting there.

She glanced down at the river again, just in time to see—

She frowned. What *had* she seen? A sudden flash of something in the air over the middle of the river, a few feet above the water. Something that reminded her distinctly of a head. But there was nothing there now. Perhaps it was just a trick of the evening light—but she'd been so certain.

Shaking her head to try to clear it, she looked at the river again, concentrating on that spot.

A jolt surged through her body as it appeared again—definitely a head. She knew for sure, because this time, a body followed it. An entire person had just *appeared* in mid-air, suspended above the river.

Suspended for a second, anyway. At the same second she took off running toward the river, whatever was holding the person up in the air like that apparently failed, and he came splashing down into the dark current.

FIVE - THE MAN IN THE RIVER

Bʏ THE TIME ELLA reached the bank, she'd realized that running straight toward a strange man who'd appeared in the air might not be the safest idea she'd ever had, and she pulled her knife from her bag, gripping the handle tightly.

The man in the water was not only fully clothed, but he wore a strange, enormous contraption on his back; she thought perhaps it was some kind of pack. Whatever it was, though, having it strapped to him wasn't an asset once he hit the water. Even though the water barely reached his waist, between the pack and the current, he couldn't keep his balance, and he tumbled sideways into the river, his body disappearing again, though the huge pack bobbed on the surface.

Ella loosened her grip on the knife.

He made what she thought was a valiant effort to right himself, but the pack kept getting wetter and heavier as he did, so after a few seconds of thrashing around, it would always pull him back down again.

"Take it off!" she called, the third time he hoisted himself back out of the water.

His head whipped around so fast it was almost comical, and his eyes widened—just before he toppled into the water again. Too late, she realized he hadn't seen her there, and she'd scared him half to death.

She slid the knife back into her pouch before tossing it to the ground and reaching down to remove her shoes.

He wasn't in immediate danger of drowning—he'd figured out how to keep his head above the water now when he fell back in—but he wasn't going to get out of that river by himself anytime soon, not with that pack on his back.

When she stepped in and felt the pull of the current against her own legs, she understood his reluctance to take the pack off. The flow of the water was strong enough to start carrying away anything much lighter than a person.

The man's face registered alarm when he felt her hand on his wrist, but he didn't pull away, and he didn't fight against her. After she had helped him regain his balance, he dug his feet into the bottom of the river and let her lead him through the water. It wasn't easy, but together, they managed to both get safely back to the bank.

Once there, Ella considered reaching for her knife again, but the man made no move to threaten her. Instead, as soon as he could balance himself on land, he took several steps back from her, moving himself to a safe distance before his hands found the first of the clasps that connected the straps of the pack securely to him.

"Are you all right?" she asked.

His eyebrows bent into a deep furrow as if he hadn't understood her.

Another electric jolt went through her center. She'd heard about such things—strange people appearing from what seemed like nowhere, people traveling through openings in the air. But these had only been stories, told late at night around the fire pit at The Dozy, only on nights when everyone there could be trusted, since talk of magic was forbidden.

Was that what this man was? she wondered. One of the magic ones? A gadab? A demon? A character from a story come to life?

Though the evening was almost stiflingly warm, tiny bumps rose all over her arms and legs, making her shiver.

"Who are you?" she asked.

This time, he answered back, uttering a single word she didn't understand, his voice a strange husky-sounding tone that made her think of leaves rubbing together in the wind. She had the strangest feeling that she should have understood it, that it was a language that should have made sense to her, but something about it was terribly off.

"I don't understand," she said, shaking her head. "I'm sorry," she added.

His eyes brightened now as if he was comprehending something new, and for the first time, she realized just how odd his eyes were.

Night had almost fully fallen now, and it was hard to tell in the deepening shades of purple, but even in this light, she could tell that his eyes were a color she'd never seen before—an odd shade of brown, maybe? A color she'd only seen on creatures, not on people. And, also like an animal, the dark pupils in the center were perfectly, unrealistically round.

Clasps finally disconnected, he shrugged out of the wide padded straps and carefully lowered the enormous contraption on his back to the ground. It was definitely a pack of some kind. Even on the ground, it was larger than any bag Ella had ever seen; it reached just past the man's waist when he was standing.

Her eyes swept up and down his frame, wondering how he'd managed to carry such a thing so far. He was tall—taller than her, at any rate—and, although she could see the faint outline of biceps beneath the wet sleeves of his long-sleeved shirt, his build was slight; he looked more like a scholar than a farmer or a tradesman. Perhaps he was a gentleman, from a family like her own, although that would make his sudden appearance in the middle of the woods even stranger than it already was.

Whoever he was, she wasn't afraid of him, she realized with a start. There was nothing about him even vaguely threatening. Even those bizarre eyes were somehow kind and safe. If anything, he was afraid of her—she could tell by the way he still kept a careful distance from her, moving so that he was always facing her, keeping a careful watch on her own motions, even as his eyes occasionally darted from side to side, appearing to take in his surroundings.

He didn't know where he was.

She cleared her throat and tried again to communicate with him, this time speaking slowly and using her hands. "I'm Ella," she said, pressing her palm against her chest. "Ella."

"Ohn," he said back, imitating her gesture.

"Ohn?" she tried the word, her tongue twisting in unfamiliar ways as she attempted to mimic the way he'd said it. "Is that your name?"

His eyes widened in pleased surprise this time, filling with the orange light of the just-rising moon. "My name. Yes. Ohin." He drew out each individual sound with deliberate slowness, and now she understood.

She'd been wrong. The man wasn't speaking a different language at all. The words were the same, he just said them in an incredibly strange way, adding sounds to the vowels, clipping the consonants at harsh angles, cutting them off before they could even get started.

She tried saying his name again, smooshing the letters between her teeth and tongue the way he seemed to, but what she said didn't sound the same at all.

He smiled at her attempt and bent down, reaching inside his pack.

This should have been the part where her sense returned and she became properly scared of this stranger, but something about him made feeling frightened impossible, and all she could do was stare in fascination as he drew something out of his bag.

She knew before she ever saw what he was holding that it wouldn't be a weapon, and it wasn't. It was a flat, square object that looked like—no, *was*—a book. The thin paper inside gleamed too-white in the moonlight as he flipped it open and began writing something on the very first page. At first, his thick, broad strokes on the paper made her think he was drawing something, but he finished almost instantly and then held the book out toward her.

She took a step closer, careful not to break the careful boundary between them and looked at what he'd written. OWEN.

"Your name is Owen," she said. In her mouth, the name didn't sound anything like what he'd said, but he smiled and nodded, and she felt an unexpected elation at having figured it out.

"Ella," she said, pointing to herself again. "Ellarowan actually."

His strange eyes crinkled in thought, and then he put his pencil to the page again for a moment, before holding it out for her to see the new word he'd written. ELLA.

She nodded, wondering if it was possible he already understood more about her than she did about him. "Where did you come from?" she asked. "How did you get here?"

He held up both hands and moved his shoulders in a motion she would have understood even if he *had* been speaking an entirely different language. Then he pointed to the river.

"You don't know how you got here?" It took effort to keep her words slow and deliberate in hopes that he would keep understanding her.

"Where *am* I?" he asked.

She cocked an eyebrow, wondering if it was the best idea to tell him everything he asked. Although she was now certain, even deep down, that he wasn't an immediate danger to her, that didn't mean everything about him was safe. She'd never truly believed the stories about the *gadab*—the travelers, but...she had just literally watched this man drop out of the air and into the river.

Of course, if he *was* magic, how could he have not at least kept himself dry?

"Where were you trying to go?" she asked. She wasn't sure why she picked this question to ask. It seemed odd to assume that someone who had quite literally fallen from the sky had been *trying* to go anywhere. And yet, it seemed to be the right question—or at least one that would produce some information from him.

This time, the answer that came out of his mouth was filled with so many convoluted syllables she couldn't understand him at all. Whatever he'd said, he was nowhere *near* his destination.

"You're in Echo Bay," she said. "In Ravensguild."

Owen thought he had prepared for this side of the gate. The river, he'd known about. He hadn't expected the current to be quite as strong as it was, but he would have managed. It was shallow; at least he'd thought far enough ahead to test that by throwing rocks first. The waterproof boots and quick-drying clothes had worked. Already, his sleeves were nearly dry, and no water had even made it to his socks. He wouldn't freeze, regardless. The night was as warm as all the other nights he'd checked. His backpack seemed intact, too. The rugged outside was soaked, but the waterproof lining lived up to its description. Even the new journal he'd bought was still dry and worked for writing.

He *had* underestimated what it would be like to jump into the shallow water from the height of the gate—the drop had jolted him a bit. But he'd gathered enough information on the times he'd peeked through to know there would be no bridge.

His plan for getting back up there to return home might need some tweaking, but he had time to figure that one out.

But the girl was unexpected. He'd prepared for this night for a long time now, peeking through the gate whenever he could get to it on an opening night, surveying the land on this side, figuring out what he'd need to land here safely and keep himself safe once he was here, and there had never been anyone around on this side.

He'd seen the small building, up there on the rise, a hundred yards or so away. But there had never been any lights, any movements, any signs of life at all. He'd even stuck most of his body through a couple of times, so he could get a good look all the way around. The lack of a bridge on this side made true surveillance challenging, but he'd been certain enough.

And yet, here she was, standing in front of him, wondering where he'd come from, looking as terrified as he felt. Not that he blamed her. If she wasn't familiar with gates—and he had no reason to suspect she would be—then it had to be more than a little disconcerting to watch someone appear out of thin air and land in a river in front of you. He was lucky her first instinct hadn't been to draw a weapon on him.

He hadn't prepared well for that possibility, either. His goal had been to land here as unobtrusively as possible and quickly find a place to hide until he could puzzle out exactly where he was and how to get from there to the capital city of Philotheum. The capital of Eirentheos would have worked, too—he wasn't picky.

But if he was understanding Ella's strange words, then he was someplace he'd never even heard—or dreamed—of.

"Ravensguild?" he asked, trying out the strange accent. Her speech scared him more than anything. It wasn't like any kind of English accent he'd ever heard before—the vowels and cadence made him imagine Old English, but, of course, he'd never heard someone speak that—and he didn't think it was quite right in any case.

He'd known quite a few people from this side of the gate. None of them spoke like this girl. While it was true the speech patterns of the people in Eirentheos were slightly different from his own, the differences were slight enough that William and Nathaniel had never had trouble blending in with the way they spoke on Owen's side and people from both sides had always understood each other easily.

Ella's accent was going to take some serious getting used to. And worse, if everyone here spoke the way she did, then Owen had no hope of blending in. As soon as he opened his mouth, he'd be marked as an outsider to anyone.

Of course, he was going to have to get through the immediate obstacle of Ella herself before he even began to worry about anyone else.

He tried to ask her again, this time saying it more slowly, while writing it out in his journal. "How far am I from Philotheum?"

She gave him the same blank stare as before when he said the word, so he held the page out to her.

A deep crease appeared down the center of her forehead, and for the first time, he noticed her eyes. There was something—not right—about them. It was hard to tell, in the darkness what exactly it was, but something was definitely off. Perhaps it was just shadows, but her pupils seemed to be the wrong shape, not round. His stomach wobbled as she shook her head and spoke again in the strange musical accent that now carried even more suspicion than before—and he hadn't thought that was possible. "I know of no place with this name. Who are you?"

"My name is Owen Robbins. I mean you no harm," he said slowly, noticing that his hands weren't the only ones trembling. "I'm just trying to find my family."

"Your family is here?" She looked around them at the darkened woods. Suddenly, he wondered where *her* family was. She appeared to be out here all alone. The one building he could see was still dark; if she lived there, she did so alone. Her clothing was in a style he didn't recognize—a long shirt over loose pants that tied just below her knees—but both items were in beautiful repair, made of fine material, and appeared tailored to fit her perfectly. He wasn't always the best judge of people, but she didn't seem like someone who lived alone in a run-down cabin in the woods.

"My family is in Philotheum," he said. "I thought I could get to them this way, or that at least I could try, but now I'm not so sure."

"How did you get here?" she asked. Her voice was quiet, almost as if she was hoping he wouldn't really hear her.

There didn't seem to be any point in lying. The gates were dangerous knowledge in Philotheum and Eirentheos. He had intended on keeping his travel through the gate a secret until he reached the safety of his sister and her family. But he was fairly certain Ella had just *watched* him travel through it. There was no way she could have arrived at the river so soon after he fell in without seeing it. She had to have been standing there—or at least near there—the entire time.

Still, his own voice was barely more than a whisper when he answered. "Through the gate above the river. I traveled here from another...place. Do you know about the gates?"

At first, she didn't respond. For several hundred heartbeats—Owen felt each one pound against the wall of his chest—she just stood there, perfectly still, staring at him. Then she looked over at the river, her eyes rising into the air where the gate was before looking back at him. She had most definitely seen. "Are you magic?"

Magic? Had he understood her correctly? Was that what she'd said? "No," he said. "I'm not magic."

Relief flooded her strange eyes, at least for a moment before confusion settled into them again, but she didn't speak. He started to think this was maybe his only opportunity to try to escape. "I'm sorry if I frightened you," he said slowly. "I didn't mean to. I didn't think anyone would be here."

This was the wrong thing to say. Her eyelids narrowed into suspicious slits. "Why not?"

Breathing was suddenly difficult; his throat felt like someone had closed a fist around his neck. He looked around, searching for an explanation as if the trees would help. "It's the middle of the woods," he finally managed to squeak.

"Not quite," she said, her voice taking on a commanding tone that surprised him. "The forest begins there." She pointed across the river. "This, here, is the Guildmaster's Estate. My family's home." Her hands swept through the air around her, indicating, he thought, the entire side of the river where they stood.

He wasn't sure what all of that meant, but he had a strong feeling this could easily escalate into far more trouble than he was prepared to deal with. Coming through a strange gate had never seemed like the *best* idea he'd ever had, but when he'd made it, that hadn't mattered in the face of possibly seeing Quinn again.

If he'd dreamed that something like *this* was a possibility, he might have been able to help himself.

"I apologize for trespassing," he said, bowing his head to show how serious he was. "I'll leave and not bother you again." He hoped this second part was only partially a lie. He would come back—barring the miracle of somehow finding another gate in the middle of a strange kingdom in this world, he would have to return to use the gate to get home again. But he would—somehow—find a way to get back here without anyone noticing. He'd figure it out.

"Where will you go right now?" she asked, in a voice that stopped him in his tracks. Not because it was powerful and demanding—though she had been both of those things only seconds ago—but because now her tone held true concern, worry, even. He could see, now, that she was younger than him, and every bit as freaked out as he was.

He sighed. In for a penny, he supposed. "I don't know. Probably I'll find somewhere to sleep in the woods, and tomorrow I'll see if I can find out how far I am from Philotheum."

"I know the names of every guild on the three continents," she said, "and the ones on the islands, too. There is no guild by that name. I'm also quite good with language, and I can't even pronounce what you wrote. Is it a city in one of the guildhavens? I don't know all of those."

He considered for a moment, trying to ignore the painful gnawing of fear rising in his belly. "It *is* the name of a city," he said. "But also the name of the kingdom the city is in."

"*Kingdom?*"

Her obvious confusion did nothing to allay the horrible thought that had just occurred to him. "Am I even in Deusterros?"

Her blank silence was enough of an answer before she even answered. "What is Deus… whatever you just said?"

Owen thought he might be sick. While it had occurred to him that traveling through a gate might land him a fair distance from his destination in Deusterros, he'd never even entertained the thought that he might end up in a different world entirely. He was so stunned that he couldn't even stop the next words that came out of his mouth. "I've made a terrible mistake."

It was like the iber and the panther all over again.

Ella knew what she *should* do—immediately extricate herself from this situation and never look back. She should leave, run to the house, report this strange man, this *Owen* to her brother, and the two of them should get a message to her father while the palades hunted him down and detained him. Let them find out where he'd come from and why he was here.

She could wash her hands of the whole thing and… And then what? Let her father dictate everything?

Almost as soon as she knew what she *should* do, she also knew she wasn't going to. Despite all logic telling her the reasons she shouldn't trust this strange man and that his appearance here was dangerous—she liked him, at least well enough to not want to see him harmed. Maybe it was the terror pouring off him in waves she could feel from several feet away. This *Owen* was more afraid right now than the iber had been last night.

Whether it was what she should do or not, Ella just couldn't bring herself to hand him over to the palades—to her father. He needed help.

"Can you get back?" She glanced back up at the spot over the river. "To wherever you came from, I mean?"

He shook his head. "Not tonight. It's already dark and the gate will be closed."

She didn't understand him, didn't know how any of it worked—although a deep curiosity about it was building inside her. If she turned Owen in to the palades—or even chased him away from the estate—she might never find out how he'd gotten here. "Tomorrow, then?"

"I… I don't know for sure. Tomorrow is possible, but I think it will be longer." His voice shook on the last words, and for a long moment all of her own curiosity and apprehension faded into concern for this strange young man.

"Well, either way, you can't sleep in the woods. It isn't safe. We shouldn't even be standing around out here by the river like this at night." She took another step back from the river, remembering, her gaze sweeping the dark outlines of the trees and the water.

"Wild animals?" Owen guessed.

"I was nearly attacked by a panther last night," she said, shuddering even at the memory.

Owen hoisted the huge pack onto his back again and stepped closer to her. "Here?"

"Right here by the river. I don't suppose you brought any weapons in that thing?"

"Only a knife—and it's buried deep in here," he added quickly. "I didn't want to show up armed and have people think I meant to hurt them. I don't think I could ever use a weapon on a person, anyway."

She frowned. "What if someone attacked you? What if there'd been someone waiting right here to grab you?"

"That would have really sucked," he answered, shrugging.

"Sucked?" She must have misheard him again. The word sounded like one she understood, but not in the way he'd used it.

"Where I'm from, that means something is awful." He chuckled softly. "But I'd rather not return home than hurt someone here—I'm the intruder, after all."

"So you were okay with just popping in and possibly being killed, right off?"

"Well, I didn't think that would happen. I didn't think anyone would be near the river. Nobody ever has been before."

A thrill of fear raced down her spine, but her hand didn't drift to her bag where her own knife hid. "You've come here before?"

"Not fully. I've never traveled all the way over before. I just…stuck my head across to look around first."

Her mouth fell open. "You can *do* that?"

"I did." He shrugged again. "I've never been entirely certain exactly how it works."

If she hadn't watched him appear, hadn't seen parts of him show up before the rest of him did, she wouldn't have believed him for a second. The things he was describing weren't possible, outside of stories. Not without magic. And she wasn't sure she believed that was real, either. But here he was, and all she could think about was how much she wanted to understand it all.

Somewhere across the river, a night bird screeched and leaves fluttered. "We should get away from the river and the forest," she said.

"You should get home and to safety," he agreed. "I'll figure out something." His already-pale skin went several shades lighter as he looked out at the expanse of trees across the river.

She sighed. "There's nowhere safe for you to go. You can't go into the forest. There's more than just panthers out there. Even a knife won't help you. And with your accent, you can't go into town. It's not safe for you there, either."

"You're very encouraging."

In spite of herself, she laughed. "Come on. I have a place where you can stay."

"That's not necessary."

"No, it isn't. But my other two options are to leave you out here and let nature take care of it, or to send the palades after you. You might as well just trust me and come."

He was silent for a moment, and his face went even paler, though she wasn't sure how. "How do I know you're not taking me straight to these palades?"

"You don't. Does it matter?"

He followed her up the hill, so she supposed it didn't.

"So you do live here," he said quietly when they reached the cottage.

"No," she answered absently, unable to focus on him for a moment because the iber was *still there*. Only it wasn't where she had left it. Now the stupid thing had perched itself on the seat of a small rotting wooden chair on the porch. Apparently Tallen had been right. Ibers could climb.

"What is *that?*" Owen whispered behind her.

"An iber. Just don't ask me what it's doing here, because I can't answer that."

"Is it your pet?"

Just as she began to shake her head, the iber hopped neatly down from the chair and did that weird float-walk thing all the way across the porch and down the steps until it was standing right at her feet. Ella let out a strangled hiss.

"It seems to think it belongs to you."

"Ibers don't belong to anyone. They can't be tamed."

As if on cue, the thing started up with the weird purring noise again and *climbed on her shoe.*

Owen chuckled. "Maybe ibers can't be tamed. But creatures don't always know what they're supposed to be. Sometimes even humans are the same way."

"Even what?" She was only half-listening to him. The vibrating sound of the iber traveled up her legs, and she could feel it everywhere.

"We don't have creatures like this in my world," he said—his voice a little too fast, but she supposed the strangeness of the situation was getting to him the same way it was to her. He bent down to get a closer look at the iber.

"Be careful," she said, "they have claws. I'm lucky this one hasn't tried to disembowel me yet."

But the warning didn't seem necessary. Owen knelt close to the creature, but kept just the right distance to not upset the thing. The iber turned its head toward Owen with what Ella thought was interest.

"I brought it up here last night after the panther attacked it," she offered by way of explanation.

Owen frowned, still crouched low to watch the animal. "Are panthers not very large here, then? In my world, a cat like that would snap this thing in half in an instant."

"That's what should have happened. I don't know how it didn't."

"Well, that explains the iber's attachment to you. It's grateful, you can tell."

"More likely its brain was damaged in the attack."

One corner of his mouth turned up in a smile, but he didn't laugh. "Doesn't look like it."

"I was joking. At least a little."

"I know. But I think it is fine. It just likes you. You need a name for it."

"I'll think about it." She nudged the iber carefully off her feet, hoping that Owen would help if the thing finally decided to use its claws, but it slipped off with little effort—though it didn't leave. It just sat there, staring at them like a fluffy rock. "You want to see the cabin?"

"So… What is this place?" Owen asked once Ella had managed to get the lamp going. The feeble yellow light cast long shadows over the aging furnishings and the destroyed curtains. The cabin looked far more decrepit and abandoned in the lamplight than it did in the daytime.

"It's a guest cottage. It looked nicer yesterday, before I trapped the iber inside last night." She crossed to the bed and pulled off the quilt, shaking it out. Clouds of fine dust rose into the air as the blanket spread across the bed, making both of them sneeze at the same time. "A little nicer, anyway. It's an old cabin; it hasn't been used by anyone in many cycles. I'm sorry."

"Sorry for saving me from sleeping in the woods at the mercy of panthers?" He smiled in a warm, understanding way that immediately melted any regret she might have held for not turning him in. "I think your standards might be a little bit high."

"They probably are," she admitted, in all seriousness. "I'm the daughter of the guildmaster. My friends have made sure to let me know that I'm spoiled—even if they're nice about it."

He chuckled, but the kind smile didn't disappear. "You can't help what you were born as—it only matters what you choose to do with it." He looked around the room, his eyes pausing on the bed, on the secure door, on the entrance to the little washroom. "You're showing an awful lot of generosity to a stranger. I don't know if you're spoiled or not, but even from here I can see that if you are, it's not the only thing that defines you."

She rubbed at her arms, wondering how she was shivering in the stuffy warmth of the cottage.

"What is a guildmaster?" Owen asked, taking his arms out of the straps of his pack and setting it on the edge of the bed.

"You don't have one where you're from?"

"No."

"It's…my father is the master of our entire guild." *Including me*, she thought, but didn't say.

"So…like a king?"

"We had a king, long ago," she said. "A man who ruled over all the guildhavens. My father says a guildmaster is different, but sometimes I'm not sure how, other than as guildmaster, he's also part of the Council of Masters. I suppose a king's powers would be more like our great master, who has authority over all the guildmasters—my father doesn't."

"Was your father chosen to be guildmaster, or born into it?"

She frowned. "Born into it. Most guildmasters are—although there are other ways. Guildmasters have been overthrown. The great master is a chosen position, which makes him different than a king."

"So will you be guildmaster yourself someday, then?"

"I have an older brother, so, no. He will be. Unless something happens to him of course. Actually, unless I can find a way out of it, I'm soon to be a guildmaster's wife."

"Unless you can find a way out of it? What do you mean?"

"Last night, my father told me that I must marry the son of another guildmaster."

"Which you don't want to do."

"No, I don't."

"You don't care for him?"

"I don't even know him."

"Is that the way things are always done here?"

She could hear, in his voice, that he was trying to withhold judgment, trying to understand something that was clearly outside the realm of things he was familiar with, trying to figure out how *she* felt about it before he said the wrong thing and offended her.

She wondered just *how* different things were done wherever he was from.

Part of her thought that she shouldn't be telling him all this, this stranger she knew nothing about. But he was remarkably easy to talk to, and besides, she wasn't telling him anything he couldn't find out in dozens of other ways. Clearly, the entire city—if not the entire guild—already knew about her engagement. She hadn't been able to keep the information from Loric at any rate.

"Apparently it's the way things are done if you're the guildmaster's daughter," she told him.

"And you're not happy about it."

It wasn't a question, but she answered it anyway. "Would you be happy if your father was forcing you to marry someone you'd never met?"

"No."

"Are you free to choose who you marry, or would your father be able to rip you away from the person you care about and force you to wed someone else?"

"You have someone else you want to marry, then." She noticed he didn't patronize her by bothering with the question she already knew the answer to. Where he was from, the choice belonged to him.

"Well, I don't know if I want to *marry* him. We've never even had the chance to make our courtship official. But I wanted to find out, and so did he—before this. Now I'm not sure he'll ever speak to me again."

Owen sucked in a breath. "Did this just happen?"

"My father told me about the betrothal last night. That's why I was in the woods; I was supposed to meet Loric. I was going to tell him, but I'm sure he already heard from someone else, and he didn't come."

There was that kind expression in his eyes again. "That was wrong of him. It's hardly your fault."

"I could have told him last night, and I didn't."

"Ah. Well, then, perhaps he just needed time to think about it, the same as you did. If he's truly worth caring for, he'll come around."

"I hope so," she said, although she wasn't sure if that was the right thing to hope for, at all. It didn't change the fact that she was betrothed to someone else. She walked over to the window, to the mangled curtains and pulled them up, trying to see if they'd still provide enough cover. "You should keep these closed," she said, pulling the edges together as best she could. "Maybe we can find something else to help cover this. Nobody ever comes out this way except me, so far as I know, but if someone did, it wouldn't be good for them to see the light."

Owen nodded and went to the lamp. He picked it up and carried it into the dark washroom, where there were no windows.

Smart, she thought, though now the main part of the cottage was almost nothing but shadows. Owen was only a dark, looming shape across the room when he emerged again. "I'll just turn it off when you leave," he told her. "If there's a chance of someone else coming out this way, I don't want it to be so obvious someone's been in here." An odd lump rose in her throat as she realized how scared and alone he must feel right now. Perhaps she shouldn't have cared—he was the one who'd decided to jump into a river in a strange world. It wasn't her fault. But already she couldn't stop herself from caring. She wanted to see him safely back, and she even found herself wishing she could help him find the family he said he'd come here looking for.

"Have you told your father that you don't want to marry this man?"

She would have been annoyed if anyone else had asked her that question. Of course, anyone who had met her father would have known better.

"He didn't ask my opinion on the subject."

"But you gave it to him anyway."

"You know me that well already, do you?"

"No. I'm sorry. I didn't mean to assume. I say things without thinking about them first sometimes."

The lump was back in her throat. She didn't know what had possessed this young man to leap into another world—or even why she believed him that this was what he'd done—but she did believe him, and it was clear that, whatever the reason, it was very important to him.

"Is there any way I can help?" he asked, interrupting her thoughts.

"Help me what? Defy my father and not get married?"

"Yes."

"I don't think it's possible. Unless maybe you wanted to take me back to your world with you."

She'd meant it as another joke, trying to lighten the mood at least a little, but he looked back at her with a serious expression.

"I could do that, of course. If that was what you really wanted."

She shivered again. "It's just that simple?"

"No." His odd eyes met hers again. "I mean, the traveling is easy enough. You just wait until the gate is open and then you step right through. But there's nothing simple about leaving your life behind and starting a new one. It doesn't matter how complicated the old one is; it's yours. What is that?"

Owen's head whipped around at the same time Ella's did, searching for the sudden loud scratching noise.

"It's at the door," Ella whispered.

Owen nodded, silent, listening. "I think… I think you should open it."

"And if it's a dragon trying to get in?"

He raised an eyebrow. "A dragon? I don't know if you're joking, but that sounds a lot smaller than a dragon. The scratching is only a few inches up. I think it's the iber."

She cast a wary glance at the door. Owen was probably right, but…

"Or we could just sit here until it scratches all the way through and then there's no door."

The scratching *was* growing louder and more determined. She reached for her bag and retrieved the knife.

"I can open it if you like. It's just…"

"If it *is* the iber, it's a lot more likely to scratch you," she finished.

"Yes, that."

It *was* the iber. As soon as she opened the door, the creature darted inside, shuffling right up next to the bed, stopping when it reached Owen's feet, making him freeze in place with a comically startled expression. Ella thought her face must match his; she hadn't known they could be that *fast*.

After a moment of shocked silence, Owen knelt down closer to the animal. "Hello Fluffy. Wanted inside, did you?"

"*Fluffy?*" Ella scoffed.

"Well, if you're not going to come up with something better, it *is* fluffy."

"I'm sure I can come up with something better."

He held out a hand, waiting.

"…Tomorrow."

"Well, it appears he's going to be sleeping in here with me tonight. If he scratches me to death in my sleep, then tomorrow you can re-name him Claws."

SIX
FORBIDDEN

A LOUD THUMPING SOUND woke Ella from what had been a sound sleep. She struggled to open her eyes, confused for a moment about where she was, though when her head was finally clear, she was in bed in her own room. Bright sunlight poured through the cracks in her shutters; it was already late.

It wasn't surprising that she'd overslept. She'd already been running on little sleep yesterday, and she'd been out quite late last night, getting Owen settled in the little cabin. The iber—the name Fluffy was going to stick—had occupied them for a long time. Ella had been afraid to leave him in the cabin with Owen, but it had become clear over the course of the evening that the iber was as content with the young man's company as it was with hers.

She just didn't know what condition she'd find the cabin in when she returned to it today.

The thumping started again, this time accompanied by a muffled, "Ella! Come on! This is ridiculous!"

Grabbing her dressing gown from her bedpost, she hurried over to the door and pulled it open. "Shea!"

"How were you still asleep?" her friend asked, hugging her around the neck before pulling the door closed behind them. "Sabelina doesn't usually let you sleep this late."

"Well, I'm of age now—no more lessons. And I'm betrothed. Hardly subject to a caretaker anymore, am I?"

Shea made a face.

"I think she feels sorry for me about the betrothal and she's being nice."

"Or she's too busy. Do you know how many servants are running around downstairs, cleaning things and accepting deliveries? Nobody even stopped me at the door, I just slipped in behind someone bringing in linens."

"The wedding." The words came out of Ella's mouth like a curse.

"You would think your father had been planning it for more than two days, considering how much is already happening."

"I've no doubt he has. It isn't as the council just dreamed something like this up and approved it overnight. He just didn't bother to tell me about it until now."

"Considerate of him," Shea said. "To make sure you wouldn't have time to do anything about it."

"Exactly. The preparations don't matter to him, anyway, he won't have had anything to do with the house. That's all Sabelina. She could pull something like this off in half a day if she had to."

Shea shook her head as she crossed over to the windows

and unlatched the heavy wooden shutters. "You weren't at The Dozy last night."

Ella shielded her eyes as the bright yellow light flooded the room. "No, I…I wasn't in the mood." Shea could be trusted with secrets, but Ella wasn't sure how to begin a conversation about someone just appearing in the river. Now, in the light of day, she was beginning to wonder if she'd imagined the whole thing.

"So you told Loric, then."

Loric. A wave of nausea gripped her insides. "No, I didn't. I don't think I needed to. He didn't even show up. I'm sure he heard it from someone else."

Shea's lips pressed together in a thin line for a second before she spoke. "Well, that's why I came here—"

"You heard from Loric?" Owen's strange appearance last night had at least been a distraction from having to think about Loric and the situation she faced. Remembering it all now in the harsh light of day was painful and she struggled to concentrate on anything else.

"No. It's just the news is all over town. I thought you said the guildmaster from Silver Island wasn't arriving for a fortnight?"

"He's not. My father said I had a fortnight to prepare." But, already, there was a sick, sinking feeling in the pit of her stomach.

"Well, I just heard that the entire port has been rescheduled to accommodate their arrival tomorrow."

"It's true," Sabelina said, five minutes later after Ella and Shea had cornered her in the kitchen. "I received the message late last evening after you'd already left. I didn't want to wake you this morning to give you such news."

"Tomorrow. They're going to be here tomorrow." Ella wondered if she was the only one who could feel the floor spinning beneath her feet.

"And the betrothal party has been moved to tomorrow night."

"Breathe, Ella," Shea said quietly. "Suffocating isn't going to solve anything."

"Actually it would," Ella pointed out. "It just wouldn't be a *great* solution."

Sabelina gave her a piercing look. "That isn't funny."

"None of this is funny. You're telling me that tomorrow—*tomorrow*—I'm expected to attend my own betrothal party with a man I've never even met. Where is my father?"

"His message didn't indicate his plans for returning. I can only imagine he'll come back sometime between now and tomorrow afternoon."

Shea scoffed. "He'll probably just show up at the party so Ella never has a chance to argue with him or plead her case."

It was a testament to the seriousness of the situation that Sabelina didn't attempt to argue or come up with a different plausible excuse for her father's absence. Not that it mattered now. Ella supposed there was plenty of work and dozens of meetings to keep her father occupied with only one more day to prepare for a formal visit from another guildmaster, especially *this* guildmaster.

"There's still some breakfast in the kitchen," Sabelina said. "You should get some food in you before the seamstress comes again. She'll be here in half an hour."

Considering everything that had happened in the past two days, Ella was surprised it was this small statement that brought all of her rage bubbling to the surface. Heat rippled through her body in waves and her hands shook as she said, "No. I'm not going to."

"Excuse me?" Sabelina blinked.

"I'm not going to stand around here all day and be fitted for dresses for parties and events I don't even want to go to. I can't." Ella looked defiantly into the wide, violet eyes of her caretaker. "I'd apologize, but I'm not sorry."

To her surprise, Sabelina shrugged. "All right. I'll figure out something. Just don't tell me where you're going, so I'm not tempted to hunt you down."

The sudden relief was so overwhelming that all Ella could do was wrap her arms around Sabelina's waist and squeeze tightly. "Thank you."

Sabelina stretched up on her toes to kiss Ella's forehead. "You remind me so much of your mother right now," she whispered. "I wish she were here to help you with this."

"To The Dozy, then?" Shea asked, once they were safely outside the confines of the house and Sabelina's earshot.

"You want to spend one of your days off at work?"

Shea only rolled her eyes at the obviously rhetorical question.

Telling Sabelina exactly where she'd be hiding would have merely upset her, but stealing Bastian's much-needed driving services on such a busy day would have had a devastating effect. And, anyway, Shea, like most workers in Echo Bay who lacked a carriage and driver of their own, depended on a bicycle for her everyday trips around town. So, although it had been a long while since Ella had ridden her own bicycle such a distance, she found herself enjoying the exercise and the quiet of the secluded paths they chose for the purpose of avoiding people in town.

She wasn't ready to face the intense curiosity and the overbearing congratulations—or concern—from everyone.

Of course, there would be attention at The Dozy, too, but somehow it was different there. This was the place where she'd found comfort after the worst thing that had ever happened to her—the people would calm her after the second-worst, too.

Before they'd even mounted their wheeled contraptions into the incongruously well-kept wooden rack in The Dozy's drive yard, Old Cecil's wife, Ollie, was waving to them from the porch.

"I've been hoping you'd come around today," she said, wrapping Ella into her buxom embrace. "How are you holding up, dear one?"

Ella shrugged. "At the moment, I'm not sure."

"Well, you must be hungry. Come on inside."

Now that she was here, she felt like she could start to think about what had happened to her in the past few days. Sitting down to be fretted over while Ollie fed her was sure to bring up questions she wouldn't have known how to answer anywhere else, but here, things felt tolerable, possible even.

About halfway through the ride, she'd realized that she'd never taken Sabelina up on the offer of breakfast. Mere hunger had long ago been swallowed into an aching emptiness that gnawed at her stomach and her nerves.

Lack of food was only part of it, really. Her mind was as starved for comfort as her stomach, so she let Shea lead her into the dining room where they were both fussed over until they were settled comfortably on cushioned stools at the long counter overlooking the kitchen.

Ollie, always patient and perceptive waited quietly until Ella had finished half a glass of milk and several bites of thick, meaty stew before she asked the first question.

"So, do we know anything about this young man? This 'guildmaster's son' from Silver Island?"

She didn't quite choke on the swig of milk in her mouth, but several drops did spray across the burnished wood counter.

Ollie merely continued to watch her with interest, as if nothing had happened, though her never-idle hands retrieved the towel from over her shoulder and the splatters disappeared.

Ella swallowed. "I'm afraid I don't know much more than you do. At the moment, I can't even remember what my father told me his name was."

"Cayloken," Shea said.

"See? Even Shea knows more than I do." She frowned at her friend. "How *do* you know that?"

Shea shrugged.

"Well, I guess now I know his name. Anyway. That's the sum of my knowledge. His name is Cayloken, and he's the son of the guildmaster of Silver Island."

"And he's your betrothed."

"That's not particularly helpful." She glared at Shea, though they both knew her anger was directed elsewhere.

"You can't fix a situation if you can't even be honest about the details of it. He'll be here day after tomorrow. Pretending it's just for an ordinary visit isn't going to change that."

Ella ran her fingers along the flat plane of the handle of the spoon, as if she could somehow rub her emotions into the same smooth shape as the metal. She knew Shea was right, but she didn't *want* to admit any of it was real. "There's nothing ordinary about the guildmaster of Silver Island visiting Ravensguild to begin with, is there?" The food was doing its job at soothing her stomach, but it had only slightly dulled the edges of Ella's nerves. She tried another bite of the stew.

This was only going to get harder, she realized. While most of the other guildmasters in the council had visited Ravensguild any number of times, and were familiar faces in the local shops and inns, Silver Island had always been the strange exception. Ella wasn't sure if their guildmaster had ever come to the mainland at all—certainly not in her memory.

She'd come here with Shea in hopes of being able to *stop* thinking about her impending doom, not to dissect it. Because of this, she was perhaps a little too desperate to change the subject, and did so without really thinking it through. "You know those stories about passages to other worlds and people traveling through them?"

"Yes." Shea frowned, looking as confused as Ella had been feeling for days. "What about them?"

"Do you think there's any way the stories could be true?"

The flicker of understanding in Shea's expression immediately told her that she'd made a grave mistake.

Ollie, by some undeserved miracle, didn't seem to find anything unusual in the question. "It's certainly something fun to think about, isn't it? I suppose that's been on your mind, then, child? If there was a gate to another world, you'd have an easy escape from your problems in this one, wouldn't you? At least for long enough to set your thoughts at ease—or perhaps even enough to work out a solution to the problem you're facing?"

She nodded gratefully at the older woman. "Something like that."

"You wouldn't be the first one, Ellarowan."

It was a simple sentence —reassuring on the surface, and logically, it should have fit right in with the conversation. But something about the way Ollie said it was *off*. It made the hairs on the back of Ella's neck stand up, and she knew, without understanding how she knew, that there was a hidden meaning in the words.

"More stew?" Ollie asked before she had enough time to consider an answer.

"No thank you. I've had more than enough."

Before Ella could blink twice, the dishes were cleared and Ollie had disappeared into the depths of the kitchen.

Shea didn't waste any time. "Are you trying to get me or Ollie arrested?"

"What? No! Of course not! Neither one of you said anything you shouldn't, anyway." But her cheeks and neck felt warm. Stories around a fire at night were one thing — frowned upon by some, of course, but not a real offense. Speaking of magic in broad daylight in a public place, though… That was illegal. And for good reason—or at least Ella had thought it was a good reason. People who spoke of magic had been known to disappear, spirited away by the magic ones.

"You're the guildmaster's daughter, Ella. It's not exactly your life you're playing with, starting a conversation like that."

"Being the guildmaster's daughter certainly isn't doing me any favors right now."

Shea's eyes narrowed to angry slits, and though her voice came out barely above a whisper, it felt like she was shouting. "Too far. I know you're upset, and I'll grant you a fair amount of leeway, but you need to stop when you start comparing your lot in life with those of folks who lost people in the Fading."

Ella blinked. "*Ollie?*" she whispered.

"Not just Ollie. Many here. It's not a topic of everyday conversation, especially around *the guildmaster's daughter*. And it's not fair of you to bring it up like it's nothing when the consequences are much greater for many others than they are for you."

She wasn't sure Shea was being quite fair in her assessment, but then, she'd felt that way before and been wrong. Learning to listen first and challenge later had been a hard-fought battle, but she had acquired the skill—at least with Shea—so for now she just nodded. The Dozy wasn't the place to argue about such things, regardless.

"But you are going to share with me later the real reason you're asking such questions in the first place." Shea was, as always, quick to understand when there was more going on than Ella was willing to say—and keeping anything hidden would be a fruitless endeavor.

"Come back to my house later and I'll *show* you."

"But not now, no matter how much I'm dying to, because you need a break from the madness there."

In truth, Ella was anxious to get back to the cottage and see if the strange Owen was actually there or if she'd imagined the whole thing, but even if she'd been certain she wanted to show Shea her whole secret, doing so in broad daylight with so many people coming and going from the house was far too dangerous. Owen likely wasn't even *in* the cottage right now—they'd discussed that the woods were likely a safer place to be in the busy daytime.

"Game of rex?" she asked.

For the first time since her father's decree, Ella was able to relax and think about something other than her predicament. Their third game of rex lusus was particularly fraught, and when a beam of afternoon sunlight fell across the board, she was startled. She realized she'd been so busy figuring out where to move her pawn that she'd completely forgotten she was at The Dozy in the middle of the day—and even, for that moment, why.

But reality always seemed to find a way to assert itself, and she found herself losing the round spectacularly because she could no longer concentrate on the marble pieces.

"Ready to return now?" Shea was on top of both games today.

She was in the middle of fitting the game pieces back into their carved slots in the table underneath the board when the light above her changed again; this time, the warm beam of sunlight disappeared. When she looked up, her mouth went dry and it was suddenly hard to breathe.

"Loric," Shea said. "I didn't expect to see you here at this time of day."

His gaze didn't stray from her upturned face. "I was told I might find Ella here. I don't suppose you'd excuse the two of us for a few moments?"

If Shea answered, Ella didn't hear it. All she knew was that she was now alone with Loric, her heart thudding a million beats per second as he held his hand out to her. "Can we go outside and talk?"

He smiled as she nodded and stood, and this small gesture calmed her considerably. He didn't hate her. This was Loric; they'd figure out a way to solve the problem between them.

The sun was in the other half of the sky, throwing blazing afternoon heat at the porch, but Loric led her into the relief of the shade on the side of the building.

She took a deep breath, knowing that she was the one who'd caused this by not talking, and that she needed to be the one to try to fix it now. "Loric I—"

"I found this," he began speaking as if she hadn't said anything. In his hand was the drawing she'd left at their meeting spot yesterday. His free hand traced over her sketched hair. "I was so angry at you for not telling me as soon as you found out. I came late to the clearing yesterday, knowing you wouldn't still be there, but I could still be mad all the same… Ella, I was hurting. And then I found this, waiting there, and I knew you were hurting, too."

"I'm sorry, Loric."

"I know." He set the paper on the porch railing and then took her in his arms, wrapping her tightly in an embrace that felt desperate. They didn't kiss; the situation was too urgent for that.

"What do we do?" she asked when they finally broke away from each other, though his hand found hers and he held it as if she'd fall over the edge of a cliff if he let go.

"Well, you're not married yet. There's still time to convince your father you shouldn't marry him. What do you know about this guildmaster's son?"

"Almost nothing."

"Your father hasn't told you *anything*?"

"Just his name."

"Well, if he's from Silver Island, I guarantee there has to be *something* about him that makes him an unsuitable match for you. You need to find out as much as you can about him. I won't be able to meet with you this evening; I promised Gaius I would work part of the evening shift in exchange for some time to come and talk to you this afternoon. But find out as much as you can before tomorrow. Once I know more, we can figure out a plan." He let go of her hands and picked up the picture again. "May I keep this?"

"Of course. I made it for you—but are you leaving so soon?"

"Yes, I'm sorry. I must get back. But I needed to see you. I couldn't go another day with this silence between us."

She wouldn't cry; it wasn't something she did, especially over something as simple as a goodbye, but still there was a thickness in the back of her throat as she stretched up to accept Loric's kiss.

SEVEN
GATES AND SECRETS

"Now you'll tell me your secret," Shea said when she was back inside.

"No. Now I'll *show* you. Come home with me." She'd almost lost Loric over not being able to talk to him, after not telling him what was going on. Losing Shea wasn't worth the risk—and that might happen if she kept something this huge from her best friend.

Fortunately for Ella and Shea, the shade of the cypresses had moved in to cover the bicycle rack. The sun was so hot today they might not have been able to touch the metal handlebars if the bicycles had been left to bake. Ollie had insisted on filling large metal bottles with fresh, cold water for each of them before she'd allow them to leave. And Ella carried something else, too—a small cloth-wrapped bundle of sandwiches. She'd told

Ollie that she just didn't think she'd be in the mood to eat with her family at home that night, and slipped her a few more coins than the normal cost. The story wasn't strictly true, but neither Ollie nor Shea blinked twice about the parcel.

Ella tried to set her bottle in the basket behind the seat, but it wouldn't go all the way in. She frowned and bent over to look at what was stopping it.

"What is that?" Shea asked.

"It's a book." Ella pulled the object out of the bottom of the basket. It hadn't been there earlier; she was sure of it. And it wasn't just a book; it was a journal, leather-wrapped and old—the leather strap tied around it felt crumbly in her fingers as she fumbled with the knot.

"Is that the secret you were going to show me? Did you find a notebook with information about a gate?"

She was halfway through shaking her head when it struck her how *odd* the question was. At almost the exact same second, she realized what had bothered her earlier about Ollie's answer. It was that word, *gate*. Both Ollie and Shea had used it, which would have been strange on its own. Last night, Ella had *watched* someone fall through the opening between the worlds. A *gate* wasn't what she would have called it. A hole, maybe, or a portal. She supposed that gate wasn't exactly the wrong word, just an unusual choice—but they'd both used it. And so had Owen.

She had questions for Shea.

But as soon as she got the knot untied and pulled open the cover of the journal, those questions seemed a lot less important than what was written on the very first page.

There were three words, written in elegant script, slightly faded from age, but still clear enough to make Ella feel as though her heart had stopped at the sight of them.

Lyonet Ellora Fullwater Lockwood

She ran her fingers slowly over the letters, tracing each familiar curve.

"Where did you find that?" Shea asked.

"Here, just now, in the basket."

"How is that possible? Who would have left your mother's journal in there while we were inside?"

She didn't answer—couldn't have answered, even if she'd thought Shea actually expected her to. She was too busy staring at the book, awestruck at the thought that she was really holding her mother's journal. The book was thick, the edges of the papers well-worn, as if they'd been thumbed through dozens of times. It was like a dream; she'd always wished she had more of her mother, her words, things she'd made. Her fingers shook as they hovered over the edge of the page, hesitant to turn it. Part of her was desperate to do it, to see what was written there, while another part knew that she'd only get to do this for the first time once.

"Do you want me to do it?" Shea had always had an uncanny knack for knowing how Ella was feeling.

"No... I need to be the one."

Even touching her fingertips to the paper was difficult; she was so afraid she'd rip it or cause some other damage, but when she finally made herself do it, the paper was thicker and stronger than she'd imagined. The page turned easily.

But there was nothing there.

The paper was blank.

Frowning, she flipped to the next page. There was nothing there, either.

Feeling frantic now, she fanned the pages back and forth between her fingers; surely something must be written in there somewhere.

But all the pages were empty.

After several times of rifling through the entire book, Shea reached over and took it from her. "Let me," she said quietly.

Ella let her take it; certain she had to be missing something—it was getting hard to see through all the blinking she was doing. It was stupid to be upset, she knew. Five minutes ago she hadn't had a book full of her mother's writing, and now she still didn't. Nothing had changed. Getting upset over something so small was ridiculous.

"I'm sorry, Ella," Shea said when she finally closed the book after her own investigation. "That has to be really disappointing."

She shrugged.

"Well, I'd be hurt."

"I think I have bigger things to worry about right now than an empty notebook."

"That being true doesn't change how you're allowed to feel about this thing."

"You don't have to be the perfect friend *all* the time, you know. It's kind of annoying."

"I'm the youngest in a large family. Annoying is what I do."

This finally made Ella chuckle.

"It's weird, though, isn't it?" Shea said, still leafing through the journal. "Why would someone go to all this trouble to give you a book with nothing in it?"

Ella reached for the book and turned back to the very first page, running her finger lightly over her mother's writing again. "I am grateful to have it. It *was* hers."

"But if there's nothing secret about it, I don't understand why whoever had it didn't just give it to you."

The words made Ella shudder a little, in spite of the blistering heat. Until Shea had said that, she hadn't considered that someone wanted to keep the journal a secret. But that would only have made sense if the book actually had anything in it. Still, it nagged at her.

"Speaking of secrets," she said, "this wasn't mine. Let's get back."

The estate was still bustling when Ella and Shea rode up the lane. Servants and delivery people darted in and out of the main house and the surrounding buildings. None of them paid any attention to two girls riding bicycles up the steep driveway and to the back of the house. They dismounted in the shade of a tree at the back of one of the kitchen gardens.

Pretending she wasn't in any kind of a hurry to do anything, Ella sat down on a stone bench and took a long drink. She patted the space beside her.

Shea's eyebrows knitted together as she sat down. "We rode all that way in this heat to sit here?"

"Nobody can know what we're doing right now, Shea. Nobody can follow us. I don't know if anyone's watching, but if they look, I want them to see us just acting normal."

The frown on Shea's face only deepened. "You're not very good at this sneaking around business, are you? No wonder your father knew about Loric."

"What do you mean?"

"I mean, if you're trying to hide what we're doing, you want *less* people to see us, not more. You don't sit here until everyone's sure you're home. You get away as fast as you can and leave people wondering if they actually saw you come home or not."

Ella supposed it was true. Until she'd met Loric, she'd never had many secrets to keep. She was, as people had often pointed out, spoiled. Although her father was strict, he'd never been around long enough to really know what was going on. Sabelina and the other servants had mostly always indulged her. She knew this, and often felt guilty about it when she was with friends who had less. It was a mistake, she realized, to have thought her father would never pay attention to anything.

"How did *you* get good at sneaking around?" she asked Shea.

Shea rolled her eyes. "We do not always live in the same world, Ella. Now where are we going?"

"This way."

A few minutes later, the river came into view, and then they turned the corner on the path that led to the old cottage.

"Is this still part of the estate?" Shea asked, wonder in her voice as she looked up at the trees all around them. "You've never brought me out here before."

"It's near where I come to meet Loric." She'd never brought *anyone* out here before Loric. Her friendship with Shea was not a secret. They'd never had reason to hide.

"I'm getting a bit shattered here, El. I'm starting to think you're leading me to a gate you've found or something equally incredible."

Ella stopped walking and turned to meet her friend's gaze. "I think I might be."

Shea gaped at her. "What does that mean? How do you *maybe* show someone a gate to another world?"

Her right hand closed around her left one, squeezing her fingers so tight it was painful. There was no easy way to say this, so she opted for just blurting it out. "Well, I can't show you where a gate is right now—but I can show you someone who came through one last night."

All the color drained from Shea's face, leaving the skin around her lips a pale tan. "Impossible."

Ella held her breath as she and Shea climbed the rise leading to the cabin, half expecting to see the place demolished. She was sure that, at minimum, there would be no more curtains on the windows, or the door would be destroyed. But when the little house came into view, it was Shea who gasped.

"It's adorable," she said. "You never told me there were buildings here that look normal and not like they're made of marble and gold."

"Most of the gold is just paint, you know."

But Shea wasn't listening. She was already up on the surprisingly intact porch.

"Wait!" Ella called.

Stopping just in front of the door, Shea turned and fixed her with a look that made Ella's insides feel like they were coming apart. "You're serious, aren't you? You've actually got someone in here."

"Did you think I *wasn't*?"

"I don't know what to think. This morning, I wouldn't have guessed Marius Lockwood's daughter would have even heard the legends of gates—or if you had, you'd be running for a palad the first time someone mentioned it in your presence—"

"That's not fair. I've never—"

Shea let out a slow breath. "You're right. That wasn't fair. You've never gone to your father about anything you've heard at The Dozy. You've earned my trust. I'm sorry. But still, you have to understand that what you're saying—Ella, if the gates exist *at all*, nobody can use them. They're locked. The keys disappeared long ago. What you're saying is not *possible*."

"I never said it was possible." She stepped past Shea and turned the knob.

The door swung open easily, revealing a perfectly tidy— and empty—room.

Nausea twisted through Ella's gut as she stepped inside the cottage; the floor felt like it was moving underneath her feet. *What was going on? Had she imagined the entire thing?*

"There's nothing here, Ella. Are you all right?"

She didn't feel all right. Her knees were weak as potential explanations flitted through her mind.

No. She hadn't imagined it. At least not all of it. The curtain was still shredded at the bottom; someone had just trimmed the worst of the edges, making the destruction less obvious.

But where was he now?

"What's going on, El?" Shea's voice now held nothing but concern. "We both want you out of this arranged marriage, but I don't see the plan here. You know I'll help however I can, but you're going to have to fill me in."

Ella heard her friend's words, but they floated aimlessly through her mind without sticking as she started exploring the cabin. Owen had been here; she was sure of that. There had to be some evidence, something he'd left behind, something that would tell her where he was now, and prove to her friend that she wasn't crazy.

She looked at Shea. "It's cleaner than it should be. Someone cleaned up, fixed the curtains, made the bed."

"Someone who also traveled through the gate to another world."

"I don't know how to answer that, Shea." She crouched down to look under the bed, but there was nothing there, either—not so much as a stray button or sock to let her know that she wasn't losing her mind.

"Where did you learn about the gates?" Shea asked quietly when she stood up again.

Ella stared at her. "What do you mean? I told you where."

"But nobody would dare discuss them in front of you. I said I trust you, and I'm trying to, but El… you must know how much trouble I could get in just for talking about this, let alone with you—*at* the Guildmaster's Estate."

"What do you mean?"

Shea's dark eyes studied for a long moment. "You don't know, do you?"

"Nobody would dare discuss it in front of me, would they?"

Shea sighed.

"So this has to do with magic, then." The word itself was so dangerous that normally just contemplating saying it would make a room feel as though the air had been sucked out. But between Owen's strange appearance last night, and his disappearance this afternoon, Ella was so deep in that she wasn't sure it mattered anymore. It couldn't be worse to speak of magic than to dabble in it.

Now her friend's stare was like glass, fixed on the floor behind Ella, and she knew she'd gone too far, whether she'd been able to help it or not.

"I'm sorry, Sh—"

Shea put a finger to her lips and shook her head rapidly. "Look!" she hissed.

Ella spun around so fast she was lucky she didn't lose her balance. There, on the floor, just inside the open doorway, was Fluffy.

She took a step toward it.

"I wouldn't do that, El. Those things can scratch and bite."

"This one won't." She didn't feel completely confident in that declaration, but at this point all her caution was gone.

And it didn't bite. Instead, it backed up exactly one step, keeping the distance between them the same. When Ella moved again, so did Fluffy.

"Friend of yours?" Shea asked, incredulous.

"Sort of." Ella took another step, and again, Fluffy retreated exactly the same distance. Now the creature was outside the door again, and it turned around so its back was to them, but it still kept pace with her movements. "I rescued it from a panther the other night, and it's been hanging about ever since. Last night, it was here when I left Owen—the man who came through the gate."

"Perhaps it will lead us to him."

"Now you think an *iber* is going to lead us to someone you didn't believe existed two seconds ago?"

The iber chose that moment to move forward on its own. Going down the steps, it looked both impossible and hilarious, like a mop come to life, tumbling end over end before landing safely in the grass. Ella might have laughed if she wasn't concentrating so hard on keeping up with it before it decided to disappear.

On the ground, it moved quickly, its long fur gliding over the ground, and Ella was slightly out of breath by the time it stopped, a good fifty yards away from the cottage, deep into a dense thicket of trees at the edge of the woods.

The iber went right up to one of the trees. Owen, stood as soon as he saw them. He brushed his hands off on his short pants, and removed the leaf that had fallen on his shoulder as he rose from his spot at the base of a tree. In the daylight, his skin was much paler than it had appeared last night, and his eyes were a shade of brown she'd never seen before. The creature skittered right up to him, perching itself almost on top of his feet

"Sorry," Ella said. "I didn't mean to frighten you."

"You didn't. I just—you didn't seem so sure that nobody would ever come to the cottage during the day, so I thought I'd hide out here until evening and work on my plans."

"Plans? Is that what he said?" Shea asked.

Owen blinked at Shea and then looked back at Ella. "You're not coming here to arrest me or something, are you?"

"No—"

"Should we be?" Shea interrupted. "Who are you? How did you get here?"

His strange pupils grew even rounder, but his voice was steady as he answered. "My name is Owen Robbins. And I—"

"Came here through a gate last night," Ella finished for him.

"Why did you come here? What do you want?"

"Coming here was an accident. I don't want anything except to get back to my home as soon as I can."

"Who sent you?"

Ella frowned. It was an odd and presumptive question, and judging by Owen's reaction, he found it as strange as she did. "What do you mean, Shea? Who could have sent him?"

But Shea's gaze didn't move from Owen; she lifted an eyebrow and waited.

"Nobody sent me. I came all on my own."

"But you're keeper? Or gadab?"

"I'm sorry. I don't know what you mean by either of those."

Shea was silent for more than a minute, and even though Ella couldn't see her face, she could read the confused expression that must be on it. Shea would be trying to make sense of Owen's answers—answers so clearly different from the ones she'd been expecting.

Ella thought her own face must look as blank as Owen's. None of the questions made sense to her. The term "keeper" triggered some faint, faraway sense of familiarity, but she didn't know why. *Gadab*, she knew. It was an old word, used only in stories. A name given to travelers from faraway places. The *gadab* weren't real. The places they came from didn't truly exist. But then, Owen's existence didn't seem possible, either, and here he was.

"If nobody sent you, where did you get the stone?"

Owen's eyebrows knitted together. "What stone? What do you mean?" But this time, for the first time in the conversation, something else flickered across his features. He wasn't lying, but the question meant *something* to him.

"The stone. A rock?" Shea arranged her hands as if she was holding a medium-sized rock. "If you really traveled through the gate, you had to have used a stone."

"I'm sorry I'm upsetting you." Owen's voice was calm and measured. "I don't have a stone."

Shea looked at Ella, desperation in her eyes. "Did you see him with a stone?"

Ella shook her head. "Not unless it was in his bag. Why? What's so important about the stone?"

"That's how the gates *work*. You have to have a key. The stones are the key. You have to have one of them to travel through the gate, but all of the ones here were taken, and nobody knows where they are." Shea turned to Owen again. "Either you have a stone, or you didn't come here through a gate."

"I don't understand most of what you're asking," Owen said, still perfectly calm. "But I'd like to learn more. I don't have any stones. You're welcome to search my belongings if you must, but you won't find one. I did have a stone once, long ago, but it was destroyed. I didn't use it on the gate—I wouldn't even know how. There must be stones already there, but I didn't find one on my side."

"What do you mean you had a stone that was destroyed? What kind of powerful magic could destroy one?"

"No magic. Only a hammer. It was smashed all to pieces."

"How could that destroy it? A single piece might not be powerful enough to operate every gate, but if you had enough pieces, it would still work."

Owen backed up so far he ran into the tree behind him. "What?"

"So where are the pieces?"

Ella had never seen Shea quite so determined or fierce. She wasn't sure whether to be afraid or impressed. Part of her thought it had been a mistake to bring Shea here to meet

Owen, but another part recognized she'd have never gotten this many answers on her own. She didn't even know the right questions to ask.

"The pieces aren't here. I didn't bring them." He reached down and pulled up his giant bag, sending Fluffy scurrying—the creature had been resting against it. "They're in my world, on the other side of the gate."

"Then how did you get here?"

"I found a gate and waited until it was open, and then I came through."

"That isn't possible." Shea's voice cracked on the last word.

The question that had been nagging at the back of Ella's mind finally burst to the forefront. "How do you know what is and isn't possible, Shea? What do you know about this gate?"

Her friend's features instantly flushed a deep purple. "I don't *know* anything, obviously. But according to all the stories…"

Ella had heard some of the old stories, around the fire at The Dozy, and sometimes in whispers, and it didn't surprise her to find out that there were other, more dangerous stories she'd never been privy to. She'd always left that part of it alone, knowing it was dangerous, knowing there were things people wouldn't share with someone like her. And she hadn't minded, really. Knowing would only complicate her own life. But now she wished she'd pressed for more. "Maybe the stories you've heard are wrong."

"Or else he's lying."

They both looked back at Owen at the same time. Just as they did, Fluffy shuffled back over and settled himself on Owen's strange white-and-green shoes.

"Do you really think he is?"

"No."

The sun had already set by the time they walked Owen back to the cabin. Although Shea's suspicion hadn't abated fully, her anger melted into curiosity and questions, only some of which Owen seemed able to answer.

The three of them walked down to the river, to the place where Ella had dragged Owen out of the water the night before. It still looked like an ordinary stretch of river, nothing indicated that there was a portal to another world here.

"Can you go back through it now?" Shea asked.

"No. I don't think so." But his fingers suddenly clenched tightly around the straps of his pack, and his breaths came quicker. "At least, not if it works the same way as the gates to the *other* other world."

This idea was so far outside Ella's comprehension that she tried to not even contemplate it. It was startling enough to hear Owen claim he was visiting from a different world; she couldn't wrap her brain around the notion that there might be dozens of other worlds, and this stranger had been to at least two of them.

Just as dusk fell, Owen began picking up rocks along the edge of the river and lobbing them through the air in a high arc, checking to see if any of them would disappear through an opening into another world, but they all fell, dropping into the water with great force, splashing the three of them.

Fluffy wisely retreated from the water's edge after the second *kerplop*.

"It doesn't mean anything," he said. "In my sister's world, ten days pass in the same time one takes in my world. The gate doesn't open there every night. This world might work the same way."

Ella gaped at him. "So you don't think you can try to go home for ten days?"

He shrugged. "If it works the same here as in Deusterros. I have no real reason to think it will or it won't. So, I'll keep trying every evening. It was always dusk on this side when I tested it."

"How did you come to live in a different world than your sister?" Shea asked.

"It's a long story."

"Well, we have time."

And so he told them the story as they walked back toward the cabin, a story of a boy who'd used the gates to help his people, and a girl who had discovered his secret and followed him, only to find out she had her own history with the world on the other side. The story of a beloved sister who'd had to leave her family behind and make a choice to close the gate by asking her brother to dig the stone from the ground and crush it to pieces.

"I shouldn't be messing with it," he said as they entered the little cabin and he set his pack on the bed. "I should have left it alone. I knew it was dangerous. That's why Quinn closed the gate in the first place. But I just missed her so much."

Shea brushed her hand across her cheek and Ella knew that all her skepticism about Owen was gone.

Ella believed him, too. She knew with deep certainty that every word he'd told them was the truth.

She just wasn't sure that he'd told them *everything*.

EIGHT - THE BETROTHAL PARTY

"*Vosh*, ELLA. WHAT DID you do, stay up all night?" Sabelina scolded after the third time Ella nodded off while Rima's fingers were still in the middle of making one of the complicated braids required of a formal occasion. Ella jerked her head back up and tried to pry her eyelids open. The hairdresser sighed and unraveled the plait before beginning again.

"No. I went straight to bed after dinner."

Sabelina crossed her arms over her chest and pursed her lips.

"I just didn't sleep."

"Well, it's going to be a very long day indeed, then."

"I know." She *had* tried to sleep. Several times she'd laid down in her bed and willed herself to fall asleep, only to have to retrieve her quilt from the floor when she'd kicked it hard enough to send it flying.

"You could have come to me, you know. I'd have made you a fresh cup of tea."

"I know, Sabbie. I'm sorry I didn't."

She was sorry. Sabelina had been exceptionally understanding of her behavior. Last night, she hadn't said a word when Ella had finally trudged back into the house several hours past dark, starving. Owen had offered to share the meal she'd brought him, but she'd refused. She couldn't promise she'd be able to sneak him something again before the betrothal party. Shea would have no trouble finding a meal after Bastian drove her home.

Normally, her caretaker would at least have asked where she'd been, if not outright lectured her about being considerate about mealtimes. But last night, Sabelina had simply gone into the kitchen and brought back a fresh plate of dinner. There had even been pie for dessert.

She knew that her caretaker would have stayed up with her and made her another cup of tea if only she'd asked. The company and warm drink would have been better than lying alone in her room, even if they hadn't brought sleep, but she hadn't even thought about it.

Before this week, Ella would have thought a cup of the hot concoction Sabelina brewed for nightmares and restlessness could solve any nighttime ill. But after the last few nights, she wasn't sure she'd ever sleep well again, tea or no.

Nothing could have quieted her mind enough for sleep last night. There were just too many ways for her thoughts to twist and jump, dragging her stomach—and her blankets— right along with them.

There was Owen and all of his secrets, the nagging fear that he'd be discovered and she'd have to answer for his presence. She'd thought that sharing her secret with Shea would make things simpler, but the opposite had happened instead. Now she had all kinds of new questions for her best friend.

Complicated as the Owen situation was, though, it hadn't been responsible for nearly as much of the sleeplessness as her mother's journal was. Every time she picked up the quilt again, she'd turn the light on and pull the little book out from under her pillow so she could look at it again and see her mother's name. After staring at the name for a while, she would carefully flip through each page, hoping that this time she'd find something she'd missed—a little note in the margins, perhaps. Maybe even a whole sheet of writing buried somewhere in the middle of the old pages.

But most of all, every time she lay down, her stomach filled with a heavy, sick dread over what was to come in the morning.

Perhaps a part of her had thought that if she never fell asleep, the morning would never come. Even an endless bout of insomnia was infinitely preferable to what awaited her in the daytime.

But it hadn't worked. The morning arrived as always, bright with cheerful sunlight that only served to remind her how dark she felt inside.

And now, here she was, perched on a cushioned bench in the side parlor, having her uncooperative hair yanked into pins and plaits by Rima, a housekeeper also tasked with Ella's hair and wardrobe on formal occasions.

Her empty stomach grumbled and churned. Sabelina kept trying to spoon broth into her, but she could only handle a bite or two at a time without beginning to feel sick.

The betrothal party was only hours away.

More than once that morning, she had contemplated sneaking out and running away. It was an absurd idea, of course. Even if there weren't dozens of servants over every inch of the house, there was nowhere to go. Nobody in Ravensguild would be able to hide her for long—and very few would be willing to defy the guildmaster in the first place. Also, the ensuing search would almost definitely turn up Owen and all kinds of questions. Perhaps she shouldn't feel such loyalty to a stranger from another world, but she didn't want to see Owen arrested and questioned. He'd never be able to return home if her father discovered him.

Loric might have hidden her, it was true, but that was a temporary solution. There wasn't anywhere the two of them could live and find work if Ella acted in defiance of the council. And she didn't want to do that to him, anyway. He had worked too long and too hard to earn the title of shipwright. She could never ask him to give that up for her. There had to be another way. But it didn't look promising right now.

"Shh… you'll muss your face," Sabelina whispered, dabbing at her cheeks with a lace-edged handkerchief. "You'll get through this. I'll make sure of it. Maybe you can fall asleep for a bit when Rima finishes."

As Shea had predicted yesterday, the first time Ella saw her father was in the grand ballroom. Although he must have appeared in the house at some point during the day to be readied himself, she had been so busy with preparations and servants buzzing around her that she'd been easy to avoid.

Now at least a hundred guests watched as she listened to a hired caller announce her name and position and then made her way across the polished floor, toward the platform where Marius and Tallen already stood.

There were whispers and gasps among the crowd as she passed; the yellow gown she wore was perhaps the most exquisite thing she had ever seen. Even she could see how the color made her olive skin glow warmer than usual. Tiny sparkling gems ran down the seams, glinting in the sunlight from the windows. She'd never hated a piece of fabric so much in her life.

When she reached the platform, her father stretched out his hand to guide her up the stairs. Every muscle in her body tightened and twitched as she held her hand over his, carefully refusing to allow her skin to touch his. The show for the onlookers was all he was going to get.

He pretended not to notice; instead smiling widely as his gaze swept over her dress. "You are a most lovely vision, my daughter."

The whole thing was absurd, clearly designed to give her no choice but to "behave" and be gracious as she was introduced to her newly betrothed. She ignored her father as she turned to face the crowd, forcing herself to smile, wondering just how many of them could tell that the gesture made her face ache and her ears ring. Truthfully, though, the smiling was easier than the not-bolting.

It didn't much matter to her what the crowd thought, anyway. Although many of the faces were familiar, few of them belonged to people who would be sympathetic to her plight. The room was filled with the powerful and wealthy landowners, craftsmen, and bankers. The dashing great master, Amalric Sandrez of Auyadel was there, as were other members of the Council of Masters, and of the guilden chamber, too—all people whose political connections with her father made them care more about the joining of the two guildhavens in peace than about the two young people whose lives the deal would irrevocably change.

There were a few friendly faces in the sea of people. Sabelina stood guard near the doors to the kitchens, her eyes never wavering from Ella's face, as if she could somehow hold Ella up with her gaze alone. It might have been working.

A few feet away from Sabelina, Shea stood discreetly near the servers and maids, wearing the dress Ella's father had given her the other night—now beautifully repaired. The message it would send to Marius was worth looking at it again.

And then, she saw him. Standing in the middle of the crowd, between his parents and Gaius Clarkin, was Loric. He wore the finery of a landowner's son, a blue silk shirt over blue-and-white striped breeches that billowed to his knees. His long, sandy hair was swept back into a neat plait. If she'd been any other young lady in Ravensguild, the fact that he was looking at her like he wanted to take her into his arms would have been a glorious victory, instead of heartbreak. He looked every bit like he belonged here, in this room, with her and her family. He should be standing up here with her, and knowing she couldn't dance on his arm tonight nearly undid her.

But there wasn't time to fall apart. She hadn't even had time to get her fill of appreciating Loric when the celica bell sounded and a hush settled over the room.

Her father's clear, deep voice rang out behind her. "Honored guests, I would like to express my profound gratitude at your attendance here tonight as my family celebrates a momentous occasion. It is my extreme privilege to welcome here tonight the esteemed guildmaster of Silver Island, Padraic Stone, along with his lovely wife, Kydwyn, and their son, Cayloken."

Ella wasn't sure what she'd been expecting. Perhaps she'd wanted them to look evil, to be armed ruffians who stormed her home and held her hostage. Or perhaps hooded thieves who stole into the estate the way they'd stolen into her life. Really, she'd wanted them to look like *anything* except a kind-faced man who entered the room with his arm wrapped tightly around his wife's waist, both of them walking slowly, protectively, in front of their son.

Cayloken Stone looked like his mother, with dark mahogany features and a slightly upturned nose. She wanted him to at least be plain, but he wasn't. His orange eyes were warm and inquisitive, even as they scanned the room with apprehension. A thick mop of curly black hair reached down just past his ears, and he hadn't done anything to tame it. Ella wasn't quite sure this had been his choice—locks like those could probably only be tamed with a blade. She imagined that, if he smiled, his cheeks would round up to his eyes, and he might be handsome.

If she was being fair, he might already be handsome. But she wasn't feeling fair, and he wasn't smiling. He looked as terrified and hesitant as she felt, and it was hard to be as angry at him as she wanted to be.

After all, this wasn't his choice, either.

It occurred to her, as he made the long walk across the ballroom, as a hundred necks craned to scrutinize his every movement, as the whispers started slowly but rose to a buzzing crescendo, that this evening had to be even worse for him than it was for her.

And so, when the Stone family finally reached the platform, and Cayloken climbed the steps behind his parents, Ellarowan stretched out her hand in greeting, and he took it, his expression melting into gratefulness as he steadied himself atop the platform. And when she offered him a tentative smile, he grinned in return, and she discovered she'd been right. His smile reached all the way to his eyes, and dimples appeared in his cheeks as he bent his head to let his lips brush her hand.

Somewhere out in the crowd, there was a small, bright *pop* of breaking glass, and when she looked down at Loric, the front of his shirt was wet.

"So, is he your favored?"

Ella looked over in surprise at the young man standing next to her on the platform. It was the first time she'd heard him speak; the two of them had been standing up there together in silence through several long, drawn-out speeches by both of their fathers and several members of the Guild of Masters about the political alliance and its promises of "peace and prosperity."

She knew she should have been listening. Likely, there was information in those speeches that could help her understand what was going on here, that might help her figure out a way to wriggle out of the arrangement, but she hadn't absorbed a single word.

All of her focus had been on Loric, watching as he bent down to discreetly sweep up the bits from his shattered glass, as he deposited the whole mess on a tray and then disappeared from the room. Her eyes hadn't left that doorway until he'd returned, just now, sporting a clean, dry shirt, looking as if nothing had happened.

"Excuse me?" she asked Cayloken.

"The young man over there who just came back in the room. Clearly he means a lot to you, I'm asking if he's your favored."

She looked around them in alarm. This wasn't an appropriate conversation.

"Relax. None of them are listening. They're too busy congratulating each other and listening to themselves talk."

He was right. After the speeches, the polite attention in the room had changed to a dull roar of mixed conversations, and their parents were no longer even on the platform. She could see her father now, over in the center of the room, speaking to two other guildmasters. Padraic and Kydwyn Stone stood just to the side of him, though Ella wasn't sure they were quite as engaged in the chatter.

She and Cayloken were alone.

"How could he be my favored? I'm betrothed, remember? To you."

It was rather satisfying to see the way he took a small step back from her at the words, and the way the muscles in his hands clenched as if looking for something to hold on to so he didn't fall off the world.

Of course, it would have been a lot more satisfying if saying it didn't elicit nearly the same reaction in her. And if he hadn't recovered more quickly than she did.

"I'm sorry, Ellarowan. I imagine this isn't any easier for you than it is for me. Or, at least I'd like to hope you and I have similar feelings about finding ourselves using that word, because it would be a lot easier with two of us, instead of each trying to get used to this alone."

She frowned at him. "And you're trying to size up your competition?"

His return smile seemed so genuine she wasn't sure whether she wanted to punch him or if she was going to have great difficulty hating him. "No."

There was a thing Ella could do with her eyebrow that had always made Tallen tease her that the palades should use her to interrogate prisoners, because it would make them give up all their secrets immediately. It seemed to have a similar effect on Cayloken. He took a small step back. "I suppose I am, a little, it's true. But mostly I would just like to know something about you. I don't imagine your life just started the moment you were told you had to marry me. You're quite beautiful, Ellarowan. It's not surprising you'd have a favored."

"Are you trying to flatter me?"

"Of course. But I'm also just being honest." He flashed that grin again and leaned in closer, conspiratorially. "Is it working?"

Loric was standing by one of the tables now, a new glass held to his lips, though very little of the yellow liquid was disappearing. He didn't appear to be looking at her and Cayloken, but Ella could see his eyes twitch to the side every minute or so, and he was much too still.

"What about you, Cayloken? Do you have a favored, somewhere in Silver Island?"

"No."

She wasn't sure what response she'd been expecting, and now she wasn't sure what to say.

"Not for lack of wanting, though. There's been a lot to keep me preoccupied for the last couple of cycles, and… Well, I knew that a…uh…political betrothal was a possibility, so it didn't seem very fair to make promises I'd never be able to keep."

Having made such a promise herself, Ella felt the sharp edge of guilt, although she knew instantly and without a doubt that Cayloken hadn't said it as a jab toward her. Irrationally, it annoyed her more that he *hadn't* meant it that way. She wanted to hate him, but he was making it difficult. She decided it was easier to focus on the rest of what he'd said. "You knew you might be forced to marry me?"

"Well, no. It might have been anyone. Whichever guildmaster had a daughter and most wanted to be considered for great master. I've only known it would be you for a few moons."

"A few *moons?*" she spat, forgetting for a second they were standing on a platform in front of a roomful of guests. Cayloken shot her a warning glance and she lowered her voice. "I've known for two *days.*"

He had his own way of knitting his eyebrows that made her feel like what she'd said was completely absurd. "What do you mean?"

"I mean, until two days ago, when my father sat down to dinner and said, 'Surprise, you're betrothed,' I didn't even know you existed. Or that my father had any intention of arranging a betrothal for me."

He was absolutely still for a full thirty seconds, and then his face melted into an expression that didn't make her feel absurd at all. Instead, he wore so much sympathy and compassion that she had to look away before she started really thinking about what she was doing up here and feeling the things she'd spent the day carefully packing away so she could get through tonight.

"I…am sorry," he said after a moment.

"Don't."

She didn't expect him to listen. In fact, part of her hoped he wouldn't, that he would pick at it and give her an excuse to be angry. She wanted to fight, and he was currently the most attractive option.

But he did listen. Instead of continuing to question her, he said, "How about we get off this ridiculous thing and get something to eat? We don't need everyone staring at us all evening."

"It could be worse," Shea said. "He's not terrible to look at."

"Why don't *you* marry him, then?" Ella took a long sip of sunfruit juice, wishing it was something stronger. She followed Shea's gaze across the room to where Cayloken was standing with his parents. It looked like he was being introduced to Gaius Clarkin, the master shipwright. Loric's boss. The whole thing made her a little sick to her stomach. He'd been kind once they were off the platform, subtly leading her to a tray of drinks and saying they should both socialize—his way, she thought, of telling her she could go and talk to Loric if she wished. But talking to Loric here in public was too dangerous. So she'd found Shea, instead.

"Yes, if only I was a lot richer, and he was less…male that might be feasible." Shea laughed. "And, anyway, it would appear he has plenty of other choices. Who *are* all of those girls?"

Ella tried to look without staring, but felt like she was failing miserably. "Most of them are the daughters of other guildmasters. The two in the blue dresses are sisters, the daughters of the guildmaster of Vraigon, but I've only met them once or twice."

Shea had none of the compunctions Ella did about observing other people at the party, and she craned her neck in every direction, studying everyone. "They all seem to know each other."

"They do." Ella picked through a bowl of nuts on the table. "As you can see, their parents bring them along when they travel to events like this. Probably other times, too. I don't really know. I only see them when they come *here*, which isn't often."

"Who's that one that keeps trying to talk to *Loric*?"

This made Ella pay attention. She stiffened when she saw what Shea was talking about. "That would be Allora Sandrez."

Shea's eyes widened. "The great master's daughter?"

"That's the one."

Shea took a long drink of juice, though this didn't distract her at all from watching what was going on. "I heard she was betrothed."

"Apparently that's not an impediment to flirting when she's traveling." Ella sighed. "Maybe I shouldn't speak. I'm betrothed, too, and I'm still courting Loric."

"That's a little different."

"Is it? I don't know anymore. Maybe her betrothal was arranged, too. I wouldn't have been told."

Shea scoffed. "Well, she could flirt with someone besides your favored. She could at least take Cayloken off your hands."

Ella almost choked on one of the nuts.

"Sorry, Ella. I don't mean to make light of it. Loric is doing a nice job of brushing her off, if that helps. It's all just... How long do we have to stay at this party?"

Ella took a drink, trying to clear her throat. "Forever. I'm stuck here until I'm officially dismissed and then I'll have to thank everyone for coming and say individual goodbyes to the guildmasters. My father will be in here all night with his friends, comparing fleets and arranging marriages. I think Cayloken and I are supposed to be 'getting to know each other.'"

"I'm not sure how you're going to do that when Loric is on his way over here."

Ella turned to look over her shoulder, just in time to see Loric setting a plate down on one of the tables and surreptitiously edging himself closer to where she and Shea were standing at the end of one of the buffet tables. When she turned back, Shea had disappeared.

They both knew how careful they had to be. Loric stopped a few feet from her and faced the table, speaking just loudly enough for her to hear. "Have you eaten anything, Ella?"

"Aside from about three nuts that just tried to kill me, no." There were three tables, piled high with every delicacy Ravensguild had to offer, including all her favorite foods. But none of it looked the least bit appetizing.

"The crab is incredible tonight." She didn't dare watch him, but she heard the clink of silver on glass as he dished something onto a plate. "I don't know what the sauce is, but you really should try it. And aren't these macamie nuts your favorite?"

He stepped just close enough to hold the plate toward her, and she accepted it, a subtle, polite gesture, but then she took several steps back. "My father knows about us, Loric. We can't. Not here."

His whole face went gray. "You told him?"

"No. He already knew. Someone must have seen us somewhere and word got back to him."

"And you didn't tell me that? You let me come here?"

"I didn't know..." But she *had* known. She'd seen him yesterday, and she could have told him then that her father knew they'd been together. "I'm sorry."

He closed his eyes, and his nostrils flared as he breathed. When he finally looked at her again, it was only for long enough to mutter, "I have to go."

She knew it was the best thing for him to do. Nothing good could come of his being here. She wouldn't be able to keep from talking to him if he was right here in the room, and then her father would see. So it was good that he left. But then he was gone, and all she could do was stand there staring down at the floor through her clear plate, pushing nuts around with her finger until one of them skidded off the edge of the glass and fell to the floor.

"Is that a custom I should adapt to?" Cayloken's voice startled her, and she nearly sent the entire plate flying, but he reached over to take it from her and set it on the table. "Is it plate, then floor, then mouth?"

"Only when there's company."

He cocked an eyebrow.

"When it's just us, we skip the plates altogether."

He laughed. "I'm not falling for that one."

"Well, I had to try."

"A journey never embarked upon is an adventure never made—that's how the saying goes isn't it?"

"Something like that."

"Sure." He smiled again, though now that they were off the platform and alone, he didn't look quite as confident, and for a long moment, the two of them stood there, staring awkwardly at each other.

"Speaking of journeys," she said, searching for a way to end the silence, "how was yours today?"

"Long. A lot of time over the water today and yesterday."

"Do you like flying?"

He grimaced. "No, not really. I get airsick if I look out the window or try to read, so it's boring and I usually try to sleep as much as I can. But this time, my mind was racing a little too much for sleep."

It was an unexpected relief to be able to stand here and engage in idle chatter with someone who might understand exactly how she was feeling. They both danced around the more serious topic between them, but she couldn't help wanting to continue the conversation. "I didn't sleep at all last night."

Continuing to hate him was going to be difficult if he kept looking at her like that. "I can't imagine why," he said, looking around the room. "Nothing like knowing you're going to have to get up in front of all these people and smile to help you relax."

She shrugged.

"What about you, do you like the airships?"

"I like to watch them. I've never been in one."

He took a step backward. "How is that possible?"

"My father doesn't think it's appropriate for me to travel with him, especially when he's going to be gone for a long time—and he always is if he travels by airship."

Cayloken bit his bottom lip and looked around the room. Ella could almost see what he was thinking, though perhaps it was only because she already knew what everyone thought. She'd always been the odd, protected anomaly among the children of the guildmasters. The girl who didn't travel to other guildhavens. The girl without a mother. Tallen traveled sometimes, but Ella had always stayed at home. She liked her life here, with Sabelina, and spending time at The Dozy. It had always seemed less complicated than trying to navigate the complex social obligations of her father's world. She'd certainly had more freedom, even than Tallen.

Until now.

"Well, that's one thing that's likely to change, at least. You'll get to take an airship to come to Silver Island."

That sentence was enough to break the spell, and she could tell he knew it, too. Conversation had been possible between them so long as they carefully avoided all mention of the betrothal, but now both of their faces were flushed, and he turned away at the same time she did to pick at the appetizers on the table. Serving spoons clinked in dishes, though neither of them scooped any food onto their plates.

It hurt, more than she wanted to admit, this mention of finally getting to go in an airship. She'd *wanted* to adventure in them, if she could have done so in freedom instead of social obligation. And Loric had promised to take her, as soon as they could make their relationship public.

A tap on her shoulder nearly made Ella drop her plate again. "Would you *quit* sneaking up on me?" she hissed, wondering how Cayloken had gotten behind her this time.

"It's me, El," Shea said.

"I'm sorry," she whispered.

"It's all right." Shea pushed the plate to the side and handed her another glass of sunfruit juice. "At least have *something*, Ella."

Cayloken was not behind her—he was still just standing there, and now he turned to face them. "Are you going to introduce me to your friend?"

She took a long sip of the juice, trying to compose herself, knowing there wasn't any choice but to keep herself together and make it through the evening.

"I'm Shea, the friend," Shea said, before Ella even had the chance. "I know who you are."

He coughed, but recovered and pulled out that smile again. "It's nice to meet you, Shea."

"Perhaps you and I could talk and let Ella have a few minutes to herself?"

Two tiny creases appeared in his forehead, but the smile stayed put and he nodded. "Of course."

So quickly nobody else could see it, Shea leaned close to Ella's ear. "Loric is in the back hallway."

For the last two days, the little hallway that connected the kitchen to a delivery entrance had been a constant bustle of people and packages, but tonight, in the middle of the party, it was empty, save for a few crates of spare glasses and silverware, and a lone figure in silky blue leaned up against the wall.

Loric stood up straight when he saw Ella, though he kept his eyes trained on the floor as she approached.

"I'm sorry," he said when she was close enough to hear his quiet voice. "I shouldn't have gotten angry with you earlier. I should have realized it wasn't wise to come here this evening."

She looked down at her hands. "Your parents are here. Did you have a choice?"

He shrugged. "I shouldn't have attempted to talk to you in full view of everyone. I knew what this party was, I shouldn't have let it bother me. I meant to stay focused on my task—to learn about this guildmaster and his son. I did overhear something interesting earlier."

"What?"

"Not here." He shook his head, but he stepped forward and took one of her hands in his, rubbing her fingers reassuringly. "I shouldn't have even had Shea ask you to meet me here, it was only that I couldn't leave things strained between us. I wanted to apologize to you, and ask if you would try and meet me at our place tomorrow?"

It was hard to breathe. Every thought and emotion that rippled through her threatened to pull her in different directions. She wanted to pause for just a moment and revel in the relief that came from knowing she and Loric weren't fighting, that she wouldn't go to bed tonight wondering just how tense things were between them, that he still wanted her. But she couldn't. She couldn't make the promise he was asking for, and every second she stood here put them in greater danger of being discovered.

"I know you can't say for sure," he whispered. "I know there are other obligations that might keep you from meeting me tomorrow. But will you at least try?"

The air finally came and she gulped it in gratefully. "Yes. I will try."

"If you can't… Maybe The Dozy tomorrow night?"

"Same thing. I can't promise."

"It's all right. We'll find each other."

She nodded. "We'll find each other."

He bent down and brushed his lips gently against hers. "I love you, Ellarowan."

It was the first time he'd said those words, and shiverbumps raised all along her arms and down her neck. She tried to pull back to look at him, but his arms held her tight against him as his lips moved to her ear. "The Stones might be sympathizers."

Behind them, someone cleared his throat and Loric let go of her so quickly she had to take a step backward to keep her balance.

Ella's heart wasn't beating as she turned around to see Tallen standing there at the end of the hallway, staring at her. She didn't have to look behind her to know that Loric was already gone, but she knew it didn't matter; her brother had already seen.

"What do you need, Tallen?"

"Father was looking for you. He wanted to formally introduce you to Padraic and Kydwyn Stone."

She pressed her fingers to her temples, fighting off the sudden painful pounding in her head.

"Ella? Are you all right? You don't look very well."

She wasn't all right. She didn't know how to do this—how to walk back into that ballroom and speak to Cayloken, how to meet a foreign guildmaster and his wife and pretend that her life wasn't crumbling to pieces in front of her.

A million times, her father had told her that she was a guildmaster's daughter, and that she'd been raised to attend to her duties and carefully socialize at important events.

It struck her then that perhaps he hadn't done as fine a job with her as he imagined.

The pounding in her head turned into sharp stabbing, and her entire body heated and then grew cold again. She took a step to steady herself and somehow missed.

"Ella!"

"Well, that's one way to escape a terrible party." Shea's voice was fuzzy around the edges, as was Ella's vision when she opened her eyes and struggled to sit up.

"Be careful," Sabelina said, pressing down on Ella's shoulder to hold her to the couch. "You hit your head when you fell."

"What?" Ella raised a hand to her forehead, managing to find a clean piece of linen wrapped around her forehead. Underneath the cloth, she could just make out the shape of a thick, tender line still a bit sticky and oozing. Sabelina grabbed her hand and pulled it away.

"Don't touch it. I just managed to stop the bleeding."

Ella didn't know if the pain in her head now was from the fall or if the headache that caused it in the first place was still raging inside her skull. Sitting up hadn't been a good idea; the room started tilting sideways, and she almost went with it before Sabelina and Shea both noticed and caught her, helping her lie back into the pillows. "How much trouble am I in?" she asked, once the dizziness had passed and she trusted herself to speak again.

"Why? Sabelina asked."Did you do this on purpose? I didn't find any bottles of poison in your pockets."

"Would that make any difference in my father's anger?"

Sabelina sighed. "I think you're all right on that account. For now, anyway. The Stones were understanding. Master Stone said to send you well wishes, and his wife asked if there was anything she could do. She's said to have some skill in healing."

Ella reached up to the gash in her forehead again, this time feeling it out gently, though even the lightest brush of her fingertips made her wince, and there was blood on her fingers when she pulled them back down again. "I'll be fine." The last thing she wanted was to have a conversation with those people while she was covered in blood—or while she wasn't, really. But it was a relief that they weren't complicating things. "And if the Stones are happy, my father is happy?" she guessed.

"He still gets his party," Shea said. "When I went back into the ballroom a while ago he seemed perfectly content to be chatting with those other guildmasters. So long as you do what he wants in the end, I'm not sure he'll notice anything else." Sabelina shot Shea a terrifying look for speaking so bluntly, but Ella appreciated the reassurance that at least someone was fully on her side.

"Why did you go back in there?" she asked Shea.

"She brought you that." Sabelina nodded to the little table at one end of the couch. There was a silver tray there, with two covered plates and a glass of sunfruit juice. The sight of the sweet yellow liquid made Ella's stomach turn again—she'd consumed a bit too much of it earlier without enough food for balance. "Ugh."

"Perhaps some water, instead?" Sabelina stood and poured water from a pitcher into a tall glass. Ella sat up and accepted it gratefully. The night was too warm, and she was sticky with sweat and blood. For a moment, before her trained manners kicked in, she couldn't decide whether to drink it or dump it over her head

"What happened, anyway?" Shea asked. "Tallen said one second you were standing there and the next you'd toppled over into a crate of silverware."

"Sounds about normal for me."

"You're lucky you only have a small gash." Sabelina dabbed lightly at the throbbing line on Ella's forehead with a damp cloth.

"I don't know, exactly. I was upset, I'd been talking to Loric and Tallen interrupted us—" Too late, she realized her mistake. Sabelina didn't know about Loric. A new wave of nausea washed over her, and the pounding in her head roared to vicious new life.

"Ella, what—" Shea leaned in close, as if to catch Ella before she fell forward off the couch. Then Shea's eyes went wide in alarm. "*Dragon's ashes,* Sabelina, look at her!"

"Hush, child," Sabelina hissed. "Can't you see she's sick? Fetch me some more water."

Ella didn't understand what was happening. Sabelina's gentle hands closed around her arms and guided her back down onto the pillows. "You must calm down," she whispered as a cool damp cloth came down across her eyelids. "Close your eyes, Ella, and don't open them again until you've rested and you feel better."

She obeyed, but this time she didn't pass out, she just lay perfectly still, willing the dizziness and the heat to go away.

"What was that, Sabelina?" Shea's voice came from the other side of the room. She was whispering, and for a moment, Ella wondered if she was really hearing it, but her mind was no longer fuzzy as it had been earlier—it was as clear as the voices in the room.

"What was what?"

A long pause, and then, "I know you saw it—Ella's eyes."

"I didn't see anything, child."

Another silence, this one so long Ella thought maybe she was dreaming when the low whispers started again, this time so quiet she wasn't sure who was speaking. "How long have you known?"

NINE
HISTORY

ELLA MIGHT HAVE MANAGED to escape the second half of her betrothal party—pleasantly or not—but when she woke the next morning, her new life was still there, immovable, inescapable, in the form of one young man seated in the chair across from her place at the breakfast table.

He stood as she entered, dipping his head in a respectful bow. "Good morning."

They weren't alone, of course. Although at the moment just acknowledging Cayloken was almost more than she could cope with, she was aware that beside him, his parents had also stood to welcome her, and that her father was already seated at the head of the table.

Behind her, Tallen was just entering the dining room. He'd been behind her on the stairs, but neither of them had spoken.

There was little choice but to play her part. She smiled politely and she dipped her own head as she was formally introduced to Padraic and Kydwyn Stone. "And this is their son, Cayloken," her father finished.

The money her father had spent on an expensive comportment tutor served him well when Ella refrained from rolling her eyes or scoffing at the final introduction. Her composure was even harder to maintain when her eyes met Cayloken's and she could see him fighting the same battle.

She cleared her throat. "Good morning. I trust you all slept well?"

"Yes. Thank you for asking." Cayloken smiled warmly across the table as he quite obviously lied through his teeth. "And did you?"

She felt as though she were on a stage at Festival, giving a speech in front of hundreds, rather than a few people in a dining room. *Of course, the consequences of a speech at Festival would be less grave.* But she smiled back and she wasn't lying this time when she said that she had, in fact, slept well. It had been difficult for Sabelina to rouse her this morning to help her dress and tend to her forehead.

"We were worried about you last night when we heard you'd taken a spill." Ella had never heard a voice as musical and gentle as Kydwyn Stone's. Turning to look at her wasn't nearly as difficult as she'd anticipated. "Are you feeling better this morning?"

"Quite a lot better, thank you." Her fingers went involuntarily up to rub at the pink line on her now-unbandaged forehead. There was no blood, nor even a scab. She must have truly been out of it last night to have imagined an injury much worse than this one had ever been.

"Looks like it was just a scratch," Kydwyn said. "But I brought some salve that might make it fade more quickly if you'd like." She opened her hand to reveal a little silver tin, small enough to fit in her palm, and held it out toward Ella.

"Thank you for your kindness," Ella said, accepting the offering. "It's beautiful!" she couldn't help exclaiming when she saw it up close. The top of the tin was engraved with an image of an opened flower—she couldn't identify what kind, but the artwork was exquisite. She ran her fingers along the delicate lines of the etching. "I'll return it to you straightaway."

"That's not necessary. Please accept the container as a gift. I'll be happy to refill it for you should you have need."

Hating Cayloken Stone was already proving to be a difficult task. Merely disliking his mother might turn out to be impossible. After thanking Kydwyn yet again, Ella sank into her chair with what she hoped was far more grace than she felt.

"Your father was telling us that you're quite an accomplished artist." Padraic said.

"Was he?" One of the servants was dishing food onto her plate, momentarily blocking her view of him. "I'm not sure how accomplished I am, but I do like to draw when I have the chance."

She picked up her fork and began moving food around on her plate—she couldn't focus enough to even see what was there, and she wasn't hungry enough to taste it, but at least it gave her something to do with her hands.

"Perhaps after breakfast you could show me some of your work?"

"Mmm—" She had to set the fork down. Her fingers were beginning to feel cold and numb.

"Gracious, Father," Cayloken interrupted. "Poor Ellarowan's had a long night, and there are a lot of extra people here. She's only had two days to adjust to the idea of us coming at all." There was a sharp edge of anger in his voice. Ella was both impressed and stunned at his bravery in speaking like this in front of her father. "Perhaps we should at least give her some time to accommodate herself and recover?"

Grateful was the last thing she'd have expected herself to feel toward Cayloken, but there it was. She suspected he wasn't being entirely benevolent. Judging by the look on his face, he wanted time to himself as badly as she did, but she didn't care. From the end of the table, her father's annoyed gaze bored into her, but he wouldn't say anything in front of these people.

"Besides, I thought that Master Lockwood was going to take you on a tour of his fine guild after breakfast?"

"Oh, that's right. Where are my manners?" Padraic said, looking apologetically at her father. "I'm looking forward to seeing the wonders of Ravensguild. I've heard many amazing stories."

Just like that Cayloken had not only given her permission to escape for a bit after breakfast, but also the freedom to do so.

"Perhaps you could bring some of your artwork to dinner this evening, then?" Padraic asked.

Dinner. There went her chances at slipping away to The Dozy. If she'd had time to consider and plan for their visit, she might have realized just how much a betrothal would consume her every waking moment, but she hadn't had that time. All she could do now was hope her temporary freedom would last long enough for her to meet Loric this afternoon.

She picked up the fork again and stabbed at whatever was on her plate. The food was a poor substitute for what she really *wanted* to stick her fork into, but it was all she had. "Of course," she answered with the best smile she could force.

Once breakfast was finally over, the only thing Ella could think about was getting out of the house before anyone could make another demand of her. Cayloken had read her well— she needed some time to "accommodate herself and recover." Her thoughts were jumbled, hopping from one topic to another before she had a chance to truly consider any of them.

She wasn't sure why, but she didn't feel like seeking comfort from Sabelina, or even Shea. It had something to do with last night—a vague memory of overhearing something she didn't quite understand. Even the thought of going to The Dozy, of being asked about the party, about the Stones, about *anything* by the people who knew her, was too much. She just needed some time *away* from everything and everyone. But she didn't want to be completely alone, either. So, as soon as she was excused from the table, she ran upstairs to retrieve her bag.

Two minutes later, after a brief stop, she was outside the kitchen doors.

The day was already blindingly hot. As soon as Ella stepped outside, her hair clung to the back of her neck in long, damp curls. She didn't care.

She had to be careful while she was still in view of the house, of course. Probably nobody was watching, but she moved slowly past the kitchen until she was in the garden and then edged her way into the depths of the fruit trees.

Once her view of the house was erased by the orchard, she took off into the woods at a run.

This time, she didn't even bother looking in the cottage first. Owen knew the estate was filled with extra guests, and no amount of telling him that nobody was likely to venture out this way had made him willing to take the risk.

Again, today, she found the creature before she found the man. The iber sat, sunning itself in the patches of sunlight just outside the first deep thicket of trees. Here, the shade made everything cooler. Ella paused to lift her hair and enjoy the light breeze that rustled up from the river.

She was still standing there, catching her breath from running, when Owen appeared between the thick trunks of two myabar trees.

"I didn't think I'd see you today," he said.

"I wasn't sure you would, either. As it stands, I'm not certain my father won't disinherit me for not accompanying him and the Stones while they tour the guildhaven today." She gave a half-smile.

"Would he do that?"

"Probably not," she scoffed. "It's not like I've come out and refused to follow his orders. The Stones are here. Unless I come up with a very good plan in the next few days, I'm going to find myself married to someone I just met last night."

"How did the party go last night? Is he terrible?"

She closed her eyes and took a deep breath. "Is there something else we can talk about right now? *Anything?* I brought food. You must be starving."

He shrugged. "I did bring food with me."

She had seen some of this the other night. Strange, dry food in odd packaging made from materials that *had* to have come from another world. He'd offered to let her taste some, but she'd hidden her hesitation behind the concern that she didn't want to deplete his supplies. He might never be able to replenish them, after all.

"Yes, but this is freshly made." She reached into her satchel to retrieve the towel-wrapped bundle she'd stopped in the kitchen for on her way out here. The soft rolls were still warm, and she needed both hands to pull out the parcel without smashing it.

As she pulled, something else from her bag slipped out and landed in the grass with a soft *thud*.

"Here, let me help you," Owen said, bending down to pick up the fallen item. He smiled when he saw what it was. "I always keep a notebook with me, too."

"This one isn't actually mine," she said.

"No?"

The question was only polite. She could see he had no intention of pressing her on the matter. He kept the journal tightly closed in his hands until she'd set the bundle of food on a rock, and then he handed it to her.

Somehow, it was the fact that he didn't ask that made her want to tell him.

"It was the strangest thing," she said. "This journal just appeared in the basket on my bicycle the other day."

"*The* strangest thing?" he asked, giving her a small smile and looking down at himself.

She thought it might be the first time she'd heard him joke, and it made her laugh. "All right. It was the strangest thing that happened that day, anyway—it was the day I brought Shea to meet you, not the day you appeared."

"Do you think someone might have left it in your basket on accident, or do you suppose it was a gift?" he asked as he opened the flaps of the towel holding the food.

"Well, I don't know if it was a gift, exactly, but I don't think it was an accident, either."

"No?" He didn't look up from the project he'd engaged himself in, breaking apart a roll and placing strips of meat in the middle of it. She'd noticed this about him—he didn't always make eye contact or ask many questions. Often, he seemed absorbed in his own tasks and thoughts, and yet he always heard everything she said.

"It was my mother's."

This was enough to pry his eyes from his breakfast. "Was?"

"She died when I was three."

He looked stricken, as if she'd physically hit him. "I'm sorry."

Ella crinkled her nose. "Just don't start thinking of me as 'that poor girl who lost her mother,' okay?"

"Someone else dying doesn't define who *you* are."

"Some people think it does."

He nodded, still a little too much pain in his eyes for her comfort. "My older sister, Quinn, is actually my half-sister. Her father died when she was little, before I was born. She said the same thing. That it was hard to have people feeling sorry for her before they even knew her. Also, she hated when people would say she *lost* him. You didn't *lose* your mother. You know where she is."

She stared at him. Coming from anyone else, it would have sounded like an insensitive joke and she'd have been annoyed. But Owen said it with a kindness and sincerity that made her swallow hard. "Actually, I don't."

"What do you mean?"

"She drowned in the river. It was during the rainy season—you're lucky you didn't try coming here then. The current gets so strong it could sweep away a small building, probably. During other times in the cycle, there's a pool not so far downstream. If you're a decent swimmer, you'd probably be okay. But past the pool…" She took a deep breath to keep her voice steady. "There's a waterfall, straight over the cliffs and into the sea."

"That's terrifying."

He didn't ask the questions other people always did. The ones that sounded innocent and curious, but underneath assigned blame. *What was she doing so near the river when it was so high?* He didn't ask the questions, and she didn't have to excuse herself to escape the powerful anger and sadness that inevitably accompanied having to explain such things. Once those feelings came, they could rarely be stopped, and though she never remembered exactly *why*, Ella knew they were dangerous. Too often, spells like that resulted in her feeling terribly sick and passing out—nothing she wanted to do in front of other people.

But Owen, somehow, was safe.

"Some people think that maybe she did it on purpose." She'd never said those words aloud before—had never even fully thought them to herself.

"What do you think?" His strange, round eyes met hers now, rapt with attention and filled with sympathy, but not pity.

And for the first time, she could think about it without heat rising in her chest and moisture pooling in her eyes. Even her voice wobbled only a little when she finished speaking. "I don't think she did it on purpose. I think it was my fault."

He frowned. "I don't know what happened, Ellarowan, but I know it wasn't your fault."

"You couldn't know that. You weren't there."

"You were three. And I doubt you pushed her in."

Her lips twitched. "If I told you I did, you'd feel terrible."

"But you didn't."

She shook her head.

They sat in companionable silence for several minutes while he ate his sandwich. It was only cold meat and bread, but as she watched him, she thought that his peaceful meal out here in the woods looked way more delicious than the fancy meal she'd eaten at the breakfast table with her father.

"Were you with her when it happened?" he asked after a while. "Is that why you think it was your fault?"

She could hear the river from where they sat. It wasn't loud at this time in the cycle; the water didn't roar and splash over the rocks or overflow its banks in slurping gurgles the way it had that day when she was three. But the water was never silent. It always demanded to occupy at least a small part of her attention.

"No. Nobody was there. She was alone…" Ella stopped, not quite sure how to continue. She'd never told the story to anyone. Not even Shea.

"I'm sorry. You don't have to tell me. It's none of my business." He picked a piece of cheese out of the cloth bundle and squeezed it between his fingers then held it up to his nose and sniffed.

She wondered if there was cheese in his world. But even more, she wondered what he'd think of her if she did tell him the story. For the first time in her memory, she wanted to share it with someone.

"I had this doll," she said.

Immediately, Owen set the cheese down and turned his full attention to her.

"I had lots of dolls, of course. I've always had lots of everything." She held a hand out at the expanse of property. "I don't know what was special about that one, or why it was such a big deal to me."

When she hadn't spoken for several seconds, Owen said, "Sometimes things are just special for no reason at all. To everyone, but when you're three, especially."

"Well, my brother never thought so. He would tease me about how attached I was to that thing. It wasn't the nicest one I had, by any means."

"Maybe it was the softest?"

"It was," she whispered, allowing herself to remember in a way that she hadn't for a very long time. "Anyway, that day while we were playing out here, my brother and I fought about something—we often did, over the stupidest things, you know?"

He gave her an empathetic half-smile.

"Did you fight a lot with your sister when you were young?"

"Well, I have two sisters," he said. "The one I told you about was—is, I hope—quite a bit older than me. I was only eight when she…left. And no, we never fought. My younger sister and I bickered sometimes, though."

"Your older sister is very special to you."

"I love both of my sisters, but yes, our connection was…I guess special is as good a word for it as any. Sometimes we connect with certain people—or things—in a way that's just *more*. There's nothing wrong with that connection being to a doll. Maybe there was a reason for it that you didn't even know."

"Maybe. But I don't know if it was worth it. Not after what happened." She picked up a blade of grass and began tearing off pieces of it.

Owen watched quietly.

"Whatever happened in our fight, I made my brother angry enough that he ripped the doll out of my hands, and he wouldn't give it back. I was chasing him and hitting him, and…we both just kept getting angrier, I think. And then…I don't remember what I did or said that finally made him *so* mad he took the doll and threw her—all the way across the river."

Owen's expression sank, like he knew what the rest of the story was going to be before she even told him. But now, she couldn't stop. It was as if she'd uncorked a bottle of shaken bubble-water and now she couldn't control the spray. It was all going to come out and get on everything, regardless of the consequences.

"I was inconsolable for the rest of the night. I couldn't even eat my dinner. Normally, my mother would have made him swim over to get it, but… No, if she'd been there, she'd never have let him do it in the first place. She always knew how to stop our fighting before it got so bad. Somehow, I think that was part of the problem that day. She wasn't home, and I didn't know why." Until that moment, Ella had completely forgotten most of the story, but especially the part about her mother not being there.

"But your father wouldn't make your brother go and get it for you?"

"My father wouldn't have cared about our argument. He's never… It was unusual that he was even home. He mostly was angry that I was throwing such a terrible fit over it. He sent me to bed early without my supper—I didn't remember that until now."

Owen looked like he didn't know what to say, but he scooted in closer.

She gave him a half-smile. "It doesn't matter. My brother couldn't have gotten the doll, anyway. It was the rainy season, and there had been lots of storms. Crossing the river wasn't safe, not for anybody. An eight-cycle boy would have drowned in a second. The doll was lost."

"Or it should have been." Owen's voice was so low, she almost wondered if she'd imagined him saying it.

"Or it should have been. My mother found me in my room when she got home. I don't know where she'd been, or why she was gone so long, I just remember that I was still crying when she came in and sat on my bed. I don't know what time it was—I thought it was late, but…"

"Memories are not always reliable."

"No." Ella sighed. "I think she was just coming in to kiss me and check on the blankets. But I was awake. I couldn't fall asleep without the doll."

The question hung in the air between them, so thick and so real Ella thought that if she reached out, she could pluck it from the air and hold it between her fingers. But Owen's mouth remained closed, his eyes on her.

There was nothing to do but finish the story. "She stayed there with me, rubbing my back and humming a lullaby…that's the last thing I remember. She was there a long time. If I close my eyes, I can still feel her hand and hear her voice. The next morning when I woke up, the doll was back, on this side of the river. It was torn and wet, but it was there. My mother was gone."

His dark brown eyebrows came together, forming a single line in sharp contrast to his pale skin. "And you know she drowned?"

Ella nodded.

"How?"

She ran her finger down the spine of the journal, feeling the edges where the leather was sewn together, frowning, thinking. Finally, she shrugged. "I was three. My mother was gone and she was never coming back. I think that's as much as I understood. It's not something that's talked about now."

It wasn't something she usually *wanted* to talk about. Even now, all these cycles later, sitting in the comfortable shade with this kind young man, she could feel it happening again. The heat of the day grew warmer, uncomfortably so, and moisture filled her eyes. It was suddenly hard to breathe.

"Ella, I'm… Are you all right?"

She didn't trust herself to speak, but she at least tried to look at him and nod. When she did, he rose to his knees, and the sides of his face went all the way white. "Your eyes…"

Her sadness was quickly turning into fear. Her pulse sped as she lifted a hand to her face, but she didn't feel anything unusual, apart from the dampness of a single tear caught halfway down one cheek. She wiped it angrily away. Crying wasn't going to change anything. She didn't cry. "What about them?"

Owen rocked back on his heels. "I don't know. I just thought I saw… Never mind. I think I've not been getting enough sleep or something."

Ella's panic didn't subside at all. Owen's expression had just reminded her of Shea's last night after the party. Shea had stared at Ella as if she'd grown a second head. And Sabelina's reaction hadn't been comforting, either. *What was she hiding?*

"What did you see, Owen?" she demanded.

Behind them, there was a loud *crack* as someone stepped hard on a fallen limb, snapping it in half.

TEN
KEEPER

IN THE NEXT INSTANT, Ella was on her feet, and she wasn't even sure how she'd gotten there.

"*Go!*" she hissed at Owen, though he was already scrambling to retreat further into the woods.

But it was too late.

"I'm sorry. I didn't mean to frighten you."

Frightened was far too mild a word for what the sound of Cayloken Stone's voice did to Ella. She'd rather have seen another panther appear between the trees than him. And this time, she was the iber.

Her mouth opened and closed several times before she could make any words come out, and her voice shook when she finally managed. "What are you doing here?"

He lifted one shoulder.

A new terrifying thought occurred to her. "I thought you were all leaving. Are your parents and my father here?"

"No. I didn't go with them. I needed some time to myself after…well…you know. And I thought I'd take a walk."

"And you came here?"

He looked around, blatantly ignoring the annoyance in her voice. "Somebody told me the woods behind the property weren't a safe place to go by myself, so, naturally, it's the first place I came." He flashed that smile of his again. She might have found it charming if she didn't hate him so much right now. "Am I likely to be eaten by a dragon?"

Ella gave him a sideways glare. "Probably not during the daytime."

"That's good then. I do apologize—I didn't realize I'd be interrupting your tryst. I have to say I'm impressed. Does the young man who was at the party last night know about this one?" He nodded toward Owen who hadn't managed to hide himself completely.

If she hadn't already been flushed with horror, her face would surely have turned nineteen shades of crimson at this remark. "*No!*" she spluttered. "This isn't… it's not…"

"No, it isn't, is it?" A second ago, his expression had been open and friendly, apologetic, even. Now, though, it was shrewd. Ella never saw the point at which it changed, but she felt it, deep in her gut. "What is this, then?" Cayloken's gaze flicked across the ground, sweeping over the journal, still sitting on a rock, then to Owen's backpack, leaned up against a tree, then to Owen himself, who stood frozen, all color gone from his face.

When that searching scrutiny landed on Ella's face again, it was so intense she thought it might make her physically sick.

And then Cayloken's eyes went wide with shock. "You're a keeper?" he whispered.

Ella wasn't sure if it was the strange question that did it, or her body had finally hit a breaking point where it couldn't deal with one more second of panic, but she suddenly felt very calm. Her hands stopped shaking and she could look him straight in the eye. When she spoke again, she didn't know where the words came from, but her voice was steady. "What do you mean?"

"*You*. You're a keeper. I see it. Your eyes. But how is that possible? Your father…"

Now she was annoyed. "What do you *mean*? What is a *keeper*?"

The moment the question was in the air between them, she knew the answer—or at least suspected it.

Except the answer was preposterous.

Shea had used the word *keeper* the other night, when she'd asked Owen if he was one. At the time it had sounded vaguely familiar, something from a faraway memory.

It had made sense, asking Owen if he was a keeper. After all, he'd appeared in the middle of the air over a river. Surely there was something at least a little magical about him.

But if it meant what she thought it did, Cayloken had just lobbed an accusation at her that would get anyone else arrested—or worse. Surely, keeper had to mean something else. She took a deep breath, purposely keeping herself from screaming at him, hoping he'd keep talking and reveal his intentions.

Cayloken stared at her blankly. "You don't know?"

For the second time that day, Ella felt like she was onstage in front of hundreds of people, expected to say something profound to the crowd, but she'd forgotten all her lines. She looked around the clearing helplessly, as if the trees would somehow come to her aid. "What is it I'm supposed to know? What about my *eyes*?"

"They changed color."

The answer didn't come from Cayloken, who was standing there with his mouth open, clearly as dumbfounded about whatever was going on as she was. But sometime in the middle of the bizarre conversation, Owen had come to stand next to her. "Your eyes changed color," he said again in a low voice. "They did it a few minutes ago, while you and I were talking, and now they've done it again. Currently, they're bright green."

"That's not possible!" she spat. "Eyes don't just change color."

"They do if you're a keeper." Cayloken seemed to have recovered a bit. "You're telling me you're not controlling it?"

For a moment, she wondered if this was some strange practical joke Cayloken and Owen had planned together. It was even a comforting thought, until she realized that possibility would be even stranger—and worse—than her eyes changing color.

"My eyes are not green," she said, in a way that dared anyone to defy her.

Cayloken tipped his head to the side and rubbed his temples with the fingers of one hand. "If you say so."

Owen's feet crunched on the dry grass and fallen leaves as he walked to his pack and reached inside. He returned a second later holding something small. "Take a look," he said, holding it out to her.

It was a little round mirror, about the size of her palm. Not big enough for much, but when she held it up she could see her eyes.

They were a deep, dark green. The shade of the leaves on a hiranthia vine.

They should have been violet.

She flipped the mirror over, searching for what had to be some kind of trick. A strange image of an animal greeted her. She thought it was maybe supposed to be a dog, but it had been drawn oddly, with bold sweeping lines. *An image for children* she thought, but she didn't know how she knew that. In any case, its eyes weren't green. They were the same peculiar brown as Owen's. Perhaps that was an ordinary color for eyes in his world. She'd have believed almost anything at this point.

Except that her own eyes had changed color. That was not possible. *My eyes are violet. Just like my mother's.*

"They're changing again," Owen said.

She looked in the mirror. Sure enough, rings of violet had appeared at the outer edges of her pupils, and they crept inward as she watched until her eyes were again the color they were supposed to be.

Ella felt the rest of her body changing color now—or at least losing all the color it was supposed to have. "Is this some kind of a trick? What does this mean?"

"You can't be serious," Cayloken said. "You know what it means. Did you think you were going to be able to hide it forever? Did your *father?*" He spit the word as if he'd tasted poison.

"I don't know what you're talking about," she said, this time allowing the edge of panic color her voice. "This has never happened to me before. It doesn't mean *anything.*"

She knew that wasn't true. A few minutes ago, she might not have known what a keeper was, but she did now. She understood. A flood of memories swept through her mind. Tiny details that she'd never put together before popped out of the mess, changing the way she saw everything.

But she couldn't concentrate on that now. If it was true, if she was one of the magic ones, she was in danger. The practice of even the simplest magic was forbidden, punishable by banishment.

This was far, far worse than a betrothal.

No. She was being ridiculous. She was the guildmaster's daughter. It couldn't be true. Whatever game Cayloken was playing at, she wanted no part of it.

"Are you all right?" Cayloken asked.

She stared up at his cheekbones, avoiding looking into his eyes as she nodded. "I'm fine."

"You're not fine. You look like you're about to collapse. Maybe you should sit down."

She pressed her lips together and breathed deeply through her nose. "I don't need to sit down. What I *need* is to not be accused of treason by some half-wit from an outer island!"

With those words ringing in the air, she turned on her heels and stormed off, retreating into the cool safety of a copse of trees a few hundred feet away. There, she sank down against the trunk of a tree and curled into a ball, wishing she could disappear. *What had just happened? What had she done?*

It took every ounce of Cayloken's resolve not to go raging through the woods himself. In fact, the only thing that stopped him was that he couldn't decide whether to go after Ellarowan or to march back up to the house and begin demanding answers. He stood there for several minutes, immobilized by indecision, trying to remember how to breathe.

It was only after he'd finally managed to remove his fingernails from the deep indentations he'd dug in his palms that he remembered he wasn't alone. The young man Ellarowan had been so absorbed in conversation with earlier was still standing there by one of the trees, though he was several feet further away than he had been, and Cayloken got the distinct impression he was trying to disappear.

Suddenly remembering his manners, he cleared his throat. "I'm sorry. I don't believe we've been properly introduced. I'm Cayloken Stone."

The stranger moved so his body was no longer half-hidden behind a tree, but he didn't come any closer. "So I gathered." He spoke in a strange accent Cayloken had never heard.

"And you are?"

"Owen Robbins."

"It's nice to meet you, Owen."

"Is it?" The young man raised an eyebrow, and that was when Cayloken noticed there was something odd about his eyes, too, though he couldn't see them clearly at this distance.

"You're a friend of Ellarowan's?"

"Something like that. There's nothing going on between us romantically, if that's what you're worried about."

It wasn't. Cayloken had believed Ellarowan from the instant she'd nearly gone apoplectic at the very suggestion. And considering Owen's accent, it was clear that he wasn't from Ravensguild—or any guild Cayloken was familiar with.

He wasn't sure where Ellarowan would have met him, but he doubted her father would have allowed her to even consider getting involved with someone from outside the league. He'd watched Marius Lockwood last night. The man knew about his daughter's intrigue with the landowner's son. He must have been quietly allowing it.

Owen would have been a different story.

But, even if there had been something between Ellarowan and Owen, he could hardly blame her. She hadn't chosen this betrothal. Unless things were terribly different in Ravensguild than they were in Silver Island, contracted betrothals were rare, even among the families of guildmasters. Until it happened to him, he'd had no reason to suspect the council would one day tell him who he was required to marry.

He certainly never would have chosen Marius Lockwood's daughter.

"I know Ellarowan has another favored," he told Owen. "I saw him last night at the betrothal party."

"So you said a few minutes ago. If I hadn't known about her young man, you would have betrayed her to me then."

Oops. "I suppose you're right. I suppose that wasn't very kind of me. Then again, she is my betrothed."

"Spilling her secrets doesn't seem like the best way to start a marriage."

If Cayloken hadn't been so shaken by what he'd just seen, he might have appreciated Owen's straightforward observation. Right now, though, he was annoyed. "I hardly think lying to me about being a keeper is the best way to start a marriage either. Why is she lying about it?"

"Do you really think she's lying?" Owen turned his head in the direction she'd retreated. "If anything, she looked more shocked about her eyes changing than you were."

Cayloken was starting to feel like a roffler, and it did nothing to improve his mood. Ordinarily, he prided himself on being kind and giving chances to everyone. It seemed particularly important to make the effort with his future wife, and he was failing spectacularly. "How could she possibly not know?"

Owen shrugged. "I—I'm afraid I don't know much about it. I only met Ella a few days ago."

"And yet she's meeting you out here in secret in the middle of the woods."

"It's complicated," Owen said, taking another step backward into the trees.

Cayloken sighed. He knew he should just let this go. Considering Ella's reaction, he was stepping into territory more volatile than he'd even guessed it could be. He knew the keepers were forbidden from practicing their craft all over the mainland, that they'd been so persecuted here that most of them had left altogether. Entire families had simply disappeared nearly twelve cycles ago, during the worst of the routing out.

His parents had told him the history, how Marius Lockwood had been among the guildmasters leading the charge to end the conflicts once and for all.

It seemed impossible that Marius's own daughter might be a keeper herself. *Was Marius one, too?*

Owen was almost completely behind the trees now. It was obvious he wished he could disappear into thin air, but Cayloken wasn't going anywhere without getting at least some answers. "Are you a keeper, too?" he asked, walking toward the other young man.

"I don't know what that means. My eyes don't change color, if that's what you're asking. At least, they never have that I've seen."

Cayloken gave an exasperated sigh. He was trying to keep from exploding on this young man he'd just met, but he wasn't sure he was going to make it. "Look, I'm trying here. I'm willing to entertain the idea that Ellarowan somehow doesn't know that she's a keeper. She's only eighteen. Sometimes keepers don't come fully into their power until around twenty, so…"He took a deep breath. The headache he'd begun feeling a little while ago was growing more intense. "But, I'm sorry. I don't believe that I'm here talking to two people who don't know what keepers are."

"You're not," a female voice broke in.

He whirled around to see Ellarowan standing there. He expected to see evidence of tears—he might have cried in such a situation himself, but the skin around her eyes wasn't puffy or red. There were no dried streaks of anything on her cheeks, though her fingernails looked like she'd pulled them through the dirt. And she looked completely calm, now. He raised an eyebrow.

"I know what keepers are—or at least enough to guess. I've just…never called them that."

"What do you mean? What else would you call them?"

"Nothing. My father calls them something else, but…"She paused, like she didn't want to tell him something. "I've always just called them *the magic ones*, but mostly I've never talked about them at all."

Cayloken gaped at her. "You just…ignored the existence of an entire race of people?" Once the words were out of his mouth though, he realized he wasn't surprised at hearing this from Marius Lockwood's daughter.

She shrugged one shoulder. "They *don't* exist in Ravensguild. Not anymore. Do they in Silver Island?"

Cayloken had to bite hard on the inside of his lip to hold in the kind of word it would never be appropriate to use in front of a young lady. This wasn't a question he was prepared to answer.

"Even if they don't live here now, surely you know the history…" he trailed off, supposing it was possible she didn't. Perhaps the Fading had been more effective here than he'd thought it could be. *Obviously not quite*, he thought dryly, looking at Ellarowan's eyes.

"You have to understand that magic is a forbidden topic in my house. When I was young, I was only sent to bed without any dinner twice before I stopped asking any questions about the magic people at all."

That would do it. "And probably nobody else would dare discuss them with you, either."

She shook her head. "People don't speak the same way to the child of a guildmaster as they probably do with each other. Especially not about things that might get them arrested."

"I might know something about that," he admitted.

"But now that I've heard the word again, I have these vague memories. I think things used to be different. I used to know that the magic people were called keepers. I never knew why."

For the first time since he'd come out here to the woods, Cayloken felt like smiling—a genuine smile, not one he was giving because he knew it would annoy her. She was surprising him. He thought he knew the name her father used for keepers—it wasn't kind. It made him feel oddly warm inside that Ellarowan would have refused to utter it, even before she knew she was a keeper. "I don't know, either. It seems like a strange name. Someone once told me that a long time ago, they were actually called gatekeepers."

Ella's face, normally a rather lovely red-brown in color, was now grayish. He didn't think he'd said anything that would upset her again. Maybe she was just getting overwhelmed with everything that was happening. "I could use something to drink, if you have anything," he said, hoping she'd get the idea to have something for herself.

She stared at him for a moment, but then nodded. "I do."

There was a leather satchel on the ground near where she'd been sitting with Owen when he'd first spotted them. Several things were spread on the ground now—food and a book he'd seen Ella holding earlier. She picked up the bag and pulled out a small metal jug. "It's not very cold anymore," she said, holding it out to Cayloken. "But it's water."

"Thank you," he mumbled, suddenly feeling awkward about drinking from a bottle that was obviously hers. He unscrewed the lid and stared at the opening, debating how to do this with both Ella and Owen watching him.

"I promise I'm not trying to poison you," she said.

He raised an eyebrow at her and lifted the bottle to his lips, taking a long swig. "That's better," he said when he was finished. "Thank you."

"You're quite welcome." Ella took the jug back from him and put it to her own mouth, drinking until a dribble ran down her chin and then onto the bare skin below her neck that her tailored shirt didn't cover.

"Is it always this hot here?" Cayloken asked.

She frowned, looking around at the lush vegetation. "It's a little cooler during the wet season. Is it not hot in Silver Island?"

"It is, but it doesn't feel like this." Already he was regretting choosing a shirt with a high neckline and sleeves that reached nearly to his elbows. "We get cross-breezes over the island; it's not this humid unless you go into the jungle."

She held out a hand toward the thick vegetation surrounding them and crooked one eyebrow.

"Point taken." This was easier, sharing a drink and chatting about the weather, even with a stranger listening in. In other circumstances, he'd have liked her immediately. But it couldn't stay this way. Cayloken still had questions he needed the answers to. He had to figure out just how much danger he might be in.

Owen had moved a comfortable distance from them, and he seemed absorbed with rustling in an enormous pack leaned against a tree, but surely he would still overhear much of what they talked about. Cayloken decided it didn't matter. The other man had already heard the worst of it. And Ella seemed to trust him.

There was no good place to start. Anything he said was likely to upset her. All he could do was jump right in. "So, you've grown up never talking about keepers, and yet, you are one."

Fire flashed in her eyes, as he'd expected. But this time they only went green around the outermost edges of her star-shaped pupils. "I'm *not* a keeper."

"Of course you are. That's the only explanation for what you're able to do with your eyes."

"I'm not *able* to *do* anything with my eyes. If you're not just playing some kind of strange trick on me—and I'm not convinced you aren't—they're doing it by themselves. I'm not controlling it."

"You just haven't learned *how*. They're still changing. That's not something that just happens to regular people."

The more frustrated and upset she got, the more green crept into her eyes. "So that's the big secret then? Magic is illegal because keepers can change the color of their eyes?"

Cayloken bit his lip, trying to maintain his own composure. "They can change the shape, too. Of their pupils, I mean. Like your friend over there with the round ones." *And failing.* That was probably the worst thing he could have said.

She wasn't stupid. She'd figure things out and start asking more difficult questions soon. Most keepers could do far more than change their eye color. He wondered where her talents lay.

ELEVEN
CONTROL

HEAT RUSHED THROUGH ELLAROWAN'S chest and up through her neck as she spun to face Owen, molten anger running through her veins.

And now, her eyes prickled, making her imagine she actually could will her pupils to change color and shape. But that was absurd. There was no way that was possible. And if it was, green was not the color she'd be choosing right now.

Owen had been keeping to himself, hiding in the trees, fiddling with his pack, but he'd been listening, she knew. Because now he stepped out to face her, his pale skin white as starlight.

"You lied to me," she said.

He shook his head. "No, I didn't. Everything I told you is the truth. I'm not magic. My eyes are not like yours, but they don't change. They're always this color and shape." His strange eyes met hers and his gaze didn't waver. "Why would I lie, anyway? My truth is worse."

She stood there staring at him for several heartbeats, but truthfully, she was just buying time to think, to try to understand. Because she believed him. Even if it was against all logic; she just couldn't help believing him. She wasn't sure Owen was even capable of lying. Withholding the truth, maybe, but not lying.

Shame replaced a small piece of the anger. "I'm sorry," she said.

"Then what are you?" Cayloken said. "What do you mean, your truth is worse?"

Owen raised one eyebrow at Ella, questioning.

She shook her head.

"He's a friend of mine. That's all," she said, turning to face Cayloken again. "He's not magic, not a keeper. We need to leave him out of this."

Cayloken was silent for a long moment. They all were. Only the river and the birds made any noise as they stared each other down, navigating their impasse.

"I think you should tell me," Cayloken finally said. "Clearly, he's already *in* this."

The anger was back in full force, but this time she aimed it at a better target. "Who do you think you are?" she growled at Cayloken. "You think you can just follow me out into the woods when I'm trying to have time by myself and then start demanding answers? Why are you even here?"

Cayloken rubbed a finger over his lip, seemingly unaffected by her outburst. "Unless you and your favored have some exceptional plan to prevent it, I'm the man who's about to be your husband. And I already know you're a keeper. How much more damage could I possibly do to you, if that's what I wanted to do? You might as well just tell me what's going on here."

Between the anger and the fear, Ella couldn't string two coherent thoughts together. All she knew was she needed to get away and get out of the situation—to get Owen somehow to safety. But she wasn't going to be able to. Cayloken wasn't giving up. She twisted and untwisted the lid of the water jug, digging her fingers into the ridges of the metal cap, trying to think. And then, she remembered what Loric had said last night.

"You're not the only one who can do damage," she said. "I know that you and your parents are sympathizers." It was a risk; she wasn't certain Loric's information was accurate. But she could hardly make the situation worse. She hoped.

His orange eyes went so wide and bright that for a second she wondered if he wasn't a keeper, too. But the color didn't change, and after a moment, he was perfectly, infuriatingly calm again. A sick feeling rolled in the pit of her stomach. "Think that one through, Ellarowan. I realize you've got to be overwhelmed right now, but take a minute. Either it's not true that we're sympathizers, in which case you won't get far with that accusation, especially since I'd then have more on you than you have on me. Or, it is true, and that's why you should tell me. Who else is going to help you?"

The only thing she really understood right now was that Cayloken wasn't going anywhere. Apparently, he was enjoying torturing her. She suddenly understood how Fluffy must have felt the night she locked him in the cabin. Ella wouldn't have minded having some bedding and curtains to shred right about now. Furniture to toss to the floor would have been even better.

"Why would you help me?"

Cayloken pressed his lips together, considering. His eyebrows quirked inward, confused. "Why wouldn't I?"

"If I'm a keeper—and you know about it… You realize that's your ticket out of having to marry me, right? You could turn me in, and then you'd be free."

He kept staring at her, not looking any less confused. "I'm sorry. Have I given you the impression that was my goal? To get out of marrying you?"

Ella was beginning to feel like she had it all wrong—that Owen wasn't the one who'd fallen into an upside-down world where nothing was how it should be. "You *want* to marry me?"

He tilted his head to the side. For a fraction of a second, his mouth curled like he'd tasted something sour, but his expression smoothed out almost immediately, back into a friendly, relaxed smile.

She narrowed her eyes at him. "That's enough of an answer. I asked the wrong question. Why don't you want to *avoid* marrying me?"

Now Cayloken chuckled. "You're smart, willing to listen and try to understand things even when they scare you or will cost you. Already I can tell you're not anything like your father—that's what I was most afraid of, but you're different." He glanced over at Owen, and then back to her, giving her an appraising look. "And you're pretty. As far as forced marriages go, I think I could do a lot worse."

Her cheeks warmed a bit at his words, but whether from his compliment or her own embarrassment about treating him far worse than she'd treated him, she wasn't sure. "But you don't want to be forced into marriage," she said.

"No, I don't. Not anymore than you do, I imagine."

"Then why…?"

He scoffed. "Any chance I could get another drink?"

She passed him the bottle and watched as he took a long sip.

When he was finished, he twisted the cap back on, but didn't hand the bottle back to her. "I'm not going to reveal you as a keeper and deal with the fallout of *that* to avoid a marriage. I couldn't do it to you, anyway. You haven't done anything to me besides be unfortunate enough to be ordered into marrying me. You don't deserve to be outed as a keeper when you don't even understand it in the first place. Which, by the way, don't imagine that I'm done with wanting to understand how *that* happened."

She took several deep breaths. Her thoughts were hopping so rapidly from one question to the next that she couldn't even remember what she was trying to think. "What color are my eyes now?"

His snicker wasn't condescending, like she was afraid hers might have been in the same situation. Instead, his was oddly reassuring, as if she were asking something almost normal. "They're red. Like iron in a fire. I can understand why."

She shook her head. "I still don't believe you."

"I wouldn't believe me, either, if I didn't know I was a keeper and suddenly people started telling me my eyes were changing. But we're even. I don't totally believe you that you had no idea."

This time, it was her turn to scoff, though she tried to be kind about it. "We'll call it a draw for now."

"Fair enough. So…?"

"So, you are a sympathizer, then."

"You're asking a lot of questions that aren't questions."

Somehow during the course of their conversation, they'd wandered back toward the little clearing where Ella and Owen had been talking. She held her hand out for the water jug. "I already know the answers," she said. "Or at least partially." The bottle was already half gone when she opened it to take a drink. They couldn't stay out here forever.

"I'm not sure exactly what sympathizer means to you," he said, watching her. "But…I have friends who are keepers, and I've never wanted them to disappear."

She froze, and this time she could definitely feel her eyes doing *something*—changing color? She imagined an icy blue. Cayloken had just revealed enough information to get himself banished, or possibly killed, along with whoever these friends of his were, and yet he was just standing there, like he'd said something completely normal.

Then he looked at her and seemed to realize what he'd done. His cheeks puffed up and then he let out a big breath. "So, yes, I guess you could say I'm a sympathizer."

"And your parents?"

"Could we leave them out of this for now?" his voice was strained.

"Why not?" There was enough to think about right now anyway. She slumped down on one of the old tree stumps. Owen had all but vanished himself, though she could still feel his presence there in the trees.

Cayloken sucked in a breath. "What is that?"

Ella followed his gaze, smiling when she saw what he was looking at. "Watch," she said, holding out her hand with her palm up and sliding down from the rock to the ground.

A second later, Fluffy was nuzzled up in her lap, having bypassed the proffered hand completely.

"No, seriously. What *is* it? It looks like a giant ball of spun wool."

The iber made a noise that sounded almost like a sneeze.

"This is Fluffy," she said, petting the top of its head gently. The rumbling noise she'd heard the other night started up again, reverberating through her.

"And Fluffy is a…?"

She frowned. "Do you not have ibers on Silver Island?"

"An iber. So this is what they look like. I've heard of them, but never seen one. No, they don't live on Silver Island. I thought it was best to leave them alone."

"Normally, it is. This one seems to be an exception."

"May I touch it?"

Ella shrugged.

Kneeling down in front of her, Cayloken tentatively reached his hand toward the little creature.

Immediately, it stopped rumbling and made a sharp hissing noise. Cayloken yanked his hand back. "Not an exception for me, I guess," he muttered.

Ella was a little wary of Fluffy herself now, after that, but as soon as the hand was gone, the creature settled back in. "I did rescue it from a panther the other night," she said. "Right over there by the river." The rumbling started again.

"There are panthers out here? This close?" Cayloken's eyes were wide again.

"You were told it was dangerous," she pointed out.

"I guess I wasn't thinking big, hungry predators."

This made her laugh. "People stopped exploring in those woods altogether after the rumors started that there were dragons in there." Dragons weren't the only rumor, but they were the easiest to explain, and she was tired and needed time to think.

He raised an eyebrow. "In your woods? Really?"

"You don't have *those* on Silver Island either, do you?"

"Actually…I have seen a dragon," he said. "They're not common, of course, but they've been spotted."

"By you?" she pressed.

"Yes…so, are you going to tell me about your friend over there in the trees, or am I going to have to try to find out a different way?"

"Do you know what a gadab is?"

For the next several minutes, the world went silent—or at least that was what it felt like to Ella as she watched Cayloken's expression and waited for him to respond. She realized she'd probably just made the biggest mistake of her life in answering him, but she couldn't see another option. Chances were he'd find out enough information to be dangerous no matter what she did. Just the fact that she was spending time alone in the woods with someone as strange as Owen was enough to cause serious damage.

"A real one?" Cayloken finally whispered.

"As opposed to a fake one?"

"Not fake so much as lying about it."

"Yes, all those characters in fireside stories seemed pretty untrustworthy."

He tilted his head. "You're the one telling me that we're standing here with a gadab, Ro, and yet, I don't see a fire, and you're not playing your lute."

"Ro?" If the point of her eyebrow could get any sharper, she would have been able to use it as a weapon.

"Well, I'm not going to spit out four syllables every time I say your name."

"People who know me usually go with Ella."

"You mean the people who've been lying to you? Who've either made an enormous secret out of one of the key elements of who you are, or who don't even *know*? Or the ones forcing you into a marriage and not even telling you until the day before you meet your new…I'm not even going to call myself your chosen. Those people?"

She didn't want to be affected by his words, but her lower lip trembled in spite of her efforts to keep it still. "Thanks for making me think of it like *that*."

"Anyway, you already hate me just for existing because of them, so, no, I'm not terribly interested in calling you the same thing they do."

She bit her lip, hard, finally steadying it at the expense of tasting blood. "And what do people call you when they can't be bothered to say three whole syllables?"

He smiled. "Cay."

"All right then, *Lo*. Why would someone lie about being a gadab? Being arrested and interrogated and who knows what else for making such a claim doesn't seem like something anyone would do just for fun."

"Be careful there, *Ella*. This situation is going to get a whole lot harder if we like each other."

"Our impending marriage, you mean?" she said, looking at him sideways.

"Yeah, that." He coughed and held out a hand for the water jug again. "Anyway, things haven't always been the way they are here, now, in the League of Guilds. There was a time when a visitor from another world might have been welcomed. In the stories, that's where some of our knowledge comes from, you know. Some of our words, even."

"In fireside stories."

"Well…" Cayloken shrugged, looking over at Owen who had now crept back out of the trees to listen to them. "What if they're not just stories?"

Ella had always enjoyed sitting around the fire at The Dozy, but she hadn't always paid full attention to all the stories. The poetry was her favorite. Stories of the gadab, though interesting, had always seemed a little too far-fetched for her, and she hadn't listened closely to all of them. They weren't told very often, anyway—at least not while she was in attendance. Now she wished she'd paid better attention.

Owen cleared his throat. "Are you saying there have been other people who've traveled through the gate before me?"

"What gate?" Cayloken asked.

Owen's eyes were wary when they met Ella's, but all she could do was shrug. Keeping information from Cayloken might be a prudent choice, but it was an impossible, meaningless one. "The one I traveled through when I came here from the other world."

"I don't see how there could be a gate up there," Cayloken said, shielding his eyes against the bright afternoon sun as he looked up at the place over the river where Owen was pointing.

"It's never visible," Owen said, in a voice so normal Cay thought they might as well have been talking about a lunch menu. "And it's closed right now—maybe it doesn't even exist right now. I don't really understand how it all works. And even when it's open, you can't *see* it; it's just suddenly *there*. One moment you're in one world, and the next you're in another, with completely different scenery."

Cay rubbed at the hem of his shirt, as he always did when he was trying to figure something out. His mother had been trying to break him of the habit for a dozen cycles at least, upset about the damage it caused, but her efforts had been fruitless. "So…when it's open, you can see through it to another world?"

"Not exactly, no." Owen looked more uncomfortable than anyone Cay had ever talked to in his life—a neat trick considering the ease with which a future guildmaster could inspire wariness in other people without even trying. "You can't ever really *see* anything."

"I didn't see anything that looked like a gate or another world," Ella confirmed. "All I saw was a body suddenly appearing in midair—and then he fell into the river."

"There's a bridge on the other side," Owen said. "But nowhere to stand on this side. I knew there wouldn't be. I didn't *fall*; I jumped. But I'm sure it looked like falling to Ellarowan."

"Then how did you *find* the gate, if you couldn't see it?"

Owen's eyes stayed trained on the ground as he spoke; he only rarely seemed to make eye contact, and when he did, it was only with Ella. "I don't really know, exactly. It took me a long time to find it; I just kept trying on different days, searching from the beginning of dusk until the sun had set, walking along the bridge with my hands held out like this." He demonstrated, taking a few steps with his arms stretched in front of him. "And then one night...my hand disappeared, and I knew I'd found it."

Cay tried to picture it and nearly gasped at the implication. "The...gate... It just opened in the middle of some bridge? You mean anyone could just walk through it at any time?"

"Well, they wouldn't be likely to. The bridge isn't in a well-traveled area. Not anymore, at least. It took me a long time to find it in the first place. And it's broken—and kind of dangerous. Normal people aren't climbing around up there at sunset."

"But you were."

"Yes."

Cay pinched the bridge of his nose, trying to head off the pounding he knew was coming. He had so many questions that he couldn't figure out where to start. And every answer he received gave him a thousand more things to wonder about.

"And you're sure you can get back to your own world through the gate?" Cayloken asked.

"No," Owen answered, and Ella felt the word like a punch in her own gut. She could only imagine the terror he must feel at the idea of being stuck in a world so different from his own. And she felt responsible, somehow, for the danger he was in every moment he remained here.

They'd been talking for hours, although only the angle of the burning sun and the growing hunger in her belly told Ella that any time had passed at all.

Owen and the gate appeared to be as fascinating to Cayloken as they were to Ella. He asked just as many questions as she did. Even the details that Ella had already heard twice felt like a brand-new story when Owen told them again.

But now the way the sunlight was coming through the leaves in a too-familiar way, she was reminded of something. "Loric will be coming near here," she said, interrupting Owen's explanation of how he'd been risking his life every evening throwing rocks up at the spot over the river, but they'd all come splashing back into the water or thudding into the grass on the other side.

Owen, lost in his own thoughts, didn't stop talking right away, but Cayloken turned to her with wide eyes. "That's your favored?"

She nodded.

"I guess I wasn't entirely wrong about you. How long have you been secretly meeting him out here?"

She shrugged. "Almost a cycle."

He shook his head, giving a little half-smile as Owen finally tapered off. "I am sorry I had to be the one your father is using to wreck whatever dream you had for yourself and him."

"You could make it a little less difficult for me to stay mad at you for it, you know."

"I'm doing my best."

"Well, your best is terrible."

She'd thought some of his smiles were genuine before, but now that she saw this one, she knew she'd been wrong.

"So, are you going to go and meet with him?" he asked.

"It wouldn't bother you if I was?"

Cayloken bent down and picked up a smooth, gray stone. He turned it over in his hand, staring at it instead of looking at her. "What? Going to meet with another man when we're betrothed?"

"Yes. That."

He flicked the stone out over the water, intending to skip it, Ella thought, but it just plopped, causing a splash. "This is not the way I pictured being betrothed, no. When I imagined the days leading up to my wedding, they were filled with sneaking off into corners just to get another minute alone with my chosen. Not watching a veritable stranger leave me to meet up with her favored." His voice caught a little on the last words, making Ella feel something she hadn't expected to.

"It's not what I imagined either, you know. I never—Loric was the first boy I ever considered as a *favored*. I was surprised when he was interested in me, honestly."

Cayloken scoffed. "You're the gorgeous daughter of a guildmaster, Ellarowan. Every single man in the guild is likely *interested* in you. Probably half the ones who aren't single, too." He bent and picked up another rock.

"Exactly. They're all interested in the guildmaster's daughter. They're hopeful I'll appear at parties and...*sneak off into corners*. Just so they'll have a story to tell—that they had a chance with Ellarowan Lockwood."

"Of course, most of them aren't interested in any of the responsibilities that would come with actually courting you." This time, his rock skipped twice before the *plop*.

She cleared her throat and bent down to examine the rocks along the riverbank. "I suppose you might know something about that."

"Oh, I don't avoid the parties, Ro. The position *can* be quite entertaining."

She chuckled. "I've no doubt parties could be fun. Depending on the specific people at them. I just… That was never what I wanted. And Loric came to *my* life, to play games with my friends, and spend time where I like to. He's different." She selected a white rock that was almost perfectly round. "I don't *want* to be sneaking around with one man and marrying another. I just wanted to be with Loric and be happy." Her rock skipped seven times, going nearly all the way across the river.

Cayloken let out a low whistle. "Well, then, I hope you figure out a plan for getting out of this that works. You should go to him, if he's waiting, don't you think?"

"I don't know," she said, nervous energy rising in her stomach. "We've both been gone for a long time. Surely our parents are back from their tour of the guild by now. Someone's going to wonder where we are."

"Ella." Owen's voice was so quiet Ella could barely hear him above the late-afternoon noises in the woods and the rushing of the water, but she turned to face him.

"Yes?"

"Does Loric know about your eyes?"

Her body seemed to be getting used to shock and terror, because her heart rate and stomach barely responded, though her eyes suddenly itched and blazed, and a word slipped through her teeth that surprised even her.

Cayloken's lips twitched in what looked like a combination of amusement and approval. "I'll take that as a no."

She glared at him.

"Sorry. That *is* a problem. Your eyes have been their normal color for the last hour or so…but now they're green again. I think they get that way when you're upset. They've really never done this before? It would be very odd for it to only just start at your age."

She hid her face with her hands. "Surely someone would have *told* me before now if they did—wouldn't they?" But almost as soon as the words were out of her mouth, she realized that, up until the last couple of days, until the announcement of her betrothal, she had very rarely *been* upset in front of people. Not since she was much younger, anyway. And when she did get upset…people weren't looking at her eyes.

"People don't upset me very often," she said. "I suppose that's hard to believe considering how I've acted since you met me, but…"

"But you're rather a spoiled rich girl?" Cayloken finished, smiling and holding his hands out in front of him, playing at escaping her wrath. "Nobody dares to upset you?"

She only chuckled softly. "Perhaps that's how everyone sees me. I suppose they wouldn't be wrong."

"I don't know," he said. "The fact that you're close to your servants, and your choice of guest at the party last night suggest that maybe *everyone* doesn't see you that way. Even if it's true." He grinned again.

"Coming from a spoiled rich boy."

"I know of what I speak. I'm a little surprised that your *father* doesn't upset you enough to ever set you off, though."

"My father's not the type to stick around and watch my eyes change color. He likes to issue decrees and then disappear, leaving someone else to deal with the fallout. Sabelina, my caretaker… That's her job."

"Sounds like perhaps you need to have a conversation with her, then."

She nodded absently, still thinking. "I've always tried not to get upset. Fought it, even."

He took her more seriously than she expected him to, pressing a finger to his lips and studying her. "What do you mean?"

"I've almost never cried in front of anyone, not since I was little—since my mother died."

"You just don't like to?"

"It's more than that—it makes me ill. If I let myself get all the way upset or start crying, then my head starts pounding and I get dizzy and hot. Sometimes I even pass out. It happened last night."

"Oh." He looked taken aback.

"Could that... Is that because I'm a keeper?"

"I've never heard of that side effect..." He was quiet for a moment, chewing nervously on his bottom lip.

"What?"

"I've heard of people—keepers—who could *do* something like that to other people. Have an effect on their bodies, I mean. Cause headaches or even people to pass out. It's usually defensive magic, though. Not because someone is upset."

Ella put her head in her hands, starting to feel a little sick right then, although she doubted it had to do with any kind of magic.

"We should get out of the woods and back to the house, though, before everyone does return and come looking for us. Will your favored come searching for you—Loric?"

She sat up and tried to think straight. "No, I don't think so. He knew I might not be able to meet him this afternoon. If I couldn't, I'm supposed to try to meet him tonight, at a taberna. But I don't see how I'll manage that, either."

"You're going to need to learn to control your eyes."

"I'll get right to that—before dinner." Her face crumpled as panic set in, again. How was she going to hide her eyes at a formal dinner?

"Breathe." This was Owen's suggestion. Coming from Cayloken, it might have turned her eyes back to fiery red, but from Owen, it seemed not only logical, but possible.

"Good," he said, when she'd taken several deep breaths. "They're back to dark purple."

"Now you need to just not get upset at dinner," Cayloken offered. "Ooh… now they're orange. We match."

She shot him a look.

"Going purple again. I used to have a toy that did something like this—changed colors if you twisted it the right way."

"Maybe you should stop trying to twist me then."

Cayloken laughed. "I wouldn't count on that happening."

She huffed in exasperation. "This is a serious problem. If you're not planning on telling anyone what you know—you could get in trouble for not reporting it."

He didn't make a joke about it, and Ella wasn't sure if that made her feel slightly better or infinitely worse.

"Don't get mad," Owen said, in his always calm, patient voice, "But you haven't *tried* to control it."

"How could I have? I didn't even know my eyes could do that when I woke up this morning."

"Exactly. So…what if you tried?"

"*How?*"

Owen shrugged. "I'm making this up as I go. In my world, magic is not real. It only exists in stories."

"Except for the part where you walked off a broken bridge and into another world at sunset," Cayloken said.

"I did. But that wasn't magic. It was science."

Cayloken twisted the cap of the almost-empty water jug. "And what is science but the explanation behind how the magic works?"

"Touché."

"What does that mean?" Ella asked, frowning at the strange word.

Owen grimaced. "Uh… Now you're asking me to explain my vocabulary. Hmm… I guess the best explanation I can give is that it means he scored a point."

She wrinkled her nose. "He's scoring points all over the place today."

"I'll take that as a compliment," Cayloken said, stooping down to hold the bottle in the cool river water, refilling it. "But you're right. It's getting late, and we need to do something before someone else sees your eyes."

"*We* need to do something? Okay, Lo. Make my eyes stay violet all the way through dinner."

"How about you just don't get upset?"

"*That* sounds like a simple thing to do at a dinner with my father right now."

"You managed it this morning. Perhaps you're overthinking it."

She narrowed her eyes at him. This time, she really could feel it; a tickling sensation just in the center of her eyeballs, strong enough to make her want to close her eyes and rub them. So she did. *Violet*, she commanded silently.

"Okay, open your eyes," Cayloken's mouth was half full of water, which he nearly sprayed at her when he spoke.

"Clearly you're taking this very seriously."

"I can be serious and thirsty at the same time. Your eyes are still violet, by the way."

"You're just losing your ability to upset me."

"All right. Fine. Let's go to dinner. We can discuss the details of our wedding. What are your thoughts on the kiss? Tongue or no tongue? Oooh! Are you going to invite Loric?"

It was more than a tickling this time. Now there was a very definite sensation of something happening to her pupils; she could almost sense the shape of them, the point of each spoke.

Water sloshed inside the bottle Cayloken was still holding. "They're getting very green."

No. Violet.

"You're doing it!" Owen said. "They're turning back to purple. It's working."

It was also starting to give her a headache, but more than that, there was a flutter of excitement in her belly. Maybe she actually could control it—at least long enough to not get caught.

Cayloken held the water jug toward her. "That was kind of incredible. I've never watched anyone do it before."

Ella took a long sip from the jug, considering her next words carefully. "So you…*know* keepers?"

"Besides you, you mean? Yes, I do. I've never watched any of them learn to control their eyes before, though."

"But…"

"It's illegal? Yes, I know. Did you want to have that discussion right now, in front of the *gadab* you're hiding, or should we get out of the woods before either panthers or our parents appear?"

"I'm not sure which one is worse. Is there a difference?" Her hands were shaking. "One time of turning my eyes back to the right color is not 'learning to control' them." In fact, she could feel them starting to turn again.

"Breathe," Owen said again. "Focus and try."

She took a deep breath, biting the insides of her cheeks, and *tried.*

"Just like that," Cayloken said. "Perfect. They're the right color."

A whole two times. "And if it doesn't work at the dinner table?"

Cayloken shrugged. "Hide your eyes. Bury them in your hands. Go relieve yourself. It's one dinner, you can manage."

"What if I just don't go?"

"Not going is not a choice. They're already going to be wondering where we were all day. I've met your father. I wouldn't put it past him to send the palades after you."

"He's not *that* bad."

"Then have dinner with him. I'll even try not to upset you."

TWELVE
DINNER AND A RIDE

"WHERE WILL OWEN go?" Cayloken asked as the main house came into view.

Although they'd been talking amiably all afternoon in the woods, the walk back had been mostly silent, the stiffness and formality of strangers settling back over them. He was still the son of another guildmaster, still the man she was going to be forced into an alliance with if she couldn't come up with a plan to stop it.

"He'll be fine." The less information she gave out—to anyone—the better.

"I'm sure that iber will protect him from predators out there."

It wasn't predators she was most worried about. "You do have a gift for sarcasm. Our parents are definitely back," Ella said, as they reached the porch.

They were back, but the timing was fortunate. Ella and Cayloken didn't have to deal with any questions until an hour later, when dinner had begun.

Tonight, the meal was being served in the dining room reserved for banquets and formal guild dinners—which, Ella supposed, this was.

For the second night in a row, all of the household servants were on duty, and she was led into the room by a liveried server who delivered her to a place at the table marked with her name card. Right next to Cayloken.

"Ellarowan," he said, bowing.

It wasn't as difficult as she'd thought it would be—as she'd spent the afternoon panicking in preparation for. Cayloken was cordial, even kind, throughout the meal, and she managed to return the courtesy, even while maintaining a poised performance for the other guildmasters gathered there.

Their whereabouts during the day were barely questioned—brushed off with nudges and winks about the betrothed couple "getting to know each other." Cayloken encouraged this talk more than she would have liked, but she had to admit it worked.

Her eyes remained under control for all but one part of the evening—when her father stood and formally invited everyone to the wedding, which would be held in three days.

It was only a polite formality. The plans had clearly been made some time ago. Ella was the only one in the room learning anything new—including Cayloken. She wished she'd thought to ask him what he knew about *that* earlier.

She stared down at the vegetables on her plate hoping desperately that her flaming cheeks would be interpreted as embarrassment at the attention. Bad manners would be far easier to live down than having her eyes change in front of these people.

Then Cayloken's hand closed around hers, and he leaned in so close she felt the warmth of his breath on her ear. "Violet. They're violet. You can do this. Take one deep breath."

She did and he helped her to stand so they could thank everyone for the congratulations and best wishes.

Compared to the party of the night before, dinner was mercifully short. The guests engaged in the customary mingling and chatting during dessert, but the good-byes started long before the teapots were empty. Ella wasn't certain she was grateful for this as the guests disappeared, leaving the Lockwoods and Stones alone together in the massive room.

"I'm pleased to see you've decided to make peace with the situation." Her father's voice startled her, nearly upsetting the liquid in the cup she held in both hands like a talisman.

She turned slightly toward him, though she didn't dare to look up and meet his gaze. He'd take it as defiance, but she didn't care. That was less dangerous than the truth.

"You don't have to like it, Ellarowan. I've told you from the beginning. You're free to do as you wish, so long as you continue to meet your obligations. Tonight was an improvement over last night. If you can manage a polite exit from the Stones, then you may have the rest of the evening to go and do whatever you like."

She gaped at him, trying to comprehend, realizing for the first time that he actually thought he was being magnanimous. That this was somehow a *favor* he was granting her. So long as she behaved as he wished in front of the other guildmasters, he truly didn't care what she did on her own time.

She tried to remember how to breathe as opposing emotions warred like dragons inside her. One wanted to just take advantage of the opportunity to escape, but the other wanted to unleash a raging inferno. Worse, if she wasn't careful, the inferno would win regardless. She had to keep the dragon fire from showing in her eyes.

Violet. Violet.

"Ellarowan! I was looking for you. Would you be so kind as to accompany me outside for a moment? There's something I'd like to discuss."

She did have to give Cayloken some credit. He knew how to play the game better than she did. Perhaps it was because he'd been raised to be a guildmaster, while Ella had only been expected to be a compliant pawn. Or maybe it was simply that he'd had more time to understand and prepare for the situation at hand. But whatever the reason, she was grateful to be leaning over the porch railing, gulping in the night air she so desperately needed.

He didn't say anything; he just stood a few feet away, staring up at the nearly full moon.

Once she thought she was in control of herself, she turned to face him.

"I couldn't see your eyes the whole time, but I think they stayed the right color," he offered.

"I suppose that's something."

"It's actually kind of awesome that you're figuring it out so quickly."

She didn't know what to do with the compliment. Ignoring it felt wrong, but acknowledging it would have been worse. She tried to meet his gaze, though, after thoroughly checking to make sure they were alone. "Kind of makes me wonder how many people…like me are wandering around with their eyes under control."

He put his hands behind him and leaned on the wide, wooden rail. "I know you don't have much reason to like me or trust me, Ella—but I would tell you. I wouldn't let you be the only one right now if I didn't have to."

She knew, this time, for sure that she'd lost control of her eyes. She even knew that they'd gone a deep shade of blue, closer to midnight than noon, and that her pupils were round.

And she knew, a moment later, when they were violet and the right shape again.

Cayloken nodded. "Just like that," he whispered. "Try another."

She thought of the bright yellow centers of the wildflowers that grew at the bottom of the steps to the cottage, and Cayloken smiled.

When she tried the pale white of the moon above them, though, he took a step to the side. "That's terrifying," he said. "Don't do that."

If things hadn't still been so tense and perilous between them, they might have dissolved into laughter.

She couldn't have explained how she did it, or how she was so certain, but she knew, now, that she could go out in public—that she could speak to Loric.

Somehow, Cayloken saw this in her eyes as well.

This time, his eyes did change. Not from orange to another color, but from amused to pleading.

"What?" she asked.

"Take me with you?"

Her mouth fell open. "Take you with me? To go and meet up with my favored?"

"I don't mean that. It's just—you said you were going to a taberna, and that sounds about a million times better than remaining here and fielding questions from my parents—and your father and brother—about what we did today while they were gone."

He didn't mean it as a threat. Not a purposeful one, anyway. But they both knew that it was one. He wouldn't set out to betray her, to give up the details of what they'd done today, but it would be impossible not to slip at all.

"If I go out with you tonight, too, it will create a buffer. More time will have passed, there will be new questions. Perhaps it will even give us a chance to make plans to keep ourselves away from questions for the next few days."

"And I'll be spending the evening with you instead of talking to Loric."

"It won't be like that. I'll leave you alone. I'm certain I can find ways to occupy myself there. People have to be curious about me anyway."

"I—"

"You can tell Loric I insisted upon coming and you couldn't get out of it."

"I don't like to lie."

He glanced at her sideways. "You don't have a problem with letting people believe things that aren't true."

"I don't mind *my father* believing things about me that aren't true. If you hadn't noticed, that's a mutual arrangement. I don't want the same kind of relationship with Loric that I have with him."

"Well then, how about we just make it the truth? Take me. I insist."

She glared at him.

"Turn them back violet, Ella. They need to be, because you're taking me."

For several moments, she buried her face in her hands, and then she sighed. "Fine. If you can get out of those ridiculous clothes and be back here on the porch as fast as I can, you can come with me."

Cayloken had thought she was joking. Well, joking wasn't the right word, because there was certainly no humor in it, but the challenge she'd issued—to be dressed for going out and back to the porch before her—had seemed facetious. He'd never met a girl who could get ready to go out for the evening faster than he could.

Not that he hadn't taken her seriously. His evening formalwear lay in a haphazard heap across the bed in the guestroom he occupied, and he was checking his hair in the mirror in the foyer when she came blasting down the stairs. He had to run outside behind her, carrying his shoes in his hands.

He wasn't even sure how, but there was a carriage waiting in the driveway already when he reached the porch. The carriage driver standing beside the door looked more than a little surprised when he saw Cayloken, and he looked questioningly at Ella.

"Cayloken asked if he could accompany me tonight, Bastian, and I agreed."

The driver was an older man, taller than Cayloken, which was saying something. His dark red hair was graying around the temples, and his orange eyes watched Cayloken with suspicion. His deep concern for Ellarowan was obvious. Despite being the subject of Bastian's scrutiny, Cayloken liked him already.

"Are you sure?" Bastian asked Ellarowan. His voice was so low Cayloken couldn't actually hear him, but he could read lips fairly well, and Ella's single nod suggested he was correct.

"Then where am I taking you?" The question was oddly pointed. Cayloken had the feeling that this driver might never like *him*.

"To The Dozy, please, Bastian."

This clearly rattled the man, and he pulled Ellarowan all the way to the side to discuss something privately with her.

Cayloken swallowed, thinking he'd probably overstepped his boundaries well and truly this time. It was impossible not to, most of the time here, considering the nature of his relationship with Ellarowan, but he didn't want to make it more difficult than necessary.

"Nev—" he started.

"Let's go," Ellarowan interrupted, returning from her private chat with Bastian. Her eyes were violet, but there was a slight green just at the tips of her pupils, and the look she was giving him suggested that he'd best just follow the plan.

"You first," he said, holding his hand toward the door of the carriage.

He hadn't considered the awkwardness of climbing into the carriage after her. There were two benches facing each other. Both options—sitting down next to her where they'd likely touch, or sitting across from each other so they'd have to look at each other the entire ride—had their difficulties. He chose across.

"Your eyes are completely back to normal," he offered, as the carriage started moving.

She nodded.

"You look nice."

He regretted saying it as soon as the words were out of his mouth. They were not yet comfortable enough with each other to handle something like that in the air between them. But to his surprise, her cheeks warmed a bit and she gave him a small smile. "Thank you. So do you."

He wasn't just trying to flatter her. So far, the clothes he'd seen her in were all for practical purposes. Formalwear for parties and meals—she probably didn't even have a say in the dresses that were chosen for these. And today in the woods— well, he'd be lying if he said he hadn't enjoyed looking at her dressed for walking and spending time sitting on the ground—but he doubted she'd put too much thought into the outfit. But tonight, the soft, yellow cotton blouse and simple blue skirt that flowed to her knees were her deliberate choices, and he saw in them something he hadn't expected.

Marius Lockwood was an imposing figure, well-known in all the guildhavens as a rich and powerful man who took what he wanted. In the last selection for great master, he'd lost to Amalric Sandrez by a very narrow margin, and there were rumors he intended to keep challenging the post. Although, considering what Cayloken had learned today about Ellarowan, he wasn't sure Marius would ever be successful.

Everyone knew that Marius had a daughter, of course, but many people had never met her. It was often assumed—and Cayloken was a bit guilty here, himself—that it was because she was spoiled and refused to leave home and endure the discomforts of traveling to guildhavens she deemed as lesser.

Now that he'd met her, he wondered how such a rumor could have ever gotten started. The girl was spoiled, certainly. She wanted for nothing. But that description fit every guildmaster's child. He wasn't an exception. The Lockwood Estate was far more opulent than any other guildmaster's home he'd ever been to, certainly. Much of it had been remodeled and added in the last few cycles—and it was fully electrified.

But Ellarowan appeared to spend as much time outside of it as she could. And her friends—well, he wasn't sure where she was taking him tonight, but he suspected he wouldn't run into the other daughters of visiting guildmasters, or even many landowners. Aside from her favored, of course.

So while she had a spoiled and shallow side, it was mostly on the surface, he thought. There was something deeper underneath.

He was almost certain, now, that Marius was the one responsible for her never traveling. Briefly, this afternoon, he'd thought he'd solved the mystery—that he was trying to hide the fact his daughter was a keeper. But now he didn't think so. Ellarowan was too determined to hide it from her father. Too legitimately scared that he'd find out. He believed her.

There had to be another reason for keeping her at home.

Outside the carriage, Echo Bay was an incredible sight at night. Cayloken's jaw dropped open as they crested a hill and he could see all of it—an entire city lit with electric lights. The lights sparkled and shimmered all the way down to the waterfront where, even now, he could see the dark shape of one of the massive hybrid airships hovering over the water, tiny lights blinking from its hull.

And then, as they neared the bottom of the hill, barreling straight into the onslaught of lights and activity, the carriage veered sharply to the left, and instead of growing steadily brighter, the lights faded.

After a few moments of bumping down an unpaved road, the only lights were the lamps on the front of the carriage. They cast strange, long shadows on the tall trees crowding the lane on either side of them.

"You're not…taking me somewhere to murder me, are you?"

The corners of her lips turned up in amusement. "If only I'd thought of that earlier."

"It would solve a lot of your problems."

"And create a lot of new ones. I don't know how to hide a body."

"I imagine Bastian would help you dispose of *me*."

She laughed, and for the first time since he'd met her, he thought he saw the mask slip, just a little. For that one moment, she'd forgotten all the terrible challenges she was facing and she was simply amused by a joke.

Of course, she remembered again almost immediately, and the carriage grew quiet.

They rode along the bumpy road for several more minutes before Bastian turned the carriage again.

Ellarowan's hands started twisting the material of her skirt. He supposed he'd be nervous too, if he had to face another girl he cared about while he was betrothed against his will.

"Breathe," he told her.

She followed his gaze to her lap and her hands stilled. "Are my eyes right?"

"It's too dark out here to tell. But I think you've got this. You'll be fine."

She buried her face in her hands. "Was I stupid to do this—to come out here in public when I'm not absolutely sure I can control them?"

There was a constant nervous roll in his own stomach about this—they could both face the consequences. He'd heard the stories of what happened to keepers in some of the other guildhavens—and Ravensguild was among the worst. In his determination to prove himself a worthy Grand Master, Marius Lockwood's policies had driven every keeper in the guild either away or entirely underground. Cayloken had no idea what would happen if he discovered his own daughter was one, but he knew it wouldn't be good.

"I don't know," he answered honestly. "It's not safe, but…your home isn't, either."

Just then, the carriage rolled into a circle of dim light—not the electric kind, but from a small circle of old, weathered lampposts, lit by hand.

"Your eyes are the right color," he told her, as the carriage rolled to a stop. "You just have to keep them that way."

She nodded.

"If you need me for something, I'll try and do what I can. But I'll leave you alone. It's a taberna, right?" He squinted out the window at the old, run-down building, starting to worry that maybe she *had* brought him somewhere dangerous. "There's food and drink—or something?"

"Yes."

THIRTEEN
AN EVENING OUT

ELLA FELT A LITTLE dizzy as she climbed the steps of The Dozy. As he was helping her out of the carriage, Bastian had asked her if she'd like him to accompany her in, but she'd shaken her head. She'd been surprised at his reaction to her wanting to bring Cayloken. While she wasn't sure about wanting to spend the evening with him, she could hardly keep her favorite place a secret from her betrothed for any length of time. He might as well come.

Unless Bastian had some new idea about getting out of the impending marriage—and he wasn't offering up any suggestions if he did—she couldn't understand why it mattered. She did appreciate his protective sentiment, even if she didn't plan on heeding his warning.

She would never have admitted it to anyone, especially Cayloken, but after today, she kind of wanted him around. It was comforting to have someone who knew her secret.

Unless he betrays me. She tried to push that thought out of her mind, though. He knew, and there was no fixing it. If he was going to betray her, he didn't need to come to The Dozy to do so. How much worse could bringing him here be?

She heard Cayloken gasp behind her when they entered. It was satisfying, hearing him react to the differences between the inside and the outside. She wondered what he'd thought when they'd first pulled into the dark drive yard. But she wasn't going to learn any of his thoughts right now. True to his word, as soon as they were inside, Cayloken left her side, drifting up to the counter, leaving her alone to do as she wished.

Shea was standing a few feet inside the door, delivering drinks to a small table of patrons. Her eyes widened in surprise, her gaze drifting between Ella and the departing Cayloken. "Give me a minute," she mouthed, glancing at the tray in her hands.

Ella thought she could define the entire last week of her life by a single feeling—that of being torn in multiple directions at the same time. She was desperate to talk to Shea, but just as she was nodding her assent to waiting for her friend, she spotted Loric, sitting alone at one of the tables in the furthest corner of the dining room.

Shea's face fell, but she nodded and this time her mouth formed the word, "Go."

He didn't see her coming. As she approached him, Ella could see that he had a deck of cards spread out on the table in front of him, and he was concentrating intently on them.

Her heart warmed at the realization that he likely meant to stay here and wait for her as long as he could.

For a long moment, she stood and watched as he pored over the cards, carefully moving them between stacks before dealing out another set. He was focused and shrewd in his play, and she was loath to interrupt the flow of his fingers over the table. So for a while, she didn't. Instead, she stood there and just enjoyed the short, peaceful interlude, letting herself imagine that everything was normal and it was just another ordinary night at The Dozy.

Finally, though, there came a moment she couldn't help but say something. "I wouldn't do that; you've got a ten of blades right there."

He looked up, surprise in his eyes, and set the cards in his hand down before he stood to greet her. "I didn't think you'd be able to come." His hands reached automatically for hers, and she twined her fingers with his, relief flowing through her at his warm touch. He leaned in to kiss her, letting his lips linger against hers for far longer than they usually did in public, but she didn't care. Just the fact that he'd been here, settled in to wait for her made everything feel a little lighter.

"I wasn't sure I would be able to come—and Cayloken is here, too," she said, wanting to get that out of the way immediately. *Please don't ask for details*, she silently willed.

Loric's nose crinkled as he scanned the room, finally spotting Cayloken standing stiffly near the kitchen, digging in a leather money pouch. His face fell. "So this is it, then. You've come to formally end things with me." His voice broke on the last words.

All the lightness was gone now—so far gone that it might never have existed at all. "That's not what I want, Loric. I still came here tonight to talk with you—to see if we can think of a plan to get me out of this."

His hands found hers again, only this time they were cold and damp. She had to focus on her eyes, on keeping them the right color as he looked into them. "I told you last night—I think I know a way." He pulled her in closer to him, further away from the few other patrons scattered around this part of the room. "Is he going to come to you once he has food?"

She shook her head. "He agreed to leave me to myself tonight. He just wanted to get away from the estate tonight, too. I don't think I can blame *anyone* for that."

One of Loric's eyebrows went up into a small peak, and she wondered if she'd told too much of the truth. Perhaps he didn't need to know that she hadn't been forced to bring Cayloken here tonight.

"*I* wouldn't mind spending as much time as I could inside your home," he said, squeezing her hand. "I've often wondered what it's like outside the ballroom."

His words were like a small dagger to the center of her heart, and her lower lip trembled in a way that had always been a precursor to feeling awful. She looked down at the floor, though she could tell that she was still in control of her eyes—for now. "I've always wanted to show you."

"I'm sorry," he whispered, setting a finger underneath her chin and tilting her head up so she was looking at him again. "That was unkind of me. I know you would have invited me in for a tour if you could have. It's just difficult—but I know it's even worse for you, especially now." He pressed his lips against her forehead. "And I shouldn't complain. I did get to see the back hallway and part of the kitchens last night, after all."

They both knew how *that* had ended, but she accepted his attempt to inject some much-needed levity into the moment. "And were they everything you imagined they would be?"

He chuckled, kissing her forehead again. "They weren't much compared to the real thing I wanted to see inside your house."

Feeling a real smile for the first time since she'd arrived, this time Ella initiated the kiss. This one lasted even longer than the first as she wrapped her arms around his neck and held tight to his curls.

"So," he said when they finally managed to extricate their lips from each other, "shall we talk about a plan?"

"It almost sounds like you have one." She slid into the seat opposite his at the table and began picking up the cards, stacking them into a neat pile.

"I wanted to tell you last night," he said. "I started to, before your brother interrupted us."

Remembering now, she shuffled the deck of cards in her hand, trying to lose herself in the soothing sound they made as they flicked over each other. A sick feeling of dread filled her belly as she realized she might not want to hear what he had to say.

"I heard some rumors down at the docks that the Stones might be sympathizers."

"How could that possibly be true?" she didn't dare look at him, so she cut the deck and shuffled again. *Sympathizers.* A word for those who believed that the Fading had been wrong—that the magic people weren't inherently dangerous and that it was possible to live with them in peace.

"You know Silver Island has always been difficult and reclusive, Ella. This alliance with them shocked everyone. I overheard Gaius saying they were forced into it under threat of invasion. It wouldn't be impossible for them to be hiding keepers in their guild."

Keepers. Loric knew the word, knew what it meant to be one. The dread in her stomach began to solidify into something solid.

"Why would they risk it?" She flipped over the first several cards in the deck, laying the foundation for a game of singlet. The question she'd just asked terrified her, both because she was afraid Loric might have an answer and because, for the first time in her life, she knew the correlating question: *Why wouldn't they?*

And it changed everything.

"I don't know *why*. Does it matter? If they are sympathizers, then we have a way to stop this, to make them go away, and for everything to go back to how it was between us."

Her father had always said that word—sympathizer—like a curse. They were the people who made his life difficult, who still dared to speak of magic. She'd even heard that sometimes sympathizers had harbored fugitives. It wasn't illegal to be a sympathizer, not precisely, anyway, but it would be no small thing to discover that a guildmaster's family didn't support the official proclamation of the council.

And she knew, after her time in the woods today with Cayloken, that it was true. If he and his family were not sympathizers, they were something that bordered dangerously close.

It was certainly something that could end the betrothal. But it would likely do far more.

Ella had never thought much about the topic of people who could do magic and their sympathizers. Her father's rationale for the Fading had seemed logical to her. Of course people who could perform magic were dangerous, a threat to their culture and way of life. How could the palades keep peace with people who could escape bonds or cast spells to make someone forget, or—she really had no idea what powers keepers actually had. She didn't know anything about them at all. Her father had told her they were bad, and she'd believed him, even dreaming up reasons why.

It had never even occurred to her that maybe the people they were talking about weren't so different from her after all. Not until the moment she'd learned that she might be one of them. A deep sense of shame flooded through her.

She couldn't look at Loric at all. Her eyes were under control, she was almost certain, but they wouldn't stay that way if she didn't keep her gaze trained on the cards. Slowly, carefully, she dealt five cards to each of them.

"We can't just do that, Loric. Accusing another guildmaster of sympathizing wouldn't just end my betrothal. It could start a war."

The words coming out of her mouth were true in every sense, and yet, she was lying when she said them.

Loric picked up his cards, arranging them carefully in his hand, taking just a little too long to answer. "It might not. And if it did, maybe that's because it *should*. If Silver Island is harboring keepers, they're betraying the entire league. We would *win*. Don't you think it's worth a chance? That *we're* worth the chance?"

Three days ago, she would have known the answer. Now she didn't.

No, that was dishonest, too. She knew the answer now, she just didn't like it. It wasn't the simple and uncomplicated answer she wanted to give. This one was hard. This one hurt.

The cards in her hand shook and threatened to spill out all over the table, but she couldn't seem to hold onto them no matter how hard she tried. "No," she said, simply, because it was the only word that would come.

"No?"

There was a sound of rustling cards and the table went blurry as moisture filled her eyes. "No. I don't think we're worth a war."

He was silent, waiting, giving her no choice but to finish what she'd started.

"I love you, Loric, and I wanted this, I did. I wanted *you*. But I'm not going to risk starting a war over this. Risk people dying? Attack another guildmaster? That's not right."

And still she was lying. As much as she wanted it to be true that she could make that decision for the right reason, to avoid a war and people getting hurt, she knew that she might have. She might have risked all of that if she hadn't learned the truth about herself, if she might not now depend on the kindness of sympathizers for her own survival.

A wave of nausea tore through her, suddenly obliviating everything else. She laid her head down on the table, fighting the urge to be violently ill.

Cayloken was beginning to regret his decision to come here with Ellarowan tonight.

He'd been warned—twice. First by the behavior of the driver, and again, when the carriage had pulled into a dark, foreboding drive yard. For a moment, he'd entertained the idea that instead of going to a taberna, Bastian had taken them to a place from which Cayloken might never return.

He should have heeded the warning.

Inside, at first, he'd allowed himself to forget the sense of danger.

The interior of The Dozy fascinated him. It was beautiful—warm and cozy and perfect. If a place like this had existed in Silver Island, he suspected he would have spent any free evenings he had there.

It was obvious Ellarowan had passed an uncountable number of hours in this place. He hadn't quite dared to venture near her bedroom at the Guildmaster's Estate, but he suspected that if he had, it wouldn't have felt nearly as intimate as this. This place, The Dozy, was hers.

She'd changed, visibly, the instant they walked in the door. One instant, the imposing implacable guildmaster's daughter, and the next a young woman melting into the comforts of the only place she felt truly safe and cared for without reservation.

He shouldn't have disrupted that.

And he wasn't the only one who thought so.

Everyone here knew who he was. That much was obvious from the scowls and looks of suspicion that seemed to hit him from every direction as he walked through the room. Those angry looks didn't bother him as much as the way a few people—the server he'd seen last night, the woman behind the kitchen counter, the driver who'd followed them inside— seemed to regard him with fear. Their glances flew back and forth from Cayloken to Ellarowan as if they were all ready to dive between them at the slightest provocation, taking a sword if necessary.

The worst part of all of it is that he liked them all immediately. *Because* they hated him so much on Ellarowan's behalf.

He wondered how many of them would feel the same way about her if they knew what he'd learned today. He hoped it was all of them, because if there was one thing they were going to need now, it was allies.

So, he steeled himself and went to the counter, pulling out his coin pouch and asking what the special tea was. Every guildhaven had one, their own blend of the unique leaves that grew wild. Sampling the offerings of different guildhavens was one of his favorite parts of traveling, and he'd never been to Ravensguild before.

The glass in front of him was a waste, though. He'd already emptied half of it without tasting anything at all, too occupied with watching Ellarowan and Loric out of the corner of his eye.

Their meeting had started well enough, he'd thought—if one could judge by the lengthy kiss at the beginning. For a moment, he'd wondered if they'd forgotten they were in public and not alone in the middle of the woods.

It wasn't his business, he kept telling himself. Or maybe it was his business. He didn't know how this worked. She *was* his betrothed, but he knew that while marriage was something that could be forced, love wasn't. Nothing good could come from being the one who made her end a relationship with someone she cared about. If their possible marriage was to be purely political, she might as well be happy with something in her life.

These thoughts hadn't stopped him from selecting a table where he could surreptitiously watch as Ellarowan and Loric sat down and began to deal out cards and talk. It might have been his imagination, or his own feelings getting in the way of the view, but things over there were starting to look a little tense.

"What are you doing here?" A harsh, feminine voice startled him out of his spying.

He looked up to see a young woman standing right next to him. She wore the same sort of apron he'd seen on the servers here. "N-nothing. I was just having a glass of tea. Should I not sit at this table?"

"I don't mean at this table, I mean at this *place*. Why would you come here with her?"

There were a whole slew of words implied in her voice, none of them good. He frowned up at the girl, wondering what he'd done to upset her so much. The arranged marriage wasn't ideal for him or Ellarowan, he knew, but it wasn't something that would affect most of the people in either of their guildhavens. Unless one counted eliminating the possibility of going to war—but this didn't seem like something that would inspire anger.

Fire blazed in this girl's eyes, though. "You couldn't leave her one place to go?" she demanded.

Ah. She was Ellarowan's friend. Yes, now that he looked more carefully, imagining her in a shimmery dress instead of the clothing of a server, he recognized her. This was the girl who'd attended the betrothal party the night before. Shea.

"I'm sorry, I-" He stole another glance over at the table where Ellarowan and Loric were sitting, and his heart sank. *Vosh.* "Can we have this conversation later?"

Without waiting for her reply, he darted across the room, not bothering to care if anyone noticed the hurry he was in. He might have knocked over a chair or two in his haste.

Loric was already gone by the time he reached the table. Ellarowan's favored had seemed in nearly as much of a rush as Cayloken was, only his goal was to exit.

Ellarowan still sat there alone on the cloth-covered bench, crumpled into a heap of arms and hair on the table. Two cards drifted onto the floor as Cayloken reached her.

He didn't know what his plan would be when he got to her. All he knew was that he should get her outside, where she could get some air—and where the darkness might hide her eyes.

But he wasn't the only one who'd noticed that she was in trouble. He was standing at the edge of the table, trying to decide the best way to get her attention when Shea blew past him and onto the bench beside Ellarowan. Immediately after that, the driver, Bastian, appeared.

Cayloken wasn't sure how it happened, but a minute later, he found himself standing by himself in the middle of a mess of strewn cards. Ellarowan was gone, spirited outside by the other two.

Chasing after them didn't seem like the best idea, not immediately anyway. Let her have a few moments with the people she knew well. A stranger, as he still was, wouldn't be likely to make her feel better. He could only hope she maintained control of her eyes. Sighing, he bent to pick up the cards.

"That was quite the performance you put on back there." This time the voice didn't startle him. He'd heard the footsteps approaching him as he arranged the deck and began searching for the box to put them in. He turned now to face yet another woman who was only vaguely familiar. This one was much older—or at least, he supposed she was. Although she had soft white hair pinned into a neat bun at the top of her head, her face was smooth as silk. She was kind, he knew that already. When he'd ordered his tea from her at the counter, she'd been the only person in the whole place who'd smiled and made him feel like something other than an intruder.

He shrugged. "I just wanted to make sure she was all right."

"Mmm. You care about her already."

"Well, I don't want to see her harmed, if that's what you mean."

The woman reached onto the bench behind him—her movements surprisingly deft considering her age—and retrieved a small wooden box from the cushion. "You're Cayloken Stone?" she asked as she held out her hand for the cards.

"Yes."

"I'm Ollie."

He waited for the rest of her introduction, but it never came. For some reason, this made him smile. "You're the proprietor here?"

"Yes. My husband and I have owned this place for… Well, since time began, it feels like." She smiled. "I met your father once, when he was near your age. He was a good man." There was something hiding behind her words, but he couldn't decide exactly what.

"He still is a good man. Or, at least, I think so." He glanced toward the door. "Do you think Ellarowan *is* all right?"

Ollie lifted one shoulder. "There are worse things than a broken heart, even if it doesn't feel that way when you're eighteen."

"I'm not sure her only problem right now is a broken heart." Once the words were out of his mouth, he wasn't sure he should have said them, but they couldn't be recaptured.

"And what do you know of her problems?" Ollie's blue eyes, which had held nothing but kindness only a moment ago, now searched him in a way that made his insides feel like melted butter.

He licked his suddenly dry lips. "I know that they're about to become my problems, too, if they aren't already."

"Do you intend to betray her?"

What an odd question. Something more was going on here, but he could only guess at what. If he'd learned anything today it was that he knew nothing about the Lockwoods or Ravensguild. "Betray her to whom?"

Ollie didn't give him an answer; she just kept waiting for his.

Taking a deep breath, he stood his ground. "I'm afraid I don't know what you mean. I met her *yesterday*. In what way could I possibly betray her?"

The older woman stared at him for several more seconds before nodding, apparently satisfied. "I'll finish up here. You should go and find her. She may not be in the mood to stay after that, and you'll not want to miss your ride."

If he hadn't been so confused and worried, he'd have laughed. It was a deft way of putting him in his place. Neither Bastian nor Shea would stop to remember him if Ellarowan decided to go home. They might even forget on purpose.

He wondered, though, if Ellarowan would leave him behind so easily.

The three of them were near the carriage when he found them, though not inside it, and the horse was still tied. Bastian was checking the fastening on the horse's harness, giving Cayloken the impression he was lucky he'd decided to come out now.

Ellarowan sat on a rough wooden bench next to Shea, staring down at her hands. She didn't look as upset as Cayloken had expected. In fact, she looked perfectly calm — when she heard his feet on the gravel and turned toward him.

The drive yard was lit only by moonlight, but he thought her eyes looked normal.

"You can't leave her alone for five minutes?" Shea demanded, standing and marching toward him

Shea was small, but she looked like she could do plenty of damage if she wanted to. And right now, she most definitely wanted to.

He understood that she was protecting her friend, but he didn't know what he'd done to make her *so* angry. Loric was the one who'd walked out on her; he'd had nothing to do with that, even if he was now rather wishing he had. Things were only getting stranger.

"Go back inside and leave us be!"

"It's all right, Shea."

"It's *not* all right. We need to talk. He can't…" She stopped herself, but not before Cayloken realized he'd interrupted more than just an attempt to comfort Ellarowan.

"Shea, stop. It's all right." Ellarowan was on her feet now. "He knows."

The effect of the words on him was immediate, sending a shock through his body as if he'd touched the inside of one of the light fixtures in the Lockwoods' mansion.

He knew immediately what Ellarowan meant, and his eyes locked on to hers. "*They* know?"

Shea stopped short. "Are we talking about the same thing?"

Ellarowan nodded. "He saw my eyes change earlier today. He knew what it meant even when I didn't."

Shea's head whipped back and forth between Ellarowan and Bastian so fast it might have been funny, if Cayloken hadn't been feeling exactly the same way. He didn't understand what was going on. "But how do they know?"

"The same way you do. Shea saw my eyes change last night, when I got upset at the party. This is the first time we've had the chance to talk." She looked at her friend. "Cayloken is the one that explained it to me. I didn't know, myself, today. This could have gone a lot differently tonight, if it wasn't for him."

"And Bastian?" he whispered, aware that the driver was well within hearing range.

"He knows, too," Shea said. "He's been keeping the secret for a long time. Last night, when I saw Ella's eyes change, we were with Sabelina."

"My caretaker," Ellarowan interrupted.

"When I saw the way Sabelina reacted to it last night—she got Ella into a private room and made her keep her eyes closed—I realized what was happening and that Sabelina must have always known."

"She's been with us since I was born," Ellarowan said. "And so has Bastian—he's her husband."

The world was growing a bit fuzzy around the edges. Cayloken gulped in several breaths of the moist night air, wishing it wasn't quite so hot here.

If there were people here who knew Ellarowan was a keeper then it meant—he wasn't sure what it meant. Were they allies, then? Sympathizers? Or even keepers themselves? It was very unlikely that there were this many keepers in this kind of proximity to a guildmaster known for his adherence to the Fading. And keepers almost never married one another, outside of the closed settlements.

Before today, he'd lost hope that there would be *any* keepers remaining in Ravensguild.

But nothing was turning out the way he'd thought.

"Are you—?" he started to ask Shea, but she turned away from him before he could even get the words out.

"I'm not talking to him," she said to Ella. "I don't care what you think he does or doesn't know. His father is a guildmaster. He could get us all killed. I cannot believe…" She turned and stomped off a short distance into the trees, presumably having the same trouble organizing her thoughts as Cayloken was right then.

"I'm not going to betray you, Ellarowan," he said quietly, another electric shock jolting through him as he wondered if *this* was what Ollie had meant inside. "I'm not going to betray any of you. Not tonight, and not ever. I know why you don't trust me. *I* wouldn't trust me, if I were you, but I wanted to say that."

He didn't know if she believed him or not.

The tension in the carriage on the ride back was so thick that Ellarowan could feel it pressing in on her chest, filling her throat, making it difficult to breathe.

Not only was she almost certain her relationship with Loric was over, but Shea was angry with her, too. Her only words to

Ella before they left had been, "Send me a message when *he's* not around. Then we can talk."

She understood her friend's feelings, but what she needed right now more than anything was to *talk about* what was going on.

Bastian was as kind as ever when he helped her into the carriage, but it was clear he wasn't interested in having a discussion about it tonight, either.

This only left Cayloken, sitting across from her, both of them tying the hems of their clothing into knots and clearing their throats but not knowing how to make the words come.

Cayloken was the first to manage to make his mouth work. "I'm sorry. I shouldn't have come."

She shrugged. "I don't know that it made any difference. The thing with Loric would have happened anyway."

"Not if I'd never come to Ravensguild in the first place, it wouldn't." His shirt wasn't going to survive the night if he kept worrying it the way he was right now. Ella barely knew him, and his existence was the source of the worst distress she'd experienced since her mother died, but right now, she wanted to comfort him. And maybe even to be comforted by him.

She wasn't at all sure either one was possible.

"Was that your fault?"

"No. But I didn't fight against it the way you have been. I didn't even have the courage to challenge it. Maybe I should have."

They were both quiet for a moment, riding through the pitch-black outskirts of the city. She thought the journey was taking longer than usual, but perhaps it just felt that way.

She didn't look at him when she finally spoke again. "Your not coming wouldn't have changed the fact that I'm a keeper."

"That does change everything, doesn't it?"

She made a face.

"Can I ask what happened with your favored tonight?"

The nausea reappeared, although it wasn't the debilitating attack she'd had earlier. This was merely a response to facing a question she didn't want to answer, but knew she should.

"I'm sorry. It's really none of my business."

"Actually, it kind of is." She rested her forehead in her hands. Maybe this would be easier if she wasn't looking at him.

"Are you all right?"

She held up one finger and took a deep breath. "I'm not going to be sick, if that's what you're asking. But, no. I'm not all right. Loric thought that perhaps I could get out of this betrothal by turning you and your parents in as sympathizers." Her hands shook and her stomach ached, but the words were out now. She braced for the fallout.

The crunching of the carriage wheels on the dirt road seemed to grow excruciatingly loud as she waited for his response.

And then he laughed.

Her head snapped up so quickly she thought she might pay for it later. "That's funny?"

"I'm sorry. I'm trying not to be a terrible roffler here. This Loric has managed to win you over enough that you'd put up this kind of fight, so he must be a decent and intelligent man. Or, that was what I was trying to believe until you just—"

"Told you he has no problem essentially threatening your life?" She knew what it sounded like—what it *was*.

"Let's remember you're the one who said it."

"Anyway…"

"Anyway," he continued, "I question his political knowledge if he honestly believes he's privy to some rumor about me and my family that your father isn't."

She stared at him, trying to make sense of what he was saying. "Do you mean that my father *knows* you and your family are sympathizers?"

"I don't know exactly what Marius does or doesn't know. The rumors about our disloyalty are rampant in all the guildhavens, last I checked. Most of them are not strictly true, but I suppose some are. My father's disagreement with what so many like to refer to as the "Fading" is certainly well-known. That's why our guild is so vulnerable we couldn't turn down this political alliance. We have a strong army and other…well… We could fight, and maybe win some battles, but there's no way we could take on a war with all the other guildhavens in the council. And the cost in innocent lives, even if we won…"

"So that's why you're not fighting the betrothal with me."

"If marrying you convinces the council that Silver Island doesn't intend to leave the league, taking our resources with us, and we avoid being invaded or even an all-out war, then it's a small price to pay."

"And it doesn't matter if you're sympathizers." Ella rested her head in her hands again.

Outside the carriage, the lights of the city were slowly coming back into view.

"If your father cares about that at all, I'm sure he thinks it's a situation he can control once this alliance is secured and he has his hands near the running of both guildhavens. It's not information some shipbuilder can use against me to end the betrothal."

Ella bit her bottom lip as she struggled to look at him again. "I told him no. That I wasn't willing to risk war just to be with him."

Cayloken nodded. "Did you tell him that to protect me, or because you realized someone who would share that information with your father would never be a safe person for a keeper to confide in?"

They rode the rest of the way home in silence, but she knew they both knew the answer.

FOURTEEN - LATE NIGHT CONVERSATIONS

BY THE TIME THEY arrived back at the Guildmaster's Estate, Cayloken was wishing he'd ordered something stronger to drink than tea. Neither he nor Ellarowan had spoken since he'd asked her that pointed question, but she accepted his hand to help her out of the carriage, and he walked her to the base of the elaborate staircase inside.

The largest guesthouse, where he and his parents were staying, was bigger and more elegant than some of the landowners' homes he'd been inside in Silver Island. Everything in it was modern, including the fully electric lights and the message-sender that could connect to any station in any of the twelve guildhavens. Ellarowan has existed longer than this guesthouse, he was certain.

He hoped to sneak inside and to his room without drawing notice, but as soon as he opened the door, he realized this was futile.

He'd forgotten how early they'd left the taberna. Both his parents were still awake, sipping drinks in the parlor. They both looked up as he entered.

"What happened?" his mother asked, glancing at the clock on the mantel and then back at him.

Cayloken sighed and slumped into one of the overstuffed armchairs. "I'm not even sure."

"Did you get her to talk to you at all today?" His father poured something from a crystal decanter into a glass and handed it to him.

He nodded, staring at the pale pink liquid swirling in the glass before tasting it. It was sweet, floral. Some kind of weak wine.

"She actually seems very sweet," his mother said. "It's a difficult time for her, obviously, but she still was polite and kind at meals."

"She is. I don't think she's much like her father at all."

"Cay," his father warned in a low voice, "let's not disrespect the man in his own house."

"Of course not. Why would we dare do that? The man who sprung a betrothal on his daughter with less than two days' notice is probably fantastic once you get to know him. Even better when you count his support of removing an entire race of people from their guildhavens, just because they're not like him."

"That well, then?" His mother stood and went to the sideboard, picking up a plate and bringing it back to him. Sweet biscuits. He wasn't really in the mood for food, but he took one to appease her.

The biscuit was delicious, of course, delicate and flaky with a creamy sweet sauce in the middle. Elegant and perfect like everything else in this maker-forsaken estate. His own home wasn't exactly a picker's cottage, of course, especially with the mark of his mother's deft touch over everything, but it wasn't like this. "That poor girl… She's obnoxious and ignorant of some basic things, and I want to be annoyed with her, and then she goes and tells me that her father didn't even inform her he'd signed a marriage contract until two days before she met me."

His parents just watched him calmly. This was probably the fifteenth time he'd repeated that bit of information.

"That's not the only thing. It's like he's deliberately kept her from knowing…*anything*." He took an angry gulp of the wine. "Anything except how to smile and put on a performance at a party where he's actively humiliating her, anyway."

"I doubt that's an accident," his father said, reaching for Cayloken's glass. For a moment, he thought it was a warning to slow down his imbibing, but his father refilled the glass almost to the top and handed it back to him. Cayloken raised an eyebrow. "Some nights call for it."

"It's not very strong, anyway," he said, taking another long drink. "I'm sure it's not an accident. She can't thwart his wishes if she doesn't even understand what he's doing."

His mother sat down on the edge of the table, facing him. "Is that what's bothering you? It's not that you went out with her and she met up with another man?"

Cayloken leaned forward, holding the glass in one hand and running his finger along the rim with the other, causing it to make a ringing sound that was both sad and haunting. "No.

I knew that before I decided to go. I can't force her to want me instead of him. It's just best not to get into the middle of it."

"I don't think it would be that easy for me," his mother said, looking over at his father.

"Well, we were never in that situation, were we?" His father leaned down and kissed his mother on the top of her head before sitting down in the chair closest to them.

He rolled his eyes at his parents, though more out of the force of habit than feeling. Not for the first time, he found himself jealous of what they shared.

"Anyway, things may have changed on that front. It appears the two of them broke things off tonight."

Both his parents turned their heads toward him in unison, eyes wide. "Because of you?"

He shook his head, steeling himself for the conversation he knew was going to happen, but didn't really want to have.

"Until this afternoon, Ellarowan didn't even know what a keeper was."

His mother raised an eyebrow. "That's an epic change of subject."

"Not really."

"How is that even possible?" His father's reaction was more like his had been. Incredulous, and a little bit angry.

"I'm not kidding when I say that Marius Lockwood has kept *everything* from her that he possibly can. It has to be on purpose. He must have instructed his servants to not discuss things around her as well. She has friends, so I don't know how that's worked, but…"

"It's not difficult. He wouldn't be the first." His father twisted his own nearly empty glass between his fingertips, then stood to go and refill it. "I imagine most of the people she associates with are servants and other people who'd face consequences for sharing such information with her, no?"

Cayloken sighed. "From what I can tell, yes. She knows a few vague details about the Fading, and she knew people who can do magic *exist*, but she didn't even know what they were called."

"Then I imagine she has no opinion on any of it—other than what her father's told her to believe?" His mother reached over and took the glass from Cayloken's hand—he hadn't noticed how loud the ringing sound had gotten until it stopped.

"Well, she does now." He grabbed the glass back and swallowed another big mouthful. "Or at least she's starting to."

Both his parents were silent, waiting.

"Ellarowan *is* a keeper."

He pretended not to look at them as they took in that information, instead concentrating on draining the wine from his glass. But he watched out of the corner of his eye, and what he saw made it awfully difficult to not lose his grip and send the glass tumbling onto the expensive rug on the floor.

Their eyes met, locking for several seconds, contemplating. Neither of them looked surprised.

He tried to take another drink and, instead, choked, spraying all three of them with droplets of the liquid. "You *knew?*" he finally spluttered.

"No!" his mother said, dashing to the sideboard in search of a towel. "Of course not."

"We would have told you, had we known something like that," his father said. "We wouldn't have left you unprepared for that."

"But we did know it was a possibility." His mother bent down to begin wiping up the spots with a plush white towel that looked as though it had never been used before.

Cayloken grabbed the towel and began dabbing up the spots of his own mess, wishing the wine had been a darker, more satisfying color that might stain. "You make it sound like such an ordinary statement, Mother. Just, 'Oh, Marius Lockwood's daughter might be a keeper. Nothing odd about that.'"

His father reached to take the towel out of Cayloken's hand. "Her mother was a keeper."

He'd had sympathy for Ellarowan before. He'd known it wasn't fair for people to keep huge secrets from her and then drop them on her when she was least expecting it. But until that moment, he hadn't truly understood what that *felt* like.

The room went blurry at the edges, and he suddenly wasn't sure which direction was up.

A million questions flooded through his brain, but so did a sense of hopelessness. He felt that perhaps there was no point in asking them, since he might not get a full or truthful answer, anyway. And if he did, it might not be an answer he wanted to hear.

How much worse it must be for Ellarowan to be finding out these secrets about herself, seemingly unable to trust anyone around her. There'd never before been a time he couldn't trust his parents. And still, they were more reliable than her father. He owed it to her to find out what he could.

"I'm just going to pour myself another drink. Sounds like we might be up for a while."

Despite his desperation for the gate to open again so he could escape, Owen was rather appreciating the time alone in the woods. It had been a while since he'd had a chance to be alone with his thoughts—something he sorely needed to deal with the reality of home right now. Ellarowan—and now Cayloken—had asked him several times if he was all right out here by himself. They clearly felt badly leaving him, but he wasn't bothered about being alone.

He only hoped that he was right about the time difference between the worlds, and that he really was only missing a single day at home. The idea that he might be gone for longer made him anxious, but he tried to keep those thoughts at bay. Nothing could be done about it right now, anyway.

He liked them well enough. Ellarowan was even beginning to grow on him a bit, and he found himself worrying about whether any of the challenges she was facing would ever be resolved. He wished he could do something to help her, but knew he was way out of his league.

Accidentally landing in a world where some people were *magic* had not been on his list of possibilities.

And now he feared he was only adding to an already fraught situation. He'd never intended to complicate anyone's life by coming here. Except Quinn's of course. He'd come here with the full intention of complicating her life, but…she would have wanted him to. He'd seen her often in his dreams lately, and while their conversations in those could never be counted upon as fact, he knew she missed him as much as he missed her.

He enjoyed Ellarowan's visits, and he was invested enough that he almost wished he could stay to find out what happened—and to learn more about the whole keeper thing—but the longer he stayed, the more danger they were all in. He wouldn't miss the chance to exit.

The cabin was a place he avoided most of the time. Although Ellarowan had reassured him that it was safe and nobody was likely to come out here, he wasn't sure he could trust her judgment on that—all things considered. Too many people seemed to be keeping secrets from her.

So, every morning, he woke up well before sunrise and gathered all of his things, checking the cabin over several times to make sure he didn't leave any traces. At first light, he headed out into the woods.

Despite Ella's warnings, he'd found the forest to be peaceful and serene. During the daylight hours, he even felt safe down by the river, where he spent a fair amount of time devising a plan to make sure he could reach the gate when it opened again. *If it opens again* was a thought that sometimes invaded, but he did his best to push it aside. He'd seen it open any number of times from the other side. In fact, as near as he could tell, it opened *every* night on the other side, the same way the gate in Bristlecone had. Surely it would be opening again soon here. Hopefully.

In preparation, he'd begun building the base of a temporary bridge out of stones he gathered along the riverbank. This was a backup plan, in case his original ideas failed. If, for some reason he couldn't hook the collapsible ladder he'd secured on the other side and pull it down to climb up.

He still wished he'd thought it would be a safe idea to climb *down* the ladder in the first place, rather than throw himself into the river. And he did wonder what would have happened if he'd just left the ladder hanging there. Would it have stopped the gate from closing? Been cut in half? Ceased to exist? He *was* grateful he hadn't attempted such an experiment. The gate had seemed so remote that he had considered it more than once.

He might not have felt as confident about spending time near the water's edge if it hadn't been for Fluffy. The little creature remained with him at all times, hovering near his feet, but never getting in the way. Twice, Fluffy had let out a short, shrill chuff that reminded Owen of a prairie dog's bark. When prairie dogs did this, it was a warning of danger nearby. So he'd hidden himself immediately, away from the river.

The first time, nothing had happened. He'd stayed hidden with the iber trembling in his lap for nearly an hour, and then the thing had hopped down and started foraging for food like everything was normal.

The second time, Owen had seen the threat. An enormous bird circling in the sky overhead, calling out to a friend who answered back, though Owen never saw the second one. That time, he'd crouched over Fluffy, hiding him completely. *Or was the iber a her?* He didn't know. Four years of medical school hadn't taught him anything about sexing furry mammals from alternate universes.

In the evenings, when nobody appeared to visit with him, he and Fluffy left the riverside at the first hints of dusk, and retreated to the trees closer to the cabin. They only went inside once it was well and truly dark and he hadn't seen any signs of movement coming from anywhere.

Inside the cabin, he kept the curtains drawn tightly, and used only his flashlight to see. Although the bed would have been more comfortable than using his sleeping bag on the floor, he didn't want to chance it. Keeping himself alive in a situation like this would never have been in his skill set, had his life stayed on the course he'd been born to. If his beloved sister had not left to go live in a universe much more primitive than his own, he doubted he'd have seen daylight once he graduated high school—three years early. But that had happened, and so he'd spent the last fourteen years dividing his time between medical textbooks and survival guides, and occasionally agreeing to camping trips with his dad.

Tonight, he was taking advantage of the peace and solitude of the cabin to organize his notes and supplies.

The quiet and time to himself were nice. There hadn't been much of either during the last few years of medical school and college. A trip through the gate *was* supposed to be a break from his real life, time to sort out his thoughts and decide what he really wanted to do. There was no reason he couldn't still contemplate that here.

Fluffy climbed into his lap, pushing his notebook to the floor. Owen smiled and set down his pen. "You're worse than a cat."

His words didn't have much weight considering he immediately started stroking the creature. Fluffy arched his back into Owen's hand and began making the contented purring sound again.

Owen's fingers worked their way into the long, soft fur until he found the two little bumps where the panther's teeth had sunk in, according to Ella. It still didn't make sense to Owen. Fluffy shouldn't have healed so quickly. Really, he shouldn't have survived the panther attack at all. Some animals did recover easily from physical injury, but this would be exceptional in any species in his world. It had only been a few days since the injury. The wounds should have still been red and scabbed over, or worse. Instead, they'd all but faded into tiny knobs of scar tissue.

All at once, every strand of Fluffy's fur puffed out straight, and the creature tensed.

"Sorry! I didn't mean to hurt you."

But even after he moved his hand away, Fluffy didn't relax. He started turning his head wildly from side to side, and then leaped off Owen's lap and ran into the bathroom.

Owen didn't waste any time. In less than a second, he extinguished his flashlight and grabbed the rest of his things, grateful he hadn't yet pulled his sleeping bag from the large pack.

The bathroom had a large window that led to the back of the cabin, a space overgrown with thick bushes and trees that nearly touched the walls. Owen had loosened this window on his first night here, sacrificing a small amount of antibiotic ointment to lubricate two spots that stuck and made noise. It slid open silently now, and he lifted Fluffy up and over the low sill.

The animal jumped down easily, and Owen hoped he was right in assuming that meant this exit was safe. He was setting his second foot on the ground when the whole cottage trembled with the sound of a heavy footstep landing on the porch.

He slid the window closed again, and he and Fluffy slunk into the forest, careful to head away from the river and not toward it.

For a long time, he and the iber crouched in silence, hidden in a copse of trees so thick he could barely make out the moonlight between the branches. After a while, he made himself comfortable, and might have even dozed off a time or two. He listened, but never heard any noises coming from the cottage, or any footfalls in the forest. When he reached the point that he wasn't sure if he'd just imagined the noise in the cabin, he picked up his pack and started walking slowly back in that direction.

Fluffy was less hesitant than he was. Though he'd woken the iber when he stood, Fluffy now bounded ahead of him, apparently carefree. The iber didn't even go to the back window, instead it circled the cottage and began climbing the wooden steps.

By the time Owen saw the shadowy figure in the chair on the porch, it was too late.

He froze and cursed under his breath as waves of alternating hot and cold coursed through him. He had no weapon; there was nothing he could do.

The iber, which had given him such good warning earlier now seemed to have abandoned any sense of self-preservation it had ever held, and it bounded straight up to the person on the porch.

"It's all right. It's just me," a voice called down, muffled a bit because its owner was bent down, greeting the iber.

The words would have been reassuring—had he recognized the voice that said them. It was a female voice; she wasn't bothering to whisper. But it was not Ella. Owen grabbed one hand with the other, trying to keep it from shaking so hard he'd cause damage. He wasn't entirely sure he hadn't wet himself.

What had he been thinking coming through that gate?

"Owen, are you all right?"

Maybe it was because he could finally hear—just a little— over the rushing blood inside his head, but now he realized that he did know who it was. Ella's friend, who'd been so suspicious of him the other day. Shea.

His legs were weak as he ascended the stairs.

"Where *were* you?" she asked.

"Just…out for a walk." He felt a bit ridiculous for not investigating the noise earlier. He could have saved himself a lot of trouble. "Have you been waiting for me all this time?"

Shea was silent for several seconds. "All *what* time? I haven't been here all evening or anything. I just got here a few minutes ago. I knocked, and you didn't answer, so I've been sitting here arguing with myself over whether or not I should go in. It occurred to me how rude it was to just show up unannounced, and then I realized I might have scared you out of your skin, and…"

He was barely listening to her. He'd been hiding in the woods for at least an hour, and probably longer. If she'd just gotten here… "It's fine," he said. "Although if I'd been inside when you arrived, I probably would have run off and hidden in the woods."

He couldn't see her face well enough to read the expression on it, but he knew he'd made her think.

"That…would make sense," she said. "I'm sorry, I don't know what I was thinking, coming here. I shouldn't have. I just…I didn't know what else to do."

"Well, you're here now," he said, trying to be kind while still attempting to calm his racing heart. Normal sensation was slowly returning to his extremities. "Would you like to come in and we can talk about it?"

"I know that Ella is a keeper," Shea said, as soon as the door was pulled securely behind them. She crossed the room, heading in the direction of the ancient oil lamp.

"Don't light it," Owen said, in his best warning tone.

For a moment, he was afraid she'd argue with him. It was pitch-black in here; he was relying on sound rather than sight.

On another night, she'd have won such an argument, but he still remembered the *thump* of the footstep. She didn't say anything, though. Instead, the sound of her stride stopped abruptly in the middle of the room and turned in the direction of the bed.

He heard the *floomp* as she settled onto the mattress, and nearly sneezed at the dust that rose into the air.

"Do you sleep?" she asked.

He almost laughed and asked if she thought he was a vampire, but caught himself. She wouldn't understand the question, most likely, and an explanation might have made her trust him less. "Yes," he answered honestly. "Just not on the bed. I don't want it to look like anyone's been in here."

As he spoke, he was listening and looking for signs that anyone had been in the cabin, but there was nothing. He'd considered, briefly, that they shouldn't have come in, just in case someone was here, but that was taking his caution too far. If someone was going to attack them, they'd have done it already.

"Do you really think anyone is coming out to this cottage to see if a *gadab* is hiding out here?"

"You did."

"That's not the same thing."

"Isn't it? You're just as much a stranger to me as anyone. I don't know your intentions. You didn't turn me in or try to hurt me the other day, but I don't know what you have waiting for me in the woods right now."

She coughed. "You're awfully calm about that possibility."

"Not really, but what am I going to do about it? I don't have any weapons, and even if I did, I'm not going to hurt anyone. Hiding in the woods only works if nobody's searching for me. I'd mess up and do something to get myself discovered in the first five minutes. So, I'm at your mercy. About all I can do is cross my fingers."

"What do you mean? What happens when you cross your fingers?"

The absurdity of the whole thing left him with no choice but to laugh. "Nothing. Anyway, if you didn't come here to turn me in or to kill me, why are you here?"

"I want answers."

There was an old, upholstered chair in the corner by the window with only a few claw marks in the fabric. Owen sat down, and the iber hopped immediately into his lap. "I gave you all the answers I have the other night."

"Are you telling me it's a coincidence that a gadab shows up at the same time I find out Ella is a keeper?"

"Yes."

"You don't think that's a little too convenient?"

"I don't really see anything convenient about any of this. I made the mistake of coming to the wrong world at what appears to be a very fraught time. But I don't even see a connection here with Ella. Do keepers and gadab have something to do with each other?"

"You tell me. You just admitted that you know Ella is a keeper. I didn't even know that, and I'm supposed to be her best friend."

Owen sighed, silently crossing "sleep" off his list of possibilities for the night. "Did you really come here because you think I have some answers that you don't? I'll tell you what I know, but I think who you really want to talk to is Ella."

"I can't if she's with Cayloken."

Owen didn't think that was true, but arguing with her was unlikely to be helpful. "And you're hoping that if you're here, you can catch her, but you didn't want to stay in the woods alone?"

She was quiet.

"Make yourself comfortable then."

FIFTEEN - A WALK IN THE WOODS

ELLAROWAN WAS ALREADY AWAKE when the knock came, but she didn't move from her seat at the dressing table to answer it. After knocking twice more, Sabelina opened the door anyway, starting a little when she saw Ella. She crossed the room to the wardrobe and began digging in it.

"Were you ever going to tell me?" Ella's voice was so low she wasn't sure it was audible, but Sabelina dropped the shirt she'd just pulled out and stood there, frozen. "Surely Bastian told you that I know now. I'm wondering if you were *ever* planning on telling me."

Sabelina turned around slowly. "I was hoping I wouldn't be the one who had to."

A fiery orange was creeping into Ella's pupils. She stared at them in the mirror until they calmed again. Her control was still weak; she couldn't always decide the color and shape, but she'd been practicing at the mirror this morning, and could get them to switch and then go back to violet again almost every time she tried now. But this conversation was putting that ability to the test.

"And how long did you think *that* would work?"

"I don't have an answer for that." Sabelina carried an outfit over to the bed and began laying it out. "It was too dangerous for you to know. It still is."

"As dangerous as it being true and me *not* knowing?"

"I don't know. We managed to keep it hidden for a long time. Now you're going to have to keep the secret, too."

"What do you mean you've kept it hidden? *How?*"

Halfway back to Ella, Sabelina stopped short again. "Where did you get that?"

Irritated at not being answered, it took Ella a second to understand that Sabelina meant the leather-bound journal Ella had been mindlessly stroking since before sunrise.

She looked down at it and then back over at Sabelina. "Why?"

"I've seen it before. Is it your mother's?"

Ella nodded.

"It's been missing since… Where did you get it?"

"I just found it in my bike basket yester— the other day. I can't keep time straight right now."

"You didn't see someone put it there?"

"Who? No, I didn't. After what I learned last night, I was sitting here almost wondering if it was *you*, but I don't know how you'd have made it to The Dozy and back in the middle of the day. Perhaps it was Bastian."

Sabelina shook her head. "He wouldn't have known about it."

Ella frowned. "What is there to know about it? It's empty."

"Are you sure?"

She felt as if she were moving underwater. Every movement she made was slow and met with resistance. But she pushed against it and held out the journal.

Sabelina flipped the pages back and forth a dozen times or more, running her fingers over the—still empty—pages. "It *was* your mother's," she said. "She would have wanted you to have it, I know that much."

"How do you know that?"

"She was writing in it all the time, before—Before she died. She once asked me to make sure you got it when you were old enough, if something ever happened to her."

Something cold worked its way through Ella's insides. "Why would she think something was going to happen to her?"

Sabelina raised an eyebrow. "That's just how keepers have lived since the beginning of the Fading, Ella. *That's* why I've kept it from you."

"Well, this can't be the notebook she was writing in. It's empty."

"I don't think so—I just think you're the only one who will be able to read it."

"What do you mean?"

Setting the book down on the dressing table, Sabelina reached for the hairbrush, but Ella recoiled, standing and taking a step back. "What do you mean?" she repeated.

"That's all I know, Ella. I know that she was writing in the notebook, for you. I know that I was supposed to give it to you when you started asking questions."

"But you didn't."

"I didn't have it. I haven't seen this in cycles! I'd almost forgotten about it, honestly."

Ella had always trusted Sabelina, always believed her, but now… "Would you have given it to me even if you *did* have it?"

"This is the first time you ever asked questions."

It took everything Ella had to not scream and throw the book across the room. "Because you were keeping it a secret from me! I didn't *know*!"

"And that kept you safe, didn't it?"

Ella's mouth fell open, and for a long moment all she could do was try to close it again, failing every time like an absurd baby bird with an invisible worm. When she finally made it work again, her eyes flashed from red to violet. "What if it hadn't? What if I'd made a mistake and someone had found out?"

"We would have had to deal with it." Sabelina stared down and the hairbrush in her hand, cleaning strands of hair from the bristles as she spoke. "It couldn't have been worse than having you keep a secret and lying to your father. We were watching, of course, ready to step in if necessary, ready to tell you if we had to. It was always a chance that we'd fail, but it was worth the risk. Telling you was more dangerous."

Downstairs, a bell rang, signaling that breakfast—another formal meal with her father and the Stones—was about to begin.

"Does my father know?" Ella asked, rushing to the bed for her clothing.

"I don't think he does, not for certain, anyway. He may suspect it's possible; he's certainly done everything he can to prevent finding out such a thing. Or he may have no idea. It doesn't really matter. You can't tell him."

"I could."

"You won't be safe if you do. He's made too much a show of his stance, Ella. You can't confront him with this, or the consequences would be disastrous. People might die. Certainly some would disappear. Permanently."

"By people, you mean you."

"Including me, yes." Sabelina's gaze dropped to the floor, though she continued to help Ella dress. "And perhaps I deserve it, but it wouldn't be just me."

Ella was angry, possibly angrier than she'd ever been in her life, but Sabelina's words sobered her immediately. Sabelina had raised her after her mother's death, tucked her into bed at night, listened as she recited her lessons in the afternoons. Her trust had been shaken; she wasn't even sure if everything Sabelina was telling her right now was true, but she did know that Sabelina loved her and believed she'd been protecting her.

Sabelina might deserve Ella's wrath, but not death—and Ella didn't want her to "disappear," either, whatever that meant.

"I won't say anything," she whispered as the breakfast bell rang again. "But this conversation isn't over."

"So Ellarowan," Cayloken said as the breakfast dishes were being taken away. "Would you accompany us on a carriage ride today?"

Keeping her composure and manners throughout breakfast had been difficult enough. Going on a carriage ride with Cayloken and his parents was the *last* thing Ella wanted to do, but already her father was smiling and nodding at them, and keeping her eyes in check was growing increasingly difficult. So, instead of the "no" she wholeheartedly wanted to give, she smiled and said, "I think that would be nice."

Twenty minutes later, when the carriage stopped on the side of the road, just outside the sight of the estate, and Cayloken pulled her out before the carriage drove away again, she nearly fell over against him in relief.

"Why would your parents do that?" she asked as he began walking into the woods.

"They thought we could use some time to ourselves. You're going to have to lead me a bit here, Ro. I don't want to get us lost and accidentally come out in your driveway."

He followed as she scurried quickly through the underbrush to the first line of trees, and then she turned and began heading in the direction of the cottage. When she was certain they were completely hidden by the forest, she stopped and turned to face him again.

"That was awfully nice of them."She frowned, a dark thought occurring to her. "Why the woods? Did you tell them something was out here?"

"I thought there was enough going on without telling them that you're keeping a gadab out here. I just figured we wouldn't get much privacy in a carriage with my parents or with curious folks following us around town."

"Privacy is good," she said. "Unless—you didn't bring me out here to murder me, did you?"

"You're the one with magic, Ro. Shouldn't I be the one who's worried?"

"Yes. I'm so terribly dangerous when my eyes change from violet to green. You'd better stand back."

"You likely have more powers than just changing your eyes. Once you learn how to use them, you might be very dangerous."

She didn't say anything for a moment, gathering her thoughts. The terrain required her attention now anyway, which was a good distraction. They'd reached a steep incline, and she could feel Cayloken looking at her thin sandals. The paths from the house to the cottage and riverfront wouldn't have been a problem, but this was uncharted territory. *Nothing to do about it now.* He wasn't precisely dressed for trekking through the woods, either. She took the next step.

Her foot slipped, nearly sending her toppling down the hill. Only nearly, because Cayloken caught her, his hands wrapping deftly around her waist, steadying her. He held on, easily pulling her to the top of the hill.

This time, it wasn't her eyes flaming red as they landed on firmer ground. "Thank you," she mumbled.

"You're welcome. See? If I was going to murder you, that would have been my chance." He smiled and stepped back, letting her walk in front of him again. "You know where we're going, right?"

"Sure." She shrugged. "We just need to keep going that way."

"Okay."

They walked in silence for a little while. Well, without talking, anyway. The woods weren't silent at all. Birds chirped and small animals chattered as if all was right with the world and everything wasn't falling apart. Listening to it made Ella feel like maybe everything wasn't so terrible. And then she noticed that all the sounds were further away than they should have been. She thought she heard something else, too. She stopped, forcing Cayloken to nearly stumble behind her.

"What is it?" he asked.

"I'm not sure. It feels wrong. Like we're not alone."

He was standing so close to her that she could feel his nervous energy, making the hair on her arms prickle. His head moved in time with hers, searching up and down the trees and under the bushes, both of them listening intently.

"I'm sure I'm just imagining things," she finally said, starting to walk again. "I'm not exactly thinking straight right now."

"Well, nobody can blame you for that."

This was easier, walking through the woods, a few steps ahead of him so he couldn't see her face when she talked. "Why are you being so nice to me?"

For a second, all she could hear was the soft crunch of his shoes against the underbrush, then, "Why wouldn't I be?"

She scoffed. "I've hardly given you any reason to be. First I hate you before I've even *met* you and then I'm spending time with another favored at our betrothal party, plotting the best way to get rid of you, and then I turn out to be a keeper."

"Do you think I didn't spend any time hating you before I even met you?"

"Did you?"

"Of course I did. I thought I was going to get here and find a spoiled brat."

"I kind of am."

He laughed. "Yes. You kind of are. But you're not as terrible as I imagined, so…"

"*Vosh!*" she screeched, stopping so quickly that this time he did bump into her.

"What is—? Oh. Is that—?"

"An iber," she whispered, nodding at the quivering ball of fluff she'd just nearly stepped on. "But I don't think—" she knelt to examine it. The creature's fur fluffed up straight and it made a loud hissing sound. They both jumped back.

"Not yours," Cayloken said.

The iber, apparently not satisfied, shuffled toward them, still hissing.

Cayloken grabbed a stick off the ground. "Run!"

But Ella couldn't. She *wanted* to, but her feet felt as if they were rooted in the ground. She stood there, her eyes flicking between the advancing animal and the end of Cayloken's stick. "No," she whispered. "Back away slowly."

She didn't know if she was more surprised that Cayloken listened to her, that her feet were willing to move now, or that the iber stilled as soon as they were a few feet away. It froze, blinking at them with its black liquid eyes as they kept moving backward, step by careful step. After a moment, Ella couldn't see its eyes anymore, and it turned and skittered back into the underbrush.

Cayloken let out a breath. "Well, your power isn't *taming* animals."

"Is that a power that a keeper can have?" She turned and walked forward. The terrain was growing more familiar now. Soon they'd come to the clearing where she and Loric had always met. She could almost hear the river up ahead.

"Honestly? I don't know. I think so. That's something some keepers I've met can do. But none of them are the same."

"I don't see how taming animals could be dangerous to anyone."

"Who said their goal was to be dangerous?"

Ella stopped short again, but this time Cayloken was paying better attention. He was learning. "I always thought their powers were dangerous."

There were a lot of cutting remarks he could have made in response. Ella thought of at least three before the words were even out of her mouth, but he pursed his lips thoughtfully, thinking before he answered. "No. I mean, some of their powers can be dangerous, I suppose. But people don't need magic to be dangerous, you know. Keepers don't even call them powers. They call them gifts."

She started walking again, mostly because it was easier than looking at him while she answered "This doesn't feel like a gift."

"Well, around your father it might not be."

"It's more like a curse, if you ask me."

"Since the Fading, it's been a curse for many people."

Ella swallowed hard as something crossed her mind she'd never thought of before. "People don't *choose* to be keepers. Do they?"

He shrugged. "They don't. But does it really matter? I'm kind of a believer in judging people by what they *do*, not by who they *are*, whether it's a choice or not. Nobody's ever hurt me just by being a keeper."

"But you don't worry that they could use their powers to hurt you?"

"People who *aren't* keepers could hurt me, too, Ella. They're a lot more likely to, actually, considering there are so many more of them. I can't strike out at keepers preemptively and still call myself the righteous one."

"You're saying you think my father is wrong."

"Among other things, yes, I think I've been making that point the entire time. Are you saying you think he's *right?*"

She stopped walking. "What if he has good reasons?"

"I don't see how that matters." Stopping beside her, Cayloken knelt to examine a group of tiny white blossoms on a bush. "People still died. Other people still live in fear. What he *did* still matters. Being afraid isn't an excuse to hurt people." He plucked one of the blooms and twirled it between his fingers.

"Nobody in Ravensguild died in the Fading."

He closed his eyes and pressed the flower to his nose, inhaling a little too deeply. His fingers went white where they were pressed against the stem. "That *is* the official story, I suppose."

Her heart felt like it had stopped beating, and she found herself unable to look him in the face. She knew people had died in the Fading, of course she did. But not here, not in her guild. Her father had always said he didn't support that.

But there were a lot of things she'd believed about her father before now, and she wasn't exactly willing to stake her own honor on his word at the moment.

"Anyway," he said, "I think I might have been wrong, at least kind of."

"Wrong about what?"

"You and animals. Your eyes…they're changing back to violet right now, but they *were* this outrageously bright yellow color—still are, just around the edges. You *did* something to that iber a few minutes ago, didn't you? You stopped it from attacking us."

"All I did was look at it."

"Yeah, and what happened the night you saved the other iber from the panther?"

"You think *I* did that?"

"You already know you're a keeper, Ro. You're going to have to stop being so shocked when that actually means something."

She made an exasperated noise. "Forgive me, *Lo*. You're changing subjects so fast it's making my head spin. I still don't understand how it's possible that I'm a keeper. How does that even happen? Can just *anyone* become a keeper?"

"No. It has to be in your bloodline. Almost always from one of your parents."

There was a small place in the back of her mind that had already realized this, of course, but the idea was so absurd she hadn't acknowledged it. "That's impossible. My father—"

"Not your father. Most definitely *not* your father. It was your mother."

Her whole body shook as she whirled to face him. "You sound like you know that for sure."

"I do. Or, at least as sure as I can be. My parents told me last night."

"How do they— Wait. Did you tell your *parents* that I'm a keeper?" Every curse word she'd ever heard raced through her mind, and then she started making up new ones. Some of them might have even flown out of her mouth.

He stood and watched, a rather impressed look on his face. *Yes, she'd definitely said some of them out loud.*

"I did tell them, yes."

She coughed. "So, I guess the wedding is off, then."

"No." He frowned. "Not from our end of it, anyway. Now, I'm quite certain that if you wanted to out yourself as a keeper, the council would be happy to nullify the contract. It's not something I'd recommend you *do*, but if your only goal is to escape the marriage, this would work."

"You would still want to marry a *keeper*?"

"We've been over this, Ellarowan. Marrying a stranger is not something I want any more than you do. But the fact that you're a keeper doesn't change anything. Everything that was true about our political situation is the same today as it was when the contract was made. Nullifying it would be just as dangerous to my guild as it would be to you. So, yes, I still intend to fulfill the marriage contract if it's an option for me. And I very much hope you'll consider not fighting against it."

She knew her eyes were changing again, but she couldn't tell what color.

"If it hasn't occurred to you yet, your secret is safe with me," he said.

"I suppose you're not at all disappointed that I broke things off with Loric."

He stared at her so intently that, for a second, she almost felt he could see into her soul. Then he sighed. "Is there any chance you could reserve your hatred of me for things I've actually said or done? This wasn't an ideal situation for me, either. But I didn't begrudge you having a favored when I arrived. And I most definitely have not taken any pleasure in the fact that you got your heart broken last night. And I *am* both disappointed and sorry that I was a catalyst for that."

In one smooth movement, he turned and stomped away from her.

She felt like a dam straining against a flooding river, and Cayloken's words were a full bucket past the breaking point. Unable to take another step, she sat down where she was, not even caring that her leg dropped straight into a thorny bush, tearing a deep scratch through her skin. She buried her face in her hands.

Cayloken's footsteps kept going another twenty paces or so, and then they stopped.

When she didn't look up for several minutes, the footsteps came back toward her, stopping when a shadow covered the little patch of light she'd been able to see between her knees.

"I'm sorry," she said. "That was rude and unkind of me, and you've been nothing but gracious. You didn't deserve it."

He was quiet for a long time, and she finally had to look up to see just how badly she'd damaged the fragile state of things between them.

She expected the worst, but he gave her a tentative half-smile. "So long as it means I get to claim victory in our first real fight, I accept your apology."

She rolled her eyes, but took hold of his proffered hand and let him help her back to her feet.

"We should get that cleaned up," he said, looking at her knee.

"It's fine. I just scraped it a little on the bush. It's tiny." It was bleeding a little too much to be called tiny, but already, it looked smaller than when she'd noticed it a few minutes ago. She tried to argue, but he pulled a jug of water out of the bag he was carrying and poured some of it down her leg and then he produced a clean wiping-cloth and handed it to her. "Thank you," she muttered, kneeling to clean up the blood running down her leg.

"See? I'm nice."

"I already said you were nice," she pointed out. "That's the problem. It's that I *wanted* to hate you, and you won't let me. And you're a lot nicer than I deserve."

He grinned that stupid grin. "Now, if only you weren't a keeper, and you weren't hiding a gadab in a cottage somewhere over here, this might have just gotten easier."

"Yes. If only."

The brush rustled a few feet ahead of them, making them both jump. Cayloken muttered something under his breath when a tuft of brown fur peeked through the tall grass, and he reached for a stick.

"Wait," Ella said. "I think it's—" The small furball came flying toward her, knocking into her feet, making her wish, yet again, that she'd worn sturdier shoes. "Fluffy." She bent down to pet the iber.

"Where does it *come from* like that?"

"The cottage is right up there," she said, pointing up the hill. "You can see the back wall from here. *Oh.*" The wall wasn't the only thing she saw.

Shea was standing right at the back corner of the little building watching them approach. She didn't look pleased.

"She really hates me," Cay said under his breath.

"No she doesn't. It's just…"

"It's okay. She thinks I'm dangerous, that I know enough to betray you and really cause problems. And she's right about that. Until I earn her trust, she has no reason to think I'm safe, so she's protecting you as best she can. Friends like that don't grow on trees. Why don't you talk to her alone for a little while? Tell her what she wants to know. Tell her what you really think of me. I'll go look for Owen."

SIXTEEN
MAGIC

CAYLOKEN CLIMBED UP THE worn steps to the little cottage, wondering if Ellarowan even remembered that yesterday she'd been trying to keep Owen's location a secret. Keeping everything straight had to be confusing for her. But there was a part of him that hoped she'd simply decided to trust him.

The cottage was unexpected. It had clearly been used as a guesthouse at some point in the estate's past, though Cayloken could see why Marius made no use of it now. The design of the little building was simple and efficient, and had probably once been more neat and stylish, but still it stood in sharp contrast to the extravagant newer buildings on the other side of the main house.

This little place spoke to a very different past.

He wondered how much of that past influenced the daughter of the guildmaster who was so very different than he'd been expecting.

He'd often had discussions with his father about how people came to be who they were. Was it that people were born to be a certain way—perhaps influenced by their bloodlines, or were their natures determined by how they were raised? In those discussions, he'd often argued that it was neither. People were free to make their own choices. In theory, anyway. In reality, in his experience as the son of a guildmaster, people rarely surprised him.

He'd had expectations of Marius Lockwood's daughter.

None of them involved housing a gadab on her father's property or hiding the fact that she was a keeper.

The gadab in question looked alarmed when Cayloken opened the door, but his terrified expression quickly gave way to a warm smile. "Hello again," he said.

"Hello," Cay answered. "Were you expecting someone much scarier than me?"

Owen raised an eyebrow. "I'm a *gadab*, or whatever, in a strange world. *Everyone* is scary. Every time I see a person— even Ella—I have to wonder if this is the interaction that's going to stop me from getting home."

Simply being forced to stay for a time in an unfamiliar guild, especially a hostile one like Ravensguild, was difficult for Cayloken. The idea of being trapped in another *world* with the possibility of never returning home was enough to speed his heart. He didn't know what would motivate someone to take the chance. "You had to have known that not being able to go home was a possibility, even if you'd landed in the right world."

Owen had a notebook open against his propped-up leg. He'd obviously been writing in it when Cayloken's entrance had interrupted him. His pen was against the paper now, and he wrote several lines before he answered. "I knew."

"How bad are things for you in your world, then?"

This was enough to pull Owen's strange round eyes up from the paper, and he chuckled softly. "No, things aren't terrible there, not really. Although that question makes sense, considering. I have a good family. Two parents who love me and have supported me. A younger sister I adore. And I'm nearly finished with the studies I've been working on for years. In a couple of years I could have a career as a doctor, and… That's all anyone is supposed to want, isn't it?"

Cayloken could tell Owen was leaving something out, but he didn't think it was any of his business. "Um, I don't know. I only understand three-quarters of what you just said."

"Sorry."

"Don't be. It sounds to me like you have a good life and every reason to want to stay there, and yet you couldn't stop yourself going through a gate into another world."

Owen shrugged, but it wasn't dismissive. "You don't have to go through a gate at sunset to find yourself in a world you don't belong in." He glanced toward the window. From here, they could both see Ella and Shea having an animated conversation, hands waving, cheeks burning.

Cay swallowed. "No. I suppose sometimes you're just born into the wrong one."

"Sometimes."

"Let me guess. Not everyone in your world is out looking for gates to other places."

"Well, no. But… I was always different in other ways, too. In my world, there's a name for it, for people like me."

"Like keepers," Cay said.

"Kind of like that, I suppose. Only I'm not magic."

"I don't think we've established *that*."

Owen chuckled quietly, but continued. "My parents love me, and have always supported me, and they work their hardest to understand me. And I love them. But my older sister, Quinn—she didn't *try* to understand me. She didn't have to. I just made sense to her."

"And she left you."

He shook his head emphatically. "There's a difference between going *to* a place and leaving *from* one. She went where she belonged, where she was supposed to be. She didn't *leave*. She's always still been with me. But I was eight when I went to that world, and…"

"It was the right one?"

"Something like that."

Cay looked out the window again. "Do you think there's a right world for Ellarowan?"

Owen's gaze followed his. Outside, the flailing limbs had calmed, and the two girls were standing much closer to each other. Owen turned to Cayloken and silently studied him before he spoke. "I think it's likely—but I don't think it's through the gate over the river."

Cay shivered as he looked back at the girls.

Outside, both Shea and Ella stopped and turned toward the window at the same time, as if they knew they were being watched. Owen and Cay stepped back so fast they nearly bumped into each other, and Cay lost his balance, toppling over backward onto the bed. They were both still laughing when the door opened.

Cay straightened up immediately. Shea was already suspicious enough. He braced himself for her anger and questions, but then, she surprised him by walking right up to him. "I think you and I might have had the wrong beginning," she said.

He lifted one shoulder. "To me it just looked like you were protecting your friend. I'd have done the same."

Her eyes narrowed and swept up and down him before her face relaxed into what could almost be called a smile. "I think I might even believe you."

It was a tentative peace, but it was a start.

"It doesn't matter," Ella said, interrupting them. "Believe each other or not—trust each other or not—we're stuck here together. Unless, of course, any one of you decides to betray me." She sat down hard on the bed, burying her head in her hands as a cloud of dust rose and then settled around her.

It was the second time this morning that she'd lost it like this, but Cayloken couldn't blame her. He'd had enough trouble getting out of bed today to face this situation of theirs, and he wasn't secretly a keeper.

Giving only the briefest thought about whether it was a good idea, he went over and sat down next to her on the bed. "It does matter," he said quietly. "It does matter whether we trust each other or not." He glanced at Shea and then Owen, and then back at Ellarowan, who was slowly lowering her hands, one fist clenched around something. "Nobody here is going to betray anybody, okay?"

She nodded slowly.

"What is that?" he asked, frowning at her hand.

"Hmm? Oh, it's yours." She held out her hand to show him the balled-up bloodied wiping-cloth.

"I think we can just call it a gift," he said, holding up his hands and smiling. "You should—" He stared, trying to make sense of what he was seeing. The wound on her leg hadn't been grievous, but it had certainly managed to bloody the wiping-cloth. There should have at least been a small, angry scab there now. But there was only a small pinkish patch of smooth new skin, a leftover remnant from a nearly healed cut. He studied both her legs carefully, just to be sure.

When he looked at Ella's face, she'd gone gray.

"What's wrong?" Shea demanded, but Cayloken couldn't focus on anything except Ellarowan.

"It's all right, Ella," he said, trying to keep his voice calm, despite the fact he'd never been quite so close to seeing someone use such a strong power. "I think we've just discovered something else you can do."

"It would explain Fluffy," Shea said. "He's so attached to you because you didn't just rescue him—you healed him."

"Do you think I can really do that? Heal other things?" Ella asked. She hadn't even told Shea yet that she thought she could maybe tame animals—or control them, or something. The encounter with the panther a few nights ago was beginning to feel like something far more impossible and dangerous than she'd thought.

Then again, that described her whole life right now.

She could barely concentrate on the lively discussion of her abilities the other three were engaged in at the moment, anyway. Part of it was because she still didn't want to believe she could do *any* of it. But mostly her thoughts were completely occupied with the *other* thing she'd learned this morning. One thing played in her mind over and over, obliterating everything else.

Her mother had been a keeper.

She thought she might have asked a question, but she didn't listen for an answer as she pulled her bag into her lap and rooted through it until she found what she was looking for—her mother's journal.

What had Sabelina said this morning? That only Ella could read it? That didn't make any sense. Ella flipped through the pages for the hundredth time. *There was nothing written here for anyone to read.*

"There's only one way to find out." A voice broke through her haze. Cayloken's voice.

"Find out what?" she asked.

Shea frowned in concern, but Cayloken just looked patient when he said, "If you can heal other people, or just yourself."

"I don't even know if I can— What are you doing? Stop!"

He'd pulled a small dagger out from somewhere—a very sharp one. Before she could get the words out, he slid the sharp blade along the side of his forearm, leaving a thin trail of red in its wake.

"Are you serious?" Shea screeched, running across the cabin. She returned a second later with a small, ragged towel and waved it in Cayloken's face.

He calmly laid the towel over his cut. "It's just a small one," he said.

The dark line of blood that immediately seeped through the cloth suggested otherwise.

"I'd love to know how you're going to explain that to your parents," Ella said.

He shrugged. "I'm not. You're going to heal it."

Her stomach felt like someone had reached inside and tied everything in knots. "I can't! I don't know how."

"What did you do with the iber? Or your leg?"

"Or your *forehead?*" Shea said, in sudden realization. "There was a huge gash on it the other night. It's completely gone now—I forgot about that."

The room shifted and spun as she touched the spot on her forehead. Shea was right. Her skin was perfectly smooth—not even the tiniest bump or bruise remained. This was impossible. "I didn't do anything! I just—"

She didn't mean to reach her hand toward Cayloken. She most definitely didn't mean to close it over the bloodied towel. It was as if she was watching someone else touch him, though the warmth of his skin, and the steady *beat, beat, beat* of his pulse radiated through her.

Everything was quiet except for that small beating, and the matching rhythm of her own heart against the wall of her chest.

The towel stopped getting bloodier.

"Um, Ella," Shea said, in a small, terrified voice. "You might want to see this."

She wasn't pointing to Cayloken's arm. In fact, Shea wasn't looking at Cayloken at all. Her eyes were locked on the journal, lying open on the bed.

Ella gasped and lost her grip on the towel.

The pages had been blank only moments ago. She'd never been so sure of something in her life.

But they weren't blank now. Both pages were filled, with lines and lines of writing, top to bottom. There were even drawings in the margins.

Shea snatched it off the bed and began flipping through the pages. "They're *all* written on!"

It was suddenly hard to breathe—and even harder to stop her hands from reaching over and yanking the book out of Shea's hands, which didn't make any sense. There'd never been anything Ella hadn't wanted to share with Shea. She gripped the ends of her shirt to stop herself.

"Wait! What's happening to it?"

Ella watched in horror as the words began to dissolve on the paper, first melting into blurry shapes and then breaking apart like so many grains of tiny black sand.

"Uh, Shea?" Cayloken said. "Maybe you should let Ellarowan…"

"Oh! Vosh! Here." Shea handed the journal over immediately.

For a second, Ella was hesitant to take the book, afraid that if they moved it too much, the tiny grains would spill off onto the ground and be lost forever. But as soon as it touched her hand, the words shifted again, the tiny flecks reorganizing themselves back into recognizable letters.

"In case you had any lingering doubts you were a keeper," Cayloken said dryly.

"Are you always this obnoxious?" Shea asked.

"I think the word you're looking for is funny."

"It's not."

Ella was barely paying attention to them, focused as she was on the words—*her mother's words*. But a small part of her appreciated that both of them were here—that Cayloken was still here, not running off to his father or to the palades, and that Shea was giving him a chance.

Cayloken cleared his throat. "So…would anyone care to explain the magic book?"

SEVENTEEN
DISCOVERED

"I CAN'T DO IT." Ella said, flopping down on the ground beside Shea.

"You didn't read *any* of it?" Shea asked around a mouthful of apple, clearly surprised by her sudden appearance. Ella had interrupted some kind of deep discussion between Cayloken, Owen, and Shea.

She'd been grateful, half an hour ago, for Cayloken's suggestion that everyone leave her alone for a bit, to spend some time with her mother's journal without them hanging over her.

She needed that. But not yet. Being alone in the cabin while they were out here had felt wrong. As soon as she was alone, she'd felt the same feeling she'd had in the woods earlier—like she was being watched. She kept waiting for someone to jump out from under the bed or something.

It wasn't doing her any good right now, anyway. She'd tried to read the first page—a collection of what seemed like garbled notes, though maybe it only seemed that way because the words kept dissolving and sliding off the page. She'd thought she'd seen her name, but then the letters had no longer made sense.

Ella had discovered that this magic worked much like changing her eye color. If she concentrated on what she wanted the letters to do, she could make them do it. Over and over, the tiny marks disappeared and reappeared on the pages. But she couldn't seem to make them stay.

"Maybe that's not because of your magic," Owen said quietly, after she explained it to them.

"What do you mean?"

"Maybe you're just not ready. It's an awful lot to take in at once. If I suddenly got a magical letter from my sister, I don't think I could read it right away. It would be too special. You only get to read something for the first time once."

She didn't know how someone so different from her—someone who wasn't even from the same *world* as she was—could so easily understand her. But he did.

"I know it has to be true that she was a keeper," she said. "But I don't know if I can read about it—about why she didn't tell me. Why she lied to me."

"That's not something it would be safe to tell a three-cycle girl," Shea pointed out gently.

"Why would my father—" A new revelation shocked her, like an electric current zapping through her chest. "Are you sure my father isn't a keeper, *too*?"

Cayloken shook his head. "That's extremely unlikely. Two keepers usually can't have a child together."

If it really had been an electric current, she'd be dead now. As it was, she couldn't guarantee her heart was still beating. "What do you mean?"

Shea shrugged. "Nobody knows why, really. It wasn't always that way, at least, not like it is now. But if two keepers marry, there are almost never children."

"Sometimes there are," Cayloken said. "But they don't usually live."

They all stared at him.

He held up a hand. "I knew of one, once. A child of two keepers. By all accounts, she was a perfect, beautiful child. She had some of the symptoms the others exhibited, but she was growing and strong. Everyone hoped that this one would be an exception. And then, shortly after she learned to walk, one morning…" He didn't finish. Nobody wanted him to.

"How are there still keepers, then?" Ella asked.

"They're like you. Born of a keeper and an omian," he said.

Her mouth fell open. "Are you telling me keepers aren't even omian?"

He shrugged. "Probably they are, if they can have children together. That's not what I meant. I just…don't have any other words to explain it."

"Okay, sorry." Breathing and thinking were hard enough right now without having to stop and consider if she was even the *species* she'd thought she was.

"Anyway, before the Fading, it was common, you know, for keepers and omian to marry, if they wanted children."

"Two omian can have a keeper child, too," Shea said.

Ella frowned. "How?"

Both Cayloken and Shea shrugged simultaneously, a motion that might have been funny in any other circumstances.

"It's very rare," Cay said, "but it happens. In some of the old stories, some of the most powerful keepers didn't have a keeper parent at all."

"That would make sense, if it's a recessive trait that's passed down genetically."

Three heads whirled to face Owen. He'd been silent the whole time, so silent that Ella hadn't even been sure he was listening, but now he wore a quizzical frown, clearly trying to puzzle something out.

"If it's a *what* that's *what?*" Ella demanded. It wasn't his accent that was tripping her up this time—these were words she didn't know. "I thought there were no magic people where you're from."

"I'm not talking magic. I'm talking science. How parents pass traits to their children."

Shea scoffed. "I don't know if you can explain any of this with science."

"Maybe not," Owen agreed. "And it probably doesn't matter—at least not to Ella, not right now."

Ella would have been interested in Owen's theories, actually. Almost everything he said fascinated her. But right then her mind was entirely occupied with a different, wholly terrifying thought. She turned to Cayloken. "So when you were saying earlier that people *died* in the Fading..."

He lifted one shoulder.

"The Fading began before the keepers were sent to live elsewhere, Ella," Shea said. Her voice was soft, barely audible, but it contained enough anger to make Ella wrap her arms tightly around her knees.

"Forbidding keepers to marry ordinary omian was essentially a death sentence in itself. Those that left and formed their own communities are slowly dying."

"Didn't they *all* leave?"

Shea tilted her head. "Did *you* leave?"

It was a rhetorical question, but Ella didn't want to deal with all of the other questions it brought up—not right now.

She grabbed the book and opened it again to the first page, which was blank again. For a moment, she found herself wishing it would stay that way. Not since her mother had died had she so badly wished she was imagining things. Surely, any moment now, she would wake up from the nightmare and her life would be normal again.

"Denial is the first part of the grieving process," Owen said.

Ella frowned. "What?"

"The first stage of grief is not believing any of it is true—that none of it really happened."

Why was he talking about that? She froze and looked around at everyone, heat rising in her cheeks. "Did I just say all that out loud?"

Cayloken nodded.

"Well, I'm not grieving. Nobody died."

She braced herself for an argument, or some long-winded explanation of how people could grieve things besides death, but nobody said anything at all, and she had to have the battle with herself. The next time someone spoke, it was Cayloken. "The words are back."

He was right—the page under her hand was now filled with writing, from top to bottom with her mother's clean, neat script.

Dear Ellarowan,

I hope there's never a day when you must read the contents of these pages. If you are reading

*them, it means I have failed for too long at the
single most important mission in my life—
returning to you.*

It was hard to breathe. Her throat felt like it had closed in on itself, collapsing into her chest. "What does she mean?" she whispered.

But nobody could answer her—the others had all averted their eyes as she read, giving her what little privacy they could, though she could see that even their visitor's eyes burned with curiosity.

And then a movement in the trees behind Owen nearly made her heart stop.

Twice this morning, she'd felt like they weren't alone in the woods. This time, it was true.

She shoved the journal under her bag and stood up quickly. "Owen! Hide!" she hissed. But it was already too late for that. Trying to leave would have made his presence far more obvious to Tallen, who was almost running toward them, his female companion trying to catch up. Ella's heart skipped a beat when the girl got close enough for her to see who it was.

"Now that's interesting," Cayloken whispered. He'd stood up beside her.

Interesting was one word for her brother sneaking off into the woods with Allora Sandrez, the daughter of the great master.

"What are you doing out here, Ella?" Tallen asked once he was close enough.

"I could ask you the same question."

"I thought you were out on a ride with the Stones."

She held her hand out toward Cayloken. "We had a detour."

"And your friends just happened to be here, too?" He frowned at Owen. "Who is this?"

Half a second before she flew into the blind rage Tallen deserved right then, she remembered her eyes. She looked down at the ground for a moment, trying to make sure they were under control—though at this point all she was really doing was staring and hoping.

Cayloken stepped in front of her. "It's nice to see you again, Tallen—and Allora."

Her brother didn't appear to have even the decency to act embarrassed about being caught out here with Allora. She wished she could have half his confidence. There was no way such a dalliance would have her father's approval. If there was one thing her father hated more than keepers, it was Amalric Sandrez—the man her father felt had stolen the position of great master.

Allora didn't appear to care either way. She flashed a smile and batted her eyelashes at Cayloken.

They were probably in more danger from her right now than from Tallen.

"I really don't think I've met this friend of yours, Ella," Tallen said again, making every muscle in her body tighten. She turned her whole body around to face Owen, mostly to keep her eyes hidden, but also in hopes of giving him some kind of subtle warning not to reveal himself to Tallen.

"Actually, he's my friend," Shea said. Her words came too fast, her voice too high-pitched. Ella hoped it was just her fear making it seem that way, but she knew Tallen was perceptive. "Owen, this is Tallen Lockwood, the guildmaster's son.

Tallen, this is my friend, Owen. He's here visiting from Whitehaven."

It was a terrible risk. Her brother could verify this information without much effort—if he could be bothered to.

"It's nice to meet you, Owen," Tallen said. Ella turned to watch in horror as her brother stepped closer.

"It's nice to meet you, too," Owen said as he did the stupidest thing possible—he took several steps toward Tallen.

Just before she passed out from sheer terror, Ella realized what he'd done—stepped directly into the brightest patch of sunlight, and then used his hand to shield his eyes as he talked to Tallen. She could almost breathe. Owen must have been spending his time alone out here practicing their accent, because he'd almost mastered it. Tallen's eyes only crinkled a bit at the corners.

"Are you staying with Shea's family, then?" Tallen asked.

Ella bit the tip of her tongue so hard she tasted blood.

A loud cracking sound toward the river made them all jump. Ella turned just in time to see an enormous branch break loose from a tree. It crashed to the ground with a resounding *thud* sending a dozen small birds flapping and squawking into the air. Her heartbeat was nearly as loud as the birds.

They were all silent for several seconds, just watching.

It was Cayloken who broke the silence. "Do you happen to know the time, Tallen?"

Tallen reached into the pocket of his shirt and withdrew the small timepiece he always carried—a gift from their father on his eighteenth birthday.

Ella had received a similar one last moon at her own coming-of-age, but she'd never removed it from its carved box.

He handed the timepiece to Cayloken.

Cay studied it for almost long enough to read it before uttering a word that was just impolite enough to be believable. "We need to go," he said. "We're meeting back up with my parents near the road in just a few minutes. I'm sorry. I wish we had more time to talk."

Reading her brother's reaction would have required exposing her eyes too much, so she directed her gaze at Owen and Shea instead. "You were heading back to Shea's house, right?"

Shea hadn't managed even a full nod when Tallen's voice interrupted again. "Won't Shea be joining you for the measuring and the first rehearsal this afternoon?"

Forgetting about her eyes, she whirled to face him. "What?"

Cayloken put a hand on her back, just between her shoulder blades, and chuckled quietly. "So many things to keep track of. I think we're all forgetting our schedules. It's almost time for the rehearsal, after we meet up with my parents."

She couldn't decide if his hand was burning a hole through her blouse or the reason she was upright. Tallen was scrutinizing Cay's protective stance.

"You've got this," Cay whispered under his breath.

And then, suddenly, she did have it. She cleared her throat. "What I meant is that *Owen* was heading back to Shea's house so the rest of us could get back for lunch and preparations for the rehearsal."

She had been so preoccupied with everything that she hadn't even stopped to have the conversations she needed to with Sabelina and the other servants. A planned rehearsal was news to her, but she could figure out what Tallen meant. It only made sense. If she was going to survive the next few days, she needed to pay more attention, to focus on the things that needed done.

"Shouldn't *you* be getting ready for the rehearsal yourself?" she asked Tallen pointedly.

"Of course," he said. "I've been discussing things with Father all morning. I was just taking Allora on a tour of the property."

Allora smiled, her gaze lingering on Cay for just a little too long. "It's lovely. I can see why you'd enjoy spending time here—if you're not worried about being kidnapped by a keeper." She giggled but stepped closer to Tallen—so close Ella thought he should take care not to trip over her if he moved. Then again, the image of her brother tripping over her and the two of them tumbling down a hill together cheered her considerably.

Ella pressed her lips together and took a deep breath, then managed to give her politest smile. "Yes, well, I hope you enjoy your tour. I suppose we'll see you at the house in just a little while then."

EIGHTEEN
NEW PLANS

"YOU DIDN'T KNOW THERE was a fitting and a rehearsal today, did you?" Cayloken asked when they reached the road.

The walk here had been brisk and silent, other than a constant stream of quiet epithets from Shea, regarding Tallen's appearance in the woods with Allora. Ella felt the same way her friend did, but knew that if she'd indulged herself, it wouldn't have been quiet. And he wasn't her biggest concern right now; there were other issues she needed to concentrate on.

After Tallen's appearance, they'd decided it was too dangerous for Owen to return to using the cabin, so now he was hidden in the woods. He said he had some kind of shelter in his bag, and he wasn't worried, but Ella was.

Now they were watching the road from behind a line of trees, waiting for the Stones' carriage to return for them.

Ella slipped her hand inside her bag, checking for the dozenth time that her journal was still safely tucked away in there. At least Tallen hadn't seen that, too.

"No, I didn't," she answered. "I haven't been keeping track of much of anything."

"You can hardly be blamed," Shea said.

She shook her head. "It doesn't much matter if I can be blamed or not, does it? There's a wedding in—"

"Two days," Cayloken finished for her.

Ella clenched her hands together tightly, steadying herself. "I'm getting married in two days. Of course there are preparations and gatherings." She looked at Shea. "I suppose I should have formally asked you to be my attendant before dragging you along to a fitting for your dress."

Shea raised an eyebrow. "You're really going to do this? You're going to get married? To *him*?"

"I'm standing right here, you know," Cay said. "And despite your opinion of me, I'm only a figurative tree slug, not a literal one. I can understand what you're saying."

"I don't care what you are," Shea said, glowering at him. "I'm here for Ella."

"I think she could do worse, you know." He flashed that ridiculous grin of his, but Shea wasn't impressed.

"The point is that *you* can't do better."

"That's very likely true," he said.

"We could walk back, you know," Shea said. "Tallen already knows you were out here, it's not like you're going to be able to hide now."

This was true, Ella realized. But, for the first time since she'd learned they were coming, she wasn't desperate to avoid

Cayloken or his parents. Perhaps it was a mistake, but she felt like they were the only people she could trust right now— besides Shea, of course.

And she understood why Shea *didn't* trust them. Appreciated it, even. Shea was the only person who was completely, unflinchingly on her side. And Ella wanted her to hate Cayloken for her, and to give him a chance at the same time. An impossible task, of course.

So she was going to have to deal with the terrible combination, at least for now.

And that meant ignoring Shea's hidden plea for time alone to talk, just the two of them again, in favor of standing here waiting with Cayloken. It meant that everything she said or did right now would be hurtful to one or the other of them.

It would have been a lot easier if she could still convince herself that Cay deserved it.

Why couldn't one thing be easy right now? Just one?

Shea sighed and looked back and forth between the two of them. "You don't *have* to get married, you know."

"Oh? And what's my other option then, Shea?"

"You could leave."

Ella crossed her arms and narrowed her eyes. "We already talked about that. I can't just run away."

"We talked about that before we knew you were a keeper. That changes everything, Ella. You can't just go about your life like nothing's changed—you can't become the wife of a blaffing guildmaster when you're a keeper! How long do you really think you can go without being caught?"

Ella and Cay both stared at her, agape. "Shea—" Ella started.

But Shea shook her hands at Ella. "You're the one who wanted me to talk in front of him!"

"Uh, no, not exactly." She looked apologetically at Cayloken.

He shook his head. "It's all right. She's just protecting you, Ella. She's not running screaming to the palades about the fact that you're a keeper, she's here, being your friend."

"Well, you're not running to the palades, either—or to my father, if she hasn't noticed."

"I haven't *yet*, Ella. And no—I don't plan to, so please breathe. But Shea has no reason to trust that. And neither do you. You're just ignoring that fact because you don't have any choice. I know, and you're down a ravine either way. Denial is useful sometimes—it lets you keep putting one foot in front of the other in impossible circumstances. Shea sees what you don't see. And she's trying to make sure to open an escape route she thinks you might need."

It took a second for her to follow his advice to breathe. Her throat felt several sizes too small. "I told her you and your family are sympathizers."

He didn't look surprised. "Nobody who lost someone they care about in the Fading is just going to take someone's word for that."

Ella's mouth dropped open and she spun to face Shea, who'd turned a pale shade of gray. "How could you know that?" Shea stammered.

"I don't," he said. "Or I didn't for sure until just now. But it's not hard to guess. You know a lot about keepers for someone your age— for someone who has a best friend who knew very little about them. And you have a clear understanding of the danger."

Shea's expression went hard again. "Yes, I do know the danger. So, forgive me if I don't think it's the best idea for a keeper to marry a future guildmaster."

Ella could hardly breathe again, couldn't keep any thoughts straight. And she had never been quite so glad to hear the wheels of a carriage on a dirt road as she was right then.

The carriage rolled to a stop on the road near their hiding spot, and Kydwyn Stone opened the door to wait. When they emerged, she didn't even question the newcomer, she simply smiled and greeted Shea as if she'd been expecting her.

It was one thing that wasn't difficult. And it was enough to let Ella breathe again.

Cay extended his hand to help Shea into the carriage, and then he held it out to Ella. It didn't feel strange or terrible this time to reach back, and she almost smiled. Just as her hand touched his, a shadow flew over them, blocking the sunlight for a fraction of a second. Ella and Cay both looked up, but by the time they did, the sky was empty.

Cay frowned, "Maybe it was the cloud?"

Ella raised a skeptical eyebrow. There was a cloud. A single, small puffy cloud on the horizon. "Sure," she agreed, letting him help her into the carriage.

After an obvious awkward glance at the seating arrangements, Cayloken settled down into the seat next to his mother, leaving Ella and Shea on the other side by themselves. Ella might have chuckled at it, if she didn't feel just as uncomfortable. She trained her eyes out the window, ready to count the minutes until they could escape.

Something was strange about the tree just out her window. She blinked, trying to figure out what.

The tree blinked back. Or, rather, a large green eye among the leaves blinked at her.

She looked away quickly, startled.

Cay frowned at her.

Shaking her head in uncertainty, she looked back, but this time, there was nothing there but the trees.

The carriage jolted forward.

"Ouch!"

"Well if you'd hold still!" the seamstress, Aramina said, exasperated as she pulled the pin back from the tender skin at Ella's waist.

The knock on the door had been the first loud sound in Ella's room in nearly an hour, and it had made her jump.

Shea, who'd been finished for several minutes now, went to open it.

"Is it safe for me to come in?" Cayloken's voice did nothing to alleviate the obvious tension in the room, but Shea swung the door wide.

Aramina made a clicking noise with her tongue. "This will have to be cleaned and re-done now," she said, and Ella looked down to see a small circle of blood spreading where the pin had jabbed into her.

"I can come back," Cay said. "But I have food."

The seamstress shrugged. "I've done what I can for now. Take it off and leave it on the bench. I'll get it in a little while."

Aramina had to be starving, too. Just the sight of the tray full of meats, cheeses, and vegetables was making Ella's mouth water. Shea didn't let Cayloken set the tray down before she shoved a cracker in her mouth.

"Let me just..." Ella didn't bother to finish; she just crossed to her dressing room and closed the door behind her before she peeled off the ridiculous layers of purple silk. At least the blood had only seeped into the wide black ribbon around the waist. It wouldn't show even if it did leave a stain She grabbed a wiping-cloth from a stack in her top drawer and pressed it against the little wound.

The bleeding stopped almost immediately, but this time Ella didn't know if it was her healing powers or the fact that it was only a tiny pinprick.

She didn't know if it mattered.

Despite the fact that what she really wanted to do with the dress was crumple it into a ball and maybe toss it into a fire, she laid it out neatly on her dressing bench before slipping into the much-cooler rehearsal dress and returning to her room.

Shea and Cayloken seemed to have agreed to an uneasy truce as they stood around the small table, both spreading soft white cheese onto hard rolls.

Ella was too hungry to be bothered with such formality right now. She picked up a piece of roast chicken and stuffed it into her mouth whole.

Once the cheese was on his bread, Cayloken set down the knife and looked around the room, searching every corner. Then he walked to the door and turned the lock.

Ella frowned, but Cay paid no attention—he went to the windows and pulled them tightly closed, despite the heat of the afternoon.

"Might want to pull the shutters if you're going to do that," Ella suggested, covering her sudden nervousness with nonchalance. "Unless you're planning on roasting all of us to death."

"How much can people hear from outside this room?" he asked, closing the shutters as she'd asked.

"Well, they'd hear me if I screamed, if that's what you're asking."

He rolled his eyes. "That's not what I'm asking."

"Not much if we're quiet, but we'd have even more privacy in my dressing room."

A minute later they were tucked inside Ella's dressing room. If the tension surrounding them hadn't been so desperate and thick, she would have felt ridiculous. And possibly embarrassed, having Cayloken in such a private space, though there was nothing particularly revealing about the neat racks of dresses and blouses, and her drawers were all thankfully closed.

He wasn't looking, anyway. As soon as the door closed behind them, his expression told her that whatever he'd come in here to talk about was the only thing on his mind.

Something was tying knots in Ella's insides again. "What's happened now?"

Cayloken's eyebrows knitted together, then smoothed again. "Nothing new happened, but I thought we should talk before the rehearsal."

"Okay?"

"Okay." A dark stain appeared on his cheeks and he eyed the dress laid out on the bench before starting to walk back and forth between the bench and the door. "First—We need to move Owen out of the woods, as soon as possible, and I'm wondering if you might be open to the possibility of telling my parents about him."

Shea made an improbable noise with her throat. "I can see why *that* question would make you nervous. Are you joking?"

Ella's throat burned as if she hadn't had anything to drink in several days. Cayloken obviously wasn't joking—and she didn't think that question accounted for all of his pacing, either.

"No. I'm not joking. I think we're out of things we can do on our own. Unless you have somewhere to hide him, Shea. Should we ask your parents instead?"

In that moment, Ella was certain Shea wasn't a keeper. If she had been, Cay would have suffered serious consequences. "And risk them getting caught and arrested—even if they could help?"

"That's why that's not the actual solution I proposed." Cay's voice was much calmer than his balled-up fists should have allowed.

"How is that safer than the woods? Unless your parents have a secret army nearby that we don't know about, how could they protect us, really?"

Cay's lips pressed into a thin, straight line, and beads of sweat broke out along his forehead.

Ella's mouth fell open at the same time Shea's did. "What are you planning?"

He shook his head. "It's not what you're thinking. There are no plans, but, let's just say we didn't trust that Marius Lockwood would for sure allow us to escape safely, so, there are a few safeguards in place."

The words that flew around inside Ella's head were probably not even real words—though they were far more colorful than any of their faces right now.

Shea was the first to recover. "I still don't see how that's better than leaving him undiscovered in the woods."

"It wouldn't be—if it were remotely likely that he'll remain undiscovered."

One of the knots in Ella's stomach twisted even tighter. "Now that Tallen has been prowling around out there…"

"With Allora Sandrez. And they've seen him. Which would be a very good reason to get Owen out of those woods even if there wasn't a dragon."

The little room grew fuzzy around the edges, all the bright silk and cotton fabrics blended into one blaring shade of brown. Ella sat down hard on the bench, not even noticing the dress crumpling beneath her. "The what?"

But she'd seen it. She hadn't known what it was, not then, but now that Cayloken had named it, she realized what the shadow and the eye had been.

"What is it *doing*?"

Cayloken shrugged. "Dragoning?"

"And we're just going to leave Owen out there *now*?" In the long mirror, Ella's eyes were changing colors rapidly; she couldn't stop them, and she didn't care.

"I don't have a better solution *now*. That's why I think we need help. I know you don't know my parents well enough to trust them, so if you have a better plan, feel free to share it."

"So, Owen could be out there, right now, being eaten by a dragon?" Shea asked.

"Dragons don't typically eat people," Cay said. "They don't even usually come this close to people. And it seemed plenty peaceful when it got close to us."

Shea scoffed. "But it's still a dragon."

"So we need to get him away from there and somewhere safe." In the mirror, Ella's eye color stabilized, though to a dark yellow. It seemed futile to be discussing any plans when she didn't even know how she was going to escape her bedroom, but she had to. "We need to get him now."

"The rehearsal is in half an hour," Cayloken said.

"You could have told us this earlier!" Now Shea was pacing the room, too. Between her and Cayloken, there were going to be holes in the rugs.

"In the carriage with my parents, or in front of all the servants dressing us?"

Shea muttered something under her breath that Ella couldn't hear.

"This would be easier if my parents knew."

"Your parents have to go to the rehearsal, too. We can't tell them now regardless."

"Do I have to be at this thing?" Shea asked. "I know I'm your attendant and everything, but what if I just wasn't here—what if I had to work?"

"People already know you're here," Ella pointed out. "And if you're not at the rehearsal, you might not be able to participate in the wedding."

Shea's eyes flicked back and forth between Cayloken and Ellarowan. "*If* there's a wedding."

Ella rubbed her temples.

"That's the other thing I came here to discuss with you," Cayloken said. He stopped pacing and leaned up against one of the tall, polished bureaus. His whole voice had changed, and for the first time since he'd come in here, Ella noticed that he was cleaned up and in his formal clothes. The orange silk shirt made his eyes stand out against his smooth, dark skin. He wasn't smiling, but still his expression was warm and kind, and, despite the chaos roiling around them, at the moment, she felt safe.

He looked straight at Ella as he spoke. His eyes squinted nervously, but his voice stayed steady and calm. "I know that once the two of you get a chance to speak alone, Shea is going to tell you all the reasons it's a terrible idea to marry me. That you should realize the gravity of the situation, and find a way to escape everything."

Ella's eyes widened, though in the mirror they were turning violet again. "I can't just—"

"She wouldn't be wrong," he interrupted, holding up a hand. "Being Marius Lockwood's daughter would not protect you. If any of the wrong people find out you're a keeper… Marriage would not protect you from the consequences."

"So you think *I* should leave?"

"I think you should let me finish. *Marriage* wouldn't protect you—not by itself." He looked up at the crystal light fixture.

"But you would?" The question had been inside Ella's brain, but it was Shea who voiced it. Ella couldn't seem to get her tongue to cooperate to form words. "She'd be magically safe if she married you?"

"Safe? No. She wouldn't be safe. Safety is not what I'm offering, nor is it something I have for myself. I have something I need to confess as well."

Ella could feel Shea's eyes boring into her, but she couldn't turn her head to look. Everything seemed to have stopped; she was frozen in place on the bench.

"Well, you might want to get on with it," Shea said. "We're kind of pressed for time."

"My parents and I… We're not just sympathizers." He spoke barely above a whisper; the racks of soft fabric swallowed most of his consonants, but Ella could hear him as clearly as if he were shouting. "We are aiding a keeper rebellion."

"That's treason against the league," Shea said.

"Yes. Of course, Ella already knew that we were committing treason by harboring keepers. I'm saying it's a lot more than that, though. We're providing funds and supplies, and even numbers."

Ella finally remembered how to make her mouth work. "So when you said you were hoping to *avoid* war…"

"We are hoping to avoid war, Ella. But avoiding war doesn't mean leaving ourselves unprotected. We'd like for our efforts to remain hidden for as long as possible, and to accomplish our goals through peaceful means."

"Like making marriage alliances and siphoning funds from two guildhavens." Ella wasn't asking a question.

His eyes were fixed on the ceiling again, and his lips pressed tightly together, but he nodded.

"So you came here to use me."

He held up one hand, still not looking at her. "It's a political marriage, Ellarowan. *You* didn't come into the equation, really."

She buried her head in her hands.

"Until you did," he continued, his voice still aimed above her head. "Until I came here and actually met you. Until I wanted to rescue you from this whole situation even before I knew you were a keeper and it was your fight, too."

The carpet under the bench was red, thick, and plush. Her father had brought it back for her from one of his journeys to another guild, she couldn't remember which one. Somewhere with renowned weavers who crafted such decadent textiles. She'd always loved it, even sometimes dragged it out into her bedroom just so she could lie upon it and read. Right now the velvety threads felt like thorns under her bare feet. "Do I even get a choice before someone tells me what my fight is?"

"That's what I'm giving you," he said.

Shea's pacing had halted. She now stood in the back corner of the dressing room, practically wedged between two shelves, as if she was trying to make herself invisible.

"I can't offer you a marriage of love, or even friendship, really. You just met me a couple of days ago, and I've been hiding at least some of my motivations the entire time."

He was looking at her now. The heat of his gaze warmed her cheekbones. "I am offering you a choice. If you truly wish to escape, I will help you. I'll send you through the gadab's gate, or I'll smuggle you to one of the keeper settlements, or even just take you back to Silver Island and not interfere with your life. Nobody will ever find you, I'll make sure of that."

"And I'll live among strangers, in hiding, for the rest of my life?"

He shrugged. "I can't control what happens between our guildhavens when this alliance is broken, so I don't know what the rest of your life would entail."

"Or?"

"Or we will be married. And I will tell you everything, and I will ask that you knowingly join the resistance, rather than secretly using your position and your guild's power and finances."

"That's not a choice," she said. "That's me being forced into one undesirable thing or another, except that one is far more terrifying—and terrible."

He chuckled. "Which one?"

"Abdicating all of my responsibility and power and giving up to let other people fight the battles on my behalf."

"I'm not sure which option you just described."

"Neither am I."

"It's still a choice, Ellarowan. You might not have the best options in front of you, but you can still make a choice for yourself instead of letting other people make it for you. I'm trying to offer you more than just living with the consequences of someone else's decisions. I'm doing a terrible job at it, but, I am trying. I can't offer you love—not now. But I can offer you my alliance, and not just politically. I can stand up beside you and be on your side. I'm asking for you to choose to marry me and then for us to choose to fight together."

The dressing room was completely still and silent as she stood to meet his gaze, trying to gather her thoughts.

Before she could say anything back to him, a loud banging noise made her heart leap into her chest. She swung her head from side to side, trying to figure out where it was coming from.

"It's your bedroom door," Shea said. "Someone's knocking."

Nineteen

Encounters

Marius lockwood's home was so expansive that, even after several days, Cayloken couldn't find his way around without getting lost.

It had been a miracle that he'd found his way to Ellarowan's room earlier to talk with her, but now that he'd left her and Shea so her maid could finish getting them ready, he was hopelessly turned around.

He'd found the stairs at least, and had made it to the main floor, but the ballroom seemed to have disappeared.

It probably didn't help that he was distracted. The last thing he wanted to be doing right now was rehearsing for a wedding ceremony neither he nor his betrothed wanted to take part in to begin with. And his thoughts were on more pressing matters—like removing Owen from the forest.

Shea skipping the rehearsal to retrieve him had actually been a decent plan, but they'd talked for too long and missed their chance. Now they'd have to somehow manage to make a new plan during the rehearsal and leave Owen in the woods until after that. He didn't know where Shea would *take* Owen, regardless. He contemplated telling his parents, despite Ella's objections—except that he couldn't find them in this infernal house. It was ridiculous. *How hard could it be to find an enormous room in one house?*

"Cayloken?" A feminine voice broke into his internal diatribe. He recognized the voice, and for a second he seriously considered pretending he hadn't heard it.

Of course, his careful training would never allow such a thing, and his body turned toward the voice without any input from his desires.

"Hello Allora," he said, giving her a warm, practiced smile.

She returned the smile, her eyes sweeping up and down him appraisingly. "If I'd have known that a betrothal would get you so nicely cleaned up, I might have tried it myself."

"You did try it," he reminded her.

Her bright violet eyes crinkled in laughter behind long yellow lashes. "So I did." She leaned in close—too close.

He took a small step back. "I'm still recovering from that broken heart, you know."

Her laugh echoed against the polished stone floor. "Just because that didn't work doesn't mean we can't still be good friends, Cay." The pigment on her lips tonight nearly matched her eyes, and she brought those lips awfully near his.

He slid back another step. "I'm not sure the two of us operate under exactly the same definition of friendship."

"Don't be silly, Cayloken. I think we still have a lot to offer each other."

"You certainly have a lot to offer to everyone. How was your afternoon with Tallen Lockwood?"

Allora's smile only grew broader. Dimples appeared in both of her cheeks. "He's very charming. Getting to know him has been—enlightening. Despite those who believe otherwise, Ravensguild does not disappoint. Although I suppose you'll know more about that than I do."

"Mmmm," he grumbled. "I suppose you could say that. What I haven't learned, however, is the way to the ballroom." He took a step to the side and turned so he was no longer facing her. "Would you be so kind as to show me the way?"

When they reached the open doorway to the ballroom, Allora gave a little gasp. "You're doing this whole wedding thing almost like it's real, aren't you?"

Cayloken didn't even have to look inside the room to know what she was talking about. The fragrance from thousands of flowers nearly knocked him over from where they stood. "Almost like," he said drily.

"I have been looking for you, you know."

He raised an eyebrow, trying to pretend he cared, though unsure why he'd bother. She wouldn't notice either way. Still, she wasn't someone he—or anyone—could afford to make an enemy of.

"I heard a terribly interesting rumor."

"Hmmm."

"Don't you want to hear it?"

He really, really didn't.

"Allora!" Tallen Lockwood was crossing the ballroom, heading straight toward them. Cayloken saw his eyes dart between the two of them, and he took one more step to the side. Not that it mattered. People always made their own judgements based on what they saw. The truth usually mattered little. And sometimes, like now, the truth wasn't much better anyway.

"I wasn't expecting to see you right now," Tallen said to Allora. "It's just a rehearsal. But I thought perhaps you'd join me later this evening?"

"Are you saying you don't want me here now?" Allora asked. Cayloken wasn't looking at her—was trying to edge himself away from them—but he could *hear* her innocent little pout. And he didn't need to see the way she was blinking her eyes at Tallen to know she was doing it. "But I love weddings. I'm fascinated with everything there is to do with them. I'd love to stay and watch—if Cayloken doesn't mind."

He took a deep breath before he turned his smile on her again. "Not at all, Allora. You're welcome to stay."

It was only after he'd walked away from her that he thought perhaps he should have listened.

After the terror of the unexpected—and apparently unwelcome—visit from Ellarowan's brother and the young woman early in the day, Owen's afternoon in the woods had been rather peaceful.

Fluffy usually left at some point in the day to go foraging (or at least that was what Owen supposed the creature did), but today he hadn't left Owen's side for a second. The two of them had found a comfortable small clearing with just enough sunlight for reading and writing, and the day had gone quickly. In fact, they'd both fallen asleep during the hottest part of the afternoon, and when Owen woke it was nearly dusk, his favorite time of day.

Ellarowan's concern over him being found made him more cautious than usual, but after sitting perfectly still and listening for several minutes, Owen thought it would probably be safe to venture out of the clearing for a bit. It was near the time the gate might possibly be opening, and he needed to check it. Staying in this world was growing more dangerous by the second, and the chance of escape was worth the minor risk of discovery.

Besides, Ella's brother would most likely also be attending her wedding rehearsal.

He headed toward the river hoping fervently that the timeline in this world was different, and that he would be able to exit tonight, before he was stuck sleeping alone in his tiny portable tent in the woods. He'd bought the thing so he'd be prepared for any situation, but he was mildly claustrophobic, and the idea of sleeping all night with a cloth roof two inches from his face was less than appealing.

Not being able to see what was going on around him would be even worse.

Maybe he'd skip the tent and just sleep in the open—while being devoured by bugs like the ones Fluffy was busily catching as they walked.

The sight of the river always made his breath catch a little. It was beautiful, the sort of scene artists painted. The massive green trees were just different enough from anything he'd seen in his world to make him feel like he really was in an alien place, and yet the peace of a tree-lined riverbank was familiar at the same time.

Rocks were a bit harder to find here than along the banks of the mountain rivers where he'd spent time as a child, but they were there, hidden among the grasses and buried in the mud. He'd managed to collect two rather impressive piles. One was of smaller, easy-to-throw pebbles he could launch into the air and test the gate. The other pile was quickly turning into a tower of larger rocks, some as large as his head.

With the rope he'd brought and enough planning, he hoped this second pile would help guarantee he could reach the overhead gate.

It was probably impossibly stupid. Each passing day made him angrier at himself for deciding to travel through an unfamiliar gate.

He'd always prided himself on his intelligence. It was the one thing he could be sure of—that he could study and learn anything he put his mind to, and that his decisions were based on research and logic.

Not this time. This time he'd made choices based entirely on emotions and dreams. He needed to see Quinn, to tell her—no, he wasn't going to think about that now.

At least the rock collecting gave him something to occupy his time and his thoughts. He'd get out of here and back home, he had to. And if what Shea had told him about the stones was correct, he might be able to use the broken ones to travel through the gate in Bristlecone.

Yes, good thoughts.

He picked up one of the pebbles and launched it into a high arc, impressing himself when it went right to the correct spot.

He'd never been good at anything remotely athletic before, but after these days of practice, he could send the rocks to the right place in the air nearly every time.

But, of course, it came plummeting right back down, landing with a soft *clunk* on the other side of the river.

He picked up another. Might as well practice. Besides, he didn't know the exact time the gate would open. Best to test it several times over the next hour or so.

The second rock went in nearly the same arc as the first, perfectly hitting the spot where the gate should be. This time, he didn't hear the satisfying clunk, though. *Couldn't* hear it over the loud fluttering sound behind him.

Cold dread crept into every inch of his body as he slowly turned to look for the source of the noise.

At first, he didn't see anything. The trees looked the same as they had a minute ago, leafy branches all tangled together so he often couldn't tell where one tree ended and the next began.

And then, some of the leaves moved. There was no breeze; the day was stiflingly hot away from the cool of the water. And the biggest wave of motion started just a little too high up to have been caused by an animal.

By a small animal, anyway.

Fluffy wedged himself firmly between Owen's feet, setting his front paws right on top of his left shoe.

He stared for what felt like several minutes—though probably it was only a few seconds—trying to see something other than leaves. He knew it was there. Even though the motion had stopped, he could feel that he was being watched. The hair on the back of his neck tickled as it stood straight. He rubbed at it with his hand, but the feeling didn't go away.

And then, something in the middle of the mass of green shapes shifted, and he could see something other than leaves.

Some*one.*

The visitor stood perfectly still; the only thing visible was the shape of a face. The face of the most dangerous creature possible—a human. *Or omian,* he supposed. He'd sort of gathered that's what they called themselves here. Owen couldn't discern a gender; he could only see the vague outlines of facial features. Even the person's hair was invisible behind a leaf, though the eyebrows were a very dark brown.

Every muscle in his body twitched as he contemplated running as far and as fast as he could to find a new hiding spot. But the rational side of his mind stopped him, reminding him he might not get very far. There was only one direction he could go, and the visitor would have a head start. Besides, there might be more of them. He didn't think that person could have made the huge fluttering noise alone.

Also, the longer they stood there just watching each other, the less afraid he was of being attacked.

Surely if they simply wanted to hurt him, they'd have done it while his back was turned. He didn't have many options. If there were more of them, and if they planned to harm him or capture him or…whatever they might do, he was already toast. Oddly, this thought calmed him.

It was usually easier to react than decide. *Just stop and think for a minute, Owen.*

The lifetime of being taught coping techniques to deal with his anxieties was turning out to be useful in a survival situation.

Action was always preferable to sitting somewhere frozen and worrying about it.

He took a deep breath and called out, "Hello?"

The eyes in the leaves blinked, and then they moved.

For a moment, Owen had the disconcerting feeling he was inside a science-fiction movie, as the trees seemed to change shape and take the form of a person.

That didn't happen, of course. It was only that the person—the woman—had blended in so well with her surroundings that she had looked like *part* of the trees. Her silky, flowing shirt and pants were the same color as the leaves on the trees, and her long, black tresses *belonged* here in the forest.

As she stepped closer, Owen could see that she was older than him, though whether by five years or twenty, he couldn't begin to guess. *Cycles*, he corrected.

He opened his mouth to greet her, but then closed it again, feeling awkward and unsure how to proceed. He'd already said hello.

She kept walking until she was only a few feet away from him. "Are you the one who opened the gate?"

His entire body blazed and then grew cold, all in the span of a single second, and the ground moved up and then down again. Or at least that was what it felt like. He stepped forward with one foot to balance himself.

The woman seemed unperturbed. She stood silently, blinking as she waited for him to answer.

"I didn't open it." It was a truthful answer, and the only one he could give. He hadn't *opened* it, he'd merely stepped through it once it was already open.

Regardless, she obviously knew *way* too much, and the alarm bells going off in his head now were already too late.

"But you came through it." It wasn't a question.

He had nothing else to lose, really. Lying was most likely pointless. She was entirely unafraid of him. It might have been because of the obvious fear pouring off him in waves, but he suspected she had other reasons to feel safe.

Which meant he wasn't safe. But there was nothing he could do about that.

"Yes, I did."

"Without using the stones."

He shrugged. He had originally assumed that this gate worked like that led from Bristlecone to Eirentheos—that there were stones already buried in the ground on both sides somewhere. Or at least on one side. They'd never found any stones in the ground on the Eirentheos side. If that were true, then he would, indeed, have "used" the stones. But he certainly hadn't carried any with him.

"So you're a gadab then."

"That's what people keep telling me, but I don't know what it means."

Her blouse fluttered as she raised one shoulder. "Did you come here by accident?"

He closed his eyes, contemplating. There wasn't a simple answer to that question, of course. And he was keeping himself at the disadvantage in the conversation by allowing her to ask all the questions. There was a way to remedy that. "Have people come here by accident before?"

The smile was entirely in her eyes—her mouth didn't move at all, but he could see it. He relaxed a little, or at least started breathing again. It didn't appear to be an ambush. Or not a hostile one, anyway.

"You would not be the first gadab to come through that gate, no."

"Without stones?" he asked.

"The gadab do not require stones to travel between the worlds," she said. "Only our kind must have them."

He stared at her in shock. It wasn't the information that was surprising. He didn't understand the stones, not really, but he'd obviously been able to go through the gate without one. With enough experimenting, he could have figured out what she was telling him for himself. His surprise had a different origin. "Why would you trust me to tell me such a thing?"

Her mouth moved a little with the smile this time—just a small twitch of her lips. "And you'd like to know if my kind have used the gate as well."

"Yes, that too."

"We haven't—not for a long time, anyway. We have not had possession of a key for many cycles now."

He heard the underlying answer, of course. That they had used the gate sometime in the past. Her trust for him went further than it should, perhaps, but not *that* far.

"As far as why I trust you, *gadab*… I don't know if I do. But you've been here for several days, and you've posed no threat to anyone. Ellarowan appears to trust you, and you've shown no signs of betraying her, so I'm willing to give you the benefit of my doubt as well. Besides, you already know more about the gate than I do."

TWENTY
KALIDA

"PLEASE TELL ME THAT'S a dagger I see you carrying," Cayloken said to Ellarowan as they reached the path at the back of the house. Escaping their parents had been far more difficult tonight than previous nights. Especially because she still refused to ask for help from his parents.

She looked at him through slit eyelids. "Am I going to need to protect myself from you?"

He chuckled. "Well, perhaps. But I'm hardly going to be the most dangerous thing in the woods right now. We should be prepared."

"Prepared," she scoffed. "Because you think that little blade you've got is going to be some kind of defense against a *dragon?*"

"We can't go into the house and arm ourselves better," Shea pointed out. "The questions would be more dangerous than the dragon will be."

"Keep telling yourself *that*," he mumbled. But he followed them down the path.

"Maybe Ella's magic can protect us from a dragon," Shea said.

"Maybe the dragon is gone. Don't they go home at night?"

"Yes, Ella. At night, dragons pack up their lunch sacks and climb into their carriages and go home to prepare dinner."

For a moment, she didn't answer him, or even acknowledge that he'd spoken. It felt like she was walking faster through the woods, too; his heart pounded as he tried to keep up. He'd gone too far; it wasn't the time for joking. The rehearsal had been rather tense, and they hadn't had a chance to discuss the things he'd said earlier. Now they were in the woods at night, and there really might be a dragon somewhere out here. He strained to listen; already he could hear the rushing of the river. But no wings. Yet. Hopefully they'd find Owen soon and get out of here.

"But the real question," Ella finally said, "is do dragons make up stories about omian when they sit around their hearth fires after dinner?"

Cayloken laughed quietly. "Everyone tells horror stories around the fire. It's just that the ones the dragons tell about us happen to be true."

There was no flutter of wings at all. Just a large, black, motionless shape blocking the path in front of them. It blended so well with the nighttime darkness that none of them had seen it until they'd nearly walked straight into their own horror story.

A pair of bright, glittering eyes blinked open in the moonlight.

Cay's hand dropped to the hilt of his blade, but it froze there. Ella had been right—the weapon was certainly no match for a dragon. He'd only anger it, which would not improve their situation in the slightest.

The dragon wasn't large. He'd known it wouldn't be. Every dragon Cayloken had ever seen had been smaller than a panther. Their small size always surprised him. All the stories built the creatures up to be larger than life, something warriors might ride.

This particular specimen was smaller than most. He'd seen larger dogs. But that didn't make it any less dangerous.

Especially when it was standing only about ten feet away from them.

Ella had come to a dead stop at first, but now she was backing up slowly, taking one deliberate step at a time. And then, she was against him, the heat of her body both oppressive in the warm night and oddly comforting.

Cayloken didn't want to die in a dragon attack, but even more than that, he didn't want to die alone.

Putting one hand on Ella's side, he inched them both closer to Shea.

The dragon took a step toward them.

Ella's heartbeat was so rapid and strong he could feel it against his own chest. It pounded through him until he could no longer distinguish hers from his.

Then, as she stared at the advancing creature, her heartbeat slowed. She took a small step forward, leaving a too-cold space between them.

She held up her hands.

The dragon stopped moving.

Shea let out a gasp.

The dragon tilted its head and looked right at Shea. It took another step forward.

"Stop!" Ella called. Her voice was strange, like it wasn't coming from her. The dragon did stop and it stayed right where it was. So did Cayloken.

For either thirty seconds or thirty hours, the three of them stood there staring down the little dragon. Nobody blinked.

And then, for no reason at all, the dragon turned around and slinked away down the path.

Again, Cayloken thought about a dog.

"Very nice, Ellarowan."

Ellarowan backed up into his chest again, this time so hard he had to rock back to catch his balance.

They all looked around for the strange, feminine voice. A voice that was somehow more terrifying than the dragon had been.

"Right here," the voice called. "I apologize for frightening you."

She was standing on the path in front of them, in almost the same spot where the dragon had been only a moment ago.

Cayloken's stomach tightened as he bit back the temptation to call out a warning about the dragon. Obviously, this woman already knew about it.

Shea's arm pressed into his, and he wrapped his hand around Ellarowan's side again. "Who are you?" he called.

The woman took several steps closer. Cayloken wasn't sure he felt any safer than he had a few moments ago when it had been a dragon before him. "What are you doing here?" he asked.

When the woman took another step toward them, Ellarowan found her voice. "These are private lands. You don't belong here."

"Oh, I'm well aware, Ellarowan," the woman said. Her voice had a musical quality. "I'm just going to have to hope you hold off on calling the palades for a bit. At least on behalf of your new friend out here. There would be a lot of questions to answer."

Ellarowan's body went so stiff they could have used it as the foundation for a building. "Owen? What have you done to him?"

"Nothing. He is perfectly safe." Now the woman sounded offended. "I have no reason to harm a gadab, nor any of you. I'm not your enemy."

"Then who are you? Are you a dragon?" Ella demanded.

Any other time, Cayloken would have had to bite back laughter at that question. Dragons couldn't turn into people. But considering what Ella had been through and learned in the last couple of days, it wasn't really such an unreasonable thing to wonder.

The woman didn't laugh, either. "No," she said simply. "My name is Kalida. I am a keeper, just as you are."

"Then where did the dragon go?"

Kalida made a soft clicking noise with her tongue. A moment later, a dark shadow trundled out of the trees, stopping a few feet behind her. The dragon perched on its hindquarters and blinked at them.

Ellarowan gasped. Cay was impressed she still had the faculties to make any noises at all. He was concentrating on not soiling himself. "Did you call it away from us then?"

"No." Kalida took several more steps, until she was standing just a conversational distance from them. "I didn't call him, Ella. You sent him away."

"No I didn't. I can't control dragons."

"Well, no. You can't. Not quite. Not yet, anyway. I think you probably will be able to. But you asked him to stop and leave you alone, and—he did."

"He?" Shea's voice shook, but she managed the question.

"Yes, this is Rinn."

"That's original," Shea muttered.

Kalida smiled. "Well, dragons don't much pride themselves on originality, I don't suppose. The great Rinn Forest has long been this one's home, so…"

"How long have you had him as a pet?" Ella asked.

Cayloken thought there were more pressing questions right now, but he couldn't wrap his mind around them, either. Easier to ask about the dragon's status as a pet to start off with.

"I wouldn't call him my *pet*, exactly. He is rather useful for protection, though. I appreciate his company when I travel like this."

"And what do you need a dragon to protect you from here?"

"I should think that would be obvious, Ellarowan. A known keeper, entering your father's territory? A dragon is not much protection at all from him."

"Then why would you risk it?"

"To see you."

Cayloken braced himself for Ella to back into him again. He saw her little stumble, heard the sharp intake of air. But this time, she didn't use him for support. This time, she took two deep breaths and then stepped forward, toward the stranger.

"Why?" she asked.

Kalida clasped her hands together in front of her. "I'm sorry—this is not how I pictured this would go. I imagined—No, I suppose it doesn't matter what I imagined. But I've started it all wrong. Allow me to introduce myself a bit more properly. My name is Kalida Fullwater."

The name meant nothing to Cayloken, but he could see the way Ellarowan reacted to it. Her entire body shuddered, and her breath came in quick gulps.

"You met me, before. A few times when you were very young, but you wouldn't remember, of course."

"How—? Who—?"

"I'm your mother's sister, Ellarowan. Your aunt."

"How is that possible?"

Kalida's eyes glinted brighter in the moonlight as they widened. "Your mother and I shared the same parents. Your grandparents."

"Are they keepers, too?"

"Not both of them. My mother was not a keeper. They married when such unions were still allowed."

"Why are you just now coming here?" Ella demanded.

"This isn't the first time, Ella. But I could never just walk up to the entrance of Marius Lockwood's home and demand an audience with his daughter."

"Does he know who you are?"

"He does. But it's not a point in my favor."

"But why are you here *now*? What do you want from me?"

When she'd first seen Kalida, Ellarowan had been terrified. A stranger in these woods—a stranger with a dragon! —was about as frightening a thing as she could imagine. When Kalida had told her she was her aunt, her mother's sister, she'd felt for a moment as if she were going to be sick.

Now, as they walked down the path toward the river, to the place Kalida had said she'd left Owen, Ellarowan didn't know what to feel.

She thought she was supposed to be grateful, that she'd finally met a member of her mother's family, that she had more family in the world than just her father and Tallen.

But she wasn't. Not yet.

Perhaps it was because of everything that had happened to her in the last week, but she couldn't bring herself to trust anything, or to feel anything except a burning desire to have her questions answered.

And to see Owen again.

When they finally reached the river and Owen was sitting there on the bank, swatting away the tiny, biting midges, she let out a breath she hadn't realized she'd been holding. There had been a part of her that wondered what they were doing following Kalida deeper into the woods. Until the moment she saw Owen with her own eyes, she hadn't trusted Kalida.

And she still wasn't sure she did. Kalida was a keeper, after all.

"Are you all right?" she asked Owen.

"More than," he answered, scooting Fluffy off his lap so he could stand. "I've learned I should most definitely be able to travel home when the gate opens."

"There's still the problem of getting you back *up* there," she said, glancing up into the air over the water.

"No. That's what I mean. Show them," he said to Kalida.

Kalida walked to the very edge of the water. When she stopped, the toes of her leather boots were very nearly *in* the river.

Acting on what felt like an unspoken signal, Cayloken and Shea closed in on either side of Ella, flanking her as they all watched.

Kalida held her hands out over the water. Moonlight reflected off her arms and face. Her lips were moving, though Ella couldn't hear her saying anything.

At first, nothing happened. Ella began to wonder if it was just some kind of odd ritual. Perhaps it was something all keepers did when the moon was nearly full.

But after a minute, something had changed. The river looked different.

Shea sucked in a breath, and Cayloken shuddered.

And then Ella saw it. The river was no longer lapping Kalida's toes. Where water had been only seconds ago, there was now solid stone.

She never quite saw it happen, would never have been able to describe *how*, or even at what exact moment it appeared, but when she looked over the river again, there was a bridge.

It wasn't enormous or fancy. In fact, it was broken. A stone half-arch started right at Kalida's feet and stretched up into the air over the middle of the river. And there, it stopped. It looked treacherous and unstable with nothing supporting it on the other side. The end was cracked and jagged as if it had been ripped right in the middle.

It was definitely magical.

And Ella was certain it led straight to Owen's gate.

She took a step toward it.

And then it was gone.

"Can you open the gate?" she demanded.

"No. Only gadab can open it without the stones. Or at least that's what I always believed. This gadab says the gate opens by itself."

"But you can just make structures appear out of thin air." Cayloken's voice was thick with what Ella guessed were several emotions.

"I did not create the bridge, either," Kalida said. "I only made it visible."

Ella looked out over the river, at the water streaming past, rippling in the moonlight. There was nothing obstructing its flow. And yet, somehow, she could picture exactly where the bridge had been a moment ago. Magic or not, it had been real. "Do you mean it's always there?" she asked.

"I don't believe in always," Kalida said. "Nothing is always. But I have found the bridge there whenever I've looked for it."

"Why are you just now showing up?" Shea asked. Her tone was belligerent, demanding—rude, even, and yet Ella had never appreciated her more. She didn't like this, this stranger showing up in the middle of the woods, claiming to be her aunt, giving half-answers to serious questions.

Ella didn't know how to voice these things herself, or maybe she was just afraid of the answers she'd get if she did, but Shea put her feelings to words.

"Why would you dare to come now, when Ella's of age, if you were too afraid of Marius to ever come here before?"

Kalida frowned. "What are you afraid I'm here to do?"

"Steal Ella."

Ella couldn't breathe, wasn't sure her heart was beating. She took a step back, toward Cayloken, though her mind raced with possibilities and she knew, logically, that a boy she'd met only days ago wasn't exactly a safe haven.

"Why would I do that?"

"Isn't that what keepers do? Steal people from these woods?"

"No," Kalida said, without any hint of *anything* in her voice. They might as well have been discussing a dinner menu. "We don't."

Shea's voice had more than a hint of anger. "Then explain the disappearances to me."

"Well, we do rescue people on occasion. Keepers who have decided they no longer want to try to hide who they are. Sometimes even keeper children whose parents want them kept safe. We've never taken anybody against their will. Never *stolen*."

Ella had always been frustrated with puzzles. And yet, she'd never been able to resist one, if it was laid out on the table in the library. It was the beginning that she hated, when all the pieces were scattered. It always felt like every piece she tried would be wrong. Two pieces would have the same colors and the same edges, but when she put them together, they wouldn't line up.

But then, slowly, a picture would begin to emerge. At first it wouldn't make sense, and Ella would still find it tedious, though at that point, she wouldn't be able to stop. And then, suddenly, that one piece that hadn't seemed to fit anywhere would just pop in, and she'd see what the whole puzzle had been meant to be.

"Why didn't you *rescue* Ella when she was a child, then?" Shea demanded.

Kalida chuckled softly, although there was no humor in it. This time when she answered, there was finally something in her voice. Something mellow and quiet and aching.

"We couldn't. *I* couldn't. To begin with, I didn't know if she was a keeper. Lyonet always believed that she was, almost from Ellarowan's birth. But even if I had known, I couldn't risk it. She was safe here. There were protections put in place. Lyonet made sure of that, even before she died."

What protections? Ella wanted to ask, but her mouth wouldn't quite form itself around the right words.

Shea took a deep breath, and Ella was grateful for the question she knew was coming.

"Did Ella's mother really die?"

That hadn't been the question. What?

"What do you mean?" Kalida asked.

Ella wanted to know the same thing. Of course her mother had died. There wasn't another explanation, wasn't anywhere else she could have gone. Unless—*No.* Ella banished that thought immediately.

"I mean, did she die, or did she travel through the gate and disappear?"

Kalida's eyes went as wide as the sudden hole in Ella's chest, and for the first time since meeting her, Ella wanted to trust her. This was her mother's *sister*. Someone who had, perhaps, loved her mother as a child. And she clearly hadn't been expecting that question.

"Lyonet was not a gadab," she said, after a long silence. "And she did not have a key to the gate."

"That's—"

Shea was cut off by aloud grumbling sound and a rustling movement in the trees behind them. Ella whirled around to face it, but as soon as she did, she wished she hadn't.

The dragon was *right there*, ambling into the clearing, only a few feet away from her.

She gasped and took a step back, holding her hands up in front of her, as if that was going to be protection against a dragon she couldn't control.

The dragon stopped. It raised its nose in the air and gave a sniff, then lowered its head until it was looking right at Ella.

In the daylight, the creature's eyes had been green and rather ordinary. At night, however, they seemed to shimmer and glow with a light that had nothing to do with the moon.

It took another step toward her, and Cayloken's hand closed tighter around her arm, but this time she wasn't afraid.

Perhaps it was because there were so many other conflicting feelings dancing in her thoughts and emotions that she simply couldn't respond to one more thing, but she didn't think so. Something about the dragon's gaze made those thoughts calm and disappear, if only for a moment. She pulled her arm away from Cayloken, and took a tiny step toward Rinn.

"I wouldn't do that," Kalida said, but Ella couldn't understand why. The dragon didn't react at all, he just watched as she moved almost imperceptibly forward. It was almost as if he was inviting her toward him.

Kalida cleared her throat loudly, this time managing to break the spell. Ella took a step back.

The dragon still didn't move, but something in its eyes changed, making Ella's heart ache, though she didn't know why.

"You need to get the gadab out of this forest," Kalida said. "He isn't safe here. If you leave him, he's going to be discovered. You're lucky he hasn't been already."

Ella wondered what her aunt would think if she knew that Owen had been—at least sort of—discovered already, by her brother. Then again, she might already know. For reasons she couldn't explain, it wasn't something she wanted to ask.

"That's why we came out here tonight," Cayloken said.

"Well, you should get going." Kalida looked around. "And avoid the woods as much as possible for now. I will come and find you two days from now, right here. Just before sunset. That is the next time it would be possible to open the gate."

They all erupted at once.

"How do you—?"

"But that's—"

"Where are—?"

It was Owen who finally managed to speak first. Perhaps because he spoke so rarely, it always seemed important to listen when he did.

"How do you know the gate will open in two days?"

"The gates were once the purview of the *gate*keepers," Kalida said. "I don't know if all our old records are correct, but if they are, two nights from now will be a time when the worlds are aligned and the gate between them can be opened."

The dragon made a low whining sound. Both Cayloken and Shea jumped and scrambled backward, toward Owen who had been behind them the whole time. But Ella still wasn't afraid. She looked into the creature's eyes again, trying to discern what it wanted. A small part of her wondered how she knew it wanted anything at all, but it didn't seem to matter.

"Come, Rinn," Kalida said.

For a moment, the dragon didn't listen. Its eyes remained locked on Ella's, and it didn't budge. But then, so quickly she didn't even know how it happened, both Rinn and her aunt were gone.

TWENTY-ONE - THE GUILDMASTER'S SON

ELLA COULDN'T QUITE REMEMBER exiting the forest. She couldn't remember saying goodbye to Owen and Shea, or walking up the path that led to the newer guesthouses. Somehow, though, she and Cayloken were standing in the shadows near the back of the largest guesthouse. He was watching her as though she might explode at any moment.

She was cold. She knew this didn't make any sense. The night was oppressively hot. But she wrapped her arms around her chest and rubbed her arms, trying to keep herself from shivering.

"Are you all right?" Cayloken asked. The strained sound in his voice gave her the impression it wasn't the first time he'd asked the question, but she didn't remember him asking her before.

"I'm not sure what that even means anymore."

"No, I suppose not."

"Did that really just happen?" she asked. "Did we see...?"

Cayloken looked around and she followed his gaze. Although they were standing next to a building, there were no windows here. The other three directions offered a clear view; they'd be able to see someone coming long before they could be overheard. So long as they didn't shout, there was little chance of anyone listening in.

"A dragon? Yes."

"And was that...?"

"I don't know what that was, Ella."

She felt dizzy and still cold. Vaguely, she remembered feeling this way before. She leaned up against the wall of the guesthouse, resting her head against the warm wood. "Where did Shea take Owen?" she asked.

He frowned.

"I'm supposed to know the answer to that, aren't I?"

He pressed his lips together, taking several seconds too long before he answered. "Shea said that sometimes, when you get upset, you're like this—you can't remember things, and sometimes you even get sick."

She wanted to be offended, to argue, to insist that this wasn't true, but the barely contained nausea rippling through her middle suggested otherwise. Also, she just didn't care. There were so many things to worry about right now, this one didn't even reach the list. "I don't even know if that's true, but I'm guessing it probably is."

She reached into her bag, thankful she'd brought it with her, and pulled out the water jug. The water inside was no longer cold, but it soothed her roiling stomach and brought things back into focus.

"I don't know where Shea took Owen," he said. "We decided it was safer for neither one of us to know right now. I think it mostly meant me, but...." He shrugged.

"You'd think I would remember that. How would I forget something that simple?"

"Do you think this is the protection?" Cayloken asked.

"What?"

"Your... Kalida said that when you were young, your mother put some kind of protection on you to keep anyone from finding out that— Well, you know." Even in almost-certain privacy, he wasn't going to say *keeper* out loud.

She took another gulp of water.

"This isn't the first time you've blacked out," he pointed out, glancing at her now-healed forehead. "That would work, wouldn't it? Making you forget things when you're upset. Keep you from revealing anything?"

"Is that possible? Could she have done something to me when I was little that still works on me now?"

"You are imagining I have more knowledge about this than I do, but if I had to guess, no. It would have worn off a long time ago. Unless someone else is...I don't know what you'd call it...maintaining it?"

"Is that possible?"

"I don't know, Ellarowan. Do you know someone who might do that, if it is possible?"

"Maybe my caretaker, Sabelina?"

"Perhaps." He shrugged. "Are you feeling better now?"

"Is that your way of changing the subject?"

"It's more my way of being awkward. And I am actually concerned."

She took another drink and then nodded, peeling herself off the wall. Now she was starting to get hot. This probably had nothing to do with getting sick. Beads of sweat dotted Cayloken's forehead, and the cicadas trilled so loudly it was hard to hear anything over them. The damp air made her clothes feel sticky. "I'm better, now that I've had something to drink. So long as no more dragons show up tonight." She turned the bottle upside down; a single drop of water landed with a tiny *plink* on the gravel path.

"Want to come in?" He nodded toward the guest house. "There are drinks in there. And we wouldn't have to be as worried about someone hearing us."

She didn't know if she did, but she knew she wasn't ready to go back into the main house. She'd either run into someone she didn't want to talk to on the way to her room, or end up alone and wound up, unable to sleep. She wasn't sure which option sounded worse. So she nodded and followed Cayloken around to the front of the building.

Just before they reached the steps, Cayloken stopped short, nearly causing Ella to run into him. "Well, hello there," he said.

Fluffy was sitting on the bottom step, looking as if he'd been expecting them. Ella wondered if the creature had been following them the whole time, or if he'd found his way here on his own.

She hated that she couldn't remember anything.

She knelt, meaning to pet him, but he jumped up the steps and then shuffled his way to the door. He leaned against it, rubbing his fur on the door frame.

Cayloken chuckled at the same time she did. "I guess he wants in."

Ordinarily, she would have cautioned against allowing a wild iber into the nicest guest house. She'd seen what Fluffy had done to the cottage.

But tonight, she had no particular inclination to protect her father's property.

Cayloken didn't appear too worried about the prospect of the creature being in the building where he slept, either. He carefully stepped around Fluffy to open the door.

"Careful," she said. "You might never get him out of there again."

He smiled and watched Fluffy bound into the lighted foyer and then held the door open for Ella. "He came for you, Ro. He'll leave when you do."

"We're back to that, are we, Lo?" She stepped past him.

"I kind of like it. It makes me feel…normal? Like…"

"Like you're not trapped in some kind of nightmare with a strange keeper girl you have to marry in two days?"

"Yeah. Like that." He walked into the parlor. "Would you like something to drink?"

"Yes, please."

She'd never spent much time in any of the guest houses. This one had been built when she was ten or so, and she and Shea had loved to play in the big, empty rooms before it was finished. But once it was complete, the guest house was a delicate, formal affair. There were so many breakable things, so much furniture that couldn't be bounced on, they'd never bothered again.

At least, that was how she remembered it. Tonight, it didn't feel as stuffy as her memories. The breakable things were still here—Cayloken was pouring them glasses of whiteberry wine from a crystal decanter—but the place felt more comfortable and welcoming than she'd pictured it.

Maybe it was the shoes piled haphazardly by the door in the foyer, or the books and papers scattered over the low table in the parlor. She had heard whispers among the servants that the Stones had insisted they didn't need their quarters cleaned every day.

Maybe it was the way Fluffy shuffled across the slightly scuffed wooden floors and hopped onto one of the couches like he owned the place, and nobody reacted at all.

Maybe it was simply the quiet, knowing she had at least a few minutes where she didn't have to worry about being confronted with something new and terrible.

Or maybe it was Cayloken, who had kicked his own shoes into the pile by the door and now hummed softly as he carried a nearly full goblet to her. His orange eyes were approving as she took a long drink and settled onto the couch next to Fluffy. After two more gulps, she took a minute to undo her ridiculously complicated shoes, slipping out of them and tucking her feet up underneath her.

Cayloken sat down in an overstuffed chair across from her. "There's plenty of the wine. You don't have to drink so sparingly," he teased.

She looked at her glass, now half-empty. "You need to catch up. It takes about five glasses of this stuff before it has any effect."

He laughed. "I know. You're probably wishing for something stronger, aren't you?"

She crinkled her nose and took another drink—only a sip this time. "I don't know. I've never *had* anything stronger. And if it's anything like losing my memory out in the woods tonight, I'm not sure I want to."

"We'll stick to this, then."

They were both quiet for a few moments, but it wasn't uncomfortable, like she thought it should have been. She sipped at her drink and Fluffy scooted over until his fur tickled her legs.

"Did you want to talk about it?" he finally asked. "Or ignore it all for tonight?"

"I want to wake up from the nightmare."

He nodded and set his glass down. There was no free space on the table, so he set the glass on top of one of the books. "And go back to what?"

She frowned. "What do you mean?"

"If this was all a dream, and in five minutes your caretaker is coming into your room to wake you up, what life are you going back to?"

"A simpler one than this."

"Was it really simpler? Or did you just not think about how complicated it was?"

"I wasn't being forced into a marriage with a stranger."

He lifted one shoulder. "You were going to be, someday, Ellarowan. Your father was never going to permit a marriage that wasn't advantageous to him politically. You might not have known that. I'm not sure what reasons he gave you for controlling your relationships, but that's always who he's been."

She couldn't even argue with him. She wanted to be angry, to shout him down, to put him in his place, but the flame wouldn't rise in her chest. The words didn't even hurt as much as they would have only a few days ago. "Well, I wasn't a keeper," was all she could manage.

"Yes, you were. You were a keeper when you were born. The best you could do is go back to not knowing about it. Is that actually what you would want?"

"I don't *want* to be a keeper."

He looked down at the iber snuggled in her lap, purring loudly. "Is that true?"

She took a very long drink.

After a moment, Cayloken stood and went to retrieve a serving pitcher from the sideboard. "There are a lot of times I've wished I wasn't the son of a guildmaster," he said as he refilled her glass, this time with water.

"I never wished that," she said. "I was always proud that my father was the leader of the guild, and that we lived in such a beautiful home and I always had nice things. My brother complained sometimes, about the expectations and the responsibilities, but I never understood that, until…" she trailed off, not wanting to finish the sentence this time.

"Until the night those responsibilities landed on you?"

She dug in her bag, not searching for anything; it was just easier than looking at him as she answered. "I suppose that makes me sound spoiled and selfish, doesn't it?"

"Yes."

Her head jerked up.

He shrugged one shoulder. "People often discover they're something they didn't *choose* to be. Powerful, selfish, sad, magical… The thing you have to decide is what you're going to do once you *know*."

"You realize you might be a few of those things yourself, right?"

His calm, interested demeanor didn't change at all. "Yes, I know. I'm the one who came to your room earlier and asked you to willingly participate in treason, defying your own father, remember?"

She couldn't sit anymore; she needed to move. Fluffy wasn't pleased when she dumped him abruptly on the cushions, but it couldn't be helped. "Are we going to talk about that now?"

"That's why I brought it up."

The parlor was large, ten steps just from the couch to the sideboard. Ella counted it three times as she tried to figure out how to answer.

"You are a keeper, Ella. Even if you could go back to a few days ago, before you even knew I existed, that would be true. You would have found out at some point. Your powers are only getting stronger. If someone did put some kind of protection on you to hide your eyes and block your memory, you're breaking through it now."

Eight steps to the other couch.

"What would your mother have wanted?" The question was so quiet she wasn't sure he even truly intended for her to hear it, but she did.

She stopped pacing.

For a moment, everything was still, even Fluffy stopped purring and blinked his liquid eyes at her from underneath the mop of fur.

She retreated to the couch, shoving Fluffy out of the way and plopping down just before she noticed that Cayloken had stood. Sighing, she reached into her bag and pulled the old journal into her lap. "Maybe I could answer that question if I could read this wretched thing!"

"I…need to excuse myself for a moment. Will you be all right?" The non-sequitur startled her and she looked up to see his cheeks darkening.

She didn't mean to laugh, but she couldn't help it. It was as if all the tension and pressure had finally broken her, and she laughed so hard she snorted. "We did have a lot to drink," she said between giggles.

It could have been awkward. He could have been offended. *She* might have been, were the situation reversed, but after staring at her for a moment, Cayloken laughed, too, and the color faded from his cheeks. "Five glasses before you feel anything, eh?"

"It's not the wine."

"Mmmhmm. I'll be back in a minute."

Well, maybe it *was* awkward. But she kind of appreciated having a minute to herself. She opened the journal to the first page again and traced her fingers over her mother's name before turning to the second page. It was blank; not even the slightest shadows of ink marred the clean page.

"If you really wanted me to read this, you shouldn't have made it quite so impossible," she mumbled. She took a deep breath and focused. After several seconds, she thought she could make out the faint outline of the word, "Dear," but it might have just been her imagination.

She slammed the book closed.

"No luck?" Cayloken asked from the doorway.

"Nothing. And now I need a minute to myself." This time her face turned colors as he laughed.

"It's—"

"I know where it is, Cay." She was pretty sure she remembered, anyway.

When she returned, Cay was sitting on the sofa where she'd been. The journal was open on the table in front of him and he was hunched over it, staring at one of the pages. She paused in the doorway, watching. His head tilted from side to side, as if he was trying to look at it from different angles. He ran a finger lightly over the page.

She cleared her throat.

He startled and looked up at her. "Sorry. I hope you don't mind."

Did she mind? She wasn't sure. It felt like perhaps she should be bothered that this stranger, who she'd only just met, was leafing through her mother's journal when she wasn't there.

She shrugged. "Did you see anything?"

"The pages don't even have indents on them from a pen. I think you're the only one who can see anything in it at all."

"If I can ever make it reveal more than a single paragraph." She plopped down on the couch beside him and picked up the book. Staring at the blank page for several seconds yielded her nothing.

"Shall I cut myself again?"

"Yes, let's just keep cutting people open to force me to perform magic. Give me the knife. I'll make the cut."

He turned to face her. "There it is."

"What?"

"You—finally having enough space to think to be angry, as you should be."

"Well it's not doing me any good, is it?" She flipped too-quickly through the pages of the book, not paying attention to them at all, only avoiding having to look at Cayloken.

"We haven't had a chance to discuss what I said to you earlier."

"What? That you're using this betrothal to me for political gain, and you expect me to go along with it just because I'm a keeper?"

He was quiet for a moment, but when he answered, his voice was as calm as if they were discussing the weather. "I don't know how much I have to gain politically here, but the rest…yes."

She flipped through the pages of the journal, not really looking at any of them. "Marriage is forever."

"I'm aware."

"You know I don't have any other real options. I can't run away from my entire life."

"There are always options, Ellarowan. You could, for example, have me killed, and then you'd be free of me completely."

His voice was so serious, she had to look up at him. He smiled.

"And then what?" She scoffed. "Provided I got away with such a thing, my father would likely marry me off to someone much worse."

"It sounds like I've moved up significantly in your world. A few days ago, I think I was 'the worst' option."

"You might not want to remind me how much I'd like to hate you right now. I'm rather angry that I can't seem to manage it."

"I'll take what I can get at this point."

She stood and collected their glasses to fill them again. "What about you? You might not be my worst option, but surely you have better prospects than me."

He didn't laugh this time. Earlier, he'd set his dagger on the table so he could sit down. Now, he picked it up by the handle and balanced the tip of the blade on the metal edge of the table. With a practiced flick of his wrist, the dagger spun perfectly for nearly ten seconds before it tipped and he caught it. "It would be too much work to start *this* all over again. Besides, you're not so easy to hate, either."

The heat in her chest was wholly disproportionate to the temperature of the room. She handed him his glass and sat down next to him again. "Give me that," she said, reaching for the dagger.

"Get your own. I'm not contributing to injuring *you*." He stretched out his hand, trying to grab it from her, but he was too late.

She cringed as she did it, expecting it to hurt, but it only felt cold as the blade sliced the skin at the base of her palm. Blood dripped onto the table immediately, falling beside the dagger as she set it down. And then it began to sting, making her suck air through her teeth.

Cayloken took her hand by the wrist and pressed a clean, white towel against the cut. She hadn't even noticed him getting up to get it.

"Seriously?" he demanded, his jaw clenched.

It was all she could do not to smack him.

The expression on her face must have tipped him off. "Is this what it felt like when I did this earlier?"

"Oh, no. When you did it earlier, you were also expecting me to magically heal you. If you'd like to call it even, how about you give it a try?" She shoved her arm closer.

"It actually works when you do it," he muttered, carefully removing the towel.

She winced when the air hit the dark red line across her palm. It was beginning to throb. "That was a huge risk you took. I'm lucky it worked once. I'm not exactly the most reliable person to count on for something like this."

"What do you mean?"

She held out her hand. "Does it look like *this* cut is going away?"

"Maybe it doesn't happen immediately." He stretched a tentative finger toward her hand. She cringed, but he only barely touched the outside of her hand, sending an unexpected shiver all the way up her arm.

It was still bleeding pretty heavily, and Cayloken replaced the towel, pressing hard against the cut.

"Maybe it was just a fluke and it will never happen at all. I don't know why you'd want to marry me. I'm not some powerful keeper, Cayloken. I'm just the spoiled, reclusive daughter of a guildmaster. Even my own mother didn't think that was worth sticking around for."

The room was deathly silent for an uncomfortable length of time, and her hand wasn't the only part of her that stung. Too late, it occurred to her that saying such a thing while they were stuck so close together had not been the best decision.

She used her free hand to brush angrily at her cheek.

Finally, Cayloken reached down to the table. She thought he was reaching for his glass, but instead, he picked up hers and handed it to her.

"Thank you," she mumbled, taking a sip and giving it back to him.

"You're welcome." He said it as if they were in the middle of a casual conversation, but then his eyes met hers. "How long have you been wondering *that*?"

She swallowed and shrugged.

"Just since tonight when Shea asked Kalida if your mother was really dead?"

It was odd that words could sting even worse than a slash from a dagger.

"I don't know," she said. Her voice didn't sound as shaky as it felt. "I was shocked when Shea said it—I kind of wanted to smack her, actually. But then…now…"

"The idea has been floating around in the back of your mind for a while?"

How did he know that? "I think maybe ever since Owen came through the gate over the river."

"And this book might have the answers." He ran his finger over the opened page of the journal. "Answers you're not ready for."

"See? How can I be a keeper? How can I help anyone? I can't even manage to read a journal that was written *for me*, because I'm too afraid of what it might say."

He peeled away the towel again. Until he did, she hadn't noticed that it had stopped throbbing. In fact, she couldn't feel her hand at all. It took every ounce of courage she possessed to look at the cut. Or at what had *been* a cut only moments ago. Now it was just a small pink line.

"You're eighteen, Ro. Not everybody figures out who they are and what they can do when they're born, you know. So what if you were a spoiled, *secluded* child? Who are you going to be now?"

She snatched the book up and flipped it open to a page in the middle, glaring at it as if it were the source of all her troubles. Almost instantly, ink covered the page. Her mother's precise handwriting suddenly filled rows and columns, tidy and dark.

"What *is* this? It looks like dates and times."

Cayloken shrugged. "Do you want me to give you some privacy?"

She knew she should want that, to be left alone to discover her mother's words on her own, but she remembered what had happened earlier when everyone left her alone. The writing only appeared when Cayloken was around. "No. I want help."

"Have you ever asked for that in your life?"

"What is *that* supposed to mean?" She narrowed her eyes at him. "I have help getting dressed in the morning."

"That's not..." He shook his head. "Never mind. I'm sorry."

"You just met me two days ago. You're not right about everything."

"I said I was sorry."

The rows upon rows of numbers didn't make any sense to her. She flipped the page, looking for more context, and was relieved to find that this page, too, was filled—at least until she saw what was written there. "More numbers." There were four more pages of numbers, and she was starting to become disheartened, but when she turned the next page, she and Cayloken gasped at the same time.

A chill slithered from her neck to the base of her spine, and she wondered if the wine was going to stay down.

This wasn't numbers. It wasn't even words—not words, plural, anyway. There was a single word.

My mother could draw, too. It was an odd first thought, considering *what* her mother had drawn there on the page.

It was the bridge.

It had been dark tonight when they'd seen the bridge, and she hadn't been able to make out the details, the shapes between the stones that were so distinct in her mother's sketch. And the bridge in the drawing was complete, stretching to both sides of the river, not broken and jagged in the middle like the one she'd seen with her eyes.

Still, it was the same bridge. The woods looked nearly the same as they still did, and the bend and curve of the river there was identical. But, perhaps most importantly, she knew it was the same bridge because of the thin, wobbly lines her mother had drawn at the top of the bridge and the single word plastered there: Gate.

She sat back hard against the cushions, away from that book, trying to remember how to breathe. Fluffy pounced into her lap as if he'd been waiting for the opportunity. She didn't understand how the words that had been so precious to her only moments ago could feel like a weapon now.

Cayloken kept leafing through the pages of numbers. He didn't stray from the ones she'd already looked at, though she wasn't sure if she cared regardless. Maybe it would be easier to have someone else reading it.

After several minutes, he sat back and turned toward Ella.

She ran her fingers through Fluffy's long, silky fur. He didn't purr, but he snuggled in closer. "She left me," she whispered.

"You don't know that."

The sideways glare she gave him should have made him flinch, but he didn't. He just watched her with a patient expression.

"Even if she used the gate, and that's why she disappeared, that doesn't mean she meant to leave you, Ellarowan. Her note in the beginning said she was planning on returning to you."

"But she didn't. She never came back. She just left me here, a keeper child with a father who hates keepers."

"He doesn't hate you."

"Oh, now you're defending *him*?" She dumped Fluffy unceremoniously onto the couch again and stood up, back to pacing the floor, the satisfying pounding of her footsteps the only thing keeping her from throwing dishes against the wall.

She made several rounds between the couch and the door before Cayloken spoke again.

"You do realize what this means, don't you?"

She paused to look at him.

"That your mother might still be alive."

Everything went still, even the air in the room. Fluffy looked more like a statue than a living creature.

"But she doesn't want me if she is."

"Or else she went through the gate and never made it back home like she meant to."

Ella rushed back over to the couch and grabbed the book, flipping frantically through the pages. But there was nothing else. Only the pages of numbers and the drawing of the gate, and even the ink on these seemed lighter than before. "Could that happen? Could she have gone to the other world and something prevented her from getting back?"

Cayloken only shrugged. "I knew about keepers before I came here, but I thought gadab and gates were only stories. I never truly believed."

"Neither did I! And now I find out that not only are they real, but maybe my mother went through one and never came home again?" Her eyes widened. "I need to find her!"

"Whoa, Ellarowan. Slow down for a minute. You can't just run off through a gate into a strange world and go looking for her."

"Why not? She did it."

"*If* she did, she didn't just do it on a whim. Look at all this research and work. These are gate opening dates I think, and times, and notes about how it all works. If she did all this and still wound up not making it back, you need to know much more about what you're doing first. You could end up stuck there, in that strange world, and still not find her. You don't even know why she went."

It was only the last part of his argument that gave her pause. Why had her mother gone through the gate? If she'd only wanted to escape her life here, there were many places she could have gone besides a different world.

Maybe she did come back. Ella's heart, only a second ago so buoyed by the thought that her mother might be alive, sank like lead in a pond. *Maybe she did come back to this world, but she didn't come back to me.*

"Don't," Cayloken said. "Don't start assuming things you don't know. Let's just start with something small. Keep trying to read more of the journal."

She started flipping through the pages, but it was all gone again. She buried her face in her hands. "Give me the dagger again."

He grabbed her hand, nearly tipping her forward, though he caught her shoulder and righted her. His thumb traced the thin pink line that was still raised and visible on her palm. Then he held out his own arm and showed her the matching line there. "No more of that. You know now that you *can*; you don't need to keep hurting yourself to prove it."

"I don't know that I can! I'm trying, right now, and I *can't*." She ripped her hand out of his and waved it over the blank page in front of her.

She'd forgotten Fluffy was there until he pushed his face against her leg and then her arm until she made room for him to climb in her lap. "You're a persistent little roffler, aren't you?"

The iber ignored her and settled his warm weight across her lap. The night was already warm, but the creature's warmth was more comforting than she wanted to admit. She set the book on his back and turned a page.

Cayloken picked up his dagger from the table and used a cloth to clean it before he slipped it back inside its sheath and carried it to a shelf across the room.

Ella shook her head.

The page she was touching filled with color.

Another drawing.

Not a bridge this time, but a man.

It wasn't a picture of anyone she'd ever seen before, Ella was certain, and yet something about him seemed familiar. He was older—at least she thought he was. His long, snow-white hair made him appear older than her father, older than Old Cecil, even. And yet, there were no lines around his eyes.

"Do you know him?" Cayloken asked.

"Never seen him before. He's strange."

"There's—" Cayloken was interrupted by the sound of footsteps on the porch steps. "My parents," he whispered.

Ella slammed the journal closed and groped for her bag.

"You don't have to leave," Cayloken said.

Her heart pounded faster with each step.

"My parents could help us, if we told them."

Fluffy hopped off her lap before she stood this time, and he hovered near her feet as she shoved the journal into her bag. "Please don't tell them anything."

"Ella—"

"Please!"

"All right. I won't."

TWENTY-TWO
SECRETS

ELLA HADN'T REALIZED JUST how long she'd stayed out until she got back to the main house and only the night lights were illuminated in the foyer and up the stairs.

She was exhausted, both physically and emotionally, but so many things spun in her head she knew she wouldn't be able to fall asleep right away. Also, she was hungry. Dinner had been many hours ago.

So, before heading upstairs to her bedroom, she made a detour to the kitchen.

She heard the voices before she saw the light, pouring out of her father's office through the slightly cracked door.

"Allora Sandrez? What could you have possibly been thinking Tallen?"

Ordinarily, Ella wouldn't have dared eavesdrop on her father, but this sentence made her stop in her tracks.

"I would think you'd be pleased with me making that kind of connection, Father."

"Why would you think that? Amalric Sandrez cannot be trusted."

"Oh, but the Stones *can*?"

"The alliance with the Stones is an advantageous one for both our guild and for your sister. All Amalric Sandrez would do is attempt to bring Ravensguild under his control and assume more power than he already has."

Oh, so you mean he's like you? Ellarowan thought bitterly. She backed into a shadow near the doorway.

"And what does Padraic Stone want out of an alliance with our guild?"

"Padraic's son is a good match for Ellarowan, and the alliance will bring peace between our guildhavens. What more do you want?"

"You know, I've heard interesting rumors about Silver Island…"

"I don't doubt that, if you've been listening to the Sandrez girl. Until tonight, you had no argument with any of it. Nothing has changed, except who you've been talking to. There is a *reason*, Tallen, that you are not yet ready for a match with anyone, let alone Amalric's daughter. If you would like to have some fun during the festivities, I really don't care, but if you humiliate me publicly, or jeopardize this alliance, then so help me, you will not be the next guildmaster of Ravensguild."

"Father!"

"Have I made myself clear?"

"What are you going to do? Hand it over to Ellarowan? And her new husband? She's not even strong enough to…"

"*Get out of my sight!*"

Footsteps scrambled over the hardwood floor and the study door flew open. Tallen didn't see her as he came barreling out of the room. She wasn't sure he saw *anything* as he flew down the hallway in the other direction, stomping his feet so loudly he was likely to wake the household.

She'd never heard her father this angry. He'd never yelled before, not in the whole of her memory. He could be terrifying without yelling, to be sure, but this…

And now the door to the study was open, and she was stuck. Her father would see her if she walked past the doorway on the way to her room. She thought about fleeing the other way, back toward the kitchen, but he might hear her footsteps if she did that, too.

She cursed herself for not removing her shoes earlier.

There was no help for it now. She leaned against the wall and bent down to start unbuckling the complicated straps.

"I'm just going to have to live forever." Her father's voice startled her, nearly making her drop one of the shoes, and it took her a moment to realize he was still in his study, not actually talking to her.

"How did you expect me to do this all on my own? What am I supposed to do here?"

She frowned. Nobody had been in there besides him and Tallen. She waited for several seconds, but nobody responded. He *was* in there alone. And then she heard a strange, muffled sound that made her take the risk of walking over there on tiptoe.

She peeked carefully around the door frame, her heart pounding in her chest.

What her father was doing now was far more terrifying than yelling. He was face down on his desk, his head buried in his arms, and he was *crying*.

She didn't know what to do. Stay? Go in to him? *No.* She couldn't see that ending well. Finally, she hugged her shoes to her chest and slunk to the other side of the hallway before crossing in front of the door, hoping his head was still down and she wouldn't be caught.

The cup of tea on her night table was still warm when Ella returned to her bedroom. She could feel the heat coming from it before she even touched it.

Sabelina always seemed to know when she was going to come up to bed, no matter the hour.

The tea.

Sabelina had made baymallow tea for her every night before bed ever since she was a small child.

When she was younger, Sabelina would sit with her, brushing out her hair, telling her stories, always staying until the tea was finished. Sometimes, Ella had been able to delay bedtime by not finishing her tea soon enough.

That hadn't been necessary for several cycles. Unable to fall asleep well without the calming brew, she didn't need prompting to empty the mug.

Was this how Sabelina had been "protecting" her? Was it the tea that hid her eyes and made her too ill to do magic?

She scooped up the mug and considered storming into Sabelina's quarters so she could dump it on her head and demand an answer. But after a few seconds of daydreaming about this, she set the cup back down on the table.

She was tired. Exhausted, even. Physically, the long day where so much had happened was wearing on every inch of her. More than the day, even. She hadn't slept well since before the betrothal party, which felt like it had happened cycles ago, not mere days.

Emotionally, the situation was far worse. She wasn't sure what to think about anything anymore. She didn't understand what had just happened downstairs with her father, and she didn't know what to do about her mother's journal, and she didn't know how to feel about Sabelina, either. It was too hard to imagine Sabelina lying or doing anything to harm her. And she didn't *want* to deal with the aftermath of dumping a mug of tea on Sabelina's head tonight.

Or maybe ever.

Perhaps this was why she'd always been afraid of learning secrets. Maybe somewhere in the back of her mind, she'd always known there were terrible things waiting to be discovered.

For the first time in her life, she left the mug sitting there on the night table, still full when she crawled under the covers and closed her eyes.

She didn't fall asleep, of course she didn't. Despite the exhaustion, and the fact that she should have been able to sleep for days, her eyes wouldn't even stay closed. She thought about the tea, and about battling it out with Sabelina, and about the evening she'd just spent with Cayloken. It felt like things had changed between the two of them, but she couldn't describe how.

But mostly, she thought about that journal. About those drawings. About whether or not her mother was still alive and maybe on the other side of that bridge.

She didn't *decide* to turn her lamp back on and get the journal out of her bag, but somehow the light was on and she was propped against her pillows, looking again at the drawing of the bridge.

She flipped through the pages of the journal, not really expecting to see anything new. The pages of numbers seemed to repeat themselves in front of her aching eyes. But then, she flipped past a flash of color and stopped to go back.

It was another drawing, in full color, and this one made something tingle from her neck to her toes.

She'd seen the drawing before, was her first thought. Not this precise one, but one remarkably like it, and she knew exactly where.

She got up and went into her dressing room, to the tall chest of drawers at the very back, and pulled open the bottom drawer. There was a box inside, and she took it out.

The picture was in a frame right on top, a little faded from when it had hung in her room a long time ago. But it had been cycles since she'd taken it out, now.

She carried it back to the bed and set it down next to the journal.

It could have been the same baby in both pictures. They had the same tiny, crinkly, just-born hands. Their noses were exactly the same, even to the tiny crease at the bottom. They even wore almost the same dresses and bows, though one was yellow and one green.

But it wasn't the same baby. This wasn't a picture of her. She wasn't sure how she knew. The different eye colors could be explained—newborns didn't always keep their eye color, she'd heard. And perhaps her mother had simply forgotten to draw the small, star-shaped birthmark on her right ankle in the other picture.

There were ways to explain the differences, but she knew none of them were right. This wasn't a picture of her. *Why would her mother draw a picture of a different baby girl? Who was she?*

"You're awake," Sabelina said when she entered the room and found Ella sitting on her bed with the journal in her lap.

Ella shrugged. She hadn't slept, not really. After putting away the picture sometime in the middle of the night, she had dozed off for a while. She'd been poring over the journal again for a couple of hours now, still unable to make anything new appear. This morning, she couldn't even find the drawing of the baby again. Or the old man. Part of her was afraid she'd imagined all of it.

For the last hour or so, she'd been developing a headache. Now the pain was raging and she couldn't make the pages display anything at all.

Sabelina sat down on the bed facing her. "I'm sorry."

"Are you?"

"I am. I didn't mean for you to find out this way."

Fire blazed in Ella's chest. "That's all you're sorry about? That I found out this way?"

"No, Ella. That's not the only thing I'm sorry about."

"Maybe you're just sorry I found out at all."

Sabelina sighed. "Your anger is fair and justified. But you're wrong in your assumptions. It wasn't something I wished to keep from you. And I wouldn't have, if I'd felt there was any other choice."

"I figured out about the tea, you know."

Immediately, Sabelina's eyes went wide and her face turned an ashy gray.

"I knew it," Ella said. She picked up the still-full mug from the table and thrust it toward her. Drops splattered everywhere as Sabelina fumbled to grasp it.

Once she had hold of the cup, Sabelina's expression turned serious and she stared at Ella. "What do you think the tea is?"

"It's how you've been concealing my magic and my eyes. There's something in the tea that takes it away."

"You've been drinking the tea the past several nights, and yet, your eyes changed and you healed that wound on your forehead."

"I…" Ella's mouth opened and closed several times, but she couldn't figure out what she meant to say. The headache was growing worse. She suppressed the urge to close her eyes and rub her temples.

"There's nothing in this tea that suppresses your magic, Ellarowan. It does help you sleep—it doesn't look like you slept at all last night without it. I'm not trying to poison you."

"Then why haven't I been able to perform magic before now?"

Sabelina's eyebrows knitted together. "When's the last time you had a cut that took more than a day to heal?"

All Ella could do was gape. She couldn't think at all. The massive showdown she'd been planning to have with Sabelina refused to materialize. Maybe it was the headache, but right now, she didn't care what was true and what wasn't. She just wanted to stop thinking about it.

"I have hidden some of your talents, it's true. But not through tea. I wish you would have come to me last night if you believed the tea wasn't safe. You might have slept. Now it's too late. The seamstress will be here in a few minutes for your final fitting and there will be no time for much of the day. I'll bring you more tea with breakfast."

"And something for a headache too, please?"

"Yes, of course." Sabelina stood and then bent to kiss her on the forehead. Ella thought she lingered just a little longer than usual, running her cool hands down the sides of Ella's face. But it felt nice, and at the moment her head hurt too badly to think about much else.

Sabelina was right; it was a busy day. Although the headache remedy helped, Ella was still uncomfortable and exhausted. By the time Shea turned up for her fitting three hours in, Ella was almost glad she was getting married tomorrow. It meant never having to prepare for a wedding like this again. She and Shea had to scramble just to find thirty seconds to talk without being overheard before Shea had to leave again.

It was late afternoon before she was finally set free from the endless dressing and undressing, pinning and practicing of hairstyles. "I think however you decide to do it tomorrow will be fine," she'd said numerous times, always to no avail.

Of course, she wasn't actually free. Wearing yet another "formal dress" she was ushered to a dining room full of people. Her father was there, of course, talking to Amalric Sandrez. Ella didn't know if there really were tight lines at her father's eyes while he spoke, or if she was imagining it after the conversation she'd overheard about the great master last night.

She looked around and noticed that her brother was standing conspicuously far from Allora, even though they kept surreptitiously looking at each other.

"I don't know about you, but I've had about enough of these events." She whirled around at the sound of the familiar voice in her ear.

"There's another awfully big one tomorrow, last I checked," she said.

"So I've heard," Cayloken said, turning to face her. "I was wondering if you would sit by me at dinner—for practice, you know? …Are you all right?"

She nodded. "I'm fine. I don't want to be here, but I'm fine." Although, now that Cayloken was standing with her, she was surprised to discover that she wasn't quite as miserable.

The hair on her arms prickled, making her feel like someone was watching her. She looked around, her eyes finally meeting her father's. He smiled and nodded, approving, before turning back to his conversation.

"Now that makes you want to knock me over the head with the nearest chair and run away as fast as you can, doesn't it?"

She laughed, but shook her head. "Two days ago it would have, but right now all I want to do is be somewhere we can have a private conversation." Her cheeks burned as she realized what she'd just shared, and she suddenly wanted to take it back. "I'm going to get a drink."

Before she could walk away, Cayloken took her hand and gently pulled her back. Somehow, she felt the warmth of his skin in the middle of her stomach. "That's what I want, too," he said quietly. "If I could get us out of here after dinner, do you know where we might find…?"

She nodded, looking around furtively. There was nothing private about their conversation. Maybe it was to be expected that guests at a wedding celebration would be interested in the couple getting married. Although Allora Sandrez would be jealous at the amount of attention they were getting from Tallen. Her father had just glanced at them again, too. It occurred to her that the more she followed her father's wishes, the more freedom she was likely to get. She moved closer to Cayloken, stretching up on her toes to whisper in his ear. "Later."

Maybe he knew what she was doing. Perhaps he was simply astute enough to know that it would help their cause. Maybe… Whatever the reason, before she could pull away, Cayloken pressed his lips to her cheek, giving her a quick, gentle kiss.

And then he had to hold her steady so she didn't topple over.

TWENTY-THREE
THE STABLES

"SO, WHERE ARE WE going?" Cayloken asked, when they'd finally managed to escape the interminable dinner and had reached the privacy of the drive yard outside the carriage house.

"Shea said to come and meet her at The Dozy as soon as we could."

"She'd take him there?"

Ella shrugged. "I don't know where is safer at this point."

"All right. Your father gave us a horse and carriage to use while we're here. I'll go and get him harnessed."

"You know how to do that?" As soon as the words were out of her mouth, she realized how pathetic it sounded. Clearly, being the child of a gatekeeper hadn't meant the same thing in Cayloken's house as it had in hers.

Even now, there was no reason Cayloken *had* to prepare the horse. It would take only a few minutes to find a stable hand to ask. And Bastian would even drive them if either of them had wanted to involve anyone else in their plans for the evening.

His smile was kind and understanding, as if she hadn't just said something stupid. "Come, I'll show you."

The pungent animal scent hit Ella as soon as they entered the stables, instantly transporting her to another time. She'd spent many hours here as a small child, finding comfort in the noises and smells.

It had been many cycles since she'd entered, though, and now she couldn't remember why. "There was a reason, though," she said.

"I'm sorry?" Cayloken paused in front of the row of light controls and turned to face her. "A reason for what?"

"Did I say that aloud?"

He nodded.

"A reason I haven't come in here in a very long time. But I don't know what it is." She squinted at the sudden brightness as Cayloken flicked on the last set of lights.

"Perhaps it's because, when you want to ride, your horse just appears in the yard, fully tacked and ready?"

She rolled her eyes at him. "I don't even have a horse of my own. I don't ride. 'It's not proper,' my father says, when I have a carriage and driver at my disposal nearly anytime. Probably he'd be appalled if he knew I rode my bicycle all the way to The Dozy the other day."

"Ah," Cayloken said, his eyes lighting up. "Now there's something you know how to do that I don't. I never learned to ride one of those contraptions."

"That is *not* the only thing."

"I didn't mean to imply that it was. I was trying to tell you I'm impressed. To give you a compliment."

Her cheeks warmed. "Thank you."

"You're welcome. Now, let's get this horse." He walked to the door of one of the stalls. As soon as he stretched out, a sleek bay head appeared, shoving its nose into Cayloken's hand. "Hello again, Bex."

Ella stopped short a few feet away from them. "One of our horses is named Bex?"

"Well, no." Cayloken shrugged. "His name is something like Benson McPompus Fancy Horse Name the Seventh. Bex is just easier."

She laughed so loudly three horses nickered, and Bex reared up for a second when Ella snorted, but she couldn't help it.

"Look at that, you've offended poor Bex," Cayloken chided, but he was laughing, too.

"I'm sorry, Bex." She walked over to him and stretched out a tentative hand.

Everything went still.

The horse's chocolate eyes looked straight into hers, and for a moment she felt like he could see her soul. She shivered. Bex stretched out his neck until she was underneath him, and he laid his head on her shoulder, nuzzling against her ear. She didn't think about what to do next; her arms just went around Bex's neck on their own, hugging him tightly.

The whole world felt somehow different when she finally stepped back.

In the next stall, there was a snuffling noise, and she looked over to see that horse hanging its head out, too, sizing her up.

"I think I might know why nobody thinks it's a good idea for you to spend time in the stables," Cayloken said. "You might have figured some things out a bit sooner."

"And we all know that the worst possible outcome of any situation is me learning the smallest kernel of truth about myself."

He didn't say anything as he began harnessing the horse.

"And don't tell me there's probably a good reason, and I've been better off not knowing and people are just trying to protect me."

"It sounds like you're doing a good enough job of that yourself."

She watched him work for a minute, his sure, steady fingers flying over buckles and straps. He'd met Bex only three days ago, and yet the horse stood patiently, allowing him to do the work, sometimes even moving his head helpfully while he made soft snuffling noises. Cayloken was even hard for horses to hate.

There was more than one way to be magic.

"What if I'm the one who doesn't want to know the secrets about myself?" She said it so quietly, she almost couldn't hear her own voice, and a bit part of her hoped he didn't hear her.

But he did. His hand fell away from the buckle he'd been fastening and he turned to face her. "What if?"

"Maybe it's all my fault that I didn't know I was a keeper, or that I was putting people in danger, or that I can't read all of my mother's journal."

He ran his fingers through the thick knot of curls at his temple. "What if it was your fault? Does it matter?"

Her mouth fell open. "How could it not matter?"

"Because none of it has anything to do with now. You know you're a keeper *now*. You can work to keep people safe *now*. If you're the one choosing not to be able to read the journal, then you can fix it. Whatever you did before is over. You can choose something different now that you know."

"I did see something else in the journal last night." She hadn't been planning on telling him this. Even though he knew the rest of her secrets, this one had felt different, private. But maybe she could learn to unravel secrets instead of hiding in them.

His full attention was still on her, as if he had all the time in existence to wait for her to speak.

So she told him about the baby. She told him how she didn't understand why, but the picture made her want to cry, and want to rip it out and throw it away, and want to put it next to her bed to look at it every night forever, all at the same time. How she both desperately wanted to know who the baby was, and yet never wanted to find out at all.

And when she finished, there were tears in the corners of her eyes, but for once she didn't feel weak or sick at the emotion. And it might have been because he placed his hand on her arm and nodded like he understood her completely.

But there were more pressing matters tonight than one drawing of a baby, so as soon as the horse was ready, Cayloken led him out into the drive yard.

They hadn't even made it all the way to the carriage when the crunching of quick footsteps on the path made them freeze.

It was that waiting feeling again. Of wondering if something terrible was about to happen. Ella would never be used to it enough to stop hating it.

After only a few seconds, Padraic Stone appeared at the entrance of the drive yard. He rushed over to them. "Oh good, you're still here. I was worried you'd be long gone by now."

Ella frowned, trying to make sense of what he was saying, mostly wondering how he'd known where to find them.

"What's wrong, Father?" Cayloken asked.

"Ellarowan received a message at the house. Her caretaker intercepted it. She said she didn't know how to find you and asked if I did." Padraic held out a folded piece of paper.

Ella looked at it as if it was something that might bite her. Why would Sabelina give *her* message to Cayloken's father?

Of course, it was true that Sabelina wouldn't know where to look for Ella and Cayloken. But why Padraic? And how did *he* know where to find them? "Did you read it?"

"No, but Sabelina said it was urgent and was worried about finding you before you went somewhere."

Ella unfolded the paper.

Don't come.
-S

There were several lines of seemingly random letters splayed across the bottom of the message, but these weren't important now. Particularly not in front of Padraic Stone. She passed the message to Cayloken.

He took it, scanned it, and nodded once. As he handed the paper back to her, he cleared his throat. "It looks as though we're staying in tonight, Father."

"What about the—? Is everything all right? Is there something I can do?"

Cayloken's eyes darted furtively toward Ellarowan, even as heat rushed through her. "You told them?" she demanded.

There was no point in him answering. Every ounce of her filled with white-hot rage, most of it directed at herself. There was no reason she should have trusted him; she'd met him three days ago for the maker's sake! *What had she been thinking?* The string of words that flew through her brain would have made a ferryman blush. She was so angry and so hot she couldn't see straight.

Too angry. Too hot. She really couldn't see straight. Shapes blurred and the night grew too dark, even under the lamp.

No! She wasn't going to do that. Not this time. She wasn't going to lose it, wasn't going to get so upset she passed out.

Ella didn't know how she'd made it to the dark area back behind the stables. She didn't remember running back here, but she must have, since the back of her blouse was wet and sticky with sweat.

She was proud of herself for remaining conscious. Or, at least she thought she had. Everything was a little foggy now, but she was upright. Sitting down against the wall of the building, she opened her bag and dug for her water jug. Her hand landed on something soft and crinkly. Cloth, with something inside it. She pulled it out of the bag.

It was a little cloth sachet. Frowning, she held it up to her nose and was immediately assaulted by the rich, sweet smell of baymallow.

Her tea. *What was that doing in here?* Sabelina must have packed it for her and slipped it into her bag. *But when? And why?* She wasn't so sure she cared why. Right now, trying to recover her composure, she only wished she had some boiling water to put with it. Still, just breathing in the scent made her calmer.

For a second.

Someone was coming. She could hear quick, light footsteps through the gravel, getting closer and closer.

She hadn't decided whether to try to run again or just to sit there and not care when Kydwyn Stone came around the corner.

Of course. He'd told both of his parents everything.

Ella wanted to get angry. To shout, maybe, or to get up and go deep into the woods where nobody would be able to find her.

But she didn't. It might have been her training, or simply the fact that she was already exhausted and not feeling well, but once Kydwyn was a few feet away, Ella stood up. "Hello."

Kydwyn didn't come any closer. "Are you all right, Ellarowan?"

Were they born with it? This natural ability to prevent people from hating them? Kydwyn's voice was so warm and unassuming that Ella wanted to crawl inside of it and sleep for days.

It was definitely the exhaustion speaking. "Did Cayloken send you?"

"He begged me not to." Kydwyn leaned up against the back of the building, matching Ella's posture, but we all wanted to make sure you were all right, too. I thought about just sneaking by and not disturbing you if I found you, but I didn't think that would be fair."

"Fair doesn't seem to be a concern for anyone right now."

"I know it doesn't. None of this is fair to you at all."

"Is he even sorry?"

Kydwyn cleared her throat and leaned her head back against the building, looking up at the night sky. The moon was full and bright. "What you asked of him wasn't fair, either."

"Asking my betrothed to keep my secrets wasn't *fair*?"

"The secrets don't only affect you, Ellarowan. The two of you are to be married tomorrow. Would it be fair of him to ask you to keep information about himself from Shea?"

If Kydwyn had asked the question about her father, she would have been able to defend herself. But this arrow struck its mark. Ella closed her eyes against the sudden damp warmth in the corners of them. *Was this what it would have been like, having a mother?* "Cayloken has a very different relationship with you than I do with my father."

"I know."

Ella nodded and ran her hand over her eyes to make sure there was nothing leaking before she opened them. The whole world was spinning; even the moon wouldn't stay where it belonged in the sky. "How much did he tell you?"

Kydwyn turned to her, her lips pressed together, considering. "I don't know. If there's something he didn't tell me, I don't know about it." She smiled.

It worked. Ella smiled back, though she still didn't know what to think or how to feel. For now, she was quite focused on remaining upright.

"Would you like to come back to the guest house with me and we can talk about it?"

This she knew she didn't want. Whatever Cayloken had told them was bad enough. She wasn't going to trust them with everything else, too. "I really just want to get back to my bed and sleep," she said. "I need to make some tea." She took a step forward, but as soon as the wall was no longer supporting her, she crumbled.

TWENTY-FOUR
THE LAST NIGHT

LATER, ELLA WOULD TELL people that she didn't remember getting from the back of the stables to the guesthouse, but it wasn't true. She remembered every second of feeling Kydwyn's cool hands on her forehead, of the shouting and then the running. And she definitely remembered Cayloken scooping her into his arms and carrying her while she fought between the urge to insist on walking herself and the desire for him to think she was too out of it to remember.

She'd also been terrified that if she *had* tried to walk, she'd have gone face-first into the gravel again.

She'd always hated her tendency to get sick at the worst possible moment. But she'd *never* been this mortified by it. She was almost grateful that her father had never insisted she travel with him. Doing something like this in front of strangers was quite possibly the most embarrassed she'd ever been. She wanted to curl into a ball and disappear. *Why couldn't that be her magical skill?*

Somehow, after a few minutes, there was a steaming mug of tea in her hands, and just breathing it in made the world stop spinning. A few sips cleared her head. And then, she stared down at the mug, the taste of baymallow suddenly bitter in her mouth. "Where did you get this?"

"My mother made it. She said it would help you feel better."

For the first time, Ella realized she and Cayloken were alone in the parlor again.

"Where did she *get* it?" Ella looked around desperately for her bag, only to realize it was sitting right next to her, tied shut.

"She made it, Ella. She has every kind of herb and concoction you can think of. Why? Is there something wrong with it? I can ask her to make you something else."

"No." She shook her head and took a long drink, feeling her strength returning with every swallow. "It's just… This is the tea my caretaker has made for me every night before bed since I was…"

"Since you were only a cycle old," Kydwyn's voice finished. Ella looked up to see her standing in the doorway.

A shiver started at the top of Ella's head and ran all the way down to her toes. "How could you know that?"

Kydwyn came into the room, though, again, she didn't get too close. She sat down on a sofa across the table from Ella.

Cayloken, still standing, looked back and forth between the two of them as if he'd suddenly found himself in a panther's lair. "How *could* you know that, Mother?"

"It was shortly after your first birthday, Ellarowan, when your mother contacted me and asked for my help."

Ella was suddenly torn between continuing to drink the tea and throwing it across the room. But she needed it, could feel that she needed it. So she took another sip. "You knew my mother?"

"We were both the wives of guildmasters, so yes, we'd met a few times. Back in those days, things weren't so tense between our guildhavens. Your mother had…*heard* things about me. About my healing skills in particular."

Despite the hot tea and the warm night, Ella was cold. "Why did she need a healer?"

"You were sick. Quite sick, in fact."

"With what?"

Kydwyn raised one shoulder. "The same condition that afflicts you now. The tea has kept it in check more than we imagined it would, or perhaps your condition isn't as bad as we feared it would be when you first exhibited symptoms."

Ella didn't understand. She sometimes had spells, but only when she was upset, only when… She wasn't *sick*. There wasn't something *wrong* with her. *Was there?* "But what *is* it?"

"I don't know, Ellarowan. For many, many cycles now we've watched the children born of two keepers develop similar symptoms, if they ever survived birth at all. It's only in more recent history that there have been babies born of a keeper and an omian with the same…difficulties. You were one of the first I knew of. Your mother would never have suspected this was what happened with you if…"

"If *what?*"

Kydwyn closed her eyes and looked down at the floor. Ella thought maybe there was a tear dripping down her cheek.

The shiver returned, and she had trouble holding her cup steady. "If *what?*"

"I don't know if anyone has ever told you this," Kydwyn said quietly. "I have a feeling nobody has, and I'm not sure I know how to be the one to tell the story."

Fear had settled like a large rock in her stomach. Even with the tea, it was hard to take a deep breath around it. Something wriggled against her leg, nearly making her spill the tea before she looked down and saw the small, gray, ball of fluff. She rested her hand in the iber's fur and somehow found the strength to speak. "It's about the baby, isn't it?"

She didn't know *how* she knew that, and part of her hoped she was wrong.

But Kydwyn nodded.

Ella set her tea down on the table so she could open her bag and pull out the journal. This time, the picture appeared instantly when she turned to the page, as if it had always been there and never disappeared. She held it out so Kydwyn could see. "Who was she?"

Cayloken had been standing and silently watching the two of them; now he sat down on the other side of Fluffy, careful to give Ella space. She was unexpectedly comforted by this.

"May I?" Kydwyn asked, reaching for the book.

The drawing remained bright and intact, even as she handed the journal across the table to Kydwyn, who stared at the image in sad, reverent awe. "Your mother was a very talented artist."

Ella nodded. "Who was she?" she repeated.

"She was the first child born to your parents. Several cycles before Tallen was born, but I don't remember exactly. Onnalia was her name, though she didn't live long enough to have a formal Announcement." Kydwyn passed the journal back across the table.

Ella stroked the image gently, running her finger across the forehead so like her own. "She had the same illness I have?"

"Nobody suspected an illness then. Certainly nothing like keeper-sickness. Even your parents, desperately grieving, believed it was just one of those things that happens sometimes. Some babies are simply too precious for this world. Later, Tallen was born, and he was perfectly healthy."

"But I wasn't."

"You were, when you were born. Even in Silver Island, I heard rumors of your brightness, your first words at eleven moons, walking by thirteen." Kydwyn chuckled quietly. "I might have heard some of those details later, from your mother, when she had me come."

Cayloken rose suddenly from the couch, making Fluffy grumble as the cushions moved, but Ella couldn't concentrate on what he was doing; her eyes remained locked on Kydwyn.

"You were beautiful and brilliant when I met you, of course. But you were very ill. When I arrived from Silver Island, you had just spent the better part of two days asleep, unable to be roused longer than a few minutes to nurse."

"How did you know it was the same thing?"

"I didn't. At the time, I hadn't even seen a child born with keeper-sickness, which is still the only name I have for it. Your mother didn't want anyone to know, which was the main reason she contacted me. I'm a gifted healer, it's true, but nobody knew how to deal with this. I didn't even think I'd be able to help you. In fact, I was convinced I'd just left my own child at home so I could come here and watch another woman's baby die."

Ella had been vaguely aware of noise and movement in the room, more than could have been caused by Cayloken moving around, but it wasn't until now, when she had to look somewhere, *anywhere* other than at Kydwyn's crumpled face, that she saw there were other people here.

Padraic Stone stood a few feet away from his wife, surrounded by Cayloken, Owen, and Shea.

Nobody said a word.

Ella thought that maybe it was supposed to matter that there were other people listening in on the conversation, that she should be bothered, or want to take this somewhere more private, but it didn't matter, and she didn't want to stop.

"But obviously, I didn't die."

"A fact for which I still thank the maker every day. I didn't know what to do; I didn't even know what was wrong. All I could think to try was the remedies I knew for the symptoms you were having. Treat the lethargy, treat the fevers that came and went. When you woke screaming and holding your head, I mixed remedies for headache. You couldn't keep much down aside from a little liquid, so I brewed herbs into teas. I still don't know *why* this tea works."

Ella picked up her mug and took a long sip. The liquid inside was no longer hot, but it still brought her a little of the comfort she needed.

Shea broke from the stunned little circle across the room and came over to her, shoving Fluffy to the side so she could sit touching Ella.

The iber sneezed indignantly and then walked across Shea's lap to sit on Ella.

She didn't want to say the words that were sitting heavy on her tongue, but she knew that if she didn't, they would stay there until she choked on them. "So, my mother didn't just leave her children, she left a *sick* child?"

"She didn't *leave* you, Ellarowan. Not intentionally. She died. She loved you, and she wanted to be with you. And the time she left on purpose, she *did* return to you."

"The time she left on purpose? There was a different time?" Nothing was making sense.

"She was gone for around ten moons when you were still only a cycle old. But not because she wanted to leave you. She was searching for someone she thought could help."

"How? Who?"

"There was a story. You could call it a legend, maybe. Or perhaps just a rumor. Or maybe there was more to it, among the keepers. I know a number of keepers who truly believe, as your mother did, that there was a man, an ancient keeper, from back in the time when keepers lived even longer than they do now. And he was said to have once cured the sickness that was afflicting the keepers' children."

Ella frowned.

"You must understand. You were still sick. The tea kept your symptoms at bay, most of the time, but you had to be kept calm, kept from ever getting too upset. This is a very tall order for a young toddler. Your mother still believed that the illness would take you from her. And she was also worried that you wouldn't be the last child born with this. And she believed that this man still existed, that she could find him, and learn his secret, and save you."

"Was he a *gadab*? Is that why she went through the gate to the other world?"

Kydwyn's eyes went very wide. "No. He was from our world. If he ever existed at all, I mean. They're not my stories;

I don't even know if I'm telling this the right way. All I know is that she returned. I don't even know if she found him. Maybe she did. You continued to live and grow. My services weren't needed, and things were growing more difficult between our guildhavens in the political realm. But I was shocked and heartbroken when I learned of her death."

It was like all the air had gone out of the room, and Ella didn't quite know why. Her mother had been gone since she was a very young child. She was used to it. She barely even remembered her. But somehow this felt like losing her all over again.

And she didn't want to talk about this anymore.

She took an enormous gulp of her tea and then shoved Fluffy off her lap so she could stand up.

After a few deep breaths, she turned to Shea. "So, what happened? How are you here?"

Shea's eyebrows came together in a sharp point. "I thought you got my message, and you sent help." She nodded at Padraic.

"I got your message, at least the first part of it. I wasn't exactly in the right state to decode the rest." And she wouldn't have been likely to send Padraic to them if she had. But they were here now. All she could do was move forward. "What happened? Why did you need help?"

Shea nodded. "After we left the forest, The Dozy was the only place I could think to go. I didn't want to take him to my house. My parents can handle a lot of things, but walking through the front door with a gadab could have led to a lot more than we're prepared to deal with on top of everything else."

Cayloken chuckled.

Ella wished that she were capable of finding anything humorous right then. Even a brief moment of levity would have drained some of the darkness that seemed to surround her.

"So, I took him to Ollie."

"You didn't *tell* her that he was a gadab, did you?"

Ella wasn't sure how it had happened, but Cayloken and Owen were now sitting in chairs, sipping at drinks. Cayloken's parents had disappeared. She wasn't sure if this made her grateful or anxious. But then, she probably couldn't trust any of her emotions tonight.

"I wasn't planning on telling her, but she took one look at him, and she knew."

If there hadn't been a table directly behind her, Ella would have simply sat down hard on the floor. She rested her forehead on her fingertips. "Ollie can tell by looking that someone is a gadab?"

"Ollie wasn't the problem, Ella. She acted like it was completely normal for me to come sneaking in the back door of The Dozy with a gadab. She waved her hand at his face and made his eyes look normal, and then she fed us."

"Wait—she changed Owen's eyes?"

Owen nodded, and Ella noticed for the first time that his eyes did look normal—for their world, anyway. He blinked at her with bright purple star-shaped pupils. It was a little terrifying. "I hope that's temporary."

"I didn't ask." Shea grimaced.

"So she *is* a keeper then," Cayloken said.

Ella blew out a breath. "So, if Ollie was fine with everything, what was the problem? Why did you tell me not to come? Why are you here?"

"After we ate, I took Owen into the main room to teach him how to play rex. He actually beat me at the second game."

"We have a similar game in my world," he said.

It was Cayloken who noticed the tension on her face. "It wasn't a game of rex that made you send that message. What happened?"

"People came in to The Dozy. People I'd never seen there before. Tallen was one of them, Ella. And…the great master's daughter."

"Allora Sandrez?"

"Yes. I'm almost positive that's who it was. And it wasn't just them. There were several other people with them. Tallen spotted me and Owen right away, and with the look he was giving us… We got back to the kitchen as fast as we could without drawing any attention, and I sent you that message. I didn't want *you* showing up there."

"What is he doing? Tallen has never been to The Dozy before! I didn't even think he knew where it was."

"And to bring all those strangers? It was weird, Ella. And, this is unrelated, but to make things worse…Loric showed up there tonight, too."

Ella swallowed. "Did he ask about me?"

"I don't know. I was a little busy hiding out in the kitchen with Owen."

Right. It was a stupid question, and it didn't matter anyway. Even if she hadn't made her decision, there was no way she could ever be with Loric. There were too many other things to be concerned about now.

Cayloken slid off the couch and onto the table Ella was sitting on. He didn't get too close—not close enough to touch—but close enough that she could hear his low, quiet words. "It's the last night, Ella. His last possible chance. Of course he was there for you. Of course he would show up and make sure, take that risk. You're worth that, you know?"

She buried her face in her hands and scoffed. "No, I'm not. I'm a keeper in a place where it's illegal to be one. And there's something wrong with me. I can't even get upset without collapsing into a useless heap. My own father doesn't seem to know anything about me except that I'm fragile, and I'm probably responsible for my mother's death."

The room got very quiet. For a long moment, the only sound was a tiny scratching along the floor that ended when Fluffy settled himself on Ella's feet.

"Stupid iber," she muttered. But the urge to shove him across the room with her foot dissipated as soon as it came.

She looked at Cayloken. "I don't know what you're even thinking, still sitting there. For what possible reason do you want to marry me tomorrow? Don't tell me it's to your political advantage. This is way more than you signed up for. Than *anyone* would ever sign up for."

"Ella…"

"What, Cayloken? Do you want to spend the rest of your life running to brew up tea because I got angry over something stupid? I'm broken. I'm sure if you go to the council and tell them the real situation here, they will find you a much more suitable match."

She wanted to stand up and stomp across the room, but Fluffy was still on her feet, and the urge to not disturb him was just enough stronger to keep her sitting there.

After several more minutes of silence, Cayloken chuckled.

Ella looked up, startled. "You think this is funny?"

"No. Well…okay, I do think it's kind of funny that you think I'm just going to disappear so easily. Our wedding is in fifteen hours or something equally outrageous. I'm not going to run to the council and tell them some ridiculous reason I can't marry a perfectly good match. You can't possibly believe I would rather spend my time dealing with someone like Allora Sandrez than brewing tea. That's absurd."

Her mouth fell open. "But I'm…"

"Not perfect? Nobody is. But you're not whatever terrible thing you've dreamed up, either. You didn't die as a baby. You're alive. You're here. And I doubt it's just because of the tea. I can just try to avoid upsetting you, you know. Considering what I've watched you survive over the past three days, I can't imagine it's going to be that difficult. Besides, I've always wanted a pet dragon. You think I'm going to pass up the chance to marry a girl who could tame one?"

Now she was laughing, too. She looked around to see how badly she'd terrified Shea and Owen, but was surprised to discover that she and Cayloken were alone.

"Oh, you ran them off a few minutes ago," he said. "They closed the door and everything. Might have even locked us in until they know you're not actually planning on summoning any dragons tonight."

She raised an eyebrow. "I don't think I'm quite there, yet."

"I don't know. You did just make it through a rather intense situation without ending face-first on the floor."

"I have a lot of tea in me."

"You also have some pretty serious healing magic. Like I said, I don't think it's just the tea."

"So, my mother might have died searching for no reason."

He took her hand in his. "I don't know what happened to your mother, Ellarowan. Maybe she found what she was looking for."

"Does it matter now? Then she died."

"You don't know that. And my mother doesn't, either. I told my parents what I thought they needed to know so they could help us, so they could keep you and Owen safe. But my mother doesn't know about the journal or that picture. She doesn't know for sure that your mother is dead. Maybe she is still alive somewhere. We can find out."

"How?"

He shrugged. "All I know is we will. I just want you to know that getting married doesn't mean giving that up. I promise I'll help you."

TWENTY-FIVE

MORNING

ELLA WOKE WITH THE first hint of sunlight, probably because the one crack in the window shades happened to cast the beam of light diagonally across her face. For a second, she couldn't see anything, and she nearly fell off the couch in her effort to sit up, having forgotten she was sleeping somewhere other than her bed.

Despite the momentary grogginess from waking, though, her memories were clear. She was in the parlor of the guest house. After a long discussion about Tallen and the people who'd shown up at The Dozy last night, they'd all decided it was best if she and Shea and Owen stayed here.

Shea had crept back into the main house to slip a note underneath Sabelina's door so there wouldn't be a panic this morning. Tallen still hadn't returned late into the night.

"Good morning," said a quiet voice. Owen was sitting on one of the chairs facing the window, a book open in his lap.

"Good morning." She looked around. On the table in front of her was a steaming mug of her tea. The scent filled the room.

"Cayloken brought that for you," Owen said. "But he didn't want to wake you. He said things would get busy and challenging enough today without needing to start extra early."

"I only usually drink this at night," she said, picking up the cup.

"You're getting married today, to someone you didn't choose, and you've only had a few days to get used to the idea. I don't care how nice he is. If it were me, I'd want that tea in an IV."

"I don't know what that means."

He chuckled. "It's the little things that would give me away in a heartbeat, even with my eyes like this." They were still purple today, she noticed. "An IV is a little tube that delivers liquids straight into your veins." He pointed to his wrist.

She gawked at him. "Is that something people *do* in your world?"

He wasn't a person who laughed easily, but when he did, it was worth hearing. "Not for fun—usually, anyway. It's done for medical treatments."

"Like healing?"

"Yes. Although it looks a lot different in my world. That's what I do, actually. I don't think I've ever told you that. I'm not called a healer in my world, but that's what I am. Or close enough, anyway."

"You know how to cure people?"

"Mmm…I know how to cure some diseases, and how to fix most injuries. But people aren't things that need to be cured."

She frowned.

"I was born with a condition, too, Ella. It has a name and a complicated description in my world, but it basically means my brain works differently than most other people's. It took me a long time to learn that it didn't mean I was broken, or something that needs to be cured." He looked at her in a way that made her feel like he could see completely through her.

"Even if there is a cure for your illness, it doesn't mean that *you* are broken or unworthy of anything."

She closed her eyes and took a long drink of her tea before opening them again. "Thank you."

He blushed and looked down at his book.

"Owen… Do you think it's possible there's a cure to my illness in your world?"

He frowned. "I don't know. I don't know what causes it. My world is…very different. There are tests I could do there, but nothing I could promise."

"But someone might *go* there, hoping they could find a cure?"

He set down his book. "Your mother, you mean?"

She nodded.

"If someone did, it would be a very dangerous decision. And it wouldn't work out how they planned. When I say my world is different, I don't even know how to explain *how* different. But…someone who came there and started walking around asking people for cures would probably find themselves stuck there forever. For her sake, I hope she didn't."

Ella took another swallow of tea.

"If you're thinking about coming to my world, you need to reconsider. You would be in danger there, and your entire *world* would be in danger if people from my world discovered the gate. Unless you have very real reason to believe your mother is there, and you have a good idea how to find her, it wouldn't be worth it. Your entire *world* would be at risk."

"From what?"

He sighed. "I've told you there's no magic in my world. Or, at least I don't believe there is. We certainly have plenty of ancient stories that suggest otherwise. But even if there's no magic, there are lots of other dangerous and powerful forces. Weapons that could destroy your entire guildhaven in one go."

"Why would anyone want to hurt our world?"

"To take it for themselves. It's a beautiful world. They'd want your resources, your land. And not just that."

"What?" Ella was starting to think she was going to need a lot more tea.

"If the discrepancy between the gate opening times is anything like how it works in my sister's world, people live longer here than they do in my world. A lot longer."

All she could do was stare.

"In my world, people remain a certain age for a year—it's what you'd call a cycle, but I don't think they're the same length of time at all. In my world, a year is only about 365 days."

She took great gulps of the tea.

"That's what I thought. So, in your terms, I've only lived about as long as a two-cycle child. Does that sound right to you?"

"I wouldn't trust my ability to do math now, but…*really?*"

"Yes, really. And with my sister's world, it doesn't appear to be connected to the people, but to the world itself. So, a traveler, a gadab, from my world to yours, would live ten times longer just by coming through the gate. And vice versa."

"You mean, if I went to your world, my life would be shortened."

"Significantly. So, it's not a proposition to take lightly, traveling to my world. If there's any way to avoid it, you should."

"Well that adds a whole new layer to why you'd come here."

He shook his head. "It was stupid of me, Ella. And while I took every precaution imaginable on my side…if I've put your world at risk by coming here, I'm truly sorry. I never thought there might be a whole different world here. I just wanted to see my sister."

"I hope you do find her someday, Owen."

He smiled, grateful. "Me too. Although at this right now, I'm just hoping to get back through the gate to my own world tonight."

There was a small click, and Owen and Ella both looked up to see the parlor door slide open. "I hope I didn't wake you earlier," Cayloken said, when he saw Ella sitting up on the couch.

"No." She shook her head. "Thank you for the tea, though."

"You're welcome."

"Where is Shea?" she asked, frowning.

"She thought it would be better if she arrived in her usual fashion at the scheduled time. If anyone noticed you missing this morning, it's probably best if they thought we just…" His cheeks got so dark so quickly she didn't need him to finish the sentence.

"Well, we are getting married today," she said. "Probably better get used to people thinking even worse."

He swallowed and sat down on the table next to her cup. "I wanted to check with you about that," he said.

"What do you mean?" The rock was back in her stomach.

Across from them, Owen was suddenly deeply absorbed in his book.

"Well, last night I told you all of the reasons I'm not planning on going to the council and stopping this thing. But later, when I was lying in bed, I realized that I didn't give *you* much of a choice in that. It isn't too late for *you* to go to the council and tell them that we're sympathizers and that an alliance with Silver Island isn't in the best interest of Ravensguild."

She stared at him. "You think I'd put all those people in danger and start a war just to get out of marrying you?"

His hands were in his lap, and he couldn't keep them still. He kept knitting and unknitting his fingers, twisting them nervously together. For the first time since she'd met him, she felt compelled to reach over and touch him, wanted to close her fingers around his, to steady and calm them.

She didn't know how he would react, and the fear that he'd shove her away almost stopped her, but then there was something inside her stronger than the fear, and she reached over anyway.

His hands went immediately still. "It's not fair," he whispered.

"No," she agreed. "None of this is fair."

"I would have wanted more for you, Ellarowan. If we'd actually had time to get to know one another without all this mess, I think I would have liked to ask you myself."

She raised an eyebrow. "You just met me."

"No, Ellarowan. Some days are short, but others can fit a lifetime inside them. And I've known you for long enough to know you're a girl who'd face a panther to save a helpless creature. You could have run to your father when a gadab showed up, but you didn't. And you didn't betray me, either. Last night…at first I didn't understand why you'd get so upset that I told things to my parents, when I knew they were safe, but now I realize it's because you'd never break anyone's trust like that. And I'm sorry."

"You were right. If you hadn't told your parents, we'd never have gotten Shea and Owen back here safely. I could do a lot better at trusting people."

"You have a lot of reasons not to. Today is one of them, and I'm sorry I'm part of that. I would have liked to hear you say 'yes' because you wanted to, not because you were afraid of the consequences if you didn't."

She bit her lip and stared at their entwined fingers.

"Don't," he said. "Don't worry about what you're supposed to say to that. You don't need to say anything. I know it's too much. But I wanted to make sure you heard that from me before we do this, because it's true."

She didn't decide to kiss him. It just sort of happened. One minute she was watching the way her fingers fit perfectly between his, and the next their lips were together. It was gentle and sweet, and when she pulled back, his smile melted away the last traces of rock in her stomach.

"Well," he said. "We did need to practice before we tried it in public."

"Really? You're going to make me regret it before breakfast?" But she was laughing.

Even Owen was smiling as he turned the page in his book. Considering the dark pink of his cheeks, he'd been watching them at least a little.

"Speaking of breakfast," Cay said, "we should get you back up to the house before anyone comes looking for you."

Ella's palms were sweating before they were even off the porch of the guest house. This didn't improve when Cay reached over and took one of her hands in his as they walked, but he squeezed her hand tightly anyway.

"Don't think," he said. "Just don't think about it. Pretend it's a normal day with some boring formal ceremony you have to attend later."

"Except at the end of it, I'll be *married*. And tonight, I won't be going back—oh *vosh*. I just missed the last chance I'll ever have to sleep in my own bed, didn't I?" A whole new set of worries came swarming into her brain like hundreds of stinging bees.

Cay stopped walking in the middle of the path and pulled on her hand until she was facing him. "Ella, breathe. Just breathe." If she'd only been listening to his voice, she would have wondered how he could possibly be so calm. But the moisture she could feel on his palms betrayed him. After a few seconds, they both had to let go and wipe their hands on their pants. "Obviously, it's not just you," he said, giving her a nervous smile.

"I just…"

"I know. And, it's true. I don't know if you'll ever sleep in your bed in your father's house again. After everything that's happened, I don't know that you'll *want* to. But, Ella, nothing else has to change today, okay? We just met. Tonight, after everything, we can drink tea and play rex, and you can sleep wherever you're the most comfortable. Okay?"

She nodded.

"Just breathe. When you get to the house, you're going to eat, drink some tea, breathe some more, let people get you ready, keep your eyes under control, and have a boring ceremony. That's all."

"Are you trying to convince me, or yourself?" she asked.

He laughed, and the sound reverberated through her, easing some of the stinging thoughts. "Both, hopefully. Although I don't have to worry about my eyes."

"Sure, rub it in."

"Come on."

Their hands were back together again by the time they turned the last corner, and they were still together when Ella realized there was a large figure standing on the porch, watching them as they approached. *Her father.*

Her whole body went rigid, and she tried to pull her hand away, but Cay held tight to it until they were nearly to the steps, then he squeezed her hand gently before letting go. "Nothing has changed," he said under his breath. "Breathe. Eyes. Boring ceremony. Do you want me to go with you?"

She shook her head.

"I'll see you in a little while, then."

She didn't watch him walk away, but she could tell when he'd disappeared around the corner again, because her father's position shifted just a little as he watched her climb the steps.

"Good morning," he said.

"Good morning."

He nodded in the direction Cayloken had gone. "I appreciate that you've decided to be reasonable about this."

Breathe. Eyes. It doesn't matter.

But it did matter. Or at least it felt like it did, right then. And she did the exact opposite of anything she should have done. She didn't know what color her eyes were when she stared up at him, but she knew they weren't violet.

She waited for a reaction. Something. *Anything.* And for a second, she thought he was breathing just a little too fast, but when he spoke again, there was nothing in his voice to indicate he'd even noticed.

"Sabelina will be waiting for you upstairs," is all he said, perfectly, infuriatingly calm. "I've left a gift with her for you. You should go and start getting ready." He took a step forward and leaned toward her, and for a horrifying moment, she thought he was going to hit her. But he didn't. He kissed the top of her head, and then turned and went down the stairs.

She was going to be sick. She couldn't move because if she did, she was going to either vomit or fall flat on her face onto the porch. Probably both. Everything started to go black.

Something rubbed against her leg, making her jump. Colors replaced the black as she looked down at the creature climbing onto her foot.

"Fluffy! You can't be here."

But the iber didn't care. And, after a few minutes of trying to shoo him away and failing, Ella decided she didn't care, either. She scooped Fluffy into her arms and carried him up to her bedroom.

"Creatures, now?" Sabelina didn't sound surprised when Ella and Fluffy entered.

"You act as if I do odd things every day." Ella sat Fluffy on the bed, where he immediately commenced sniffing at the box sitting in the middle of the bed. Ella ignored this, determined to not acknowledge her father's gift at all.

"It's been an unusual week for everyone," Sabelina said.

There was a fresh tray of food sitting on the table under one of her windows. Not wanting a repeat of what had just happened on the porch, Ella went straight for the steaming mug. After a careful sip of the hot liquid, she turned to face her caretaker. "Why didn't you tell me I was sick?"

"What would it have changed? Your father didn't want you to have a childhood where your only memories were of your illness. He said it was bad enough that you had to be kept at home so much, and that he had to be away from you so much of the time. He wanted you to be as normal as you could. And you were. You've done so well, for so long, very few people even know."

"So long as I drink the tea."

"So long as the tea keeps working."

"Does he know it's because I'm a keeper?"

"I don't want to know the answer to that, Ella. It doesn't matter. All that matters is that you're safe, and that we get you through this wedding. Please tell me that nobody saw you with your eyes green like this."

"Just my father."

"All right." Sabelina looked at her for several seconds. "They're the right color again. It normally lasts for a day or two, but if you do something, I can't…"

There were a million questions Ella wanted to ask Sabelina, things she wanted to demand, things she was angry about. But right now, all she could see was the tears in the corners of her caretaker's eyes, and the lines of worry in Sabelina's forehead.

Whatever Sabelina had hidden from her, or might know, none of it mattered right now. Sabelina had always loved and cared for her, always been on her side. Maybe it was time, as Cayloken had said, to take a chance on trusting someone. She needed Sabelina's help to focus, breathe, and get through the day. Questions could come later.

She set down her tea and threw her arms around Sabelina's neck.

Sabelina's response was immediate. She wrapped her arms around Ella and pulled her close, bathing Ella in the sweet scent of her hiranthia lotion. "All I ever wanted was for you to be safe," she whispered. "To protect you when your mother couldn't."

Ella nodded against Sabelina's shoulder, and for now, it was enough.

TWENTY-SIX
A WEDDING

She really was beautiful.

Considering everything else that was going on, Cayloken thought this might be the wrong thing to have on his mind right now, but he couldn't help it. Besides, he was never going to have another wedding, he might as well appreciate the way his chosen looked on this day, even if he hadn't *chosen* her.

Her dress was the same glowing shade of violet as her eyes, a fact which both fascinated him and made every muscle in his body feel shaky and tight. Any slip in her control would be noticeable from a hundred feet away.

She looked calmer than he expected—calmer than he felt, too. Although waiting in this room might have been easier for him if his best friend was standing next to him and chattering lightly, the way Shea was with Ella.

But since Mari was both a girl and a keeper, he hadn't thought it was wise to bring her as an attendant at his wedding in Ravensguild. He didn't regret this decision, considering the danger he and Ellarowan were now in, but he did miss her.

It didn't matter. *Breathe. Move forward. Don't stare at the way her skirt moves when she walks—not where she can see you, at least.*

The head of a man he was probably supposed to recognize popped through the door. "I need the attendants, please."

There was only Shea, but she disappeared through the door like she'd simply been called to carry a drink to a customer at The Dozy.

It shouldn't have been hard to walk over to Ellarowan, but he felt like he was dragging heavy limbs through water as he took the few short steps toward her. "She's not going to give them the satisfaction, is she?" he asked, nodding toward the door.

"Do you *always* make jokes?"

"No. Sometimes I just make really awkward statements that fall flat and make people uncomfortable."

Her smile was small and nervous, but it was there. "Shea doesn't give *anyone* the satisfaction."

"That's why I like her, even if she's not so sure about me."

"She's warming up to you."

He wanted to ask Ellarowan if she, too, was "warming up" to him. There were a lot of questions he would have liked to ask her, actually. But his tongue felt too large for his mouth, and by the time he'd figured out how to move it, the door opened again.

Now all he could do was take her hand in his and lead her out onto the platform.

Her hand trembled in his as they stepped in front of the crowd. He knew she wasn't as used to this as he was; she'd told him at the rehearsal that she'd never even *been* to a wedding before, and yet here she was, standing in front of an oversized crowd, attempting to navigate her own.

"You can do this," Shea whispered as she took Ella's flowers when they reached the middle of the platform and stopped so that everyone could see them. Cayloken hoped so, but Ella's hand was growing cold and clammy in his, and he was desperate to get through this and get her down from there.

When the introductions were finally over, and he could face her instead of the crowd, the first place he looked was her eyes.

The outermost edges of her pupils were blue.

Vomiting on the stage would not be helpful. Neither would letting her know. It was only the edges right now; probably nobody else could tell. At least they weren't bright yellow.

His own hands were sweating now as he took her other hand.

The vows were traditional, so many ancient words he'd never understood. In his mind, marriage had nothing to do with endless journeys over unending seas, or discovering new lands. And the words that made sense to him didn't exactly apply to their situation. In his imagination, his wedding ceremony had been much more meaningful, but at least it didn't involve too much thinking.

And she was calming down, her eyes turning back to solid violet even as she held onto his hands for dear life.

Maybe that was all that mattered.

First my favored, then my chosen, today you become mine forever.

He didn't hear most of it, though the words came out of his mouth on cue. Ella repeated her lines dutifully. At least once, as she looked into his eyes on the word *chosen*, he almost believed her.

They turned together to cross the stage and walk through a giant arch of flowers—the "doorway to a new life as one," and he was allowing himself to be thankful that at least wedding ceremonies were short when he remembered.

He almost froze right in the middle of the archway. If Ella's elbow hadn't been locked so tightly with his, and she hadn't taken a step at just the right time, he might have interrupted the ceremony.

Ella pulled a little harder to keep him going, and he wondered if she'd forgotten, or if she didn't realize.

They'd walked through this part of the ceremony at the rehearsal, of course, but it had been brushed over. Best not to spend too much time dwelling on what "must" be done. For tradition's sake, of course.

Many of the weddings he'd been to no longer included this part. Couples found other ways to mark their connection. But, he'd never been to any other ceremonies that would result in the joining of two guilds, either.

He was being unfair, he knew. The churning in his stomach made it impossible not to be. He liked tradition. In different circumstances, he might have asked his chosen to include this.

Ella was following his advice better than he was. Breathe and move forward. She was moving forward with such confidence that Cayloken was now almost certain she didn't realize.

Another step closer and the shining, silver blade on the table came into view.

There it is. Ella's hand felt like a brick inside his and her entire body gave a single, violent shudder.

The pain meant nothing to him. The cuts would be small, simple and quick. And he knew already that Ella wasn't afraid of that, either. But they were both shaking so badly when they reached the table that he wasn't even sure he'd be able to *do* it.

And now, Ella's eyes blazed green.

He yanked her arm, turning her the rest of the way away from the crowd as he picked up the small knife.

"Cry," he whispered between clenched teeth.

Her eyes widened as if he'd just asked her to take flight. *Of course they did,* he realized. For Ella, the two tasks were probably equally difficult. She'd spent a lifetime fighting off tears as if they were dragons.

"You have to," he said, poising the blade over her middle finger—the center of both her hand and the concentration of lifeblood. According to tradition, anyway.

"You have to purify the blade," she said, nodding to the candle on the table.

She was stalling, but she was right.

Ella knew she was stalling. This was her worst nightmare. Whatever she'd learned about herself in the past days about having actually been ill her entire life, didn't matter. She'd never been weak in front of a crowd of people. She'd never *cried.*

The cuts would be small, though deep enough to leave a scar, since that was the point. Not something to look forward to, but certainly not enough to make her cry in front of five hundred people.

Or, at least, they were supposed to leave a scar.

Despite the audience, Ella and Cay were utterly alone at the very back of the platform. This part of the ceremony was meant to be the sealing of a private bond between them. Even Shea stood a good ten feet away, watching attentively, but too far to hear their quiet voices. The words were written on a card on the table, as a reminder, but nobody would hear them spoken.

And nobody really wanted to see the blood. It was the evidence they'd ask for later. The scabbed-over fingers tonight. The permanent little *x* marking each of them at the point their lives had joined together.

The evidence that was wholly unlikely to exist half an hour from now.

Which meant that Ella either needed to figure out how to *not* heal both of them, or else be so distraught over the whole thing that nobody dared ask. That *might* solve the problem for today, anyway.

Crying would give her an excuse to hide her eyes, too. Or at least make the black and gold powder decorating her eyelashes and eyelids run so badly over her face that nobody would notice what color her eyes were.

It might work. *If* she could make herself cry. But the chances of that seemed remote.

"Then make me," she whispered.

"I'm not a dragon. I can't breathe fire on you." As soon as the words were out of his mouth, he got a strange look on his face, like he'd just thought of something.

Keeping his grip on her hand, he held the tip of the blade over the candle, sliding it back and forth in the flame. Red and yellow reflected off the knife, bathing them both in flickering light. The blade could be purified in a quick pass through the fire, but Cayloken held it there much longer. He was stalling, too.

And then he held it in the flame for just a little too long, and Ella suddenly felt like all her muscles were made of jelly. There was a small porcelain bowl of water next to the candle, for cooling and wetting the knife, but it could only do so much.

The tip of the blade nearly glowed by itself when Cayloken finally pulled it from the flame. He held it over the bowl, and lowered it, but the blade fell just to the side of the bowl, touching the table instead of the water.

It didn't leave a burn mark on the purple cloth, but Ella's eyes were already filled with moisture when he held the tip over her finger again.

She squeezed her eyes shut, and willed the tears to come, though once the searing metal touched her fingertip, it didn't matter. The pain reached deep into her bones, and for several seconds it was only Cayloken's tight grip on her wrist that kept her upright.

Her face was soaked.

And her fingertip wasn't going to heal anytime soon.

Ella's whole body shook as she did what she had to do next, holding Cayloken's wrist with her good hand, and forcing herself to watch as he repeated the procedure on his own finger. Dancing flames on the blade, clink of metal on glass as the blade touched the side of the bowl instead of the bottom, smell of searing flesh.

Tears ran down Cayloken's face, too.

This hadn't been the plan, yet they worked together seamlessly. Mouthing nonsense at each other as they touched the tips of their burned fingers together, the pain shooting all the way up her arm again. There were supposed to be words about their blood mixing, but there were no words, and there was no blood. There was only searing pain and hands wrapped tight around wrists as they held each other up.

Cayloken somehow managed to dip the set of clean white cloths into the little bowl before they wrapped each other's wounds. Ella expected relief, but the damp cloth only stung.

"Are we all right?" Cayloken whispered near her ear.

She nodded, startling herself with the knowledge that yes, *they* were, this *we* of her and Cayloken that had existed for a time that could still be counted in minutes.

They were fine.

In one sense, anyway.

They had no choice but to hold their burned hands together, wincing as they touched, when they faced each other again at the front of the platform.

There were words spoken, but Ella didn't hear them, she just hoped Cay was listening while she let the tears flow freely down her face, closing her eyes against the crowd, even as she was certain her eyes were violet again. That was the one thing perfectly under her control.

When he turned her toward him and bent to give her the customary kiss, she buried her lips in his, letting their tears mingle together. Blood wasn't the only thing that could join two people.

TWENTY-SEVEN

THE GATE

"ALL I WANT TO know is that you're all right," Shea said, dabbing at Ella's face with a damp cloth in one of the side rooms. "Do not tell me what you did." This last part was directed at Cayloken, who, even after dinner, still looked a bit like he was going to vomit.

"We got married," Ella said. "That's all."

Hard as it had been, she was rather appreciating the genius of making her cry. People could think whatever they wanted so long as it gave her this excuse to be away from the crowd and attend to her face. It had worked so well after the ceremony that she'd accidentally-on-purpose allowed her fingertip to touch her steaming mug of tea at the end of dinner.

The tears weren't fake ones.

Maybe it hadn't mattered, anyway. If there was one wedding tradition she'd discovered she liked, it was that the newly married couple was not expected to linger at the party for long after dinner.

This was a good thing considering their next problem.

They had to escape the house before sunset and get Owen down to the gate.

"Yes, I'm sure that's *all* that happened," Shea said. "It would be enough, obviously, but…you both still have fingertips under those bandages, right?"

"I'm not that clumsy with a blade," Cayloken said, holding up his hand. "It hurts, but it's still there."

Considering how *much* her finger hurt, Ella was beginning to wonder if her healing powers worked on burns at all.

Cayloken sat down next to her on the padded bench. Afternoon sunlight poured through the window, which would ordinarily have made him warm and sleepy, but right now he only noticed the sun slipping a little lower in the sky. "You didn't answer Shea's question," he pointed out. "Are you all right?"

"Not even slightly. Are you?"

He shrugged. "I suppose it's a stupid question. Do you need anything else from out there? I need to go and make our formal farewell."

"Should I go?" she asked, standing up beside him.

His cheeks grew darker. "It's, uh, not expected of the bride."

"Why not?"

"This is the part where your attendants are supposed to take you to the bridal bedroom and prepare you to complete your wedding obligations." Shea had little regard for subtlety.

"Fortunately for you, the tradition of asking the attendants for proof seems to have faded."

Ella rolled her eyes. She knew that one of the guest houses had been prepared specifically for her and Cayloken, but none of this had been on her mind. Getting through the wedding itself and getting Owen safely home was all she'd thought about.

And that wasn't going to change now. She definitely wasn't going to begin thinking about what it meant to now be married to Cay. All the tea in the world wasn't enough for that right now.

Cayloken's hand was throbbing. He hadn't planned on his little stunt working out quite so well. He'd wanted to leave enough of a mark on each of them that nobody would ask questions, but now he wished Ella's healing powers would work just a bit better. Or at all. His finger felt like it was touching the flame of the candle right now.

He hoped Ella wasn't feeling quite as bad, but there wasn't anything he could do about it if she was. His mother would have some salve, if he asked, but he was afraid to do anything that might speed the healing too much.

The party was still in full swing, as it would be for most of the night. Marius Lockwood knew how to throw a wedding, that much was certain. It was hard to imagine that the servants had only had a week or so to make most of the arrangements. But he preferred believing that they had accomplished all this in a short time over the idea that they'd all been lying to Ella for several moons.

Speaking of Marius, he was standing only a few feet away from the door when Cayloken emerged, almost as if he'd been waiting.

Perhaps he had been, because now Marius was walking toward him.

"Do you and Ellarowan have everything you need?" Marius asked, as soon as he was close enough.

The question was so unexpected, so strange, that for a moment, all Cayloken could do was blink in confusion. *Did they have everything they needed? What did that even mean?* No, they didn't have "everything they needed." They didn't even have the freedom to make their own choices about who to marry. And they didn't have any guarantees about getting Owen safely home tonight, or about keeping Ella's abilities from being discovered.

Marius wasn't going to give them any of those things.

But they were fed, and they had a place to sleep tonight—a whole guest house of their own. So Cayloken allowed his eyes to meet Marius's and he said, "Yes, we do, thank you."

"It is I who should be thanking you." Marius's voice was too quiet to be overheard by anyone else, though his tone was entirely sincere. "You and your family have been gracious to my daughter, and I know she'll be well cared for. I hope the gifts I've had sent to your home will demonstrate my gratitude, but if there's anything else you should need, please never hesitate to ask."

It was a strange conversation. Cayloken was saved only by his cycles of training and experience at diplomatic meetings. He smiled and thanked Marius for his hospitality and generosity with the lodging and the wedding.

There was some sort of code in the exchange that he might have been able to understand if his mind hadn't been on getting Ellarowan, Owen, and himself through the evening in one piece.

Politically, Marius's speech about gifts and gratitude was terrifyingly wrong. On an official level, their families were equal. One guildmaster implying that another guildmaster needed assistance in caring for his family—or worse, that a price was being offered to take a bride—was dangerous.

Cayloken could, and possibly should, take serious offense at the suggestion. But instead, he was simply confused.

There was no reason—no political reason, anyway—that Marius would dare overstep in that way. Cayloken was almost certain that Marius was sincere, and not insulting him. It was almost as if Marius wasn't speaking to him as a guildmaster, but as a father.

An obvious conclusion, if Cay had been speaking to nearly anyone else in the world. But, to Cay's knowledge, everything Marius had ever said or done was political. Even his interactions with his own daughter.

Which meant…no, he didn't know what it meant.

He might have been wrong about Marius all along, but that wasn't a comfort right now.

Instead of acknowledging the situation further, he just smiled. "Do you know where your son might be? I wanted to pay my respects to him as well."

"He seems to have disappeared," Marius said, with a resigned sigh that was yet another misstep in the expected etiquette. "But I will give him your regards when I do see him. You and Ellarowan must be ready for some rest and privacy. It's been a long day for both of you."

"Thank you, Sir."

Cayloken was halfway turned around to walk away when he felt a hand on his wrist. For half a second, the only thing he could think about was how grateful he was that it wasn't his hand.

"Sorry, I didn't mean to do that," Marius said, when Cayloken was facing him again. "I just wanted to say that I am sincere in my offering of assistance and privacy. You've done your part. I will not place any additional demands on the two of you. Neither one of you will be required to make any further public appearances here, and you have no obligations to fulfill in Ravensguild. Arrangements and explanations will be made for you. Our guilds are allied, now, and Silver Island will enjoy my full support."

"What does that mean?" Ella asked, as she and Cayloken walked up the steps to the guest house that had been prepared for them.

The lights were already all on inside, but Ella wasn't ready to open the door. Something about crossing the threshold with Cayloken was too much, too soon, even though right now they were only going inside to find Shea and Owen.

It shouldn't have mattered, entering a place she would share with Cayloken. They'd slept in the same house last night. And they were married now. Walking into a building didn't change anything.

"I don't know," Cay said. "I couldn't tell if he was being oddly nice, or if it was some kind of veiled threat, like he doesn't *want* us appearing in public in Ravensguild."

"Maybe he doesn't." She looked up at him, purposely forcing her eyes to turn bright yellow. "Perhaps he'd rather I stay as hidden as possible, and you along with me. Easier to explain things if we're just not around." She knew she sounded more callous about it than she probably should. It ought to have bothered her more, this being discarded by her father. Maybe it would have, if her emotions weren't already stretched well past anything she'd ever dealt with before.

There wasn't time to think about it right now, anyway. There wasn't time to worry about what going inside the house meant, either.

At least it would be easier to do now, while warm evening sunlight covered the porch than it would be later in the darkness.

She opened the door with her good hand.

Until she saw the empty parlor, she didn't realize she'd been half-expecting something terrible to happen. She still jumped when Cayloken pulled the door closed behind them.

"Hello?" Cayloken called.

Nobody answered.

Ella was certain her frown matched Cay's.

"The bedrooms?" he asked, in a voice low enough that she knew he didn't feel right about this, either. Shea and Owen were supposed to be here.

She trailed behind him as they walked down the hallway, wishing her magic was something a little more defensive than changing her eyes and healing people.

At least Cayloken was wearing his ceremonial dagger.

There were three bedrooms in this guest house, ridiculous for just Ella and Cayloken, but of course her father would never have put them in one of the smaller cottages. The first two bedrooms were dark, curtains closed against the heat, but Cayloken checked inside them anyway.

By the time they approached the open door to the largest bedroom, Cayloken's hand was on the hilt of his dagger. Ella didn't know what there was to be frightened of, but they were both feeling it.

The curtains were pulled closed in here, too, but the lights were on, and it was obviously empty, aside from the enormous bed that occupied the entire center of the room. There might have been other furniture, too, but all Ella could see was the soft quilt on the bed and the small piece of paper sitting in the middle of it.

Cayloken reached it first. His eyes scanned the paper, frowning, and then he shook his head. "I don't know what it says."

Ella took it from him. The paper was covered in random, garbled letters, just like most of the note Shea had sent her the night before. Then, Ella hadn't taken the time to decode the message written in the secret code she'd shared with Shea ever since they were small.

Today, she had no other choice, so she stared at the letters, unscrambling them in her head.

"They've gone into the woods already," she told Cayloken. "They heard someone walking around near the guesthouses and got worried that if they waited too long, they wouldn't get out of here without being caught."

He nodded. "Well, we didn't see anyone when we were out there, so I suppose we should go now, too. Do you want your bag?" He tilted his head toward the foot of the bed.

There *was* other furniture in the room. A long wooden bench at the end of the bed held both her bag and the gift box from her father that she hadn't opened earlier.

Cayloken was already lifting the bag without waiting for her answer.

She raised an eyebrow at him. "You think you know me so well already?"

"I think you always have a water jug in here, and it is a hot night."

"You could carry your own water, you know."

"If you let me change out of this ridiculous outfit first, I'll carry the whole bag."

Whatever Shea and Owen had heard that had spooked them out of the guesthouse, there was nobody nearby now. Perhaps there had just been servants making the last few rounds of evening preparations for the guests. Although the sun was still above the tree line, all the porch lights were on, and the pleasant smell of clean sheets drifted out of windows as they walked by.

The servants would have wanted to finish in time to enjoy the later festivities.

Still, Ella couldn't shake the feeling that something wasn't right, and Cay seemed to feel the same way. They clung to the sides of the buildings, tucking themselves out of sight of the main paths, even though there was no reason the two of them couldn't walk wherever they pleased without offering an explanation to anyone.

Ella let out a sigh of relief when they reached the tree line, and Cayloken's shoulders relaxed a bit, though he still looked around warily. "Do you think it's the dragon again?" he asked.

"Maybe." She stood silently for a moment, listening. "I don't hear any signs of it, but didn't Kalida say she'd be meeting us out here? The dragon would make sense."

There was nothing else to do but move forward. At one point, Cayloken reached for her hand, but they quickly realized that wasn't going to work. Both their fingers were still too hot and raw for touching.

Twice, they stopped cold, both at the same time to listen for another twig snapping that wasn't quite right. The second time, Cayloken chuckled. "We might be a little too unsettled. What are we even worried about?"

Nothing, it turned out. When they finally emerged at the slope leading to the river, Shea and Owen were sitting there, only half-hidden by the trees, talking as they tossed rocks into the water.

Shea nodded, acknowledging she'd seen them, but they finished their conversation before standing to greet Ella and Cay.

"The wedding went well?" Owen asked.

"Yes, thank you," Ella said. She supposed it had, anyway.

"As well as could be expected," Cayloken said, echoing her thoughts.

"I would say congratulations, but, I'm not sure that's the right sentiment."

"It works as well as anything else." Cayloken's head turned as he surveyed the riverbank. "Any sign of Kalida yet?"

The sun had dipped lower as they'd walked through the woods and was beginning to take on the distinct orange-purple glow of dusk.

"Nothing. No Kalida, no dragons, just him." Shea pointed to the ground near Ella's feet.

The ground that looked like it was moving. Ella swallowed back a squeal as she realized what it was, and she bent down. "How did you know we were coming out here, you little ball of fur?"

The iber tipped his head up and sniffed suspiciously at her bandaged finger.

"Ibers never reveal their secrets," Owen said, picking up another rock. He tossed it in a high arc, way up over the river. Ella waited for it to *plop* on the other side, but it never did.

She stood. "Was that…? Did it…?"

"It went through the gate." Cayloken's voice held the most reverent sound of awe she'd ever heard. "One second it was there, sailing through the air, and then it just disappeared. The gate is real."

This seemed like an obvious statement. After all, the gate was the entire reason they were out here. And yet, Ella felt the same way. Hearing about, and even believing, the stories was different than having a portal to another world hanging open in the air above you.

"What do we do now? Where is Kalida?"Ella looked around, scanning the ground and the trees. They'd spent the entire walk over here terrified they'd catch a glimpse of someone else out here, and now that they *wanted* someone to appear, the forest was empty.

"How long is the gate open for?" Shea asked.

Owen held his hands up in a helpless gesture. His face had gone pale and he was pacing in a small circle. Ella was almost worried he was going to take a running start and try to jump for the opening. His only way out of their world. His only chance to get back home.

Ella started to feel a little panicked, too.

Maybe the gate would be open for hours, but maybe it would close again in a few minutes.

They had to get him up there.

"What is our plan if Kalida doesn't show?" Cayloken asked. He sounded calm and businesslike, but Ella could see the way he rubbed the fingers of his good hand on the hem of his shirt, and the way his eyes darted from one person to the next.

"Did you say you had a ladder on the other side you were going to try to get?" Shea asked Owen.

He nodded, and without another word bent down to open a pocket on his bag. He pulled out a strange, long cord made of some material Ella didn't recognize. A rope of some sort, though it was thin and lightweight.

Too lightweight to make it all the way up to the gate, she thought, even with the small metal hook he was now attaching to one end.

It felt like an invisible hand was tightening around her stomach.

And somewhere up in the trees, she could hear voices.

Owen's hook fell to the ground with a small *clink* as they all stared at each other in horror.

It wasn't Kalida. At least one of the voices was male.

"They're not close enough to see us, not yet," Cayloken said under his breath. "What do we do?"

Ella walked up to the edge of the water and stared up at the spot where the rock had disappeared, silently willing Kalida to appear between the trees. There was a part of her that thought this was ridiculous. She'd only met the woman two days ago. Even if Kalida was her mother's sister, there was no reason to trust her. They couldn't stand here all night and wait for her, allowing the gate to close while they watched.

While they waited to get caught.

She closed her eyes, imagining the bridge that had appeared the other night at Kalia's command. The imposing half-arch of stone leading right up to the gate.

Behind her, someone gasped.

And when she opened her eyes again, the bridge was there.

She looked around frantically. "Where is she?"

Cayloken shook his head. "It's only you, Ella."

"Well I didn't do that! I can't…"

As if to prove her point, the bridge went pale gray and then blinked out of existence.

Owen, kneeling by his bag to re-pack his rope, let out a strangled sound.

"Put it back, Ella," Shea said. "Put it back and we can finish this."

"I can't—" But she could. She didn't know how she knew it, but she knew she could. She turned around and closed her eyes, and imagined the bridge there again.

It didn't appear right away. Even though her eyes were closed, she knew this. There were voices behind her, the others talking, but the only thing she could concentrate on was the bridge.

And then it was there. She could tell it was there even before she opened her eyes. To prove it to herself, she kicked her foot forward, marveling when it connected with solid stone.

"Okay, go now!" she hissed at Owen.

It felt wrong, too abrupt, too…something. As Owen climbed up the first step, she found herself wishing they'd had more time, felt like there should be more to the good-bye than this. But there couldn't be. There wasn't time. The voices in the woods were getting closer. He had to go now.

Owen hurried up the steps, stopping only when he got to the top. He turned around and looked down at them. "Thank you for everything. I wish…"

Ella nodded. She wished, too.

Watching Owen step into the gate was something she thought she'd never forget in her life. He seemed a little hesitant about actually doing it, perhaps remembering his fall into the water on this side. He put one foot slowly through and it disappeared as if it no longer existed.

Ella's skin buzzed as if it were electrified.

A movement out of the corner of her eye made her look away from Owen.

A small ball of fluff zoomed up the steps, faster than she'd ever seen a creature move.

"Fluffy!" Ella screeched, as the iber hopped straight over Owen's leg, grabbing on to his shoe, just as he was putting his other foot through the gate.

Cayloken darted past her, running up the stairs after the iber.

It was too late, Ella thought, they were already gone.

But just as Cay reached the top of the bridge, Owen's head appeared through the opening, and then half his body, an arm curled tight around a trembling iber.

Cay reached for Fluffy.

Fluffy made a hissing noise and Cay yelped and pulled his hand away, bitten.

"For the…" Ella muttered, and ran up the stairs for herself.

She was a little afraid as she reached toward the iber, wondering if she, too, would be attacked, but the iber hopped into her arms and began purring innocently. Ella briefly considered dropping him into the water from that height. "You'd deserve it," she said, holding him near the edge.

He didn't look concerned.

"Thank you, Owen," she said to the half of him she could see.

"I didn't know what else to do," Owen said. "I don't know if he'd do so well on our side. There aren't animals like him, here, and he probably doesn't like pizza."

"I don't know what pizza is." She didn't really care to know the answer to that right now, either. She was far too intrigued at the way his body could be half here, half in another universe.

Suddenly, more than anything else, she wanted to try it for herself.

"Do you think I could step through?"

Owen shrugged. "I don't see why not."

Cayloken cleared his throat, but he didn't say anything. Ella glanced back at him long enough to see that he, too, was warring with his curiosity.

Owen disappeared, making room.

She held her foot out over the edge of the broken bridge, but it didn't disappear.

They were too late. The gate must be closed. She sighed. At least Owen was safely on the other side.

Cayloken grabbed her upper arm. "Ella."

"I know, we need to go."

"No, Ella, *look*." He pointed out over the forest.

Ella followed his gaze, and her heart nearly stopped.

She'd been worried about the voices, but mostly she'd thought it would be some servants out wandering around. Or perhaps her brother and Allora Sandrez, if he was still playing that game.

But it wasn't Allora Sandrez she could see from her vantage point, though maybe Allora was somewhere nearby.

Because she *could* see Amalric Sandrez, the great master. One of the main architects behind The Fading. And here she was, standing on a magic bridge, cradling a creature that shouldn't be able to be tamed.

Being discovered would cost her everything. It would cost her father and Cayloken's family, too. And they were headed directly for the place where Shea stood by the riverbank.

There was another figure half-hidden behind Amalric, but the gathering darkness made it impossible for her to see.

"They haven't looked up yet," Cayloken whispered. "Let's get out of here quickly."

They hadn't even taken the first step when Owen's head suddenly appeared behind them again. "I think you have to be touching me," he said, putting one hand on her shoulder.

"Owen! Go back!" Ella said through gritted teeth, but just as she said it, Amalric Sandrez's head tilted upward, right in their direction.

A terrifying screech rose into the dusk, and something enormous flew out of the trees just in front of them, blocking Ella's view, confusing her, and then, it flew *at* them. By the time she realized it was the dragon, she'd stumbled backwards.

They should have gone over the edge, into the water. Both of them, since Cayloken's hand was still tightly clasped around her arm.

Instead, her back hit something soft, and by the time they landed in a pile, on solid ground, she realized there weren't two of them, but three. Four, if she counted the iber on her chest. Owen's leg was under her back.

There was no dragon, and there was no broken bridge. They were on a bridge, Ella thought. She could hear the river flowing below them, but this bridge was wide and whole, no broken precipice in sight.

As they stood and brushed themselves off, Ella realized the forest they were in wasn't the same one. Even though it was almost completely dark.

Cayloken muttered a word she'd only heard out loud one time before. One she was yelling over and over again inside her head.

Nobody spoke; they all realized the same thing.

They couldn't go back, even if the gate was still open. If they weren't immediately assaulted by a dragon, they'd face an even greater danger at the bottom of the steps.

They just stood in a circle and stared at each other as the last bit of sunlight blinked out over the horizon.

"Well," Cayloken finally said. "I hope the bridge disappeared when you did."

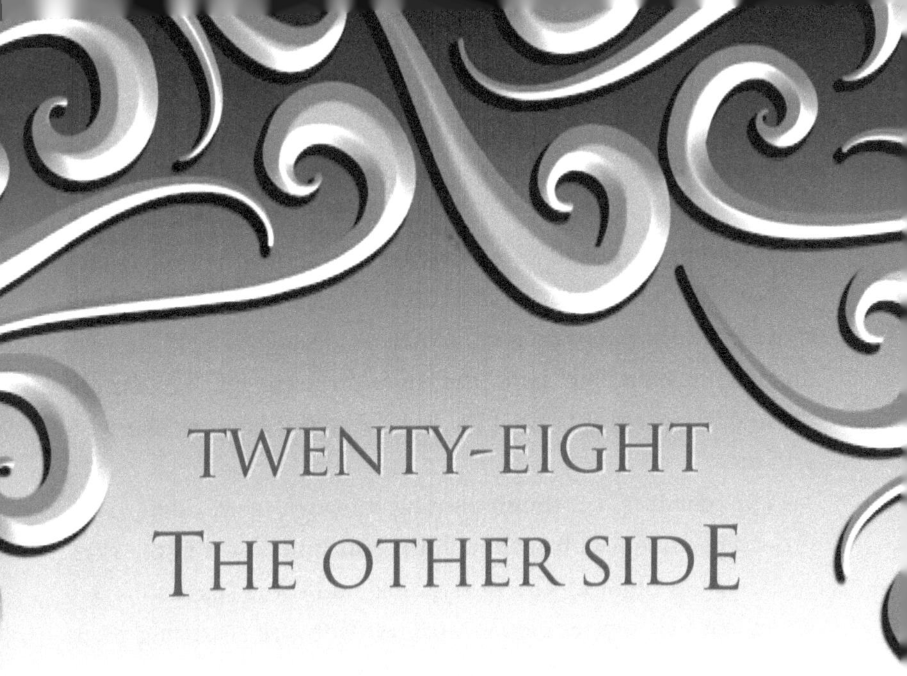

TWENTY-EIGHT
THE OTHER SIDE

AND JUST LIKE THAT, they were gone.

Shea's heart was still pounding, her lips still desperately mouthing a plea that Ella and Cayloken *get down here,* the iber be cursed, when everything had just disappeared.

Everything except the dragon and the shouting, anyway.

She didn't know where the dragon had gone. It had flown straight up in front of the bridge and then into the trees, in the same direction as the shouting. She suspected it was the *cause* of the shouting.

But she didn't know *who* was shouting.

Ella had known, Shea was certain. Whatever she'd seen from her vantage point up there on the magic bridge had terrified her. Running into anyone out here would have been risky of course, but whoever Ella had seen was downright dangerous.

Shea didn't want to be here when they arrived.

But she didn't want to abandon Ella and Cayloken if they came back through the gate, either. At least, she told herself that the reason she kept the river in view as she darted through the trees was for Ella and Cay—not because she was curious.

The chances of them coming through were slim, and growing slimmer with each inch the sun sunk lower in the sky.

After last night at The Dozy, Shea had some suspicions, so when the two figures came into view, she was searching their silhouettes for proof more than anything.

She tried to pick out Tallen's form in the gathering shadows.

But it wasn't him.

There was an older man and a younger one, but the younger one didn't have Tallen's close-cropped hair. His hair was longer, curling to just past his shoulders.

For several moments, she didn't believe it, it didn't make sense, couldn't be.

But just as the sun sank behind the mountains, she could no longer deny that she was looking right at Loric Allsdale.

Now she wished she hadn't looked, wished it was something she didn't know. But she supposed it didn't change anything for now. She had to seek help, to tell somebody what had happened to Cayloken and Ella before someone else discovered them missing.

Before last night, she would never have dreamed of going to a guildmaster for help with anything. Certainly, she'd never have approached Ellarowan's father. But now, she didn't see that she had any choice, and she ran back to the guest house she'd slept in the night before, to wait to tell the Stones their son had just vanished into another world.

"So, what do we do *now*?" Ella asked, still staring in disbelief at the place where they'd just crossed over a few minutes ago.

"Well, I suppose you're stuck in my world for a bit the way I was in yours," Owen said. Ella normally appreciated how calm he seemed about things, but right now it was irritating. "It's a much shorter time on this side, at least. The gate will most likely open tomorrow again here, and you can go home."

"But it will have been much longer on our side," Cayloken said, removing Ella's bag from his shoulder so he could rub his arm.

"Yes," Owen agreed.

Ella closed her eyes and took a deep breath. "There's nothing we can do about it now, is there?" This was what Owen had said, several times over the time their positions were reversed. Now she knew he hadn't been as calm as he looked. She felt like she was going to crawl right out of her skin, but that simply wouldn't help.

"No, there's nothing you can do. Just rest for the night, and I can bring you back to the gate tomorrow."

"We're not going to stay here?" Cayloken asked.

"Well, we *could*," Owen said. "But we're literally in a forest in the middle of nowhere. There's no food and no shelter. It will get colder here at night than you're used to. The tent I have won't fit all three of us. Better to leave and go get a hotel room for tonight, and just come back."

"You don't live here." This was an obvious statement, Ella realized, but this was so far removed from how things worked on her side that she was having trouble understanding it.

"No. I don't live anywhere near here. It takes several days to travel to my home by car, even."

"Car? Hotel?" Cayloken was having the same difficulties as Ella.

"I'll explain as I go," Owen said. "It'll just be easier. There's too much."

"I thought you said this world was really dangerous," Ella said as they started to climb down from the bridge. Already, she was feeling the difference in weather. A light wind cut through her thin shirt, making her shiver. Fluffy shuddered in her arms although he was the only one who seemed dressed for this. Aside from the weather, though, this world didn't look much different than hers.

Owen paused. "It *is*, but not in ways I can explain easily. Hopefully, we'll get you back to your world before it becomes an issue. Do you think you can do something about your eyes?"

"I can try."

A *car* turned out to be a kind of carriage that Owen said he could operate without a horse. Ella didn't understand how, but then, she didn't understand airships, either, and they flew. By the time they reached the car, she didn't much care, anyway. Her teeth were chattering and she was covered in shiverbumps. The only thing she noticed about the car was that she could get inside it.

At least until Owen climbed into the seat in front of her and did something to it that made it rumble and roar.

"I thought you said this world didn't have magic."

"It's not magic," Cayloken said beside her. His eyes—still orange despite her efforts—shone as he stared at the wheel Owen was now turning. "It's a machine."

The *machine* suddenly lurched forward, pressing both Ella and Cayloken back against the seat. Fluffy hopped off the seat and huddled underneath Ella's legs. "There are seat belts," Owen said. "I just realized you wouldn't know. They're long straps that go over you and connect so you stay safe in the car."

Ella might have asked what the straps would keep them safe *from* if just then the car hadn't turned suddenly to the side, tipping her over into Cayloken's arm. A light appeared over their heads as she and Cay worked together to figure out how to pull the straps across them and buckle them into the seats.

The car bumped and jolted over the dirt road, rocking them back and forth, and twice the seat belt stopped her from bumping her head on the roof.

This machine seemed ill-suited to the terrain of the place, but she didn't know if Owen would be offended if she said so.

She was beginning to feel nauseous. Going back and facing the great master and a dragon suddenly didn't sound so terrible.

"Are you all right?" Cay asked. "We have your bag, at least. That tea is still in it, I think."

It was. She was stranded in another world with little more than the tea, a water jug, some drawing supplies, and her mother's journal. But it might have been much worse without the tea. She still didn't understand why Sabelina had put it in her bag, but she was grateful. "No hot water to make the tea right now," she pointed out.

"Is there anything I can do?" Cay asked.

She shook her head, staring at the strange lights of the machine in front of Owen. Lots of blue numbers and dials and things she didn't understand. "You don't have to take care of me," she told him.

"I'm pretty sure I do, actually." Cayloken set his hand on top of where hers was pressed against the seat, briefly allowing the bandage of his burned finger to brush against her.

She bit her lip and tried to breathe. "I don't think I can think about that right now."

He chuckled quietly. "No, neither do I. But we're trapped in another world together right now. Maybe we can take care of each other a little, at least?"

There was yet another huge bump that sent both their hands into the air. Cayloken sucked a breath through his teeth as his hand landed on top of hers again, a little too hard.

Owen cleared his throat. "Can I ask what happened to your fingers?"

Ella looked out the window while Cayloken explained. After that last bump, the road seemed to even out, and now the car glided smoothly in the darkness, alleviating some of her nausea. She'd told Cayloken she couldn't think about the marriage right now, but the truth was, she couldn't really think about anything. It was just too much, all of it. The dark night flew by outside; they had to be going faster than Ella had ever traveled in her life.

The stars in the sky were so different from the ones at home. This made sense, of course, but it was disconcerting to search for the shape of the familiar dragon's wing in the sky and not see it.

"Ellarowan? Ella?"

"Sorry, what?" She sat up straight, rubbing her eyes. Everything felt wrong for several seconds until she realized the problem: they were no longer moving. Also, there were lights, not just the blue ones in front of Owen, but outside the window, too, shining down on her. "Where are we?"

Cayloken shrugged. "We're in another world. Owen went into that building. He said he's getting us some rooms for the night."

Ella looked where he was pointing and tried, not so successfully, not to panic. The similarities between the woods here and at home had lulled her into a false sense of security about this world. This was like nothing she'd ever seen.

The building was enormous, with lights everywhere, and dozens of doors. Three stories of doors. She turned her head back and forth, trying to make sense of it. An enormous green-and-yellow illuminated sign read *Val-U-Tel.* Bright red letters underneath announced *Rooms Available $69.* She understood the rooms part, sort of.

There wasn't much time to think about it. Owen appeared outside the car while she was still trying to make sense out of that strange $ symbol. It must refer to money, she thought. *Did Owen have money?* She'd never given any thought to the kind of life he had in this world. She knew he wasn't the son of a guildmaster, but only because he had told her these didn't exist in his world.

He must have had at least enough for this place, because he opened the door and waved two little squares at them. "Come on."

Cayloken carried her bag again and stayed right behind her as if he was afraid she'd stumble on the stairs as they followed Owen to one of the dozens of doors.

Electric lights. Everything here was a flurry of electric lights. Ravensguild paled—quite literally—in comparison to this world. Owen flicked switches on the wall to reveal a rather small room with two beds and some other furnishings. A strange, large black thing dominated most of the dresser top.

Fluffy took one look and yelped, then hopped out of Ella's arms and ran underneath one of the beds.

"I made sure to find a place that allows pets," Owen said. "If anyone asks, Fluffy is a dog."

Ella raised an eyebrow at the suggestion, but nodded. Fluffy seemed like the least of their concerns right now. It was the creature's fault they were here. She was still half-tempted to drop him into a river.

"There are laws about animals here?" Cayloken asked.

Owen's sigh was pained and exhausted. "Not exactly."

Ella looked dubiously at the two beds. "Um…"

"I got us two rooms," Owen said quickly, reading her mind.

"You're sure you're not a keeper, too," she asked him.

"I'm not sure about anything anymore, Ella," he said. "One of you open that door over there." He pointed to a door in the wall near the head of one of the beds.

Cayloken went to do this as Owen went back out the door they'd come in. A minute later, Owen reappeared at the second door. "More beds, a second bathroom," he said. "We can figure out how we want to do this in a bit."

Ella was feeling a bit dizzy again, and she sat down on the bed.

"There's a coffee pot," Owen said. "We can use it to brew some of the tea."

"Okay," Ella said, as if it were some perfectly normal evening, and she had any idea what he was talking about. Tea sounded good, though. She scooted herself back so she could lean against the pillows.

After a few minutes, Cayloken came over with a little brown cup made of some material she didn't recognize. He set it on the little bedside table and sat down on the bed beside Ella.

"None of this makes any sense to you, either, right?" he said with a half-smile.

She shook her head.

"Do you want to sleep in a room by yourself? Owen and I can share."

The question only made her dizzier. She picked up the cup. The tea was still too hot to drink, but inhaling the steam was soothing.

"Sorry," Cayloken said. "We don't have to make any decisions right now." His eyes met hers for a minute, but then kept darting around the room, landing on one strange object after another—a task that might never end now that Owen was unloading his pack onto the table.

She sat up and put her free hand on his leg, a motion that felt more natural than she was expecting. "This isn't how I imagined my wedding night either, you know."

He laughed, and she was struck by the way the musical sound was even more comforting than her tea. "Can we just say this one doesn't count?"

"Definitely."

He leaned in and gently pressed his lips against her forehead, as if it was a natural gesture that he'd performed a thousand times before, without thinking.

She felt less dizzy.

"I wonder if my magic even works here," she said, looking at his still-orange eyes. At least Owen's eyes had faded back into his usual brown.

"I don't think we can gauge by that," he said, clearly understanding what had brought it up. "You're barely able to control your own eyes when you're not terrified by landing in another world. Maybe you should start with something simpler."

"I'll just have to buy some dark sunglasses for you tomorrow if we're going to be seen by anyone," Owen said. "Or you could say they're contacts. I've seen people do much stranger things than purple with star pupils."

Ella only understood enough of this to wonder exactly what kind of people were in this world, but she nodded. "Contacts, got it. Sometime you'll have to explain that to me. But not today."

"It's strange, I know," Owen said. "I spent a lot of time in your world thinking about the differences and wondering how I'd ever be able to explain any of it to someone who hasn't seen the things I'm talking about. The reality is even harder."

"Maybe you should try your magic on something simpler," Cayloken said. "Like your mother's journal."

"Will you hand me my bag?"

Her heart pounded as she ran her hand over the leather cover, although she wasn't sure why. She already knew what was in the book, and nothing could be worse than what they'd already dealt with today. But she couldn't control it, and it wasn't going to stop. Might as well just open the book.

It was like a floodgate had opened. As soon as she flipped to the middle of the book, every page seemed to fill with charcoal and ink. She didn't even have to concentrate. If she wasn't watching the pages go from blank to covered in front of her eyes, she might have wondered if the book was magic in this world at all.

"Wow," Owen breathed, coming over to sit on the corner of the bed with them.

Ella flipped through the pages with fervor, not taking any time to read just yet, wondering at first if the pages had the *same* content as they had in the other world.

They did. There was the picture of the baby, and the bridge, and then the perplexing old man.

Owen let out a noise she hadn't known people were capable of making. Perhaps humans were truly different than omian.

"What is it?" Cayloken asked, concerned.

"I know who that is."

Ella's head snapped up so fast she was lucky it didn't fly across the room. "What do you mean?" In her mind, she replayed the last several days with Owen. He hadn't had time to go running around in her world meeting people—had he?

"Not in your world," Owen said, with that uncanny ability he sometimes had of guessing what she was thinking. "And he's not just someone I've seen before. I *know* him."

"He's from *your* world? A gadab?" Her head spun as she tried to figure out why her mother would have a picture of a gadab.

"Not from my world, no. Although he has been here before. I suppose, actually, that I don't know what world he's from. I met him, spent time with him, in my sister's world. He's not…usual."

"What do you mean?" She looked down at the drawing again, searching for clues. This time, she noticed there was something written underneath the picture. Words that hadn't been there before. *The Traveler,* it read. *Ancient gatekeeper who may have cured keeper sickness before.*

She was suddenly so cold she began shivering. Cayloken quickly pulled the blanket from the end of the bed and wrapped it around her shoulders. "This is who my mother was searching for. Do you know where he is?"

"I believe he lives in my sister's world, Ella. Not in this one or in yours. My sister knows him well, as well as anyone does, anyway. Or at least she did. He even performed her wedding. But that was a long time ago."

"Do you think you could find him?" She wasn't sure why she would want to, but there was some part of her that felt like it was important, that she wanted to meet this man whose picture was in her mother's book.

"I don't know. If I could get to my sister's world, I probably could. But you see how well that turned out last time I tried it."

"You could do it if you had the stones," Cayloken said quietly. "Couldn't you?"

Owen shrugged, but Ella could see the answer hidden underneath. He'd learned something in her world that had changed his ideas about the other one.

Her brain was not equipped to handle this level of information right now. She could barely process anything. She was grateful that the burned finger was on her left hand, because her right one couldn't stop flipping through the pages of the journal. Hoping to find some comfort this time, she flipped back to the very first note that had appeared for her.

Dear Ellarowan,

I hope there's never a day when you must read the contents of these pages. If you are reading them, it means I have failed for too long at the single most important mission in my life— returning to you.

This time, the words continued.

Of course, if you're reading this note at all, it must mean that all my searching has not been for naught. If you're alive and reading this, then my search was worth it.

I have gone through the gate, to the other world to search for the great gatekeeper, known as the traveler. My plan was to return with the traveler before you'd even missed me—too much, at least. I know that I will miss your sweet smile every minute we're apart.

But I know the trip is dangerous, and I know that if you're reading this, I didn't make it back. I don't know what you'll be told about my disappearance. I've had to make some sacrifices to continue to search for the cure for you. I was told to give up hope, to just enjoy the time I had with you and to keep you comfortable. But I couldn't, Ellarowan. I couldn't sit in that big house and

*watch my daughter fade away into nothingness.
Not this time. And if you are reading this, then
my sacrifices were worth everything.*

*Nobody knows about the gate, except the
person who helped me through. The person who
was to give this journal to you when you were old
enough. As much as I never want you to read this,
I also pray with all of my being that there is a day
you are old enough, and healthy enough, to see
these words if I am not there to tell you the story of
how I came back.*

*Please know that I love you, and that I'm
still trying to make my way back to you. Please be
there when I return.*

*I love you my sweetling,
Mother*

When she finished, she shoved the book toward Cayloken and Owen, who had both been politely looking anywhere else as she read. The little hotel room was silent for several minutes, until Cayloken let out a long, low whistle.

"Well," he said a few minutes later. "I'm guessing by that look on your face that we're not going to be returning to Ravensguild tomorrow night."

Ella took a long drink of her tea.

OTHER BOOKS BY BREEANA PUTTROFF

THE DUSK GATE CHRONICLES

The bestselling series that started it all. Meet Owen for the first time, and his sister, too.

Available for Kindle, Audible, iTunes, and Paperback

SEEDS OF DISCOVERY: BOOK ONE
ROOTS OF INSIGHT: BOOK TWO
THORNS OF DECISION: BOOK THREE
BLOOMS OF CONSEQUENCE: BOOK FOUR
CANES OF DIVERGENCE: BOOK FIVE
LEAVES OF REVOLUTION: BOOK SIX
BLADES OF ACCESSION: BOOK SEVEN

RUMPELSTILTSKIN'S DAUGHTER

"My father says there are three sides to every story: yours, mine, and the truth."

The first time Raya Trinklus hears the story of a goblin who could spin straw into gold and once tried to steal the queen's child, she believes it's only that – an impossible story. But as she learns more about the fabled royal family of Auria, and her own family's past, and is drawn in to a budding rebellion, Raya discovers that the truth in a story depends upon the storyteller, and that history is never as simple as it seems.

ABOUT THE AUTHOR

Breeana Puttroff is the author of the bestselling Dusk Gate Chronicles, a former elementary teacher, and a current homeschooling mom. Her true loves are reading, writing, and children. These days, she can nearly always be found plotting adventures in alternate universes and chatting with amazing people on Facebook—when she's not too busy building the periodic table out of marshmallows.

She loves to connect with her readers on her website, Facebook, Twitter, e-mail, and old-fashioned snail mail.

Sign up for her newsletter to receive a free novel from The Dusk Gate Chronicles—Crossed Roses, an alternative viewpoint of the first book.

Newsletter Sign Up - smarturl.it/bpnewsletter

Facebook Page - www.facebook.com/duskgate

Reader Group - www.facebook.com/groups/duskgatefun